Game Changer

FALLING IN FRISCO BOOK 1

CINDY TA

Flutter & Bloom Press

Game Changer

FALLING IN FRISCO BOOK 1

CINDY TA

Flutter & Bloom Press

For those who let their doubts keep them from chasing their dreams. I hope one day you find the strength to silence the voices that say you can't—because you were born to shine.

Content Warnings

This book is intended for readers 18+ and includes mature themes and explicit sexual content.

Please be advised of the following trigger warnings: marijuana and alcohol use, mentions of cancer and cheating, blackmail, gun violence, attempted murder, and death.

Pronunciation and Translation Guide

Names:

Kamado: ka-mah-do
Masashi: mah-sah-shee
Asami: ah-sah-mee
Izumi: ee-zoo-mee
Satoshi: suh-tow-shee

Words:

Baka: baa-kuh (idiot)
Arigato: ah-ree-gah-toh (Thank you)
Daisuki: dye-sue-kee (I love you)
Kuso kare: koo-so kah-reh (Eat shit)
Kono kusottare: koh-noh koo-soh-tah-reh (You piece of shit)
Gomenasai: go-men-nah-sai (I'm sorry)
Mahalo: muh-haa-low (Thank you)
Na'u ka hau'oli: nah-oo kah how-oh-lee (The pleasure is mine)

Playlist

Icebox - Omarion
Lose Control - Teddy Swims
My Boo -Usher, Alicia Keys
Coaster - Khalid
Ghost - Justin Bieber
Hold On - Chord Overstreet
Heartbreak Anniversary - Giveon
The Heart Wants What It Wants - Selena Gomez
Thinkin Bout You - Frank Ocean
Hate That I Love You - Rihanna, Ne-Yo
Touch It - Ariana Grande
Always Been You - Chris Greay
Kiss It Better - Rihanna
Anyone - Justin Bieber
Make Up Sex - Somo
Style - Taylor Swift
Free -EJAE, Andrew Choi
Red Rose - Johnny Huyhn
I Won't Give Up - Jason Mraz
Die For You - The Weeknd
This I Promise You - NSYNC
Infinity - Jaymes Young

DRAGONS
24
ADO
24
初志貫徹

CHAPTER 1
Maddox

There are only a few seconds left in the game, and the New York Werewolves are leading by two. Determined to keep our winning streak alive, I steal the ball from their point guard, Christian Baker, and launch a shot from half-court.

Everything around me moves in slow motion. The roar of the crowd is so loud it fades away, blending with the too-fast beat of my heart. My eyes flick to the clock again before locking back in on the ball.

Please, please, please go in.

I chew the inside of my cheeks, my heart pounding like a drum.

I swear, if it's an airball, I'm quitting. A loss would be less humiliating.

I can already imagine what they would say about me on the sports news.

"What was Kamado thinking? I can't believe this guy is in the running for MVP."

"They said he would be the next Kyrie Lyons. What a joke. These young players don't know what they're doing."

The ball drops into the net, swishing on its descent right before the buzzer sounds.

Fuck yes! I jump up, pumping my fist in the air as I watch the score flip in our favor.

I did it. Thank God! I really wasn't looking forward to starting a new career at twenty-two.

"Dragooooonssss wiiiinnnnnn!" the commentator bellows.

The entire arena erupts with cheers. Everyone is on their feet, embracing one another and jumping with excitement. My teammates rush to me, smacking my shoulders as they dole out high fives with wide smiles, celebrating our win.

"Let's fucking go! That's what I'm talking about!"

"MVP! MVP! MVP!" The crowd chants in unison as they wave signs with my face on them.

From the moment I was four years old, I knew I wanted to play basketball. I would sit in front of the television, mesmerized, watching Kyrie Lyons dominate the court with his unmatched skills. He was drafted into the NBA straight out of high school and signed with the San Francisco Dragons, playing his entire career with them. He led the Dragons to multiple NBA championships, year after year.

The Dragons haven't seen a playoff game since Kyrie retired a decade ago. I'm determined to change that. I want my name in the Hall of Fame. I want to be the next legend.

Family and friends have started to join our celebration on the court. Okāsan pulls me into a warm hug, her eyes shining with pride. I glance around, searching for Otōsan, but—like always—he's nowhere to be found. Still, I'm grateful to have at least one parent by my side. "Masashi, you were amazing out there!"

I smile at the sound of my Japanese name. Masashi. Ambition. A pretty fitting name for me given the circumstances around my birth. I was premature. The doctors told my parents I might not survive, but there was a nurse named Maddox who refused to give up—who believed that I would be a little fighter.

He was right—I pulled through, so my parents decided to name me after him.

"I would've never let you live it down if you'd missed," my older sister Asami teases. "That would not have been a good look for someone in the running for MVP."

Grabbing her, I dig my knuckles into her skull. "I think next time I'll aim for your face."

"Stop! You're messing up my hair!" She pushes my arms, attempting to break free.

"Your hair is already messed up. I don't know how you left the house like that."

"That can be easily fixed—unlike your ugly face."

Okāsan shakes her head, chuckling softly. That pretty much sums up my relationship with my sister—constant jokes, but solid as a rock. When push comes to shove, we always have each other's backs.

"Otōsan got caught up with work and couldn't make it," Okāsan says, her voice tinged with disappointment.

Otōsan is the CEO and founder of Kamado Tech—the largest electronics company in the world. My parents moved from Osaka, Japan, when Asami was one to help expand his business. He was never too fond of my love for basketball. He wanted me to follow in his footsteps—to take over the company one day. But that was his dream, not mine.

Okāsan, on the other hand, has always been my biggest supporter. She bought me my first basketball, and I've kept it all these years. It's old, worn out, with most of the leather peeled away—but it holds so many memories.

Against Otōsan's wishes, she signed me up for basketball lessons and took me to my very first NBA game. I still remember the rush of seeing Kyrie play live. Despite her demanding schedule as a Michelin-starred chef, she always made time to be there for most of my games.

I smile to mask the sting in my chest, and pat the tops of their heads. "It's okay, Okāsan. You and Asami are here. That's all that matters."

"Bro, that shot was fucking wild!" Elijah Callahan—our point guard and my best friend—shouts as he smacks me on the back.

We've known each other since childhood. In high school, we were an unstoppable duo.

After graduation, Elijah stayed in San Francisco while I moved to Chicago. During our sophomore year of college, we were drafted to different NBA teams—me to the Houston Phoenixes, and him to the Seattle Sphinxes.

So when we reunited this year to play for our top-choice team, I was beyond thrilled.

"I still can't believe I made it in." I grab a bottle of water, gulping it down. "I would've died from embarrassment if it had been an airball."

"The look on Baker's face was priceless," says Andrés Navarro, our power forward, grinning like he'd just won the lottery. "That smug bastard acts like his shit doesn't stink."

Andrés and I were roommates when we attended Millennium University in Chicago. Having my two closest friends on the same team feels like a blessing.

Our chemistry is off the charts—which is probably why we're ranked the number-one team in the league right now.

"I wish we could skip the post-game interview," Elijah mutters, tugging off his sweat-soaked jersey. "I'm ready to hit the club."

"Same. I'm ready to celebrate," I say, grabbing a fresh towel. "They reserved a VIP section for us at Blackout—you know, that new spot that just opened."

"Oh, sweet! Are we allowed to bring a plus-one?"

"Yeah, everyone can bring a plus-one," I tell him. "You thinking about bringing Lauren?"

"Oh nah." Elijah shakes his head. "Had to cut things off with her. She was trying to be exclusive, and I'm not about that life. I'm only twenty-two—I'm not trying to be tied down to anyone."

"I couldn't agree more," I say with a smirk. "Single life is the best life."

"Amen to that!" Elijah throws up a fist, and I meet it with a grin and a solid bump.

"Being single is boring. Just wait until you find the one, and your life will change," Andrés says, grinning as he glances at the photo of his wife hanging in his locker. "Being in a loving, committed relationship is the key to happiness."

He's been with the same girl since he was eighteen, and they got married last summer.

Elijah rolls his eyes. "Don't you ever get tired of sleeping with the same person over and over again?"

"Don't you get tired of worrying about catching an STD?" Andrés snaps back.

Elijah hurls his sweaty jersey at him, smacking Andrés right in the face. The whole locker room booms with laughter.

"Fuck, man! You're disgusting!" Andrés wrinkles his nose, wiping the sweat off his face.

"I never have to worry about that," Elijah says with a shrug, a cocky grin spreading across his face. "I'm God's favorite."

"Oh, yeah, because He *totally* approves of you having sex out of wedlock," I say, sarcasm thick in my voice.

"Please. You're no saint yourself," Elijah fires back.

"I never said I was."

I have a bit of a reputation for sleeping around. After celebrating a big win, my usual routine involved hitting up a club and then bringing a beautiful woman back to the hotel. And it was usually never the same one. I've hooked up with countless celebrities, from Oscar-winning actresses to global pop stars.

I never led them on and always made it clear from the start that this is purely sex and nothing more. But the moment I start to notice they're getting too attached is when I have to cut things off.

I don't have time for relationships, nor do I have the desire to be in one. Not after what happened the last time.

I gave someone my heart once just to have it stomped on. Over the years, I built an impenetrable wall and made a vow to never let anyone else in.

Love isn't something I need to feel fulfilled. What matters most to me is bringing a championship home for my team.

"So I was thinking about inviting Riley to come out with us," Elijah says.

I stop in my tracks. "Wait—one of the cheerleaders?"

"Yeah. Is that a problem?" He lifts a brow.

"Bad idea, bro. Don't shit where you eat." I shake my head. "I learned that the hard way. Last year, when I was playing for Houston, I hooked up with two of the cheerleaders. They got into a huge fight during the halftime performance and slashed my tires after the game."

He waves his hand, brushing me off. "Dude, I make millions. I'm not worried about that. If it happens, I'll just buy new ones. She's smoking hot, and I'd love to see what's underneath that cheerleading uniform."

I don't even know why I bother giving this guy advice—he never listens.

"Always thinking with his dick," Andrés mutters under his breath.

I step off the elevator and take a moment to admire the stunning design of Blackout. The space is tastefully decorated with sleek, modern furniture, glossy black epoxy floors, and a massive disco ball spinning above the dance floor. Floor-to-ceiling windows frame a breathtaking view of the Golden Gate Bridge glittering in the night.

I spot my teammates gathered in the back and weave through the crowd toward them.

"Well, if it isn't the man of the hour!" Chandler shouts over the blaring music.

"What's up, Chan Man!" I fist bump him then move around the table, dapping up the rest of my teammates.

Our server arrives with a bottle of their most expensive tequila and pours it into shot glasses.

"Let's raise a glass to our MVP, Maddox Kamado!" Elijah cheers.

We clink our glasses together and down the shots in unison.

"I think we have a real shot at the playoffs this year," Darius says, clapping me on the back.

Darius Booker is the veteran of the team. He played alongside Kyrie Lyons before the legend hung up his jersey. Since I joined the Dragons, he's taken me under his wing, giving me advice I still rely on every time I step on the court.

The server brings my drink of choice—a Moscow mule—and I sink into the soft velvet couch.

Elijah spots Riley—the cheerleader he invited—and waves her over. She's with another girl I don't recognize—a curvy woman with deep bronze skin and long braids.

"Damn," Elijah says, eyeing her up and down. "I thought you looked good in your cheer uniform, but this dress"—he whistles —"I'm speechless."

Riley leans in and whispers something in his ear that makes him grin like an idiot.

"I hope you don't mind that I brought a friend," she says.

"Not at all. The more the merrier." Elijah gives her a wink.

"This is my best friend, Alicia. She's visiting from Louisiana."

Alicia-from-Louisiana looks me up and down like she's mentally undressing me. I flash my famous dimpled smile and she instantly gets flustered. Scooting over, I pat the open space beside me, and she wastes no time sliding in—getting as close as possible.

"I was at the game earlier," she says. "Watching you play? You looked so hot." Her hand slides up my thigh, and she brushes it against the tip of my cock.

She's a bold one, that's for sure.

"Oh, yeah?" I casually drape my arm over her shoulder. "What was your favorite part of the game?"

"When you made that winning shot," she purrs.

She swings her legs over and slides onto my lap. "It's no wonder you shoot so well. Your arms are so big and sexy."

She bites her lower lip and grips my biceps like she never wants to let go. "I wonder what else is big…"

She's about to find out real soon.

The DJ blasts "Get Low" by Lil Jon & The East Side Boyz, and her eyes light up.

"Oh my God, I love this song!" she squeals. "Come on! Let's see if you're as skilled on the dance floor as you are on the court."

Grabbing my hand, she pulls me towards the center of the club.

"Damn, that was amazing." Alicia lies sprawled on the bed, out of breath after our session. "I swear, I'll have such high expectations for men after tonight."

"I'm quite flattered," I say with a chuckle.

"I wish I could stay for more, but I have to be up early tomorrow." She reluctantly climbs out of the bed to get dressed.

I pull out my phone and call my driver to arrange a ride for her back to Riley's.

"Um, can I get my phone back?" She chews on her finger-nails, avoiding my gaze.

"Oh, right. Sorry." I reach into the nightstand drawer and hand her the phone.

After catching someone trying to record me without my consent, I had to start taking extra precautions. Now I make sure the women I spend the night with always put their phones away before we get started. So far, none have had a problem with it.

If a sex tape ever leaked, it would be a massive scandal.

"Thank you for making my stay in San Francisco memo-rable," she drawls, lingering by the door frame.

"Glad I could be of assistance," I say, flashing her a wink.

After she leaves, I slip back into bed and drift off into a peaceful sleep, still riding the high of my victory.

CHAPTER 2
Annalise

My eyes grow heavy as I sit at my desk, struggling to stay awake while organizing the stack of files before me. I stayed up all night binge-watching *The Heart Ripper*, a true crime documentary about the murder of college students in a small town in Oregon called Misty Hollow. I was so invested that I lost track of time.

The day just started and I'm already ready for it to end.

"This is the wrong material!" I hear my boss, Veronica, shout.

I spin my chair around, curious to see what could possibly be upsetting her now.

Veronica Zhang, founder of Dauntless, the athletic wear brand I work for, is quite literally the boss from hell. She treats anyone that's not in a position of power like the scum of the earth, and as her assistant, I'm not lucky enough to escape her wrath. I can't count the number of times she's fired someone for challenging her. I've learned that it's best to just keep your head down and your mouth shut to keep the peace around here.

Her fist tightens around a pair of pants, and she shoots Clara a look that has the poor intern trembling with fear. "Were my instructions not clear enough?" Veronica seethes.

Clara's fair skin flushes to a deep shade of crimson, sweat staining her satin blouse. She stares down at her feet and wrings her hands together. "I—uh—think it—it could still w-w-work." She smiles weakly at Veronica.

Veronica hurls the pants at the window, making Clara jump. She scoffs and hangs her hands on her hips, leveling the redhead with a glare. "If I wanted your opinion, I'd ask for it. Now get the hell out of my face before I really lose it."

Clara runs to the bathroom, tears streaming down her face.

"Sheesh. Let me make sure I don't make any mistakes today," I mutter to my coworker Ivy.

"She's on edge," Ivy whispers. "I overheard one of the fashion designers say that someone famous wants to collaborate with us. They're supposed to be here soon."

Ivy is the head of marketing, and the only reason this place is bearable. Everyone here is so serious—mainly because they are terrified of Veronica—but Ivy has a carefree personality and is easy to get along with.

Working for an athletic brand is not what I had in mind for the start of my career. I thought graduating Devereaux Fashion Institute in New York—the top fashion school in the nation— would mean something, but it didn't. I originally applied for a fashion design position at Dauntless, but they said I didn't have enough "experience."

So I'm stuck working as Veronica's personal assistant. I have to do anything and everything she asks of me, no matter how ridiculous the task. She once made me search nearly every grocery store in San Francisco for a specific brand of kale.

This is not how I pictured my life playing out.

Ever since I was a little girl, it's been a dream of mine to become a fashion designer and have my own clothing line. I would spend hours sketching clothes and hoping one day I'd see celebrities wearing my creations.

That dream seems so out of reach now. I had a fantastic internship lined up when I was in New York, but instead I returned home when my abuelo was diagnosed with lung cancer.

My parents have been divorced for a while, but even when they were together, my father was absent from my life. Abuelo helped raise me, and I owed him so much for all that he'd done for me. I wanted to be by his side while he fights this battle.

"Amanda. I'm going to need you to stop daydreaming and make yourself useful," Veronica barks from behind me, pulling me back to reality. There's still an air of annoyance in her voice.

"It's Annalise," I politely correct her. I've been working here for over a month, and she still doesn't know my name.

She waves a hand in the air, dismissing me. "Whatever. I don't have time to learn everyone's name around here. Anyways, I need you to go to Rise and Grind for a coffee run." She passes me a long list of orders, hers being the most complicated. "Our special guest will be arriving shortly, so please hurry."

"Right away, Ms. Zhang." I plaster on a smile and rise from my seat.

Once outside, I pull my coat tighter around me, the cold biting at my cheeks as I stroll past Lombard Street. A cluster of tourists huddles nearby, trying to capture the perfect photo in front of San Francisco's famous crooked street.

When I arrive, I push the door open and step inside the coffee shop. Sarah, the young barista, greets me.

"Hi, welcome to Rise and Grind—the best coffee in the Bay Area." Her smile gleams, but her expression quickly shifts when I approach the counter.

"Oh, it's you." She lets out a long sigh, rolling her eyes. "Fucking fantastic."

I hand her the list of orders and manage a weak smile. "I totally get why you're frustrated. I would be too. I used to work as a barista during college, and these types of orders would piss me off.”

“Well, you’re not the one behind the counter making coffee now, are you?” she mumbles as she inputs the order on the screen.

Well, alright. Let me just keep my mouth shut next time.

“It’ll be $58.46,” she says flatly.

I leave her a large tip. It’s coming out of Veronica’s pocket anyway.

By the time my order is ready, the coffee shop is packed with customers. I squeeze past them and exit through the door. Although the office isn’t far, navigating the steep streets of San Francisco while carrying eight cups of coffee is a challenge.

Against all odds, I make it back to the office without a single coffee spilling along the way.

I knock lightly on Veronica’s door. “Ms. Zhang, I have your coffee.”

“Come on in,” she calls out.

As I open the door, the sharp scent of expensive cologne hits me instantly. Facing my boss is a tall man dressed head-to-toe in designer clothing.

I step quietly into the corner, keeping my eyes low, waiting for their conversation to wrap up.

“I can assure you that you made the right decision in choosing Dauntless,” Veronica says. “We have an amazing team of designers. I look forward to working with you and bringing your ideas to life.”

“I think we will work very well together, Ms. Zhang,” the man replies.

I freeze. That voice—deep, smooth, unmistakable. I know it far too well. I’d recognize it anywhere.

No… no… *NO!*

My heart hammers in my chest, and all the air escapes from my lungs.

He snaps his head toward me, shock flooding his face. "Annalise?" His eyes widen like he's just seen a ghost.

Sitting across from my boss is the last person I ever expected to see again—the one who's haunted me for years. The one I've tried to erase from every memory.

Maddox Kamado.

My *fucking* ex.

CHAPTER 3
Maddox

FOUR YEARS AGO

I gently caress her hair as we sit at our secret spot—a beach cove we stumbled upon years ago—watching the sunset together. Streaks of gold and pink fill the horizon. A week from now, we'll be eight hundred miles apart, attending different colleges. Each passing day fills me with dread. I inhale deeply, trying to memorize the smell of freshly bloomed roses and summer sun that seems to always cling to her.

"I really wish you were coming to New York with me," Annalise says with a sigh.

I place a kiss on her forehead and interlace her delicate fingers with mine. "I know. Me too, Rosie. I hate the thought of being apart from you."

Suddenly, she sits up straight and pulls away from me. I can tell by the distant look in her eyes that her mind is racing. "What if we don't have time for each other? Or what if you meet some hot cheerleader in college and forget about me?"

"Hey, stop thinking like that." I gently cup her cheeks and stare deeply into her eyes, trying to erase all the doubts from her mind. "You have nothing to worry about, my love. You are the most beautiful girl in the world." I gently brush a stray strand of hair from her face, tucking it behind her ear. "I love you, Annalise Rose Monroe. I only have eyes for you."

The worry in her expression begins to soften, melting away at my words. "There's no one else for me."

"I love you too, Maddy Bear." She wraps her arms around my neck, kissing me passionately. I melt into her, savoring this moment.

"I know most couples split after high school, but we will not be a statistic," I reassure her. "*You* are the person I want to spend the rest of my life with. *You* are my soulmate. No one else."

Annalise's eyes glisten, a huge grin spreading across her face. "And you are mine. I can't wait to go to your games and cheer you on when you make it to the NBA."

"And I can't wait to sit front row at your fashion shows when you're a world-famous designer." I grin, reaching for her hand. "*Maddalise* forever."

"You are sooo corny." She chuckles, shaking her head.

"Says the one who calls me *Maddy Bear*!" I laugh, scooping her up and tossing her over my shoulder. She bursts into a fit of giggles as I take off running toward the water.

CHAPTER 4
Annalise

Maddox Kamado is the *last* person on Earth I want to see. As if I didn't already dread working here—now I'm forced to be in the same room as him? I've avoided watching sports like the plague, so I had no idea he was even back in San Francisco.

My feet remain planted, fingers tightening around the paper cup as if it could shield me from the pull of his gaze. Despite my hatred for him, I can't bring myself to look away. He's undeniably handsome. Deep brown almond-shaped eyes, soft lips, and a perfectly chiseled jaw. His sense of style certainly enhances his appeal. He's donning a crisp, pale blue button-up shirt paired with navy slacks and Louboutin oxford shoes. The accessories he chose add a nice touch to his polished look: a gold Cuban link chain, a Rolex Submariner, and diamond stud earrings.

"Wait, you two know each other?" Veronica's eyes flick between Maddox and me.

"Yeah, we used to date." Maddox shifts his weight, tapping his foot and rubbing the back of his neck. He looks as uncomfortable as I feel.

"What a small world. That won't be a problem now, will it, Amy?" Veronica crosses her arms and narrows her eyes at me.

Oh, it's going to be a huge fucking problem…

"Well?" she asks when I don't answer her.

Placing the coffee on her desk, I shake my head. "Of course not! My history with Mr. Kamado will have no effect on my ability to remain professional."

The tension in the room curls around us like thick clouds of smoke, suffocating us. A thousand unspoken words hang in the air.

"Good, because he'll be working with us for a while. Collaborating with someone as successful as Mr. Kamado here could bring a lot of profit to our company," Veronica says. "We can finally be number one and beat Velocity."

Velocity is another athletic wear brand that happens to be our biggest competitor. Veronica consistently seeks to develop new ideas to outperform them in sales, but Dauntless always falls short.

She picks up her coffee, taking a sip. "Did you make sure it was soy milk? I do *not* need a repeat of what happened last time."

I try to stifle a laugh as I recall the incident. I forgot to ask for soy milk, and Veronica took multiple trips to the restroom during a very important meeting. I was shocked she didn't fire me on the spot.

"Yes, it's soy milk," I reply.

"So, Annalise," Maddox starts, shifting his gaze to me, "will you be one of the designers on the team?"

Veronica nearly spits out her coffee. "Oh, please! She's just an assistant," she snorts. "She can barely get my coffee orders right. There's no way I'd trust her to handle designs."

Heat floods my cheeks as I stare up at the ceiling, fingers twisting the hem of my shirt. Drawing in a shaky breath, I fight back the tears that are threatening to spill over.

I can feel Maddox's gaze lingering on me, heavy with pity. I straighten my spine. I won't let him see me break. Being belittled by Veronica has become a normal occurrence, but having Maddox of all people hear it is humiliating.

"That's a shame. Ms. Monroe is extremely talented. I've seen what she's capable of," Maddox says.

Veronica ignores his comment and quickly changes the subject. "Mr. Kamado, would you like some coffee? I'm sure Ava here won't mind going back to Rise and Grind to grab you a cup."

"Annalise," Maddox grumbles.

"Pardon?"

"Her name is Annalise," he says firmly and I pinch my eyes shut. Him correcting her isn't going to get us anywhere. She won't learn it. And it'll only serve to piss her off.

"Isn't that what I said?" she asks, feigning innocence.

Maddox gears up to say something but I cut him off.

"I don't mind going to get you something." I smile through gritted teeth. "What would you like?"

"I'll have an iced macchiato." He smiles at me, dimples creasing his cheeks.

Those damn dimples.

They still have the same effect on me after all these years. His smile, paired with that ridiculously handsome face, can make any girl swoon. I was foolish enough to fall victim to his charms.

I return from my second coffee run of the day—thanks to him—and hand over his iced coffee. "Here you go, Mr. Kamado."

"Thank you so much, Ms. Monroe. I appreciate it." He takes a sip from his coffee and it spills all over his shirt—which probably costs more than what I make in a week.

I may have "accidentally" loosened the lid slightly before handing it over to him. *Oops*.

"Oh, my goodness!" I gasp, putting on my best innocent act.

Maddox's glare lets on that he knows it was no accident.

"Mr. Kamado! I'm terribly sorry!" Veronica pulls tissues out of the Kleenex box and hands them to him. "I'll pay for your dry cleaning and if the stain doesn't come out, I'll buy—"

"That won't be necessary," Maddox interjects, waving her off. "Do you have a shirt I can borrow?"

"Oh, of course!"

On her way out the door, she pauses in front of me. Her upper lip curls into a sneer. The vein on her temple pulses. "We need to have a chat later."

The loud slam of her door reverberates throughout the office.

Oh, I am completely fucked.

I swallow hard, the lump in my throat tightening as nerves twist painfully in my gut. My promise to remain professional flew out the window when I saw him—I completely lost my cool. Now, I'll probably have to pay the consequence.

"Thanks for ruining my shirt," Maddox snaps.

"You make all that money bouncing balls for a living. You'll be alright."

Maddox unbuttons his shirt, revealing the glorious physique only a professional athlete can achieve. I try not to stare but fail miserably, completely captivated by the man standing in front of me. He's always been in shape, but now he's even more ripped than ever before.

A dragon tattoo coils around his sculpted arm, the artwork so well done it's practically coming off his skin. My eyes wander upward, catching on the familiar characters inked on the side of his neck: Japanese Kanji for *"never give up."* Those words slam me back to the past, to the day he turned eighteen, when I sat beside him in that dimly lit tattoo parlor, my fingers laced with his. I'd gotten roses etched into my thigh that day, a quiet rebellion we shared.

My eyes drop lower and a flood of sinful memories surges forward. Like how I once touched him like he was mine. And how we danced, tangled in sheets. Or how we talked about getting more tattoos together. I wonder what the canvas of our bodies would look like if we had kept that promise.

"If you wanted me to take my clothes off, all you had to do was ask." Maddox smirks, clearly amused by the fact that I've been staring at him for what feels like an eternity.

I huff, rolling my eyes. "Please, don't flatter yourself."

"So, what brings you back home?" Maddox asks. "I thought you would be on your way to becoming some big-shot fashion designer in New York by now."

"That's none of your damn business," I snap.

"Come on, Monroe. Can you be an adult for a second? We need to talk about what happened."

"There's nothing to talk about."

Maddox takes a step forward, reaching for me. "You can't stay mad at me."

"Oh, you have some damn nerve. How the hell are you gonna tell me how I should be feeling?" I jab a finger into his chest. "You have no right, after what you did."

He lets out a frustrated groan, raking his fingers through his hair. "Damn it, Annalise. How many times do I have to explain myself to you? I didn't—"

"Save your breath, Kamado! Everything that comes out of your mouth is a lie anyway."

"You haven't changed one bit." His nostrils flare as he leans in, our faces merely inches apart. "You're still so fucking stubborn."

"And you're still a self-absorbed asshole," I bite back, shoving him hard in the chest.

"Mr. Kamado, I brought you a—" Veronica drops the shirt

she was holding. "Oh my!" She blushes furiously, gawking at Maddox's half-naked body.

Realizing that her eyes have been lingering on him for far too long, she clears her throat and bends down to pick the shirt up off the floor. "I, uh—I brought you a—a polo. I'm sorry I don't have a nicer shirt for you. I plan on creating a business casual line with comfortable, sweat-resistant clothing."

"That sounds incredible, Ms. Zhang. I'm sure it will be a huge success." He smiles.

"You can call me Veronica," she drawls, twirling her hair.

So disgusting.

Veronica's attention snaps to me. "What are you doing still standing here, Alexa? Get out of my office."

I hold back an eye roll as I leave. For fucking *once*, it would be great if she got my name right.

"You used to date Maddox Kamado, and you didn't tell me?" Ivy stares at me, her brows knitted together as a mixture of bewilderment and curiosity dances in her eyes.

"Announce it to the whole world, why don't you?" I grumble. Her mouth stays hanging open for a solid ten seconds.

"Were y'all serious?"

"Yeah… We were together for three years."

Maddox and I started dating during our sophomore year and remained together throughout high school. He was my first and only serious relationship.

I dated around when I went to college, but it never went further than a few dates. Even now, my trust in men is nonexistent. I can't allow myself to be vulnerable.

She gasps. "Three years?"

"Unfortunately…" I mumble.

"You know, I've heard some rumors about him." She drops

her voice, glancing around the office to make sure no one is within earshot. "Is he really that big?"

I rub my temples. "I am *so* not having this conversation with you."

"Ugh, fine! You're no fun." Ivy frowns, scooting her chair farther from me.

"Will you at least hook me up with one of his teammates?"

"Nope," I reply flatly.

"How dare you not help me find a sugar daddy! This friendship is over."

"Who said we were ever friends?" I arch a brow at her.

Ivy gasps and dramatically clutches her chest.

The door of Veronica's office opens, and she walks out with Maddox. She introduces him to Trang, one of the fashion designers. They continue to converse about the collaboration. Of course, the role was given to Veronica's niece. Nepotism at its finest.

Veronica turns her attention to me, shooting me a death glare that causes me to slump in my seat. "Andrea, come here. I would like to have a word with you."

Uh oh. This can't be good.

Reluctantly, I get up from my seat, my shoulders sagging as I walk across the office to where she's standing.

CHAPTER 5
Maddox

"This is Trang. She will be the lead designer on our team." Veronica gestures to a petite Vietnamese girl with straight, shoulder-length black hair.

"Hey, it's nice to meet you!" I extend my hand to her, and she shakes it with enthusiasm.

"It's such a pleasure to meet you, Mr. Kamado!"

"Please, call me Maddox."

"I'm such a huge fan. I've watched every single one of your games," she gushes. "When Veronica told me you wanted to start a clothing line with us, I nearly fainted. I threw up this morning because I was so nervous." She shuffles her feet and clears her throat. "Sorry. I, uh, tend to overshare sometimes."

"Don't worry about it. You're good." My mouth curves into a half-smile. "It's always nice to meet one of my fans."

Trang continues droning on about how much she loves watching basketball, but I've stopped paying attention.

My eyes scan the room and lock on *her*. Annalise Rose Monroe—the first girl to steal my heart and the first one to break it. Waves of emotion washed over me when I saw her again. I spent the last four years trying to erase her from my mind, distracting myself with basketball and burying myself in other women, but nothing seemed to fill the void. She's like a tattoo on my skin, an indelible part of me forever.

She looks more stunning than I remember. Her mesmerizing sapphire and emerald eyes draw me in like a moth to a flame. Silky, wavy, brown hair cascades gracefully down her shoulders, contrasting beautifully against her tan skin. And those luscious pink lips bring back memories of the moments when I had the chance to taste their sweetness.

I've been with a lot of attractive women these past few years, but they all paled in comparison to her. Annalise is the whole package. Drop-dead gorgeous, intelligent, and blessed with a voluptuous figure.

Our reunion was not what I've envisioned. The love she once had for me has turned into hatred. Maybe if we had gone to college in the same city, we would still be together today.

"Andrea, come here. I would like to have a word with you." Veronica's sharp voice slices through my daze like a whip crack. I blink, dragged back to the present. She stands in the middle of the office with arms crossed and a scowl on her face. How in the hell she can't remember a single name is beyond me.

"You have no idea how much you embarrassed me from that stunt you pulled earlier," she hollers, her voice echoing through the office.

"Stunt?" Annalise furrows her brows. "I don't know what you're talking about."

"Oh! Don't act stupid. I know you loosened that lid on purpose so the coffee would spill on him," Veronica snaps, eyes blazing with fury. "You said having your ex here wouldn't be a problem, but it clearly is."

"I swear, I—I didn't!" Annalise's hands fly up, palms out. "It was an accident."

"Cut the bullshit!" Veronica snaps, losing the grip on her professionalism. "You obviously don't know how to separate your personal life from your work life."

Annalise's eyes widen, her voice trembling as she speaks. "But Ms. Zhang—"

"Save it," she shouts, cutting Annalise off. There's venom dripping from her every word as she nonchalantly brushes a hand down her front and says, "You're fired. Effective immediately."

Annalise stands there frozen, her breaths coming in short, ragged gasps as she stares at her boss.

"Well? What are you waiting for? I said you're fired," Veronica articulates, her voice shrill. "Pack up your stuff and go."

I'm pissed about the encounter with Annalise, sure, but I can't stand here and watch this vile woman continue to disrespect her.

Excusing myself from Trang, I march over to Annalise's side. "Ms. Zhang, this really isn't necessary. It was an accident, and it's just a shirt. Firing her over that is hardly justified."

"Just a shirt?" She places a hand on her chest, clearly appalled by my nonchalance.

So what if it's a five-thousand-dollar custom shirt? Annalise was right—bouncing balls for a living earns me a fuck-ton of money. I could buy one for every day of the year and still have more money than I know what to do with.

"You're saying that as if you bought that from a thrift shop." Her gaze shifts to Annalise and I don't miss the way she looks her up and down like she's scum. "I'm sure you know all about those, don't you, dear? I can spot that cheap fabric from a mile away."

Annalise shoots her a glare but remains silent, her lips pressed in a tight line.

"Mr. Kamado, consider this a favor. You'll no longer have to see your ex here," Veronica says.

"I have no problem having her here. My problem is with *you*," I snap.

Veronica stumbles back, startled by the sharp edge in my tone.

Bringing myself to my full height, I stare down at her, and she shrinks beneath the weight of my gaze. "With all due respect, Ms. Zhang, you're an extremely talented woman, but how you treat your employees is downright repulsive."

Her mouth pops open as she stares at me, dumbfounded. I can tell she's about to say something else offensive about Annalise, or any of the other people that work for her, so I start instead. "I was looking forward to working together, but I think I'll be taking my business elsewhere." Pausing for a moment, I let the words hang in the air before adding, "Maybe I should call Velocity back. They offered me a much better deal."

With that, I turn on my heel, walking toward the exit.

"Mr. Kamado, please wait!" Veronica chases after me and nearly trips in the process.

Standing there with my arms crossed, I wait to see what she has to say.

She closes her eyes, inhaling deeply before looking at Annalise. "Arya, I—"

"Annalise," I practically growl.

Veronica clears her throat, her cheeks flushing. "*Annalise*, I apologize for lashing out at you. It was very out of character for me."

"Out of character, my ass," Annalise mumbles under her breath, and I can't help the silent chuckle that shakes my shoulders. Everyone here knows that's a load of crap.

"You are no longer fired. As a matter of fact, why don't you take an early lunch break?" Veronica plasters on a smile. "It'll be my treat. You can order whatever you like. You can even take two hours!"

"Wow, that's so thoughtful of you. You're sure you wouldn't

mind if I treated myself to the wagyu from Roka Akor?" Annalise asks, arching a brow.

"The t-t-two hundred dollar s-s-steak?" All the color drains from Veronica's face. She looks like she's on the verge of fainting.

"Yeah. Is that a problem?"

Veronica twists her pearl necklace between her fingers as she slips her mask back on. "No, of course not."

"Perfect! I'll leave the waiter a nice fat tip, too." Annalise grins. "I'll see you after lunch!" She walks to the elevator, and I follow after her.

The elevator doors shut, trapping us both inside, and I give Annalise a sidelong glance. "Fuck. Is she always like that?"

"Yeah. I usually get the brunt of it. She's been out to get me since day one."

My lips tilt into a knowing smile. "The Annalise I knew would've ripped her a new one."

"Well, a lot has changed since then." She turns away, avoiding eye contact.

The remainder of the ride is filled with an awkward silence. She sighs with relief when the elevator doors finally open, scurrying to the exit like she can't get away from me fast enough.

I chase after her and grab her wrist, turning her to face me.

"So I don't even get a thank you for saving your ass from getting fired?"

She shakes her wrist free from my grasp. "I didn't need you to defend me. I could've spoken for myself."

"Oh, really?" My brows soar upward. "Because from where I was standing, you were too busy looking like a deer in headlights."

Rolling her eyes, she reaches for the door, but I stand in front of it, blocking her.

"Get out of my way. You're cutting into my lunch break."

Using all of her strength, she tries to push me out of the way, but I don't move an inch.

"Can I join you for lunch? I don't have practice today, so maybe we can—"

"Just stop, Maddox!" she snaps.

"Stop what?"

"Oh, don't play dumb. You're trying to make up for what you did in the past," she scoffs. "I appreciate what you did for me in there, but nothing you do could ever fix things between us. So do us both a favor and stop trying, okay?"

I open my mouth to reply, but the words catch in my throat.

"You may have your dream career, a nice car, and all the money in the world, but you sure as hell will never have me."

Her words slice through me like a blade, reopening old wounds I thought had healed.

Many people would look at my life and be envious of it. I have it all: money, power, fame. But what does that matter when you don't have anyone to share it with? Sure, I could probably have any girl in the world, but none of them would ever come close to making me feel the way Annalise does.

I haven't been the same since the day she walked out of my life. She's the reason I can never be in another relationship. It wouldn't be fair, because my heart will only ever belong to her.

I hate how much power she still holds over me. She makes me feel weak, and I despise that. I'm too prideful to show her how much her words affect me, even though it feels like she just ripped my heart out of my chest and tore it into a million pieces.

"Quite bold of you to assume that I'm trying to get you back." I snicker. "I don't waste my time chasing after someone who doesn't want me. I'm quite offended that you think I'd be so pathetic."

She stares down at her feet, pretending to pick lint off her shirt.

"I simply wanted to keep things cordial between us since

we're going to be seeing a lot more of each other now," I state, tucking my hands into the pockets of my slacks. "But if you'd rather us not speak, then I'll respect your wishes and stay out of your way."

I push open the door and step through. "I'll see you next week, Monroe." I feel her gaze lingering on me as I walk away.

CHAPTER 6
Maddox

SEVEN YEARS AGO

After crushing on her since she transferred to my school in second grade, today is the day I will finally ask Annalise Rose Monroe out on a date. I've been a bundle of nerves all day and could barely focus on what Mr. Nguyen was going over in chemistry class.

"Alright. I'm gonna do it." I rub my hands together, taking a deep breath.

"Do what?" Elijah says, eyeing me curiously as he dials the combination to his locker.

"I'm gonna ask Annalise out on a date."

Elijah laughs. "Bro, are you still high from earlier? You don't date, remember?"

"Well, there's a first time for everything." I shrug. "I'm tired of messing around with these girls I don't even care about. I want something more."

He cackles, patting my back. "Dude, what the fuck did that weed do to you?"

"I'm not high, you moron." I smack him in the back of his

head. "I'm dead serious. Shit gets old. I want my homecoming date this year to be someone I actually care about."

"Okay, well, good luck with that." He stuffs his geometry book in his backpack and zips it. "She rejected half the guys in our class already, so I doubt she'll say yes to you."

"Well, none of those guys were me, were they?" I say, a cheeky grin appearing on my face.

"I'm gonna be laughing if your ass gets rejected, too." Elijah shakes his head.

I flip him the middle finger and stride over to where Annalise is standing.

"Hey, Monroe." I casually lean against the lockers, smiling at her.

"Oh, hey, Kamado." Annalise smiles back at me, making my heart flutter. "What's up?"

"What are your plans for the weekend?"

"I'll probably just hit up the mall with Mazi and then study for next week's geometry exam."

"How about you skip studying and come see *The Haunted Trails* with me?"

I absolutely hate horror movies, especially if they involve ghosts. I never understood why people pay money to get scared. But I know how much Annalise loves them, so I figured I'd suck it up. She's been gushing about the release since the trailer came out.

"I got tickets to an advanced screening," I add.

She pauses for a moment, a smile forming on her lips.

My pulse quickens. This is it. She's about to say yes, about to smile and say how excited she is for our date—and then she'll be mine.

I can already picture us walking the halls together, hand in hand, sharing laughs.

My smile widens, anticipation buzzing in my chest.

"Tempting. But I'm gonna have to pass."

The words hit like a record scratching to a halt.

She shrugs, closing her locker. "I'd rather watch grass grow than go on a date with you."

My smile cracks and fades, heat creeping up my neck at the sting of her rejection.

"What's the matter, Kamado? Not used to being rejected? Hate to break it to you, but you're just not my type. Have fun at the movies. I'll see you later." She wags her fingers and takes off, leaving me with my humiliation.

Elijah hurls over, laughing so hard he can barely catch his breath. "Dude, that was fucking brutal! I don't know what's worse—getting kicked in the balls or being rejected by her."

"She's just putting on a façade. She totally wants me," I say.

"You're delusional, man. Just give it up."

"I never give up on what I want. It'll happen one day, trust me." I sling my arm around him, smiling. "Ten years from now, you'll be the best man at our wedding."

Elijah chuckles, shaking his head. "Bro, you are fucking stupid."

CHAPTER 7
Annalise

"Okay, spill. What's wrong?" Mazi asks, interrupting the romcom we're watching that I've completely zoned out on.

I light up my second joint of the night, inhaling deeply. I don't smoke weed often, but after the day I've had, it's *much* needed. "Nothing, Mazi. I just had a very long day. You know how Veronica can be." I shrug my shoulders.

"Oh, bullshit! You've been dying to watch this movie, and you're barely paying attention."

Mazikeen Rivera has been my best friend since I was eight. I transferred to her elementary school in the middle of the year. One day during recess, I was trying to get on a swing when a group of bullies pushed me down. They surrounded me, throwing dirt at me while calling me an alien freak because of my heterochromia.

Mazi marched over and pushed down the biggest kid in our class, Martin Tanner. She climbed on top of him and punched him in the face, giving him a bloody nose. All the other kids ran away crying. No one's messed with me since. She's always been extremely overprotective of me and will fight anyone who tries to hurt me.

"I have been paying attention."

"Okay." She sits up straight, turning her body toward me. "Then what's the name of the cat?"

I pause for a moment, thinking. "Uh, wasn't it Snowball or something like that?"

"There was no fucking cat!" Mazi throws a pillow at me and turns off the television.

"What are you doing? Turn it back on!" I reach over for the remote, but she snatches it up.

"Not until you tell me what's going on," she demands.

I take another puff of my joint before answering her. "I ran into Maddox today…"

"What the fuck?" Mazi's hazel eyes bulge out in bewilderment. "You've been home for three hours and you're *just* now telling me this?"

"I'm still trying to process everything. Seeing him again after four years…" I lean forward, placing my hands on my thighs, breathing in and out.

Don't cry. Don't cry. Don't cry.

"It's okay, Annalise, we don't need to talk about it. You can tell me another time." Mazi rubs soothing circles on my back.

"I saw him at Dauntless. He's collaborating with us for his own line." Hot, angry tears stream down my cheeks as all the emotions I've been suppressing resurface. "Ugh! What did I do to deserve this?" Grabbing a pillow, I throw it on the floor out of frustration. "First Abuelo, now this! Why can't God let me be happy?"

Mazi pulls me into a hug, consoling me while I sob uncontrollably.

"What's He gonna throw at me next?"

"I'm so sorry, Annalise," she whispers. "I hope things start looking up for you. I hate seeing you like this."

Lately, it seems like nothing in my life is going right. I feel like I'm trapped in a relentless rip current, desperately struggling to reach the shore. No matter how hard I fight to break free, every effort feels futile. The harsh waters pull me under every time, leaving me completely exhausted.

"If it's too much for you, why don't you just quit Dauntless?"

I sit up straight, staring at her. "What? Are you out of your mind? How am I supposed to give you money for rent?"

"You don't have to give me anything. A rich couple hired me to shoot their wedding photos, and they offered me a lot of money."

Mazi is an extremely talented freelance photographer. She started gaining popularity a few months ago, after a famous influencer hired her for an engagement shoot.

She places her hands on my shoulders. "You're already miserable at Dauntless, and now you have to see that asshole. What kind of best friend would I be if I let you stay in a situation that causes you harm?"

If the roles were reversed, I would've done the same thing for her in a heartbeat. As much as I dread seeing Maddox again, I can't allow Mazi to let me live here rent-free. She's already covering most of the bills and other expenses, like groceries, herself.

I shake my head. "I don't feel right freeloading off of you, Mazi."

"You can pay me back by cooking me your delicious meals." She bumps her shoulder into mine, smiling. "It'll only be temporary until you can find another job."

"It was already hard for me to get a job at Dauntless. I don't have any other options. Plus, it would look bad on my resume if I quit after a month." I grab a box of Kleenex and blow my nose. "Hopefully he won't be there for too long, since it's just a collaboration. I'll just have to suck it up."

Mazi sighs, knowing she won't win this argument. "Well, if

he ever does anything to upset you, best believe I'll drop every-thing I'm doing and kick his ass."

I laugh, even though she is being dead serious.

"Anyways, enough about that piece of shit. Has anyone else on SwipeMates piqued your interest?"

SwipeMates is an app designed for users to find their "soul-mates," but so far I've had no luck.

"No. I haven't been on it since the last date went so horribly."

The last guy I matched with took me to a cheap buffet that cost ten dollars per person. I wish I had left after dinner, but he suggested we watch a movie I'd been wanting to see.

When we got to the ticket booth, he said, "Since I paid for dinner, you got this, right?" I felt too awkward to say no, so I ended up paying for the tickets—which ended up costing more than dinner.

"Oh, yeah. That guy was such a weirdo," Mazi says, making a face.

"He actually thought it went well because he texted me the other week asking for a second date."

"The only date he's gonna have for a while is with his right hand." Mazi snickers.

I shake with laughter, my mood slowly lifting.

"By the way, when's the last time you got laid?"

"I don't know. Like, seven months ago?"

"Seven months ago?" She blinks twice, her eyes wide with disbelief. "Girl, how are you functioning? It must be dryer than the Sahara Desert down there."

I roll my eyes while she cracks up at her own joke.

Unlike Mazi, I don't particularly enjoy having casual, mean-ingless sex. Over the years I've been single, I've slept with a few men, but it always left me feeling unfulfilled. And I don't mean that in the sense that they couldn't satisfy my needs—although some couldn't. I just felt empty after the encounters. I craved a deep emotional connection, which was something I would never find in these casual hookups.

A new text buzzes on Mazi's phone, and she unlocks it to read it.

"Serena says she needs a break from studying for her boards. She wants to meet up at Lush Lounge later."

A couple of months ago, Mazi met Serena Trinh when she hired her to take graduation photos. They hit it off during the session and have been friends ever since. Mazi usually has trouble making new friends, but I can see why she liked Serena. She has a warm, inviting energy and is easy to talk to.

Since I returned to San Francisco, I've hung out with both her and Mazi several times. Currently, Serena works as a nursing assistant at Greenwich Memorial. She's studying for her NCLEX exam to obtain her license as a registered nurse.

"I think I'm gonna sit this one out." I stretch my legs out on our sectional, throwing a blanket over my body.

"No, you're not!" Mazi yanks the blanket from me. "I'm not gonna let you stay home and get high."

"I don't wanna go anywhere right now. I just wanna stay here and sulk."

I *do not* have the energy to put on makeup or rummage through my closet to find the right outfit.

"Come on! It'll be fun." She grabs my hands, smiling. "We're gonna dance the night away, and maybe you'll meet a guy who will help you get your mind off of stupid Maddox."

"Nope. I'm staying home. Go and have fun with Serena."

I, in fact, *did not* stay home. I'm currently standing at the entrance of Lush Lounge with Mazi as an intimidating bouncer checks our IDs. He gives us a curt nod and steps aside, allowing us to pass through.

Lush Lounge is the perfect spot for a ladies' night out. The vibrant magenta walls and glittery dance floor create a lively atmosphere. The back wall is adorned with flowers, and there's an adorable white wooden swing hanging from the ceiling. A group of girls eagerly take turns on it, giggling and striking poses as they try to capture the perfect Instagram-worthy photo.

We spot Serena at the bar chatting with a burly man who has greasy, sandy-brown hair. He looks out of place in his loud yellow plaid button-up and baggy khakis.

He could definitely use some fashion advice.

"Thank you so much for coming!" Serena pulls us in for a hug. Even in heels, she's barely over five feet tall. "I felt like my brain was gonna explode if I took another practice exam."

The man beside her opens his mouth and a creepy, nasally voice oozes out, immediately sending a wave of discomfort through me. "Aren't you gonna introduce me to your friends?"

Serena hesitates, her fingers nervously toying with her glossy black hair. "Oh, sorry, babe." She forces a smile, clearly trying to smooth over the awkwardness. "This is my boyfriend, Randall. And these are my friends, Mazi and Annalise."

"Nice to meet you." He extends his hand, and I shake it reluctantly. His hands are clammy and soft, as if he has never experienced a hard day's work.

He reaches his hand to Mazi, but she doesn't take it.

"I thought we were having a girls' night." She glares at Randall, revulsion twisting in her face.

"I have to make sure to protect my baby girl from all the creeps." He possessively wraps his arms around Serena's waist, kissing the side of her neck.

She lets out a nervous laugh, shooting us an apologetic glance.

"The only creep she needs protection from is you," I mutter under my breath, just loud enough so Mazi can hear.

We each take one of Serena's arms, linking ours through hers.

"Come on—let's take some shots and then take pictures by the flower wall."

"While you ladies do that, I'm gonna hit the restroom," Randall says. "Don't go dancing with any other guys while I'm gone." He smacks Serena on the ass as he passes. "Or you'll be in trouble."

Even though he said it playfully, the flicker of unease on Serena's face says she knows he's not playing around.

"Order me a strawberry margarita, yeah?" he says over his shoulder as he saunters off.

Once Randall's out of earshot, she turns to us. "I'm so sorry!" she groans, burying her face in her hands. "When I told him I was going out tonight, he insisted on coming. He told me he was worried about me going out without him since I can't handle my liquor. Truthfully… I don't think he trusts me."

She waves down the bartender to get his attention. "Hi, can I get a strawberry margarita? And—uh—are you girls okay with lemon drops?"

Mazi and I both nod.

"And three lemon drop shots, please," she adds, sliding her card across the bar.

"I don't understand why he doesn't trust you," Mazi says, shaking her head. "You go to work and then come straight home to study!"

"Exactly! I barely have time to do anything!"

"That man is way too controlling," I say. "I would feel suffocated if I was with someone who wanted to do *everything* together."

"What do you even see in him?" Mazi asks, her brows furrowed. "You're gorgeous, and he's, well…"

"A walking red flag," I cut in, finishing her thought.

Serena doesn't disagree with us or try to come to Randall's defense.

The bartender slides our shots across the bar, and we raise

our glasses in unison. After a quick *clink*, we down them in one smooth motion.

"When I started nursing school, he became unbearably clingy," Serena says, setting her shot glass down. "I thought things would get better, but lately I—"

She spots Randall nearing us and quickly drops the conversation.

It's impossible to enjoy ourselves with Randall in our presence. Every time we start talking, he butts in and makes it about himself.

"Mazikeen! Annalise! Ah, it's so good to see you two lovely ladies!" Mazi and I turn toward the voice. Standing before us is a lanky man with red hair and freckles across his cheeks.

"Oh, hey," I reply, giving him a wave.

"Girl, who is that?" I whisper to Mazi.

"Hell if I know," she replies. "He is pretty cute, though."

"Do you remember me? I'm Austin Roberts," he says, flashing me a toothy grin. "We went to high school together."

"Oh, that's right! We, uh, had biology class together." I pull something out of my ass, hoping he doesn't notice that I'm completely blanking on who he is.

"Ah, so you *do* remember!" His smile widens.

"I had the biggest crush on you in high school." He steps closer to me, and I nearly pass out after I catch a whiff of his rancid breath. This man clearly hasn't picked up a toothbrush since we graduated high school.

I glance at Mazi, wanting to signal for her to save me, but she's deep in conversation with a beautiful woman next to us.

He leans in and I hold my breath, trying to control my face.

"So… are you seeing anyone right now?"

"No, I'm riding solo," I reply, forcing a smile.

Austin is pretty cute, and I might've gone for it if it wasn't for his poor dental hygiene.

Sifting through my purse, I reach in and retrieve my pack of gum. "Do you want some?" I ask, holding it up.

Please say yes.

"Nah, I'm good," he says.

Fuck me.

Mazi taps me on the shoulder. "Hey, do you mind if I go dancing?"

The woman she's been chatting with rests a hand on Mazi's hip, staring at her with pure lust.

I want to scream *Please don't leave me*, but I don't want to clamjam her.

"No, you go ahead! I'll join you in a bit."

Mazi gives me a quick smile, takes the woman's hand, and disappears into the crowd.

I scan the bar, looking for Serena, but she's nowhere to be found. Maybe she and Randall got into an argument.

Austin stares down at his phone, letting out a long sigh. "Ah, damn, my buddy just canceled on me." He slings his arm around my shoulder, and my body stiffens at his touch. "So you get the pleasure of keeping me company for the rest of the night."

I let out a nervous laugh. "Well, aren't I lucky?"

I wave at the bartender to order another drink. This is going to be a long night…

I lost count of how many drinks I had last night and can't even recall how I made it home. I haven't been this wasted since my freshmen year of college. I pray I didn't do anything stupid last night.

I should get up and make something to cure my hangover, but I don't want to leave the comfort of my bed.

Wait. This bed is too comfortable to be mine.

Slowly, I open my eyes.

I take in my surroundings and freak out when I realize I'm not in my apartment.

Fuck. Did I go home with Austin Stinky-Breath Roberts?

The bedroom I'm in is larger than my entire apartment and looks like it was pulled straight from a design magazine. Dark hardwood floors stretch across the space, and floor-to-ceiling windows flood the room with light. The stunning art pieces displayed above the modern king-sized platform bed bring the room to life.

This man may have bad breath, but he sure is rich—and he has an eye for interior design.

Scrambling out of bed, I get up to look for my belongings, and I'm instantly hit with a wave of nausea.

I scan the room, and spot a sliding barn door on the left and sprint to it, hoping it's the bathroom.

I stumble to the toilet and everything I consumed last night comes up, burning my throat.

The shower shuts off and footsteps echo, drawing closer while I continue to heave.

"Rough night?"

I glance up to find Maddox standing there, completely naked, with a smirk on his face.

I did indeed do something stupid, after all.

CHAPTER 8
Maddox

18 HOURS AGO

Snuggled on my couch with my dog Tsuki, I let "Coaster" by Khalid blast through the speakers and close my eyes, singing along. His *American Teen* album has been on repeat since I got back from Dauntless earlier today. I skip the happy, upbeat tracks and focus on the melancholic songs that reflect my current feelings.

My phone buzzes with an incoming call from Elijah.

I release a groan. Knowing him, he's probably calling to invite me to the club tonight, but I'm not in the mood. Hitting the green button, I accept the call while trying to come up with excuses for why I can't go.

"Hey, what's up, man?"

"Not much, bro. What are you up to right now?"

"I just woke up from a nap."

If he knew what I really was doing, he'd never let me hear the end of it.

"What are you doing napping so late?" he asks, a hint of confusion lacing his voice.

Glancing at my watch, I check the time—it's seven o'clock. It was a little past one when I came home.

Damn. Have I been sulking for that long?

"I don't know, man. I was just watching a show and passed the hell out," I reply.

"Well, I was calling to see if you wanted to come over and chill. I invited Andrés and Santiago. We can grill some burgers and have some drinks."

Santiago is a year older than Elijah and me, and we all grew close when we were on the basketball team in high school. He was pretty damn good at it, but decided to pursue a career in healthcare instead.

"By 'we,' you mean you and Santiago, right? I think I'd end up burning your penthouse down."

Elijah chuckles on the other line.

Unfortunately, Okāsan's skills in the kitchen were not something I inherited. I've attempted to cook a few times, but it's always a disaster. Being back home and having easy access to her cooking is a blessing. When I lived in Houston, I had to hire a private chef. Although the meals were good, nothing beats a home-cooked meal.

"So you coming over or what? You can sit there and look pretty while us men do all the work," he teases.

"You act like Andrés does much of anything." I scoff, rolling my eyes. "But yes, I'll be there."

"Alright, man. I'll see you later."

The line disconnects, and I get up to change. Listening to sad music for hours on end probably isn't the best way to spend a Friday night. Hopefully kicking it with the boys will help me get my mind off of *her*.

"So what do you think?" Elijah watches me as I take a bite of the burger. He tends to seek validation every time he cooks.

"It's not bad." I shrug, keeping my expression neutral. "Could use a bit of seasoning."

"Not bad?" His expression shifts into a frown. "I even added mushrooms to your burger, just like you like it."

The burger is delicious and cooked to perfection, but watching Elijah's reaction is priceless.

"How's your burger, man?" He turns his attention to Andrés in hopes that he'll give him a better response than I did.

"It's a bit dry," Andrés says flatly. "Good job on fries, though, Santiago." Reaching over, he grabs another handful from the plate, stuffing it in his mouth.

"Thanks, man. It was my first time making them from scratch," Santiago says.

Elijah stares at the ground, his shoulders slumping in defeat.

We exchange glances, suppressing our laughter.

"What's so funny?" he snaps, shooting us all a glare.

"We're just messing with you." I punch him playfully on the arm. "The burger tastes amazing."

His face lights up, a cocky grin sliding across his lips. "I knew you boys were just bullshitting. Everything I cook is top tier." He grabs the burger and takes a bite, a satisfied hum escaping his lips. "Damn, I did a good job. If I wasn't an NBA player, I could be an award-winning chef."

"This is *exactly* why we don't give you compliments." Santiago rolls his eyes. "You always get a big ole head."

Santiago's four-year-old son Isaiah walks up to him, showing him his plate. "Papi, I finished my food. Can I get some ice cream now?" All of his fries were gone, but he's only taken a small bite of his burger.

"No, mijo. You need to eat at least half of your burger."

"But I want ice cream," he pouts.

Santiago crosses his arms, fixing him with a stern look. "If you don't eat more of your burger, you won't get any ice cream."

"Okay." Isaiah sighs, climbing on the couch and squeezing between Santiago and me as he munches on his burger.

The resemblance between the two of them is uncanny. Big hazel eyes, the same upturned nose, and thick curly hair.

Santiago's ex, Gabriela, left without a word when Isaiah was only a year old. He hasn't heard from her since. The fucked-up thing is he later found out Gabriela had been cheating on him a few months after their son was born. I guess she couldn't handle being a mother.

He was accepted into medical school, but had to give it all up so he could raise his son. Santiago's father helps out when he can, but he's busy running his own business.

"I ate more of the burger! See?" Isaiah says, grinning widely.

"Good job, mijo! I'll get you some ice cream now." Santiago smiles, ruffling Isaiah's hair.

Santiago returns with a bowl of Oreo ice cream, and Isaiah claps his hands. He takes a big spoonful and the ice cream smears all over his mouth. "This is so yummy. Do you want some ice cream, Uncle Maddox?"

"No, I'm not ready for dessert yet," I say, shaking my head. "I'm gonna eat another burger."

"Another one?" He gasps, his big brown eyes bulging out. "How can you eat so much?"

The guys erupt in laughter.

"He always eats like he's been starving for days," Elijah says.

"Be a dear and fix me another plate."

"Get your own damn plate," he replies, settling deeper in his seat. "I'm comfortable right now. I don't feel like getting up."

"You're a bullshit-ass host." I get up from my seat, and Elijah flips me the middle finger.

When I return from the kitchen, Andrés glances up. "So, how did the meeting at Dauntless go?"

I haven't brought it up, and I was hoping they would forget about it. But I've been talking about the collaboration with the guys all week because of how excited I was.

"It went well." Picking my beer up, I take a swig. "I'm going back next week to discuss in more detail what I want."

"Sweet. I'm so excited for you, man," Santiago says with a smile. "I love their clothes. They have the best quality."

Elijah wiggles his brows, a devilish smirk dancing on his face. "Were the fashion designers hot?"

The encounter I had with Annalise flashes through my mind, her harsh words replaying.

"Nothing you do could ever fix things between us. So do us both a favor and stop trying, okay?"

The bottle digs into my palms as I grip it tighter, my knuckles whitening. My vision blurs and the world around me begins to sway out of focus.

"Hey, man, you good?" Santiago pats me on the shoulder, worry etched in his face.

Taking a deep breath in, I stare at the ground. "I, uh… I saw Annalise today."

The room falls silent at the mention of her name. Everyone stops what they're doing. They stare at me, anxiously waiting for me to continue.

Tipping my beer back, I chug the rest of it and then bring them up to date on what happened.

"Damn, bro. That must've been hard," Santiago says softly.

"Seeing her again… Did it bring back any old feelings?" Andrés asks.

I wave my hand in the air. "Nah. That ship sailed a long time ago. I've moved on with my life. If she doesn't want to try to be cordial, so be it." The lie tastes sour on my tongue.

"He'll be fine, boys. All he needs is a sexy lady to warm his bed tonight." Elijah holds his fist out, and I bump it.

"Yep. Nothing a good lay can't fix." I smile, but I can tell it doesn't quite reach my eyes.

"Fucking around and avoiding your feelings isn't healthy, man." Santiago shakes his head.

"What feelings?" I scoff. "I'm over her."

Pulling my phone out, I scroll through my contacts and shoot a text to Hannah Chen, a model I've hooked up with in the past.

> What are you doing tonight?

She replies within seconds.

> HANNAH
>
> Hopefully you 😏

Andrés leans forward, letting out an exasperated sigh. "Come on, man. Annalise broke your fucking heart. You're gonna sit there and tell me seeing her again didn't hurt?"

Ignoring him, I continue texting Hannah.

"You pretend like you don't care," he presses, "but I know—"

I slam my palms against the couch cushions. "I don't want to talk about her anymore! I just want to have a nice night with my boys," I say, forcing a smile. "I am *fine*. Trust me."

Santiago clears his throat and starts telling us a funny story about Isaiah in order to ease the tension. No one has the balls to mention Annalise again.

From the moment I enter Hannah's apartment, she wastes no time. Dragging me to her bedroom, she gets on top of me and starts kissing me aggressively.

"I want to feel you in my mouth." She licks the side of my neck while rubbing me through my jeans.

My phone starts buzzing. I pull it out of my pocket to silence it, but my stomach somersaults when I see who's calling.

Annalise's name lights up my phone. Her smiling face fills the screen, a photo I took of her on the beach, sunlight dancing on her skin. It was from our summer before college—before everything changed. I couldn't bring myself to delete her number after we broke up.

So much for getting her off my mind tonight…

"Hey, I gotta take this call." I gently push Hannah off of me and climb off the bed.

She stares at me in disbelief as I walk out of her bedroom.

"Monroe? Are you okay?" I ask, pressing the phone to my ear.

"Hey, Kamadooo," she drawls.

I hear the muffled thump of music in the background—she's definitely at the club.

"You know, I really hate yooou. But I really wanna fuuuck yooou."

Okay—she's plastered.

"Oh, is that so?"

"I want you to bend me ooover Veronica's desk."

I start imagining her bent over a desk with her skirt hiked up as I pound into her. My hands tightly grip her ass as I drive myself deeper. Her loud moans fill the—

Shaking my head, I blow out a breath.

I need to get a hold of myself. Now is *not* the time to be having sexual fantasies about my ex.

"God, you must be hammered right now," I say, chuckling.

"Nooo, I'm not," she slurs.

"Where are you? I'll come pick you up."

"Heey, yooou. Where are we?"

I hear a girl's voice answering her in the background.

"I'm at Lush Lounge," Annalise says.

I do a quick search of the place on my GPS app—it's only ten minutes away. With my Ferrari, I could be there in no time.

"Hang tight. I'll be there soon, Monroe."

"Please hurrry, Maddy Bear! I'm sooo hooornyyy!" She bursts into a fit of giggles and the line disconnects.

"Everything okay?" Hannah comes up behind me and wraps her arms around my waist.

I turn to face her. "I gotta take care of something important. I'll be back later."

"Okay. Hurry back. I'll be waiting." She nibbles on my ear, and then opens the door to let me out.

I search the packed club for Annalise and spot her standing in the back by the bar, barely able to hold herself up.

Lowering my cap over my face, I weave through the crowd, praying that no one recognizes me. Normally I don't mind entertaining my fans, but I don't want to lose sight of Annalise. She's drunk and alone in a bar. I don't want anything bad to happen to her.

"Kamadooo, you maaade it!" She throws her arms around my neck, the pungent smell of liquor radiating off of her. "I can't waaait to shooow yooou the new moooves I picked up."

I shake my head, chuckling. "Come on, Monroe. Let's get you outta here." Wrapping my arms around her waist, I guide her as she stumbles out of the club.

I head to the valet stand and hand the attendant my ticket. While I'm waiting for him to bring my car around, a couple next to me erupts into a heated argument.

"I wasn't flirting with the bartender!" a petite Asian girl with dark black hair shouts at a hefty man.

"Then why the hell was he giving you free drinks?" he

shouts back. She pulls at her hair and lets out a loud groan as they continue to argue back and forth.

The valet pulls up with my car, clearly ecstatic that he could drive it even for a short period. I hand him a generous tip and help Annalise into the passenger seat.

"Woo hoo! Let's keep this party going!" Kicking off her heels, Annalise sprints to the living room.

I spent the entire thirty-minute drive back to my house listening to her sing along to Taylor Swift. I thought she would be exhausted by now, but she is clearly full of energy.

Tsuki comes out of my room and jumps on Annalise. I expect her to growl or bare her teeth, but to my surprise, she wags her tail wildly and sticks out her tongue.

Annalise squats down to pet her. "Oh my goodness, who is this precious fluff ball?"

Tsuki covers her in kisses and Annalise lets out an excited giggle.

"Hey, Kamadooo! Where the hell is the music? I wanna dance!"

"You can dance tomorrow. You need to go to bed." Taking her hand, I lead her toward my room.

"No! I wanna dance!" She yanks her hand free, strutting to my living room. Her smile widens the moment she spots my Echo. "Alexa! Play 'WAP' by Cardi B and Megan Thee Stallion."

The bass booms through my surround sound as she hops up on the couch, belting out the lyrics and rolling her hips to the beat.

I can't help but laugh and shake my head as she sings every filthy word.

Her phone buzzes against the floor where she dropped it at

the start of her impromptu solo dance party. The screen lights up with an incoming video call from Mazikeen.

Scooping it up from the floor, I swipe to answer it. Mazikeen hates my fucking guts, so I know she's about to go ballistic when she sees my face.

"Annalise, where the hell—"

Mazikeen's eyes practically pop out of her skull when she sees me on the screen. "What the fuck are you doing with her?"

"Hello to you too, Mazikeen." I smile, waving at her—which ticks her off even more. "She was drunk out of her mind at the club, so I came to rescue her. Where were you?"

She glowers at me, nostrils flaring. "Maddox, I swear if you lay one hand on her, I'll fucking kill you."

I roll my eyes. "Relax. I'm not going to do anything to her."

"Where is she?"

I flip the camera, revealing Annalise twerking on the couch.

"See? She's fine. She's having her own little dance party."

"What's your address? I'm coming to get her."

"No, you're not," I say firmly. "You've been drinking. You shouldn't be driving right now. Enjoy your night. I'll take care of her and bring her back in the morning."

"I fucking hate you," she snarls.

"The feeling is mutual."

I hang up and look over to find Annalise slumped over on the couch, fighting to stay awake. Looks like the dance party is over.

Scooping her up, I carry her to my bedroom and gently lay her on the bed. After stripping down to my briefs, I climb in next to her. It's been a long night and I don't have the energy to walk to the guest room.

Annalise reaches over, tugging on my briefs. "Why aren't you naked yet?"

Chuckling softly, I grab a pillow and place it between us. "Go to bed, Annalise."

"I'm not"—she lets out a yawn—"sleepy… yet… I want you to fuck…" Her eyelids start drooping and she begins to doze off.

Turning to the side, I watch her chest rise and fall as she drifts off into a peaceful slumber. Her wild hair is spread all over the pillow, her makeup smudged, but she still looks so beautiful.

When morning comes, she'll go back to hating me. I want to enjoy this moment while it lasts.

The next morning, I step out of the shower and find Annalise bent over the toilet, puking her guts out.

"Rough night?"

Her eyes go wide as she sucks in a sharp gasp. "What the hell am I doing here?"

"How much do you remember from last night?"

Pushing herself to her feet, she leans against the wall, scrubbing a hand down her face. "Not much. Everything's a blur. I overdid it last night—had four, maybe five drinks?" She pauses, chewing on her bottom lip and rubbing the back of her neck. "And an edible…"

A laugh bubbles from my lips and I shake my head. "Geez. No wonder you were so fucked up."

I catch her staring at me, her gaze lingering when it drops below my waist.

I clear my throat and she quickly looks away.

She wrinkles her nose and shields her eyes. "Can you please cover up?"

Cocking my head to the side, I smirk. "Why? It's not like you haven't seen it before."

"Well, I don't want to see it." She folds her arms over her chest, rolling her eyes. "It'll make me throw up again."

Reaching over and snagging a towel off of the rack, I wrap it around myself. "You seemed to be enjoying it last night."

Heat rises to her cheeks and her eyes go wide.

Taking a step closer, I place my hands on the wall, caging her in. "You were screaming my name over and over…"

"Oh, God! We slept together?" Her hands fly to her mouth. "Fuck, this was a mistake!" she blurts, burying her face in her hands.

"Relax, Monroe." My hand moves to her inner thigh and I lean in, my lips grazing her ear. "You should already know that if we *did* sleep together, you'd be struggling to walk right now."

Goosebumps rise on her skin as I slowly slide my hand up. She bites her lip, arching her back when my hand reaches the hem of her skirt.

For someone who claims she wants nothing to do with me, she clearly seems to want me to pleasure her. But I'm not going to give her what she wants just yet. She's gonna to have to beg for it.

Removing my hand, I take a few steps back. She frowns, her face crowded with disappointment.

"Why the long face?" I ask, flashing her a devious smile.

She places her hands on her hips, shooting me a glare. "How did I end up here?"

"You drunk dialed me."

"Oh, bullshit. I deleted your number years ago," she scoffs.

I place my hand over my chest, smiling. "Aw, I guess you remembered it by heart then. I'm quite touched."

She rolls her eyes and an impatient groan escapes her lips. "Just tell me what happened, Kamado."

As I catch her up on the events from last night, a deep shade of crimson flushes her cheeks.

"Oh, God! This is so embarrassing." She shakes her head. "I can't believe I said those things to you. I hope you know I didn't mean any of it!"

"Whatever you say." I shrug. "You could really use a shower, by the way. You smell like shit."

"Yeah, sure! Let me hop in the shower and then put my *dirty* clothes back on. Great fucking idea!" She rolls her eyes at me.

I walk to my room and grab the bag that's sitting in the corner near my nightstand, then hand it to her.

"I had my assistant buy some clothes for you this morning. I figured you wouldn't wanna go home in the same clothes from last night."

"Oh… um, thanks. You didn't have to do that," she says, her tone softening. "How much was it? I can pay you back."

"Don't sweat it, Monroe."

I grab my fresh clothes that are lying on the counter and step out of the bathroom, shutting the door behind me.

Dropping my towel to the floor, I change into grey sweatpants and an oversized Dauntless tee.

I walk to the living room, plopping down on the couch and pull out my phone to check my notifications—which I haven't done since last night.

There are several missed calls and a string of texts from Hannah.

I forgot I told her I'd be back. *Oops.*

HANNAH

Maddox! Where the fuck are you? It's been over an hour.

Hello? Why aren't you answering my calls?

You can forget about the blowjob! Don't ever contact me again, asshole!

I start to type something back but then decide to leave it alone. There's no use in trying to apologize, because the truth is, I'm not sorry. Not even in the slightest.

Annalise walks into the living room wearing the clothes my assistant picked out for her—a cropped sweater and high-waisted jeans that does wonders for her hips and thick thighs.

Turning my attention back to my phone, I try to clear out the explicit thoughts of her that are running through my mind. Containing myself is going to be a challenge.

Tsuki lifts her head from the bowl and trots over to Annalise, tail wagging with excitement.

"Oh, hi, pretty girl! What's your name?" Annalise crouches down and pets her soft, fluffy fur.

"Her name is Tsuki. I found her wandering around campus a couple of years ago and decided to take her in."

Growing up, I always wanted a dog, but Otōsan was never fond of pets.

"Oh, who could abandon this sweet girl?" she coos while rubbing Tsuki's belly.

"She seems to really like you." I smile. "It usually takes forever for her to warm up to people. She's still not a fan of Elijah. She's house trained, but she pissed on his shoes a few weeks ago." I laugh, recalling the look on his face when he found his limited-edition sneakers drenched in urine.

She chuckles. "I bet he wasn't happy about that. He's always been obsessed with his sneakers."

"He has a whole room full of them at his penthouse."

"He sure knows how to spend his money," she quips, shaking her head.

Stretching out my legs, I lean back into the couch. "Man, I wish I had videos of you from last night. You were hilarious."

"Well, I'm glad you don't, because I would rather not die from embarrassment."

"Wait—you know what? I think the security camera in my living room might've captured the footage."

Opening my app, I scroll through the footage from last night. I find a thumbnail of her dancing and press play. I turn the phone around and show her the video of her dancing to the 'WAP' song.

She narrows her eyes, fists clenching at her side. "Maddox! You better delete that shit right now!"

"I think I'm gonna upload it to YouTube," I tease. "It'll get loads of views."

"You better fucking not!" Marching toward the couch, she lunges at me. "Give it to me, *now!*" She wrestles with me, trying to grab my phone, and ends up on top of me with her legs straddling my hips.

"This feels familiar," I drawl, staring deep into those captivating sapphire and emerald eyes.

I manage to play it cool, but in reality, I'm losing my mind. Having her on top of me fully clothed turns me on way more than the women I've had naked in my bed. The countless flings I've had over the last few years never amounted to what I had with Annalise. All of that was meaningless, empty, and purely for pleasure.

I craved her touch, to feel her body on mine.

Man, have I missed being between her legs.

I try to contain myself by focusing on my breathing, but it's no use. My cock is already fully erect.

"Are you gonna get off of me anytime soon?" I lift a brow, a smirk tugging at my lips. "Or do you plan on staying on top of me for the rest of the day?"

She doesn't move a muscle but continues to stare at me, mouth agape. Gripping her thighs, I pull her closer to me so she can feel how much I want her.

She gasps loudly, her eyes burning with lust.

Reaching up, my thumb brushes across her bottom lip. "Am I making you nervous?"

"Not at all," she answers breathlessly.

"The look in your eyes tells a different story. I've seen that look many times before." I drag my fingertips inside the waistband of her jeans and her breathing becomes erratic.

"I hate you..." she whispers.

"Oh, yeah? Then why aren't you resisting me?" My fingers dig into her hips and I grind into her.

"Maddox…" she moans softly.

She takes control, fisting my shirt as she rocks her hips, rubbing herself against my erection. Her breathing turns shallow, quickening with each movement.

Fuck. If she keeps moving like this, I'm going to make a mess in my pants.

Need overwhelms me. I slip my hand between us and pop the button of her jeans, desperate to feel how wet she is for me. "If you don't want this," I murmur, "just say the word and I'll stop."

CHAPTER 9
Annalise

His words echo in my ear and I can't for the life of me bring myself to ask him to stop. Feeling Maddox pressed against me makes me forget about all the anger I have for him. All I can focus on is the friction between my legs and how much pleasure it brings me.

My body remembers him even though I've tried my hardest to forget. It wants to relive being with him. To relive being *claimed* by him.

Damn my raging hormones for having a mind of their own.

Maddox slips his hand into the front of my jeans and my lips part in anticipation.

The front door creaks open, footsteps quickly approaching. "Masashi, I brought you some—"

Fuck!

Mrs. Kamado nearly drops her bags when she locks eyes with me.

I quickly scramble off of him and approach her, heat that's entirely fueled by embarrassment crawling up my spine. After all these years, why did our first encounter have to involve her catching me in a compromising position with her son?

Waving my hand, I give her a faint smile. "Hi, Mrs. Kamado."

Izumi pulls me into a warm embrace. "Oh, Annalise, it's so good to see you. I have missed you so much."

"It's good to see you too," I say, giving her a warm smile.

She squeezes my hand, her eyes lighting up with joy. "I'm so happy you gave him another chance."

I open my mouth to respond, but the words escape me. My eyes flick to Maddox, who's shifting uncomfortably on the couch.

"You two have always been so perfect for each other. Poor Masashi was so devastated when you broke up with him, I had to—"

"Okāsan!" Maddox gets up from the couch and stands behind us with his arms folded across his broad chest.

Izumi whips her head around. "What?"

"We're not together," he says, his tone firm.

Her brows draw tight, the corners of her mouth turning down into a frown. "What do you mean? Because it sure looked like you two were—"

He sighs. "No, Okāsan," he says, shaking his head.

"Oh… I see." Izumi drops my hand, the light in her eyes fading.

He rakes a hand through his hair. "You have to call me when you come over. You can't just barge in whenever you please."

"But you gave me the code to your house so that I can drop off food for you. You've never had a problem with it before." She strokes her chin, eyes ping-ponging between Maddox and me. "Was I interrupting something?"

"Yes, you were," Maddox says.

"If you want, I can leave so that you can—"

"No. No. You don't have to do that." I throw my hands up, chuckling nervously. "You weren't interrupting anything, I promise. I was, uh… trying to grab something and fell on top of him." I flash a smile in her direction, but she doesn't look convinced.

Maddox leans into me, whispering, "I bet you enjoyed being on top of me, didn't you, Monroe?"

"*Please.* Nothing involving *you* is enjoyable." I roll my eyes at him, but my core starts throbbing madly as memories of how good he used to make me feel surge through me.

It doesn't help that he's wearing those damn grey sweatpants that do nothing to hide the outline of his thick cock.

His lips curl into a sly smile when he catches where my eyes have landed. "Your jeans are still unbuttoned, by the way."

Heat flushes my cheeks and I quickly button them up, hoping his mom doesn't notice.

I've made a complete and total fool out of myself this weekend. I have to get out of here. I have to get away from *him.*

"Um, I should really get going. Can you give me a ride home?"

"Uh, yeah, sure," Maddox says, his tone laced with a tinge of disappointment.

Izumi pouts, looking at me with sad eyes. "Do you have to go now? I made some tonkotsu ramen. There's enough for all of us."

My mouth waters at the thought of my taste buds being blessed with her ramen. There's no way I can say no to her. There are a lot of good Japanese restaurants in San Francisco, but none come close to being as phenomenal as Izumi's. She's a Michelin-starred chef, after all.

I pass by her restaurant every day on the way home from work, and I always contemplate getting dinner from there, but I didn't want to run the risk of bumping into Maddox.

Oh, what the hell. Sharing one meal with my ex and his mom can't hurt, right?

"I am pretty hungry," I reply with a smile. "And your ramen

is exactly what I need." My eyes flick to Maddox. "Do you mind?"

A crooked smile ghosts his lips as he shakes his head. "Not at all."

"Perfect!" she beams. "Masashi, go show her to the dining room, then come back and help me prepare."

Following Maddox down the hall, I trail behind him as he leads me to the dining room. I pause as we enter, captivated by its beauty.

It's a traditional Japanese dining room with shoji screens and tatami mats on top of the wood flooring. There is a low table in the middle, surrounded by floor mats. With natural lighting streaming in and the presence of bamboo trees, the space carries an effortless sense of tranquility.

I'm sure sitting on the floor to eat isn't comfortable for someone as tall as Maddox, but his culture has always been important to him.

"You still like your ramen with an extra boiled egg?" Maddox asks.

I settle down on the cushion. "Yes, that would be great. Thank you."

He gives me a quick smile before walking back to the kitchen.

My phone buzzes in my pocket. I pull it out and see a new text from Mazi.

MAZI

Bitch, are you alive???

Barely. I feel like shit 😫

MAZI

I'm so sorry!!! 😭 😭

I should've never left you. I honestly thought you were vibing with Austin.

> Girl, fuck no! His breath stank so bad 

MAZI

OMG I feel so bad. I'm sorry for being such a crappy friend.

> It's okay. I still love you 🖤

MAZI

I could barely sleep all night. I was so worried about you when I found out you left with Maddox. Y'all didn't hook up last night, did you?

> Come on, Mazi. I'm not so desperate to get laid that I would hook up with that asshole! 🙄

MAZI

Okay. I just wanna make sure.

Even though Mazi is my best friend, there's no way in hell I can tell her about what happened earlier. She can't stand Maddox and would be livid if she knew how close I came to giving in to him.

"Thank you so much, Mrs. Kamado. It was delicious." I slurp up the last bit of my rich, creamy ramen, not wanting to leave behind a single drop of the flavorful broth.

Izumi smiles at me, her eyes crinkling. "I'm so glad you liked it." She turns her attention to Maddox. "What would you do without me? You would probably be malnourished and not have those big strong muscles."

He rolls his eyes, slurping down another spoonful of ramen.

"Damn, Kamado. You still don't know how to cook?" I tease.

"I can cook. I just choose not to," he replies with a shrug.

Izumi snorts. "Putting bread in the toaster is hardly *cooking*."

"Hey! It always comes out perfectly toasty!"

"Annalise, remember that time he tried to bake me a birthday cake and you had to come help?" She glances in my direction, chuckling softly.

The Kamados' kitchen looks as though a curious toddler has been left unattended. Their marble counters are dusted with flour, and eggshells litter the floor.

Maddox flashes me his adorable dimpled smile as I assess the mess. He's wearing his mom's pink apron that's way too small, and there's cake batter all over him.

Dipping my fingers into the batter, I give it a taste and immediately gag, spitting it into the sink. "This tastes like concrete."

"I don't know what I did wrong. I followed the recipe." Maddox pulls out his phone to show me.

Glancing over at the counter, I spot a measuring cup sticking out of a bag of salt.

A laugh escapes my lips. "You used salt instead of sugar, you big goof."

He slaps a palm on his forehead. "Ah, dang it! How did I miss that?"

I place my hand on his shoulder. "Aw, it's okay, Maddy Bear. We can fix this. Just help me clean up the kitchen, and I'll make some new batter."

Izumi and I shake with laughter at the memory.

She squeezes his shoulder. "It's okay, Masashi. It's the thought that counts."

One of the hardest things about the breakup was not being able to see his family. His dad mostly kept to himself, but his mom and sister, Asami, treated me like family. Izumi always looked out for me and made sure I was fed.

Asami and I became really close, but our friendship ended when Maddox and I broke up. Having to cut ties with people I shared a bond with was not an easy thing to do.

"So, Annalise, what brings you back to San Francisco?"

Izumi asks. "I thought you wanted to live in New York and start your fashion line there?"

Taking a sip of my water, I avert my eyes. "I got really lonely and I missed my family." Not a lie, but not the full truth either. Maddox doesn't need to know any more about my life than he already does.

My body may have forgotten his betrayal, but I sure as hell haven't.

Maddox fixes me with a puzzled look, doubt flickering in his eyes and letting on that he doesn't fully believe me, but I brush it off.

CHAPTER 10
Annalise

FOUR YEARS AGO

"My mom's gonna kill you if she finds you here," I whisper as I quietly shut my bedroom door. "Please, she loves me more than you," Maddox teases.

He plops down on the bed and pulls the covers over himself, getting comfortable.

I join him in bed and he pulls me close, running his fingers through my hair.

"I just had to come see you. I missed you too much," Maddox says, pouting.

"You saw me at school today, you dork." I chuckle, leaning in to kiss his cheek.

"It's not the same as getting to sleep next to you, and waking up with you in my arms." He presses a tender kiss to my lips. My stomach flutters as a warm blush spreads across my cheeks.

Everyone at school sees Maddox as a popular jock, but there's so much more to him. Beneath that tough exterior is the sweetest and most caring person I know. And he only ever shows his soft side to me.

"I really hope we get accepted to the colleges we applied to in New York," I say with a sigh.

"We'll get in, without a doubt," he says, squeezing my hand.

"Easy for you to say—you're the valedictorian," I scoff, rolling my eyes. "You'll get accepted anywhere."

He props himself up on an elbow, resting his head on his hand. "And so will you. Your portfolio is amazing, and your designs will blow them away."

"I feel like it won't be good enough." My fingers twist in the sheets as doubts creep into my mind. "What if they hate it?"

"Annalise Rose Monroe! Talk down to yourself one more time and I'll leave," he says, his tone playful. "If you give yourself a compliment, you'll be rewarded later." He whispers the last sentence, trailing kisses along my neck as his hand slides up my inner thigh.

A rush of heat floods through me.

"Fine." I roll my eyes. "I, Annalise Rose Monroe, am a talented, creative, strong, and beautiful woman." I lift my gaze to him, a smirk tugging my lips. "There. Are you satisfied now?"

"You forgot to add: with a big ass, and a mouth that can—"

He chuckles as I shove him playfully. "Shut up, you idiot."

"You're going to be a world-famous fashion designer, and I am going to be an NBA star and make it to the hall of fame." An adorable dimpled smile stretches across his face. "We'll be the ultimate power couple."

"Together, we'll be unstoppable," I add.

Maddox climbs on top of me, kissing me softly.

"Now it's time for me to give you your reward," he murmurs, smiling against my lips.

CHAPTER 11
Maddox

After lunch, a notification pops up on my phone alerting me that the Uber driver is arriving. I was planning to drive Annalise home in hopes that we could spend more time together, but she insisted I stay and visit with my mom.

I could tell that she didn't trust herself to be alone with me. Especially since she nearly lost control earlier when we ended up with our bodies tangled together on the couch.

Watching Annalise and Okāsan share laughter over a meal filled me with a warm wave of nostalgia. I know she only stayed because she didn't want to appear disrespectful by turning down Okāsan's food, but part of me clung to the hope that she wanted to continue being around me.

I wish I knew the real reason why she was back home. Annalise is not the type to give up on her dreams so easily. Her returning home because she felt homesick doesn't make sense to me. Especially since she spent the last four years living in New York.

It's never been easy for Annalise to open up to people. She likes to pretend everything is okay because she doesn't want to burden anyone with her problems, but I've always been able to tell when something is bothering her. She can wear a smile on her face, but I can still see the pain behind her eyes.

"Don't be a stranger! Swing by the restaurant any time. You will never have to worry about paying." Okāsan pulls Annalise into a tight embrace.

"I will! It was so nice to see you again, Mrs. Kamado." Annalise smiles. "Thanks again for lunch!"

"It was nice to see you too, Annalise. You have been missed."

Annalise waves her goodbye and slips on her shoes.

"I'll walk you out," I say, holding the door open for her.

The door clicks shut behind us. With a nervous glance, she stuffs her hands into her pockets, eyes darting to meet mine. "Uh —thank you for the clothes, and for last night. I'm sorry for all the trouble I caused and for ruining your weekend."

"Oh, don't apologize, Monroe. You didn't ruin my weekend," I say, reassuring her with a smile. I could never be mad about spending time with Annalise. It's clear that she may hate me, but this was one of the best weekends I've had in years. All those nights I spent partying till sunrise and losing myself in various women don't even come close to how it felt to wake up next to her.

We stand there in silence, looking at one another. There are so many questions I want to ask her, so many things I want to say.

What would have happened if we hadn't been interrupted earlier?

Can we meet up somewhere private one day, so we can finally talk and I can tell you all the things I've been wanting to say to you all these years?

Before I can say anything, the driver lightly honks his horn, and I miss my opportunity.

She clears her throat and throws her thumb over her shoulder. "I—uh… I should get going."

"Right. Don't want to keep him waiting."

I start to lean in for a hug, but decide against it. I don't know if I would be able to handle the sting of her rejection. Letting out a shaky breath, I tuck my hands into my pockets instead. "Text me when you get home so I know you made it safely."

She nods, giving me a quick smile and walking toward the car.

Her eyes linger on me for a brief moment before she slips into the back seat.

The car peels away, and a part of me leaves with it.

Opening the front door, I step back inside and walk to the kitchen to help Okāsan with the dishes. I always tell her to load them into the dishwasher, but she insists on hand washing.

"Why didn't you tell me Annalise was back?" she asks, arching a brow at me as she scrubs the pot.

"Because I found out less than twenty-four hours ago. She works at Dauntless, the athletic brand I'm collaborating with."

"See! That's clearly a sign from God!" She passes me the cleaned pot, smiling at me giddily. "You two are meant to be together."

I roll my eyes to conceal the warmth swelling in my chest. Maybe it *is* a sign from God. I lived away from San Francisco for four years, and during all my visits back, I never once encountered Annalise. Maybe the timing wasn't right then, but it could be now.

But then Annalise's words slice through my mind, destroying whatever hope I had.

"You may have your dream career, a nice car, and all the money in the world, but you sure as hell will never have me."

No matter how needy she had been in my lap, she wants nothing to do with me. I need to see her again so we can finally talk about what happened. At the very least, I need closure.

I can't allow myself to be vulnerable again. If she breaks my heart, I don't know if I'll be able to recover this time.

"What was she doing here, anyway? Did she spend the night?"

As much as I love my mother, she can be extremely nosy. *Especially* when it involves my love life.

"She was at a bar last and got really drunk, so I picked her up."

"Oh, my boy is such a gentleman!" A smile lights up her face. There's a twinkle in her eye I haven't seen in quite some time. "I knew you still loved her."

"I don't love her," I reply dryly.

She turns off the water and looks me dead in the eye. "You can't lie to me, Masashi. I saw the way you looked at her."

"It's been years, Okāsan," I say with a shrug, keeping my voice steady. "I've moved on."

She shoots me a look that says, *You're full of shit.* "If you've moved on, then why haven't you gotten into another relationship?"

I throw my head back, letting out a groan. "Geez! Just because I've been single since we broke up doesn't mean I haven't moved on. I'm not interested in dating anyone. My career is the most important thing to me right now."

"There's a reason why she came back into your life. Don't let her walk away again."

"So, what do you think?" Trang asks, chewing her bottom lip as her fingers drum against the table.

I've been staring at her sketches for a good ten minutes now, and I'm trying to come up with a nice way to tell her that I abhor her designs. The clothes she drew are fitting for a sixty-year-old man—

not someone in their twenties. I want to incorporate my Japanese culture in this clothing line, and it's as though she completely disregarded that vision. I need to work with someone who knows me.

I need to work with Annalise.

She would know exactly what I want.

"The designs are great… But they're not exactly what I had in mind." I give her a smile, hoping to lessen the burn.

"Oh." Her face falls as she pinches her forearm, unable to meet my gaze. "What's wrong with them?"

Everything. Where should I even start?

"It's not my style. I want something more modern. The color choice is a bit loud."

"Oh. I see…" She clears her throat, grabbing the sketchbook and clutching it tight to her chest. "I'll get started on some new designs to show you next time you're here."

"Sounds great. I'll see you then," I say.

She forces a smile and walks out of the conference room with her head hung low.

Damn it. Was I too harsh?

I wasn't about to lie to her and tell her it was everything I wanted. Plus, in her line of work, you would think she'd be able to accept criticism.

I glance around the office, and my pulse ricochets when I spot Annalise. She's at her desk, typing away, completely focused. My heartbeat quickens when I catch sight of her skirt—cut just high enough to reveal the tattoo of roses inked along her thigh.

Earlier, when I arrived at Dauntless, she wasn't here. I asked her coworker, Ivy, where she was and she told me Annalise was out buying supplies for Veronica. She gave me a funny look when I asked about Annalise, but I didn't care. I had to see her again. I would've found an excuse to stick around until she returned.

I had basketball practice earlier this morning, so I made sure to pack a nice outfit to change into and to wear my best cologne.

Before I approach her, I quickly glance at my reflection in the mirror that's hanging on the wall to make sure I look presentable.

"You wanna get some phở for lunch?" Ivy asks Annalise.

"Ooh, yes. It's the perfect weather for that," she replies.

"Okay! I need to go to the restroom. I'll meet you out front!" Ivy says as she steps inside the elevator.

Annalise gets up from her seat and grabs her purse, knocking over her sketchbook in the process.

"Damn it," she mutters with a sigh.

"Here, let me get that for you." Crouching down, I reach for the sketchbook, which is open to a page with a beautiful green gown.

I stare at it in awe, admiring the intricate details. "Your talents are wasted here. You should quit and start your own clothing line. I know it would be a huge success."

She snatches the sketchbook from me. "Unlike you, I don't have rich parents, nor am I a millionaire. Am I just supposed to pull the money out of my ass?"

I mean, it's big enough...

"If you need help starting your business, I can help you. I have plenty of connections, and I'd promote your fashion line on my social media. And if you're worried about the money, I'd be more than happy to give you—"

"I'm not a damn charity case!" she snaps.

I let out a heavy sigh, shaking my head. "You confuse the hell outta me, Monroe. A few days ago, you were practically *begging* me to fuck you. And now you can't even stand being in the same room as me? Make up your damn mind."

She shoots me a glare. "I was drunk. Don't read too much into it."

"What is it they say? A drunk mind speaks sober thoughts?"

If looks could kill, I'd be six feet under. "But I wasn't talking about that." I flash her a cocky smile, keeping my voice low. "I'm talking about what happened on my couch."

Her eyes widen, heat flooding her cheeks. My cock strains against my slacks from thinking about the look in her eyes and the sound of her soft moans as she straddled my lap.

The office begins to clear. Everyone is heading off to their lunch break, leaving me and Annalise alone.

"You were one hundred percent sober, and I know you wanted it as much as I did."

She blows air out of her cheeks, rolling her eyes. "Okay, Kamado. Whatever helps you sleep at night."

Stepping closer, I take her hand in mine, slowly tracing circles on her palm. "You don't have to pretend like you didn't enjoy feeling me between your legs."

She parts her lips slightly, an insatiable gleam igniting in her eyes.

"How about we pick up where we left off?" I whisper, brushing my lips against her ear. "We can go to your boss's office, and I'll bend you over her desk and fuck you just like you've been wanting me to."

The ache I have for her is unbearable. I need her now.

Suddenly, she shoves me off of her and the moment is over. "You are fucking unbelievable!"

I stare at her, thrown off by the sudden shift in her mood.

"You think you can waltz back into my life and pretend like nothing ever happened?" she snaps.

"What are you talking about? *You're* the one sending all these mixed signals! And now you're getting mad at me for what?" I drag my hand through my hair, the frustration boiling over. "You are fucking impossible."

"What happened last weekend shouldn't have happened," she says, crossing her arms tightly over her chest. "And what happened now... That was a mistake. A lapse in judgment." She lets out a short, bitter laugh. "Thank God I came to my senses before it went further."

"Why do you keep lying to yourself, Annalise?"

"I'm not. I *hate* you. And I will always hate you. I'll *never* forgive you for what you did."

Before I can reply, the elevator door slides open and Ivy walks through.

"Girl, I've been waiting down there for ten minutes. Everything okay?" Ivy asks, her eyes flicking between us.

"Sorry! Veronica needed me to answer some emails," Annalise says, pushing her purse straps over her shoulder. "Let's go."

She walks off to the elevator with Ivy, leaving me behind in the cold, empty office with a hole in my heart.

CHAPTER 12
Annalise

FOUR YEARS AGO

"Hey, gorgeous!" Maddox's grin lights up my phone screen. He's lying in bed wearing a Millennium University hoodie, black hair falling over his forehead in messy waves. Our freshmen year of college has been extremely hectic, and we've only been able to see each other twice since the semester started.

Even though some of our calls don't last long because we're both too exhausted from a long day, we make an effort to Face-Time each other every night.

"Hey, Maddy Bear. I have some bad news."

Maddox sits up straight, brows knitting together. "What is it? Is everything okay?"

"I won't be able to make it next weekend," I say, sorrow lacing my voice. "I have a major project due and I'm already so behind."

His expression shifts into a frown. "So we have to spend our three-year anniversary apart?"

"I'm sorry, babe. This project is a major part of my grade."

"It's okay… I understand." He releases a sigh, twisting the drawstrings of his hoodie around his fingers.

The pained look in Maddox's eyes tugs at my heartstrings and almost makes me ruin my plan. I don't actually have a project due, and I'm still planning on flying to Chicago to celebrate our anniversary. It's killing me to keep this from him, but seeing his reaction when I surprise him will be worth it.

"Even though we don't get to spend our anniversary together, we'll have plenty more to look forward to. You're stuck with me for a lifetime." He gives me a wink, and that adorable dimpled smile returns.

"I wouldn't have it any other way." I smile softly, fingertips hovering over the screen as if I could reach through it and touch him.

Many people said that we're too young to know what "true love" is, and that we wouldn't last after high school. But they don't understand the magnitude of what we feel for each other. This isn't just a phase. Maddox is my soulmate—the person I'm going to spend the rest of my life with.

"I wish I could come to you, but I have a game that Friday."

"I guess we'll have to wait until winter break to see each other…" I put on my best sad face, trying my hardest not to break character.

I can barely contain my excitement. We haven't seen each other for nearly two months, and I've been counting down the days until I get to hold him in my arms and kiss that handsome face.

"Going another month without seeing you…" he whispers, his voice strained. "I don't know if I can do it. I miss you so much."

"I miss you too, Maddox," I murmur.

"Why don't we take a trip during winter break?" he asks, his voice bubbling with excitement. "We can make it a late anniversary celebration!"

"That sounds perfect! Since our finals end the first week of December, we can go somewhere the following week."

"That's a great plan. Where do you want to go, my love?"

"Hmm… Let's go somewhere warm. I'm sick of the cold."

"Tell me about it." He nods. "This snow is too much. I miss California's weather."

"How about Hawaii? I've always wanted to go there."

"Let's do it. That's one of my top travel destinations, too." He beams. "I'll start looking at flights soon!"

"Maddox is gonna be so happy to see you." Andrés pulls out the keys to the apartment he shares with Maddox and hands them to me.

He's been in on my plan for a few weeks now. After I landed in Chicago, I met up with him at his girlfriend Katie's apartment.

"I can't wait to see the look on his face when he sees me," I say, a rush of excitement flooding my chest.

"He's been bummed out all week. He couldn't even enjoy the party we had at our place after the game."

"Aw, my poor Maddy Bear."

Andrés wrinkles his nose in disgust. "That nickname is *so* freaking cringey."

"He loves it."

"Of course he does," he says with an eye roll. "Anyways, I'm staying at Katie's this weekend, so you two have the whole place to yourself. But please do not have sex in my bedroom."

"Sorry, no promises there," I tease, shrugging my shoulders.

He glares at me and holds his hand out. "Alright, give me my keys back. You and Maddox can stay at a hotel."

"I'm *kidding*. Thanks for helping me orchestrate this."

"No problem." He nods. "I hope you have a great anniversary!"

I quietly open the door to Maddox's apartment, careful not to wake him up. There are empty liquor bottles all over the kitchen counter and red cups scattered throughout the apartment.

I tidy up the kitchen, wiping down the counter before setting a gift bag on top. Inside is a scarf and beanie I spent hours knitting, each stitch woven with care. Tucked beside them is a glass jar packed with handwritten notes folded into origami hearts. I've filled them with reasons why I love him, and lyrics from songs that say everything I can't always put into words.

As I'm writing a heartfelt note in the anniversary card I picked up from the store, the door to his bedroom creaks open.

Instead of Maddox, out walks Charlotte—dressed in his hoodie and sweatpants.

My stomach clenches, nausea rising like waves.

She stops in her tracks, letting out a startled gasp.

"W-what are y-you doing h-here?" I'm shaking so hard I can barely speak.

"Wait. You and Maddox are still together?" she asks.

"Why wouldn't we be?" I snap, my teeth clenched.

Charlotte widens her pale blue eyes, clapping a hand over her mouth. "Oh my God! I feel awful. If I would've known, I never would've…"

My grip tightens around the pen until the plastic gives with a sharp crack. "What happened?"

Charlotte opens her mouth and says words that flip my world upside down, "We slept together last night."

Anger courses through me as tears spill from my eyes. They splatter onto the card, smudging the ink and distorting the message I'd poured my heart into writing.

"During the party, he told me that you two broke up," she continues. "He flirted with me all night. If I had known he was lying, I would've never done that… I'm so sorry, Annalise. You deserve better." She walks up to me, placing a hand on my back in a failed attempt to comfort me before walking out the door.

I sink to the ground, painful sobs wracking through my body. A black hole opens inside my chest, swallowing my heart.

I feel so betrayed. It makes me question whether he's cheated on me during the entirety of our relationship. Here I thought I had found my Prince Charming and the love of my life, but everything has been a *fucking* lie.

Am I not good enough?

Am I not worthy of love?

"Annalise! You're here!" Maddox's voice rings out, bright and full of surprise.

But his smile falters when he sees the state I'm in. "Wait. What's the matter?"

When I don't answer, he continues. "Babe, look at me. Tell me what's going on." He crouches down in front of me, reaching for my chin, but I flinch—recoiling from his touch.

"How could you? And on our anniversary, too…" I say through choked tears.

"What?" His brows draw tight. "What are you talking about?"

Pushing him off of me, I get up and storm out of his apartment.

"Annalise! Wait!" he calls out.

Snow falls from the sky, blanketing the ground in a thick, powdery layer. The frigid air slices through my lungs with every breath as I dash across the street to Millennium Park.

Maddox quickly catches up with me, reaching for my hand and holding it tightly as concern flickers in his deep-brown eyes.

Or is it guilt behind treacherous eyes?

"Annalise, please come back inside. It's freezing out here."

I yank my hand away, freeing myself from his hold. "Get away from me! I can't believe you cheated on me, you piece of shit!"

He stares at me, baffled. "What? Where is this coming from?"

"Oh, don't you dare try to deny it!" I snap. "I saw Charlotte come out of your bedroom! She told me that you were flirting with her all night long and that you said we broke up."

"What the fuck? I got wasted last night, but I sure as hell would never say that. Are you seriously going to believe her over me?"

"She came out of your fucking bedroom, Maddox! Wearing *your* clothes! What more proof do I need?"

Maddox tucks my hair behind my ear and swipes my tears with his thumb. "I swear, I would never do anything to hurt you." He leans forward, touching his forehead to mine. "I love you more than anything in the world. I would never give up what we have."

I want to believe him. I want to believe that what he feels for me is real. That he is the person I am destined to spend eternity with.

But my mind floods with vivid images of Maddox and Charlotte's naked bodies entwined together in bed, igniting a rage within me like flowing lava. Each moment I envision them together deepens my sense of betrayal.

I step away from him, creating a distance between us that's more than just physical. I won't allow myself to be weak again.

"You know, back then I kept rejecting you because I heard you had a reputation for being a player. But something told me there was more to you. That I should take a chance on you and not listen to what everyone else was saying. I thought maybe you just hadn't found a girl that was worth committing to, but I was clearly wrong," I shake my head as the tears continue to fall down my cheeks. "You'll never change and will always be a player. I bet you were unfaithful throughout our whole relationship."

"Do you really think that?" Maddox asks, his eyes searching mine.

"I do," I reply without hesitation.

His shoulders sag, tears trickling down his cheeks. "How could you think so low of me, Annalise? If it were any other girl, I would've given up after being rejected the first time. *You* are the first girl I let myself be completely vulnerable with," he says, his voice cracking. "I'd never been in love before I met you."

"Stop saying you love me!" I snap. "You *clearly* don't have a clue what it means to love someone. The only person you're capable of loving is yourself."

A wave of hurt clouds his face, but I couldn't care less. I know that it's yet another act of deception crafted to manipulate my feelings.

"How could you say I never loved you? Charlotte and I only slept together once in high school, and it happened way before you and I got together. I promise I haven't been with anyone but you. You are the only one I want, Rosie."

"Enough!" I shout, tears searing my cheeks. "I'm *sick* of your lies! You're exactly like my father."

Maddox stares back at me in disbelief, my last words cutting him deep.

"I don't want to see you ever again! We're done."

I turn on my heel to walk away, but he catches me, pulling me back into his arms. He leans down, his forehead pressed to my chest as a broken sob escapes him.

"Annalise, please don't walk away from us," he begs. "I need you in my life. I love you so much." He reaches between us and gently grabs the dainty gold rose dangling from my neck, the gift he bought me for our one-year anniversary. "The necklace you're wearing symbolizes my eternal love for you. Doesn't that mean something?"

"You can have the stupid necklace!" I unclasp it, tossing it into the snow. "It means nothing to me. *You* mean nothing to me."

He kneels to the ground, collecting the necklace and clutching it tightly, his cries echoing through the park.

"Have a nice life, Maddox," I spit.

As I turn my back to him, an icy chill wraps around my heart. Not only am I leaving him behind, but the remnants of my former self—the naive girl who believes in soulmates and so foolishly fell in love.

determined to work harder after my shitty performance last night. I may have scored the game-winning basket, but that doesn't excuse the rest of the game.

I drop my bag on the bench and open up my locker before Elijah taps me on the arm and kicks his head to the side, signaling for me to move in closer.

"What's up? Are you about to profess your undying love for me or something?" I tease.

He doesn't laugh, a serious look settling on his face. "Don't cause a scene," he says, keeping his voice low. "But I just saw Lucas Hilton walk out of the general manager's office."

My blood runs cold. Lucas Hilton is my nemesis and the bane of my existence. Everyone in high school thought he was a nice guy, but I saw him for who he really is—a conniving snake who tried to go after Annalise when we were together.

She would always brush it off and tell me I was being dramatic, and that Lucas was just being friendly. But I knew what his true intentions were.

"What the fuck is he doing here? Isn't he in the G League?"

"I've been hearing rumors about how we're trying to get a new sixth man. Simmons's knee has been acting up a lot lately. I don't think he fully healed from his injury last season."

"Thompson must have lost his marbles. There are so many other great players out there. Why him?" I ask.

"It could have something to do with the budget. I mean, look how much you and I make," he says.

"I need to find out what's going on." Turning on my heel, I march out of the locker room.

"Dude! I told you not to make a scene," he whisper-yells before he shakes his head and jogs after me.

Burning rage crawls through my spine as I see Lucas standing in the hall, chatting with our general manager, Gary Thompson, and our coach, Zachary Watson.

"What the fuck are you doing here, Hilton?"

Lucas's head whips around. A sardonic smile spreads across his face when he sees me. "Is that how you greet an old friend?" he asks, his tone laced with mockery.

"We have *never* been friends." My fists clench at my side. I want to punch him in the face and wipe that smug look off of it.

Coach glares at me. "Kamado, go change and get ready for practice. I'll talk to you and the team later."

Lucas grins. "Oh, I don't mind sharing the news with him now. I just signed a deal. I'm going to be part of the San Francisco Dragons."

"You've got to be fucking kidding me," I mutter under my breath.

When I graduated high school, I thought I was finally free of him. Now, at the peak of my career, he's returned. And his timing couldn't be worse, with Annalise being back in town.

"So, how much did your dad have to pay to get you into the NBA?" I snicker.

"Show some respect, Kamado," Gary says as he narrows his eyes at me. "Lucas has worked his ass off and has been proving himself in the G League. He has a lot of potential and will be a great asset to the team."

"Wow, you really haven't changed since high school, huh? You're still a bully," Lucas sneers.

Heat surges inside of me. He always tried to give me a bad rap by starting rumors and playing the victim. I may be an asshole to him, but it was always warranted.

I try to charge toward him but Elijah holds me back. "Bro, calm down before you do something stupid," he whispers. "You're a professional basketball player now. Don't let this fucker get to you."

When it comes to Lucas, I have a tendency of losing my temper. Elijah has always been my voice of reason. In high school, I got into a fight with Lucas once, which caused me to get suspended. There were countless times where I almost beat him up again, but Elijah prevented me from doing so. Otherwise, I probably would've been expelled.

I can't let him get under my skin. Unlike high school, I have a hell of a lot more to lose now if I lash out.

Clapping Lucas on the back, I plaster a smile on my face. "I'm just messing with you, man. I'm beyond thrilled to have you on the team. Welcome to the Dragons."

I extend my hand and he takes it. I smirk when my grip tightens, causing him to wince.

"I'm ecstatic to be here. It's going to be a great season," he says.

Great? More like a clusterfuck. He's going to ruin our team's dynamic.

Asami gnaws on her fingernails while she stares at her phone. Okāsan invited us over for dinner and now here we are, watching my sister refresh her email every ten seconds. She's waiting to see if the results for her boards—which she took a couple weeks back—are in yet.

"Anything yet?" I ask.

"No, not yet. I don't know what's taking so long. I thought the results would be in this morning. I've been a nervous wreck all day."

"Just eat, Asami. Your udon is gonna get cold. Check later," Okāsan says, placing her hand on top of Asami's.

"Sorry, Okāsan. I'm just so nervous" She sets down her phone. "If I don't pass, I'm gonna have to wait another six months to retake it."

"You're going to pass it. You're *my* daughter," Otōsan says, smiling at her.

There is no denying that Asami is his favorite child. He's always praised her for everything, no matter how small. Me, on the other hand? I don't get so much as a pat on the back for my achievements.

Asami takes a spoonful of udon then grabs her phone again.

"You really couldn't wait a whole ten seconds?" I ask.

"*Kuso kurae*," Asami snaps.

"Guess I'll just eat your udon, since I'm already done with mine." I reach for her bowl and she swats my hand away.

"Oh my gosh, the results are in!" Her knee bounces under the table and, with trembling hands, she clicks on the results.

I close my eyes, silently praying that she passes. Even though I have a funny way of showing it, I do love my sister. She's been busting her ass in medical school for the last few years, and it would make me incredibly happy to see her succeed.

"I passed." Her mouth falls open and she places her hands on her head. "I PASSED! AHHH!" She squeals, leaping from the chair and bouncing up and down. "You are now looking at San Francisco's newest dermatologist—Dr. Asami Kamado."

"That's amazing, *onee-chan*!" I say, beaming. "I'm addressing you as Dr. *Baka* from now on."

"Shut up." She chuckles, shaking her head.

Okāsan wraps her arms around Asami, pressing a kiss to the top of her head. "This makes me so happy. You're going to be the best dermatologist in the nation."

"Now I can tell everyone we have a doctor in the family. I'm so proud of you, Asami," Otōsan says, his eyes gleaming.

My father has never once uttered those words to me. Despite all of my achievements, in his eyes, I'm still a failure. I thought he would start respecting my career once I got drafted into the NBA, but I was wrong.

He still hasn't come to any of my games. At every home game I look to the crowd, hoping he'll show up, but he never does. Nothing I ever do is good enough for him. All I've ever wanted was for him to accept me.

"Is your fiancé almost off work? You should tell him the

news and invite him over. There's still plenty of udon left," Okāsan says.

"I texted him earlier, and he said he had to stay late to finish working on a case," Asami answers. "He doesn't know when he'll be home."

Hotaru Tsukino—Asami's fiancé—works at a major corporate law firm, and recently got promoted to junior partner. He's an arrogant prick who doesn't deserve my sister, but my parents seem to like him—especially my dad.

"I'm so glad my future son-in-law is someone who is worthy of you," he says.

"I don't know. I kinda thought she would end up with Steven —the guy who claimed the multiverse is real and that he's from Earth 119," I say, adding a smirk. "I think attending a wedding there would've been dope."

Asami rolls her eyes. "I need to start finalizing my guest list soon, before we send out save the dates. Have you thought about who you're going to bring as your plus-one?"

I shrug. "I'm not bringing anyone—I already told you. My date for the wedding will be a bottle of champagne."

"Ugh, come on," she groans, slapping her hand on the table. "There has to be someone you want to bring."

"I know someone who he could bring." Okāsan waggles her brows suggestively.

Asami crosses her arms. "It's not Mrs. Tanaka's daughter Hina, is it? She's so stuck up. I can't stand her.

"No, not her," Okāsan replies. "I would never let that gold digger anywhere near my son." She reaches for my hand, giving it a squeeze. "You should ask Annalise, Masashi."

I shoot her a look, and she just chuckles.

"Wait—Annalise is in Cali?" Asami asks. "I thought she was living in New York."

"No, she's back now. As a matter of fact..." Okasan looks at me, a smile hovering her lips. "I saw her the other week. She was over at Masashi's place."

"Wait, what?" Asami sits up straight, her eyes widening. "Why didn't you tell me y'all were back together?"

"Because we're not," I reply, my tone firm.

"Yet…" Okāsan nudges me in the side with her elbow.

"My wedding will be the perfect place to rekindle your love." A wide smile blooms on Asami's face.

I groan, shaking my head. "Why do you two insist on meddling in my love life? There's *nothing* to rekindle. I'm not gonna ask her to go with me. Annalise made it very clear that she wants nothing to do with me."

"That's not true." Okāsan shakes her head. "I know deep down she still loves you too. Keep fighting for her and remind her why you two belong together, Masashi."

I let out a heavy sigh. I don't know if I have the strength to fight again. Trying to win Annalise back will be a losing battle.

CHAPTER 14
Annalise

My head is pounding. Veronica doubled my workload today and I barely had time to take a break. As soon as five o'clock hit, I rushed out of there before she could find something else for me to do. Thank God it's Friday and I don't have to be back in that hellhole for another two days—though, honestly, two days is never enough.

I didn't see Maddox at Dauntless this week. Maybe he's been busy traveling for games. I thought I would be relieved that he's not around, but I find myself craving his presence.

Why does he have to be so damn caring? It would be easier for me to keep hating him if he acted like an asshole. I've tried to block it from my mind, but I can't stop thinking about how he went out of his way to take care of me the night I was drunk and the morning after.

I would be lying to myself if I said I wasn't still attracted to him. Maddox Kamado is irresistibly sexy, and my body betrays me when I'm around him.

The moment we shared on his couch has replayed in my mind more times than I care to admit. When I'm in my bed late at night, my hand wanders between my legs as I imagine Maddox thrusting inside of me.

I bet he would get a kick out of it if he knew my self-indulgence sessions were because of him.

Maybe if I started dating, I could get him off of my mind—but I refuse to go on a dating app ever again. Sure, it works for some, but all the dates I've been on have been a disaster. I want to meet someone organically, but even that is hard. All the men I meet at bars are creeps who only want one thing.

Now, relieved to finally be done with work for the week, I push my shopping cart toward the vegetable section to pick out some tomatoes and potatoes. Mom called me earlier and asked if I could stop by the grocery store to pick up a few ingredients for her.

She's cooking ropa vieja for dinner—my favorite Cuban staple—but needed some ingredients for side dishes. I've attempted to make it myself a few times, but it never comes out as tender or flavorful as hers.

After I get what I need for Mom, I head toward the bakery. I'm craving some brownies. They usually run out by this time of day, but I remain hopeful.

"Damn it." I release a sigh when I see that they're gone.

My eyes scan the grocery store, hunting for another dessert to satisfy my sweet tooth. That's when I spot Lucas Hilton, an old friend from high school, reaching for a container of freshly baked croissants.

"Lucas, hey!" I say, waving at him.

He glances up, a wide grin spreading across his face. "Hey, Annalise!" Lucas sets the croissants in his cart and struts toward me. "Wow, it's been forever," he says as he pulls me in for a hug.

When we finally step back, his eyes sweep over me. "I didn't think it was possible for you to become more beautiful than you already were."

I wave my hand in the air, smiling. "Oh, stop. You're embarrassing me."

"So, how have you been?"

"I've been good! I just moved back to San Francisco a little over a month ago. How are things with you?"

"I'm doing well. I actually moved back recently, too. I've been living in Colorado for the last four years. I'm sorry I haven't kept in touch."

"Don't worry about it. I'm horrible at keeping in touch with people, too. Mazi is the only person from high school I still hang out with."

I was considered popular in high school. I was part of the cheer team, won prom queen, and dated the star athlete and most desirable guy at Seymour High. All the girls that used to tease me in elementary and middle school suddenly wanted to become my friend when I started dating Maddox. Mazi was the only genuine friend I had, so I didn't bother to keep in touch with anyone else from our class.

"Yeah. I still keep up with Brian, but I only see him a few times a year."

"It's so hard to find time as we get older."

Lucas glances at his phone. "Hey, I need to get going soon, but we should catch up over dinner. Next Saturday, if you're free?"

I hesitate, trying to decide if I should go.

Lucas is a nice guy—and he's handsome, standing about six feet tall with sandy blonde hair and soft hazel eyes—but I never saw him as anything other than a friend. He's not my type.

Yeah, because your type is a dark-haired tattooed man with dimples who you haven't been able to get out of your head.

The fact that Maddox Kamado is occupying my mind at all is more of a reason why I should go out with Lucas.

"Dinner sounds great," I reply with a smile.

"*Hola*, Mami." I place the grocery bags on the counter and walk over to Mom, planting a kiss on her cheek.

Abuelo is sleeping soundly on the couch. He had a chemotherapy session today—they always leave him feeling drained.

"Anything new going on with you lately, *mi rosa*?" Mom asks while she peels the potatoes.

Grabbing another cutting board from the drawer, I begin chopping the tomatoes. "Not much, besides Veronica driving me crazy."

Mom and I are only eighteen years apart. She's practically my best friend, and I share everything that's going on in my life with her.

But I haven't told her about seeing Maddox again. She doesn't even know the real reason we broke up. I told her that being in a long-distance relationship was too much for us to handle, so we decided it was best to part ways.

When I was a senior in high school, I stumbled upon my father cheating on my mom with his secretary—a woman nearly half his age. Seeing that broke something inside of me and I haven't been able to get over my trust issues since.

Talk about emotional damage.

He was too much of a coward to tell my mom, so I had to do it. She was beyond devastated when I broke the news to her and lost a part of herself that she still hasn't fully regained. Despite the rocky nature of her relationship with my father, she still loved him deeply.

I knew she would be heartbroken if she found out that I had experienced the same fate, so I decided to keep it from her. Mazi is the only person who knows what happened.

My little brother Ollie walks into the kitchen and grabs a bag of chips from the pantry.

Mom waves a knife at him. "Ah, ah! Put those back right now, Oliver. You're not gonna eat junk before dinner."

"But I'm hungry now," he pouts, his shoulders sagging. "I just wanna eat a little."

"You can wait fifteen more minutes. Go and clear the table please."

He groans, placing the chips back on the shelf.

"How was school this week, Ollie?" I ask. "Did you make any new friends?"

"Not really. I don't have anything in common with anyone in my class," he says quietly. "I only get to see Jake during first period and lunch, so the rest of the day drags."

"Are you going to try out for the basketball team this year?"

He shakes his head. "I doubt I'd to make it. I would rather not embarrass myself during tryouts."

Ollie is such a sweet kid but he's very timid, which makes it hard for him to make new friends.

The popular kids in school often pick on him, and now that he's in high school, I'm worried about him more than ever. Teenagers can be brutal, and they don't understand how damaging their words can be.

I really hope he's able to break out of his shell and gain some confidence.

"I'm sure you'd make the team," I say gently, hoping to reassure him. "You've been practicing every day. It's something you're passionate about, and it would be a great way for you to make new friends."

"Do it for me. I don't have much time left, and I want to see you play on the court before I die." Abuelo rubs his eyes, giving me a sleepy smile. "*Hola, mi rosa.*"

I stroll over to the couch and he greets me with a big, warm hug. There's something so special about his hugs. They wrap around me like a cozy blanket and always make me feel safe and loved.

"Enough with this negative energy, Abuelo—you're going to live for another twenty years. And Ollie, you're going to make the team."

"It's funny that you're being so positive, but when it comes to something related to your life, you're the complete opposite." Ollie rolls his eyes.

"What do you mean?" I ask.

"Oh, you know exactly what I mean. You're always saying, '*I don't know if I can do it,*'" he says in a mocking tone, earning chuckles from Mom and Abuelo.

"Your brother is right," Mom says with a nod. "You do tend to doubt yourself a lot."

For as long as I can remember, I've struggled with thinking I'm not good enough. Not deserving enough. That nothing I do could ever be praised or appreciated. The voices in my head spew negativity on a daily basis, making sure I keep myself in check and don't get too proud of anything I accomplish. No matter how hard I try to drown them out, the voices are always too loud.

I choose to be a glass-half-empty kind of person, because it's easier than getting my hopes up only to be met with disappointment.

Mom finishes cooking, and Ollie and I help her set the table.

"Let us say a prayer before we dig in," Abuelo says, holding his hands out.

We all join hands and bow our heads as Abuelo leads us in prayer.

"Dear Lord, we pray and honor you. Thank you for bringing us together for this meal. May this food refresh and nourish our bodies, minds, and spirits. In Jesus's name, Amen."

"Amen," we say in unison.

Abuelo had never been a religious person. When Abuela was still alive—she passed away when I was in elementary school—

she used to force him to go to church with her and attend church events.

But after he was diagnosed with cancer, he turned his life over to God. He felt like he hadn't been living life correctly because he lacked God's presence. Building a relationship with God helped him cope with his cancer diagnosis and has allowed him to remain positive.

"Mmm. This is delicious, Valeria. It tastes just like your mother's," Abuelo says.

I swallow a spoonful and tilt my head back in satisfaction. It's incredibly savory, and the tender meat melts on my tongue.

"Is La Diabla still giving you a hard time?" Abuelo asks.

I can't help but chuckle at the nickname we gave Veronica. "Oh, you know it. I swear she gets worse every day. Today she misplaced her car keys and blamed me for it."

"Maybe you can get her some of those special gummies you like to eat to help calm her down," Ollie says.

I cast a glare in his direction and kick him hard under the table.

"Ow!" he yelps.

"I really wish you hadn't left New York because of me," Abuelo says, staring down at his hands. "You wouldn't have to deal with her, and you would've been happy."

After I graduated, I returned home to visit before I started my internship. Abuelo had a worsening cough that wouldn't go away, and he had lost a lot of weight. Mom said she'd been begging him to see a doctor, but he was too stubborn to go. It took a lot of convincing, but I finally got him to agree.

He got a scan done that showed a mass in his lung. The biopsy confirmed that he had stage-three small cell carcinoma. The doctor informed us that the cancer was very aggressive and urged us to start treatment right away to prevent it from metastasizing.

Abuelo used to smoke Cuban cigars daily, but he hadn't

touched one in over fifteen years. I was angry at the fact that someone so kind and pure had to be punished.

We got into a huge argument when I told him I was moving back home permanently. He knew how hard I had worked to get that internship and hated to see me give it all up.

I give his hand a squeeze, smiling. "I am happy, Abuelo. My job may not be what I wanted, but I have so many things to be grateful for. I was so lonely in New York. Being able to spend more time with my family is what makes me happy."

He squeezes my hand back, his eyes crinkling into a smile. "*Te quiero, mi rosa.*"

"*Te quiero*, Abuelo."

CHAPTER 15
Annalise

The elevator door slides open and Maddox steps through, looking like he just walked off a magazine cover. He's wearing a forest-green button-up shirt with black slacks, and his signature gold chain. The sleeves of his shirt are rolled up to his elbows, revealing his toned forearms and the tail end of the dragon tattoo. Everyone in the office—including myself—turns their heads to steal a glance.

There are only two men that work here—Reginald, who's fabulously gay and dresses better than anyone I know, and Henry, the sixty year old maintenance man for the building. It's safe to say the women in this office have been dying for an attractive man to come through the doors.

So when Maddox is here, everyone seems to find an excuse to talk to him or be near him. I don't blame them. He's gorgeous. It's like God took extra time and care when creating him. But I hate the way my stomach flips every time I see him.

"Remind me why you haven't banged him again?" Ivy asks, resting her hand on her cheek as she stares at him with heart eyes.

"Because he's my ex, and a million other reasons."

"You can be exes with benefits." She winks at me, nudging her shoulder against mine.

I shake my head. "Absolutely not. No matter how good he is in bed, I'm not going down that path." *Even if the space between my legs is begging me to repeat history.*

Maddox walks by and my stomach does a full-on somersault.

"Good morning, Maddox!" Ivy chirps.

"Good morning, Ivy. Morning, Monroe," he says, flashing me his dimpled smile.

"Good morning, Kama—*ah!*" My vision goes blurry and my lower abdomen twists with pain. *You've got to be kidding me… Why now?*

Since I've been on this birth control, my periods have been super sporadic. I can never tell when it's coming, and when it does, I'm hit with the worst cramps that make me want to curl up in the fetal position.

Maddox's brows pinch together, lines of worry etching his face. "Are you okay?"

"I'll be fine." I flash him a weak smile before my lips twist in pain. "Ooh, *fuck*, that hurts," I hiss, clutching my stomach as I turn my back on Maddox. I reach into my purse for the bottle of ibuprofen that I usually keep there, but it's nowhere to be found. I must have forgotten to put it back after I took it the other day for my headache. "Ivy, do you have any ibuprofen?"

She sifts through her purse and shakes her head. "No. I'm sorry." She hands me a pad and tampon instead. "I'll add hot water to a bottle so you can use it as a heating pad."

"Thank you." Pushing myself up, I hobble to the restroom with the pad and tampon. The first two days are usually heavy, so I always use both.

"Damn it," I groan when I get into the stall. There's a small stain on my underwear, so now I have to spend the next eight hours feeling absolutely disgusting.

I wipe up as much as I can before heading back to my desk.

"Here, put this on your stomach." Ivy hands me the hot water bottle and I place it under my shirt. The warmth lessens the intensity of the cramps, but it's like putting a Band-Aid on a bullet wound.

"If I have some free time, I'll stop by the store to get you some meds," she says.

"Thank you."

Veronica walks out of her office, her head swiveling around the room. "Has anyone seen Mr. Kamado? I thought he would be here by now."

"He was here earlier, but just left. Said he had to take care of something and will be back later," Reginald tells her.

"Oh, I see." Her eyes flick to mine and her expression immediately changes. "I need you to go to the storage room and organize the materials. I want everything in there neatly organized by the end of the day."

"I'll get it done." I give her a tight-lipped smile and drag myself to the storage room, bringing the water bottle with me.

I open the door and nearly faint when I see the mess inside. The fabrics are supposed to be organized by color and type of material, but they're all jumbled together. There are scraps of fabrics all over the floor, along with threads that have been unraveled or tangled up. I have a feeling Veronica purposely created this mess to make my life harder. I wouldn't put it past her.

As I reach for the stack of fabrics, a sharp stabbing pain shoots through my abdomen. I double over, gripping my stomach tightly as sweat drips down my forehead and a groan of agony escapes my lips. The water bottle has already cooled off, so it isn't providing much relief.

Crawling over to the thread section, I attempt to roll them up neatly and organize everything while sitting down.

I've managed to get a few done when there's a knock on the

door. I huff a sigh. It's probably Veronica coming to ask me to do another ridiculous task.

Using the wall, I push myself up and smooth down my skirt. "Come in."

The door swings open and Maddox walks in, bags in hand.

My brows shoot up in surprise. "What are you doing here?"

He strides over and hands me the bags. "I went to Target to buy you some things," he says, blush creeping on his cheeks. "Hopefully they'll make you feel better."

I open the bags and examine the contents. It's filled with different types and sizes of pads and tampons, a bottle of ibuprofen, bananas, chocolate bars, and a large bottle of water. He even threw in five pairs of seamless panties and a wearable portable heating pad. Warmth spreads through me, settling in my chest.

I said some harsh words to him the last time we saw each other, but his attitude toward me never wavered. He continues to be as sweet as ever, which only makes hating him even harder.

I lift my eyes to his and I'm so happy I could cry. "Thank you. I really appreciate it."

A grin pulls at his lips. "You're welcome. I remember how bad your cramps can get."

When we were together, Maddox would always take care of me when I was on my period. He would run to the store to get what I needed and buy me whatever food I wanted to satisfy my cravings. Even as a teenager, he was never embarrassed to walk in a store and purchase feminine products.

I sit down on the ground and pop three ibuprofen in my mouth, swallowing them down with water. Since I don't want the medicine tearing up my stomach, I peel one of the bananas and take a bite.

Maddox plops down next to me and pulls out the heating pad. "Do you need me to help you put it on?"

I nod and pull my blouse out of my skirt, lifting it up to expose my abdomen.

His fingers skim along my side while he secures the heating pad, sending goosebumps racing through me. "What setting do you want it on?"

"The highest, please."

He presses the button three times and warmth slowly spreads through my stomach.

"Oh my gosh, this feels amazing," I say, leaning my head back on the wall.

"Can I help you with anything?" he asks, glancing around the room.

"No, it's fine. I'll get it done eventually."

"Come on, Annalise. You can barely stand for more than a few seconds, and you're as pale as the walls."

Shaking my head weakly, I lick my lips. "Don't you have to go meet with Veronica and Trang?"

"They're in a meeting right now. Veronica said it would take about thirty minutes. Tell me what you need to do and I'll do it."

I point to a pile of fabric. "You can help me organize that. Separate it by material and color. The type of material should be labeled at the top. If there's no label, just set it to the side and I'll figure it out."

"Got it." He smiles, his dimples pitting his cheeks slightly. "Just relax for a little while until you're feeling better."

Maddox manages to organize a decent amount of fabric in the span of thirty minutes. We don't speak much, but I sneak glances at him when he's not paying attention. There's still more work to be done, but Maddox has definitely lightened the load.

"How are you feeling?" he asks.

"Much better. The meds are starting to kick in, and this heating pad is a lifesaver. Thank you." I shoot him a smile and blush spreads on his cheeks.

"I gotta go meet them, but I can come back and help you when I'm done."

"No, no, I'll manage. Plus, if Veronica sees you in here,

she'll probably call me lazy and accuse me of forcing you to do my work."

A small laugh escapes him. "True. I want her to stay off your back as much as possible today."

"You and me both. Thanks again, Kamado."

"Anytime, Monroe." He gives me a wink before stepping out the door.

Maddox doing what he did today is exactly why it's so damn hard to hate him.

"Are you excited about your date tonight?" Mazi asks.

She's sitting on the bathroom counter with a huge grin on her face while I apply my makeup. When I told her I ran into Lucas and that we made plans for dinner, she squealed with excitement and begged me to go shopping with her for an outfit.

She is definitely more enthusiastic about this than I am.

"It's not a date. We're just grabbing a bite to catch up." I shrug and swipe a coat of mascara on my lashes.

"He's taking you to the best Brazilian steakhouse in the city. It's a damn date. Plus, he always had a crush on you. I remember he used to follow you around like a puppy dog in high school."

"Oh, please." I laugh, rolling my eyes. "He did not have a crush on me."

"Yes, he did. And so did half the guys at our school. You were just too oblivious to notice."

I never paid attention to anyone else because I only had eyes for Maddox. I dated a few guys before him, but it never developed into anything serious. He was my first real relationship, and the one I gave my everything to.

When I transferred schools, he was the only person apart from Mazi who was kind to me. Maddox always hung with the popular crowd, but he was different from the rest of them. He was genuine and always stood up for anyone being bullied. It was one of the things that made me fall for him.

My phone chimes with a text from Lucas stating that he's here. I pull up the app to let him inside our apartment building.

Slipping into my favorite comfy wedges, I spray on some perfume before heading to our living room to meet Lucas.

I pull open the door and greet him with a smile. "Hey, Lucas!"

"Wow, Annalise," he says, eyeing me up and down. "You look beautiful."

"Thank you."

"Oh, these are for you!" Lucas grins, thrusting a bouquet of carnations into my hands, half of them already wilting.

"Oh, thank you… They're lovely," I say, doing my best to keep my smile from slipping.

I wasn't expecting flowers, but the bouquet he chose feels like an insult—like I'm not worthy enough to get nice flowers.

Maddox's voice pops up in my head. *"Not only did he get you the cheapest bouquet, he gave you the worst-looking one. What a fucking tool."*

"Get out of my head, Kamado," I mumble.

"What did you say?" Lucas asks.

My cheeks flush with heat. "Oh, I said I need to find a vase for these."

While I search for a vase in our cupboards, Mazi comes out of the bathroom pretending like she hasn't been eavesdropping this whole time.

"Hey, Lucas."

"Hey, Mazikeen," he says. "Good to see you again. How have you been?"

"I've been doing good! My photography business has been taking off lately."

"That's amazing! I've seen some of your work on Instagram. You're so talented."

"Thank you. Well, you two have fun tonight." Mazi points a finger at me. "And make sure you're back no later than midnight."

"Got it, Ms. Rivera!" Lucas says, giving her a salute.

We arrive at the restaurant, and I feel out of place amongst all the rich people. Everyone's dressed in designer clothing and decked out with expensive watches and jewelry.

I can't help but feel self-conscious in the green satin dress I bought on sale at Macy's.

The host looks me up and down before she leads us to our table. Round booths line the outside and long tables for larger parties are scattered throughout the middle.

A sax player fills the room with a soft jazz tune, really selling the romantic ambiance of the space. Couples are nuzzled closely together, staring deeply into each other's eyes as they engage in conversation.

"So what was it like living in Colorado? Do you miss it?" I ask after our server takes our drink orders.

"Oh yeah, for sure. I loved living there. The apartment I stayed in had an incredible view of the mountains."

"That sounds a whole lot better than the view I had. There was an old man in the building next to mine who would always walk around naked." I shudder as the image flashes through my mind.

Lucas chuckles, shaking his head. "New York is something else."

"Did you go snowboarding or skiing while you were there?"

He nods. "Snowboarding. I completely underestimated how

difficult it would be. I didn't take lessons, and I fell on my ass more times than I can count."

"Oh no! Did you get better, at least?"

"Yeah. I made sure to take lessons when I went again. I haven't gone down a black diamond yet, but plan on doing it next year."

"Are you still playing basketball?"

"I am. I actually have some news." Lucas's eyes light up, a grin stretching from ear to ear. "I recently signed with the San Francisco Dragons. I'm going to be their sixth man."

"Wow! That's incredible. Congratulations, Lucas!"

He smiles shyly. "Thank you. I don't know if you keep up with basketball at all, but Maddox and Elijah are on the team too."

Great—now I'm back to thinking about Maddox and his stupidly handsome face.

"Is it weird playing with them? I know you guys didn't exactly get along in high school."

Lucas shakes his head. "There haven't been any problems so far, but I've only practiced with them a few times. Kamado can be a ball hog, so we'll see how it goes when I play a game with them in a few days."

As if we spoke him into existence, none other than Maddox fucking Kamado walks into the restaurant flanked by Elijah, Santiago, and Andrés.

Just my luck.

I pull my phone out, pretending to check my messages.

Please, please sit them somewhere else.

The host leads them to the table directly in front of us and I curse under my breath.

"Here's your table, gentlemen. Your server will be with you shortly."

"Oh, shit!" Elijah blurts, eyes widening when he spots Lucas and me.

"What?" Maddox asks, giving him a puzzled look.

Elijah tips his chin in our direction and Maddox follows his gaze.

Fury ignites in his eyes. I can feel the heat of his rage surging through the restaurant.

"What the fuck are you doing with her, Hilton?"

SEVEN YEARS AGO

Annalise's cheer practice ended early, so she came to watch me at basketball practice. We're planning on stopping by Fisherman's Wharf after I'm done to grab a bite and watch the sea lions.

It's been a few weeks since we had our first date, and things have been going extremely well. It took a while for her to finally agree to go out with me, but it was worth the wait. The fact that Annalise Rose Monroe gave me the time of the day feels like the biggest win.

The other week, we went to a carnival and shared our first kiss at the top of the Ferris wheel. As cheesy as it sounds, I saw fireworks going off when her soft lips touched mine.

I find myself falling harder for her every day. Everything feels easy around her. I share things with her that I can't share with my family or friends. Everyone at school sees me as a popular jock, but with Annalise, I can be my true authentic self.

Homecoming is a couple of weeks away, and I'm planning on officially asking her to be my girlfriend after the dance.

"Nice shot, Dimples!" Annalise cheers after I slam dunk the ball into the net.

I've been purposely showing off since she arrived.

I blow her a kiss and watch as a blush creeps over her cheeks, along with a radiant grin that blossoms on her face.

"Y'all wanna go get some In-N-Out?" Elijah asks after practice ended.

"I have plans with Annalise." I grin.

"Damn, it's already starting." Santiago shakes his head. "Soon you won't have time for us anymore."

"Dude, shut up. I always have time for my boys." I laugh, rolling my eyes.

Annalise climbs off the bleachers and shuffles toward me, but Lucas stops her in her tracks. "Hey, Annalise!"

"Hey, Lucas!"

"Do you plan on going to homecoming this year?" Lucas asks.

"Yeah, I think so."

"So—I, uh…" Lucas clears his throat, rubbing the back of his neck. "I was wondering if you maybe wanted to go with me?"

You've got to be kidding me.

Santiago elbows me in the gut. "Aren't you gonna intervene? He looks like he's trying to go after your girl."

I roll my eyes, crossing my arms. "*Please*, I'm not worried about Hilton."

I'll never admit it to the guys, but I can't help but feel insecure when I see other guys flirting with Annalise—*especially* Lucas Hilton. There's something about him that has me on high alert. I view him as my biggest threat.

"Oh, Sorry. I already have a date. I'm going with Maddox." Annalise's eyes shift to mine and her mouth curves into a smile that shoots straight to my heart.

"Wait—Maddox Kamado?" Lucas's brows lift up. "I didn't think you would go for someone like him."

What the fuck is that supposed to mean?

My jaw tightens in an attempt to keep my rage from boiling over.

"Well, I've been hanging out with him outside of school and he's different than I thought he would be." Her cheeks flush and there's a dreamy look in her eyes. "He's sweet, down-to-earth and so fun to be around."

A wide grin slides across my face. I feel myself relax, some of the worry fading away.

"Just be careful around him, Annalise." Lucas shakes his head. "Maddox isn't exactly relationship material. He's probably slept with the entire school by now. I'd hate for him to break your heart and use you for sex, because you're worth so much more than that."

My fists clench at my side as I march toward him, stepping between him and Annalise. Bringing myself to my full height, I fix my gaze on him, anger radiating through my stare. "Instead of dragging my name, why don't you stay back and practice some more? You could use it if you want to get actual play time instead of warming the bench."

Lucas's face reddens, his upper lip curling into a snarl. He mutters something under his breath before storming off to the locker room.

"Don't listen to a damn thing he says, okay? You know me, Annalise."

She chews her lip and nods. "I know," she says weakly, but I can't help but wonder if she's only saying that to appease me.

CHAPTER 17
Maddox

As if being on the same team as him wasn't bad enough, now I find out that he's on a fucking date with Annalise? The mere thought of her being with another man makes me furious, but seeing her with Lucas brings out a whole other level of rage within me that I can't contain.

I want to fucking kill him.

"What the fuck are you doing with her, Hilton?"

"What does it look like, Maddox? We're having dinner." The sarcasm in his tone pisses me off even more.

Elijah glares at him. "Come on, dude, have some respect for your teammates. There are boundaries you shouldn't cross."

"Wait—was he the one who kept going after Annalise in high school?" Andrés whispers.

Elijah and Santiago nod.

"I didn't think you would lower your standards so much, Annalise," I say.

She shifts uncomfortably in her seat, avoiding my gaze.

"Nice outfit, Lucas." I smirk, nodding at his sweater-vest-and-khaki combo. "Did you steal it from your grandpa's closet?"

Lucas rolls his eyes and the guys burst into snickers behind me.

"Maddox, stop being a dick," Annalise groans.

"That's impossible." Lucas lets out a bitter laugh, shaking his head. "He will *always* be a dick. He's still the same ole Maddox from high school."

"And you're still the same ole Lucas," I snap. "You're still trying to go after what's *mine*."

My eyes lock with Annalise and hers widen in shock. She clears her throat and I catch a blush on her cheeks before she quickly glances away.

"I'm sorry—yours?" Lucas snorts. "Last I checked, she's single. And she's not a fucking item."

I take a step closer to his table. "I am this close to fucking you up."

The restaurant goes quiet, all eyes on us.

I want to beat him to a pulp. I'm sick and tired of him acting like he's innocent. He's a deceitful scumbag. A real wolf in sheep's clothing.

Santiago tugs on my arm. "Come on, bro. Let's just sit somewhere else."

I pull out a chair and plop down, making a point to sit directly in their line of sight. "Nope. I'm perfectly fine sitting right here."

Our server comes around and brings us silverware and glasses of water. "Hey, I'm Logan. Thank you for joining us tonight. Can I get you all started with something to—"

His eyes widen when he notices who we are. "Whoa! I can't believe I'm serving the San Francisco Dragons! I've been watching you all play since college. Can I, uh, get a picture?"

"Of course," I reply with a smile.

"I can take the picture," Santiago offers.

"Thanks." Logan hands him his phone, and we all crowd together for the photo.

"You know, I also play for the San Francisco Dragons," Lucas chimes in.

"Oh, really? What's your name?" Logan asks. "I don't think I've seen you before."

"I'm Lucas Hilton. I recently got signed. I'll be the sixth man. I'm playing my first game with them in a few days."

"Oh… That's cool." Logan shifts his attention back to us. "What would you boys like to drink? Some wine, perhaps? Or champagne?"

"I'll be more than happy to take a picture with you if you want," Lucas says.

Annalise stares down at the table, covering her face with her hand. She's clearly suffering from secondhand embarrassment.

"Oh, no. I'm good. Thanks." Logan gives him an awkward smile and continues taking our orders.

The boys and I share knowing glances and burst out laughing.

"I can't believe this guy thinks he's some kinda all-star basketball player," Santiago says with a laugh.

"He sure thinks highly of himself for someone who's never played in an NBA game. Never thought I'd meet someone who has a bigger ego than Elijah," Andrés adds with a smirk.

Elijah flips him the bird, grinning from ear to ear. "Unlike him, I live up to my ego."

They continue throwing jabs but my attention is elsewhere.

Lucas scoots closer to Annalise and drapes his arms over her shoulder. He catches me staring and shoots me a sly smile.

It takes everything in me not to walk over there and punch him in the fucking face.

Logan comes back with a bottle of pinot grigio and pours it into our wine glasses.

I reach for a glass, my fist clenching the stem as I gulp it down.

"Don't even worry about him, man. She's probably just

going out with him out of pity. Hilton will always be a loser," Santiago says, sensing my uneasiness.

"I'm going fucking crazy. What if their date goes well and they kiss tonight? What if they have sex?"

"Why does it matter if they have sex? You act like you haven't been fucking around with multiple women," Andrés scoffs.

"That's different." I shake my head. "I didn't have feelings for them, nor have I taken them out on dates. What if they go on more dates and it turns into something serious?"

Elijah gives me a pointed look. "I thought you didn't give a shit."

"I don't."

Lucas leans into Annalise, whispering in her ear.

My jaw tightens as heat simmers in my veins.

"Alright, what can I get for our MVP?" Logan asks.

Lucas's head on a fucking platter.

CHAPTER 18
Annalise

"**I**'m sorry tonight didn't go as planned," Lucas says as we walk down the quiet hall of my apartment building. "It's just my luck that your ex showed up at the same restaurant."

"Don't beat yourself up over it, Lucas. There's no way you could've known he would show up. I still had a great time." I smile, hoping he doesn't see that I'm lying through my teeth.

Nothing about tonight was great. It was the most awkward ninety minutes of my life. I should've texted Mazi and told her to call me with a fake emergency.

Maddox kept shooting death glares at Lucas all night. I'm pretty sure he was imagining Lucas's face on the steak he was cutting into.

"I had an amazing time, too. Did you enjoy the food?"

"Yes, the steak was delicious, and those empanadas were to die for."

"I'm glad the food didn't turn out as bad as the night did," Lucas teases.

I chuckle softly. "It was really nice to catch up with you, Lucas. I'm happy to hear that you're doing so well."

"I loved catching up with you too." He shuffles from side to side, a blush creeping on his cheeks. "Do you want to hang out again next weekend?"

"Sure." I smile. "I'd love to."

His mouth lifts into a grin. "Hopefully we won't run into Maddox again."

"I hope so too." I laugh, shaking my head. "Thank you again for dinner. Goodnight, Lucas."

"Goodnight, Annalise."

I give him a quick hug then slip inside my apartment. As I open the door, Mazi jumps in surprise.

She throws her arms up in defense. "I totally wasn't eavesdropping!"

"Mmm hmm." I place my purse down and walk toward my room.

Mazi calls after me. "Um, hello? Where are you going? I want details!"

"Geez, woman!" I laugh, shaking my head. "Can I change? I'm ready to take off this bra."

"Fine! But hurry up! I've been waiting all night."

I pull on a T-shirt and a pair of shorts and wander into the living room, dropping onto the couch beside Mazi.

"Sooo how did it go?" She smiles widely, pulling a blanket over her lap. "You ran into Maddox? Did I hear that right?"

Raising a brow at her, I fold my arms over my chest. "I thought you weren't listening?"

She shrugs unapologetically. "Well, I didn't hear *everything*. What happened?" she asks, eyes burning with curiosity.

"Things were going fine," I start. I grab a pillow and begin picking at the loose threads. "We were catching up and he was telling me what it was like living in Denver. Then Maddox showed up." My voice voice tightens. "And it became a complete disaster."

Mazi widens her eyes, her mouth falling open. "No fucking way!"

"To make matters worse, he had a table right next to us. And he was not happy with the fact that I was there with Lucas."

She balls her fists at her sides. "Are you fucking kidding me? He has no right to get upset. Who you go out with is none of his concern."

"I know. He was being so possessive, and we're not even together."

You're still trying to go after what's mine.

Butterflies flutter in my stomach as his words replay in my mind. I enjoyed hearing those words and seeing him get jealous more than I cared to admit.

"Was he with another girl?"

I shake my head. "Nah, he was with Santiago, Elijah, and Andrés. It was so awkward. I wish I had a cloak of invisibility so I could've slipped out of there."

"How typical of Maddox to fuck things up." She rolls her eyes. "He needs to grow up." Scooting closer, she rests a hand lightly on my shoulder. "I'm sorry your night didn't go well, babe." She pauses, searching my face. "How do you feel about Lucas? Was there something there?"

"Not really… I mean, he's a really nice guy, but—"

He's not Maddox.

I hate that my head reminds me of this fact, but I can't deny that it's true.

"There were no sparks." I pull the pillow close to my body. "We didn't have any chemistry. But… I'm hanging out with him again next week, so we'll see."

"I hope it develops into something more," she says, her voice warm. "You deserve to find love again."

I give her a small smile as I glance her way. "How's everything going with that girl you met from the bar? What's her name again?"

"Aretta," she says with a sigh, her shoulders slumping. "Yeah… It's not going."

"Wait, what? I thought you two clicked." I frown.

"I thought so too," she says quietly. "But I guess she doesn't feel the same way. On Tuesday, I texted her asking if she wanted to go on a date this weekend, and she completely ghosted me." She lets out a heavy, defeated sigh, her hands twisting in the blanket.

"I'm sorry, Mazi. That was a jerk move. She could've at least communicated."

Her eyes glaze over and she sniffles softly. "Is there something wrong with me? All of my relationships have been failures and they never last longer than a couple of months."

Reaching over, I give her hand a squeeze. "There's absolutely nothing wrong with you. You're Mazikeen freaking Rivera —smart, talented, and a total badass."

She swipes her eyes, a small chuckle leaving her lips.

"One day, you'll meet someone worthy of you and everything is going to fall into place," I say, my voice steady and reassuring. "They won't ever make you feel like you did something wrong."

"I'm praying that this love finds us," she replies, the corners of her lips lifting into a soft smile as warmth returns to her hazel eyes. "But right now, I'm in the mood to watch a K-drama and fall in love with a Korean man. Wanna join?"

I laugh. "I'm always in the mood to swoon over Korean men. What are we watching?"

CHAPTER 19
Maddox

I wake up in a panic, my body drenched in sweat and my pulse hammering. Tsuki sensed that I was upset and nuzzled her head against my chest to wake me up.

Ever since I saw Annalise and Lucas together, I've been restless. When I do manage to fall asleep, I have the same recurring nightmare that Lucas and Annalise are getting married.

When the officiant asks if anyone objects, I try to speak up, but no words come out—my entire body is paralyzed. I'm forced to watch him marry the love of my life and I can't do a damn thing about it. I'm sick to my stomach envisioning Lucas living the life I want with her.

It's dangerous being alone with my thoughts. I can't get the images of them together out of my mind. When we were dating, Annalise would always reassure me that her relationship with Lucas was purely platonic. But seeing her on a date with him makes me wonder if she had feelings for him back then.

My phone buzzes on the bedside table and I grab it, seeing an incoming call from Veronica.

"Hello, Mrs. Zhang," I answer. "How's everything going?"

"Good morning, Mr. Kamado. Everything is going splendidly. I was wondering if you were coming by this week? Trang has the new designs ready and we are eager to show you what she came up with."

"Sorry, I've been so busy with practice and games that I haven't been able to stop by. I'll swing by first thing tomorrow morning."

"Okay. We look forward to seeing you, Mr. Kamado."

The truth is I've been avoiding going to Dauntless because I don't want to run into Annalise. I even contemplated pulling out of the collaboration. It would be hard seeing her every week knowing that she's with someone else.

That night after dinner, Elijah suggested we go out to a club so I could find someone to hook up with. Several women approached me hoping I'd take them home, but I turned them all down.

The guys were all shocked, considering that falling into bed with women is how I usually deal with things, but I didn't have an ounce of desire to be with anyone in that way.

I don't need to have meaningless sex to help me numb the pain.

What I need is *her*.

I refuse to let these nightmares become a reality.

I need to win her back.

I pull my car into an empty parking space next to a rose-gold SUV and see Annalise inside. "Don't Blame Me" by Taylor Swift is blasting on full volume.

I chuckle softly, watching her sing her heart out.

She glances to the side and catches me watching her. Her cheeks turn a deep shade of crimson before she shuts off the engine and climbs out of her car.

"Nice singing," I tease.

"I was trying to unwind before work, but of course you *had* to ruin it." She rolls her eyes, slamming her car door. "Don't know why I'm not surprised. It's typical for you to ruin things for me."

"Are you referring to your little date with Lucas?" I ask, my voice tinged with bitterness.

"Yes, among other things. I don't get why you can't stand the fact that I've moved on. You did," she says, her voice sharp. "At least that's what the paparazzi photos of you and countless different women coming and going from hotel rooms seem to suggest."

"It's been weeks since I've hooked up with anyone, and none of those hookups ever meant anything to me."

She claps her hands slowly, letting out a bitter laugh. "Congratulations, Maddox, you learned to keep your dick in your pants. If only you'd done that while we were together."

I shut my eyes, pinching the bridge of my nose. "When are you going to believe me? I didn't cheat on you. I would never do that to someone I lo—" The word is at the tip of my tongue but I swallow it down, my cowardice taking over. "Of all the people in San Francisco, you go for Lucas Hilton? The biggest fucking douche to ever walk the planet?"

"I don't understand why you never liked him. He's a good person."

"Oh, don't be so fucking dense, Annalise. He's never been a good person. He's been obsessed with you since high school and always tried to come between us."

"There is no more *us*!" she snaps, her harsh words slicing through me. "So it doesn't really matter that I'm spending time with him, does it?"

I step closer to her, my voice softening. "It matters because you deserve better."

"And what exactly do I deserve?" She folds her arms over her chest, narrowing her eyes at me.

You deserve me.

I shove my hands into my pockets, biting back the words I want to say to her.

"Great. Now I'm late because of you," she huffs, pushing past me.

I watch her as she crosses the parking lot and enters the building.

"Fuck!" I shout, slamming my hand down onto the hood of my car.

I need to stop being a fucking coward or else I'm going to lose her. To Lucas fucking Hilton, of all people.

CHAPTER 20
Annalise

"Okay, so I came up with some new designs based on what you suggested last time. Let me know if you like these or if there are any changes you need me to make," Trang says to Maddox.

I feel his gaze on me as I sort through files in the corner. He doesn't seem the slightest bit interested in what Trang has to say, or in her designs.

Veronica catches on to where Maddox's attention is and shoots daggers my way. "Ms. Monroe, my office. Now."

The files slip from my hand. "What? But I—"

"Now," she repeats.

I follow her into her office, shutting the door behind me.

She crosses her arms, narrowing her eyes. "Do I need to remind you that Mr. Kamado is a client and you need to keep it professional?"

"Where is this coming from? I haven't said or done anything."

"It has nothing to do with what you say or do. It's the way you dress. Your clothes are far too revealing."

I stare at her, shocked. "What? I'm not even wearing anything inappropriate!" My hands skim down the front of my outfit in disbelief.

I'm wearing a turtleneck sweater and a skirt that falls just above my knees—there's hardly anything showing.

"Don't raise your voice at me," she snaps, glowering. "I know exactly what you're trying to do. You're trying to seduce him so you can get what you want. You want him to convince me to give you Trang's job."

My cheeks flush as frustration boils inside of me.

This bitch is fucking out of her mind. Do I think Trang should've been given the job? No. But the fact that Veronica thinks I would seduce someone to get ahead is outrageous.

"People like you always try to use their pretty faces and bodies to move up in the industry," she sneers. "Mr. Kamado is our client and having a sexual relationship with him is strictly prohibited. So unless you want to be out of a job, I highly suggest you refrain from getting involved with him."

My nails dig into the palm of my hand, helping me fight the temptation to lunge at her and slap her across that stupid fucking face. "Trust me—you don't have to worry about that. Was there anything else you wanted to add?" I ask through gritted teeth.

"No, that is all," she says, smoothing her hand over her skirt. "Just make sure you start dressing more modestly."

As I leave her office, I fight the urge to slam the door on my way out.

I storm into the break room and start kicking the trash can over and over. "I can't fucking stand this place! Veronica needs to rot in hell."

"Everything okay?"

I gasp, clutching my chest. "Shit, you scared me."

Maddox is standing in the corner with a cup of water in his hands, eyeing me with concern.

"What are you doing here?"

"Getting water." He holds up his cup. "Is that a crime?"

"No. I just thought someone else would bring it to you."

Maddox shrugs, gulping down the rest of his water. He strides over to where I'm standing and rests his hip against the counter. "What's going on, Monroe?"

He looks genuinely concerned, and after my conversation with Veronica, I don't have it in me to pretend like he isn't a comforting presence for me. We went through a lot together, and despite the fact that he cheated, I still trust him with certain aspects of my life. This is one of them.

I can hate him all I want, but Maddox Kamado will always listen.

"I don't know how much longer I can take it," I groan, raking my hands through my hair. "I am absolutely miserable here."

"Is Veronica still treating you like shit?" he asks, his expression tight with worry.

"Yes," I sigh. "And she's worse when you're around. She accused me of trying to seduce you and said my clothes were too revealing." My fists ball at my sides. The anger bubbles up, rising in my chest as I replay the conversation.

"Are you fucking kidding me?" He shakes his head, stunned.

"I wish I was," I say, exhaling sharply. "She thinks I'm doing this to steal Trang's position."

A laugh slips through his throat. "Wow, she really is something. I didn't know she would be like this when I agreed to work with her."

"I guess now I have to go fucking shopping for a new wardrobe," I groan.

"She's out of her mind if she thinks changing your attire would make you any less attractive. You could be wearing a trash bag and you would still be the most beautiful girl in the world." He flashes me a smile, dimples sinking into his cheeks.

Blush spreads across my cheeks and flutters stir in the pit of my stomach.

Damn it. Why does he have to say stuff like that?

"She said having a sexual relationship with you is prohibited," I continue, shaking my head.

"Damn. I guess your little fantasy about me bending you over her desk can't happen then," he says, his mouth lifting into a smirk. "That's a shame."

My cheeks redden further, and heat pools to my core. "Maddox, this isn't funny," I say, slipping back into serious mode, trying to push away the explicit thoughts circulating through my mind. "I'm so tired of coming to work and wondering if today will be the day she'll fire me."

"I'm gonna have another talk with her. Just because she's your boss does not give her the right to disrespect you like that," he says, his tone firm.

"There's no point, Maddox." I shake my head, letting out a defeated sigh. "She's a horrible human being, and there's nothing you can say to her that will change that."

"I can't stand seeing you unhappy," he murmurs, letting out a long sigh.

I exhale slowly, my eyes fixed to the ground. "I just gotta learn to accept the fact that this is my life now."

"But it doesn't have to be," he says, taking a step closer to me. "New York might be the fashion capital, but I know you'll be successful no matter where you live. God gave you this gift for a reason. You're not only robbing yourself but also the rest of the world of your talents if you don't share those beautiful creations in your sketchbook."

Warmth spreads through me, chipping away at the ice encasing my heart. I've been trying to guard my heart from him, but when he says stuff like this, it makes it impossible for me to not feel something.

Maddox always believed in me, even when I didn't believe in myself, and it's clear he still does after all this time.

"I know you said you don't want my money, but..." He pauses, lifting his eyes to mine. "What if I gave you a loan?"

"I don't want to be in your debt, Maddox. I'll probably die before I can pay you back in full."

He chuckles. "You're always so pessimistic. I wouldn't invest in something I didn't think was promising. You *will* be successful, Annalise. You'll make the money back in no time."

I chew the inside of my cheeks, shuffling my feet. "I don't know..."

"Will you at least consider it?"

"I'll think about it."

"Sweet." His lips tilt into a smile.

"How's everything going with the collab?" I ask.

"Not to sound like an asshole, but Trang's designs are atrocious. I tell her what I want and she does the *complete* opposite." He lets out a groan, dragging his hand down his face. "Veronica told me Trang is the best, but I don't see it."

I throw my head back, unable to keep from laughing.

Maddox quirks a brow. "I take it you're not a fan of her either?"

"Not really. I'm sure she only got the job because she's Veronica's niece. I don't even know if she went to school for fashion or had any previous experience."

Maddox clicks his tongue. "Well, Dauntless is gonna be out of business if she continues to give Trang design roles. If you were the lead designer on the team, I'm sure you would've killed it on your first try."

I can't help the grin that breaks free. Just like that, another shard of ice around my heart chips away.

I clear my throat, quickly glancing away. "I need to get going before I have to face Veronica's wrath again."

"Right. Well, I hope the rest of your day goes well," he says, holding the door open for me.

"Thank you." I flash him a smile, stepping out of the break room in a better mood than when I walked in.

How does Maddox always know exactly what to say to lift me up?

CHAPTER 21
Annalise

The crash of waves blends with the laughter of children and the sharp barks of sea lions splashing around the pier. I finish the last of my clam chowder and toss the empty container into a nearby trash can.

Grabbing my bag, I pull out my sketchbook and colored pencils.

I'd been holed up in my apartment all morning, staring at blank pages and crumpling every attempt at a new design. So I came to the pier, hoping a change of scenery would cure my creative block.

Sketching used to be effortless. A flower, a bird, even a plate of food could spark an idea that blossomed into a beautiful piece of clothing. But ever since I returned to San Francisco, I've struggled to find inspiration. Between Veronica's ruthless demands and the constant worry over Abuelo, I haven't had the heart to create. Lately, I've felt like I'm losing myself.

But then Maddox's words of encouragement sparked something within me—something I thought had been fading away. I feel butterflies fluttering in my stomach when I think of him and the way his eyes lit up as he encouraged me to keep chasing my dreams.

Those *beautiful* warm brown eyes.

Suddenly an idea strikes me, and I pull out a brown colored pencil that closely matches his eye color. I smile to myself as I glide the pencil across the paper. Each stroke brings me one step closer to creating something beautiful.

When I hold up the finished sketch, a sparkly brown mermaid gown stares back at me, and for the first time in months, I'm proud.

I shake my head, wondering who would've thought I'd find inspiration from my ex.

"Tsuki, get back here!"

I glance up just as a fluffy white blur barrels toward me, leash dragging behind her. Maddox is sprinting after her but Tsuki beats him to me, leaping onto the bench and smothering me in kisses.

"Hi, pretty girl," I coo, scratching behind her ears.

"I'm so sorry about my—" Maddox skids to a stop, then freezes when he sees me. "Annalise. Hey."

It's cloudy today but he's wearing sunglasses—probably so people won't recognize him—along with a hunter-green sweater, dark blue jeans, and—my heart stumbles—the same grey beanie I knitted for him years ago.

He slides onto the bench, eyes dropping to my sketch. "Wow. This is stunning." His fingers brush mine as he lifts the page, and a jolt of electricity shoots through me.

"Did you get inspired by those lazy sea lions?" he asks, nodding toward a group of them lounging on the dock.

"Yeah, the sea lions," I say quickly, eyes darting away as heat creeps onto my cheeks.

"The way your mind works never ceases to amaze me," he says, a warm smile touching his lips. "Remember that time at the store? You spotted that funky lamp, and by the end of the night you'd turned the idea into your prom dress." He closes the space between us until our thighs press firmly together and locks his eyes with mine. "You are extraordinary, Annalise."

A smile ghosts over my lips and the flutters in my stomach multiply. I clear my throat and tuck my sketchbook and colored pencils back into my bag. "So… you're playing against Boston tomorrow?" I blurt out the first thing that comes to mind.

If he keeps saying things like that—keeps pulling up old memories—I don't stand a chance of containing these damn butterflies.

His brow arches, a slow knowing smirk curving his mouth. "Oh, so you've been keeping up with my game schedule, Monroe?"

"No," I say, a little too quickly. "My coworker, Ivy. She's a huge basketball fan. She mentioned it."

"Uh-huh. Whatever you say." He chuckles, low and warm. "But yeah, I'll be in Boston. Supposed to be, what, twenty degrees?" He tugs at his beanie and grins. "Good thing I've got this to keep me warm."

My cheeks turn a darker shade of pink. My gaze lingers on the beanie and I notice how worn it is—fuzzy edges, a few loose threads. My chest tightens. "I didn't think you still had that."

"I wear it every winter," he admits, his own cheeks tinged pink. "None of my other beanies keep me as warm."

Warmth blooms in my chest. *If he kept the beanie… what else did he keep?*

"The other ones you have probably don't use quality yarn," I say, smiling softly.

"Nor were they made by you," he notes, his hands settling over mine. The simple touch sends my heart into a frenzy. My mind screams at me to pull away—yet I don't. I can't.

Weeks ago, when we were tangled together on his couch, I was unable to pull away because I was fueled by lust and the desperate need to dull the ache between my legs. But this… this is different. This is slower, deeper, and dangerous in a way I don't want to name. A feeling I shouldn't allow myself to have.

Then Tsuki's head snaps up, a low growl rumbling from her chest. She hops off the bench, teeth bared. Maddox's hand slips from mine as he tightens his grip on her leash before she can lunge.

Disappointment flickers through me—but maybe it's for the best. Sitting here with his hand on mine felt far too familiar, too easy. A path I can't let myself wander down again.

"Tsuki, calm down!" Maddox urges. He pulls a treat from his pocket and sets it on the ground but she ignores it, eyes locked, growl unrelenting.

He sighs, shaking his head. "I don't know what's gotten into her."

I rise from the bench and crouch beside her, reaching out gently. "Hey, Tsuki... What's wrong, baby girl? Do you want to go for a—"

"Annalise?"

The voice freezes me. My breath stalls, the hairs on the back of my neck prickling.

Tsuki must've sensed negative energy, because standing before me is my father, hand in hand with the woman he betrayed my mother with.

"Why isn't it working?" Maddox groans, swiping our hotel key over and over before rattling the handle.

We're in New York for the weekend, exploring potential colleges. Devereaux Fashion Institute is only a few blocks from NYU, and we could easily commute together and grab food during our lunch breaks. I'm so excited, thinking about living in New York together.

"Maybe we need to go down to the lobby and get a new key." He sighs.

I glance up at the number on the door and laugh. "This is 268. Our room's 286."

Maddox groans, dragging a hand down his face. "Damn it. Guess I was too distracted by your beauty."

"You are so cheesy." I grin, slipping my hand into his as we walk down the hall.

"Think we'll have time to check out Central Park before our flight tomorrow?" he asks.

"Yeah," I nod. "I wanna see the—what the hell?"

I glance up and my pulse spikes, heat flooding my chest.

Pressed against a doorframe is my father—his hands all over his secretary, his mouth on hers.

He told us he had to go out of town on business. Apparently that "business" involves groping his secretary.

His head jerks up, eyes wide. "Annalise. W-what are you doing here?"

"Touring colleges," I snap, tears already stinging. "Not that you'd remember—I guess you were too busy screwing your assistant to care." My voice cracks, anger and grief tangling in my throat. "How could you do this to mom? She stuck by you all these years, despite you being a crappy husband and father! She's done so much for you, and this is how you repay her?"

He drops his gaze, shifting on his feet. "Your mother and I... We've been drifting apart for years."

A harsh, bitter laugh bursts from me. "And that gives you an excuse to cheat on her? You are unbelievable. And you"—I turn, cutting my glare to the woman still frozen beside him—"sleeping with a married man. Do you not have any self-respect?"

She fumbles with the sleeves of her dress, refusing to meet my eyes.

"Annalise, I'm so sorry," my father mutters weakly.

"No. If you were sorry, you wouldn't have done it in the first place." My chest aches, fury burning through me. "I hate you."

Before he can answer, I storm down the hall, my vision blurred with a torrent of tears.

"How have you been, Annalise?" he asks, scratching the back of his neck. "I've been, uh, trying to call you."

"I know." My reply is clipped, sharp. "I've been ignoring you."

He clears his throat, forcing a weak smile. "It's nice seeing you two still together. And, uh—congratulations on the NBA, Maddox."

"Thanks," Maddox answers flatly, his jaw tight, muscles twitching.

My father turns his attention back to me. "Annalise, can we please talk?"

"I have nothing to say to you, Julian."

He sighs, shoulders sagging. "I know I made mistakes, but please give me a chance to make things right. Let me be a part of your life again."

"My life is just fine without you in it," I snap, every word dripping with the bitterness I've carried for years. "You were never there for me while I was growing up, so it wouldn't really make much of a difference now."

"Can you please find it in your heart to forgive me?" He takes a careful step forward, only to freeze when Tsuki growls, her lips curling back. He retreats, hands lifted slightly.

I cross my arms over my chest, the anger boiling over. "Why should I? You destroyed our family! You ruined Mom!"

"Your brother gave me another chance," he says quietly. "Can't you do the same?"

"Ollie was too young to understand what was going on, which made it easier for you to manipulate him," I bite back.

He opens his mouth but nothing comes out. Silence stretches between us before he shoves his hands into his pockets, eyes dropping to the pavement.

My gaze flicks to the ring glittering on his mistress's hand and fury knots in my gut. "Congratulations, by the way. If you two start a family, I hope you'll be a better father to them than you ever were to me."

I shoot them a scathing smile before turning on my heel. Maddox and Tsuki fall in step behind me.

My grip tightens around the railing near the dock as I blink back angry tears. "I can't believe he's still trying to ask for forgiveness," I mutter, shaking my head.

"He's got some fucking nerve for that," Maddox say, his jaw clenched. "What he did was unforgivable."

"I can't stand the fact that he's still with her. That he's happy," I say, my voice trembling with rage. "Meanwhile my mom is still trying to piece herself back together."

"It's not fair," he says, shaking his head. "One day, karma's going to catch up with him. Then he'll know what betrayal feels like."

"Yeah," I whisper. "I hope so."

He's quiet for a beat before asking, more softly, "Your mom hasn't dated since the divorce?"

I shake my head. "Says she doesn't need anyone—that me and Ollie are enough—but I can see it in her eyes. She's lonely. She wants love, even if she won't admit it." My throat tightens. "She deserves someone who will treat her right."

"Your father doesn't deserve either of you. I hope she finds someone worthy of her love." Those brown eyes hold mine, full of words he doesn't speak. "And I hope you do too."

Another shard of ice cracks loose from my heart. Here he is again—lifting me up when I'm about ready to crumble, steady and grounding. And yet... Maddox is the one weakness I can't afford. I have to be careful—before the whole wall shatters and nothing is left to protect me from him.

CHAPTER 22
Annalise

I sift through my closet and grab a pair of jeans and a pink sweater. Lucas is taking me to a rooftop movie theater, so I want to dress comfortably. We were supposed to go out last weekend, but he's been busy with practice.

My phone buzzes with a new text, and I step out of the closet to retrieve my phone from the bathroom counter.

I let out a quiet sigh of relief. I'm not the least bit disappointed that our plans got canceled again. The last few days, the pull toward Maddox has been impossible to ignore, a constant tug I shouldn't give in to. I find myself scrolling through his Instagram page and lingering on his photos longer than I should. I even shamelessly watched his game in Boston on TV the other day before Mazi got home.

And as for Lucas? My chest doesn't flutter. His text barely

stirs me. Maddox has me wrapped around his energy, and I hate that I want it.

No worries! We can reschedule for next week.

LUCAS

I actually wanted to see if you want to come along?

Oh no, it's okay! I don't wanna intrude!

LUCAS

You won't be intruding! Come on, please go! I'll have a lot more fun if you're there 😌

I don't know. Won't Maddox be there?

LUCAS

Probably. But don't worry about him. I won't let him mess with us.

I think I should stay home. I don't want there to be any drama.

LUCAS

Are you sure? Chandler told me Adriana Garcia will be performing.

No fucking way! 😱 Are you serious? She's my favorite artist.

LUCAS

Lol 😆 does that mean you're coming now?

Is it a bad idea to agree to go, knowing that Lucas and Maddox will most likely kill each other? A thousand percent, yes. But I can't resist seeing Adriana Garcia for free!

Yes, lol. I will be there.

Ditching the casual outfit I'd set aside earlier, I slip on a tight red dress with a sweetheart neckline and paint my lips to match. Maybe the outfit change is due to Adriana, or maybe it's to get a rise out of a certain shooting guard…

With the amount of VIP guests in attendance tonight at The Reverb, they had to double the amount of security. I'm probably one of the few people in the crowd who's *not* a celebrity.

"So how do you two know each other?" Chandler asks.

"We went to high school together."

"Yeah, we were really good friends," Lucas adds, resting his hand on my hip.

"Oh, wow! It's like a high school reunion." Chandler chuckles. "I heard Callahan and Kamado also went to the same school. Were you friends with them as well?"

I'm guessing he doesn't have a clue about my history with Maddox, and I'd rather keep it that way.

"Yeah." I nod. "We all hung around with the same crowd."

Lucas and Chandler dive into stories from their high school days.

I stifle a yawn, their conversation already lulling me into boredom. Hopefully the cosmo I'm sipping will kick in soon to make the night a little more bearable.

As I bring my glass to my lips for a sip, I see him—the man I've been waiting for—and suddenly my night becomes a lot more interesting.

Maddox steps into the club accompanied by Elijah, Andrés, and Andrés's wife, Katie. He has a way of commanding attention every time he enters a room, and I'm immediately drawn to him.

My heart throbs at the sight of him. He is looking *especially* fine tonight. The short-sleeve white button-up shirt he's wearing accentuates his muscular build and showcases his large biceps.

He catches a glimpse of me in the crowd, halting in his

tracks. My knees go weak as his eyes sweep down my body. His gaze lingers on my breasts before moving to my lips.

When our eyes meet, I casually flip my hair over my shoulder and bite down on my bottom lip, knowing it drives him wild. He draws in a sharp breath, his muscles tensing, proof that it worked.

The way he's looking at me has my core throbbing with need.

"What's up, boys!" Chandler throws his hands in the air when Maddox and his friends arrive at our section.

"Hey, man. Happy birthday!" Maddox greets him with a smile.

They pull each other into one of those classic bro hugs.

The server brings over a tray of shots and we all take one to celebrate Chandler's birthday.

Maddox leaves his friends' side and walks over—stopping directly behind me. "I know what you're trying to do," he whispers.

Our close proximity and the feel of his breath on my skin sends shivers down my spine.

"I don't know what you're talking about."

Grabbing my hips, he pulls me closer, pressing his hard cock into my ass. My breath hitches in my throat, the wetness between my legs increasing. "You're trying to make me jealous. Wearing this dress and showing up with *him.*"

I glance over at Lucas, who's too busy taking more shots with Chandler to notice what's happening.

"*Please.* As if I care enough to make you jealous," I say, pushing my ass back further and causing him to grunt.

"Two can play this game, Monroe." With a wink, he steps away from me, extinguishing what was building between us and leaving me craving his presence.

A busty blonde woman wearing a dress that barely covers her

nipples stares at Maddox from across the room. She twirls her fingers through her hair and gives him a seductive smile.

He smiles back at her and weaves through the crowd to get to her.

Rage sears through me seeing him interact with this woman. He leans in close, whispering in her ear. She throws her head back laughing and rests a hand on his chest.

A playful smile dances on his lips as he glances at me, clearly amused by the angry look on my face.

Okay, Kamado. Game on.

Strutting toward Lucas, I grab his hand, pulling him away from his teammates. "Let's dance."

His mouth tilts into a smile and he happily follows me to the dance floor. He holds me close as I grind my hips against him, moving to the beat.

"Fuck, you're so hot," he murmurs, moving his hands down my legs.

I shift my gaze to Maddox, satisfied to catch the scowl on his face and the way he's gripping his drink tightly.

Bringing the drink to his lips, he gulps the rest of it down and sets it on a nearby table. He places his hand on the small of the blonde woman's back, guiding her to the dance floor.

Maddox draws her close to him, their hips swirling together rhythmically.

The blonde bends over, nearly flashing everyone as she moves her ass against Maddox.

Flames of anger lick through me seeing them dance together. Unable to watch them for another second, I excuse myself and go to the restroom.

My mind starts to race as I stare back at my reflection in the mirror.

I keep telling myself that I don't have feelings for Maddox—but if I don't, then why the hell am I so jealous of the blonde getting his attention? I'm sure it's just a normal reaction to seeing your ex with another woman. Anyone else would have acted the same way I did, right? There's no way I could have any romantic feelings for him. Not again.

Although I did wear this dress because I knew he would be here. And I knew it would make him want me.

But that's also normal, isn't it? A lot of girls try to look their best when they know they'll be seeing their ex. That doesn't mean they still want them.

But I do want him.

The restroom door swings open and pulls me out of my thoughts. In steps Maddox, wearing that irresistible dimpled smile.

"So you started something you couldn't finish, huh, Monroe?" He leans against the wall, amusement flickering across his face.

"Did you seriously follow me in here?" I shoot him a glare.

A laugh bubbles from his lips. "You're in the men's restroom."

I spin around, spotting the urinals lined up in the back. I guess I was so angry that I didn't even notice.

"You should pay more attention next time," he says, stepping closer to me. "What if some creep had walked in here instead of me?"

"I'm perfectly capable of handling myself. I'm not some damsel in distress," I snap, folding my arms over my chest. "You can go back out there and dance with that girl. I didn't think blondes were your type."

"They're not." He laughs.

Then Maddox's strong arms spin me around, pushing me against the counter. I can feel him growing hard against me, and the contour of his sculpted abs.

"I like seeing you get jealous, Monroe." His eyes darken as he licks his lips.

"I'm not jealous."

"I know you're lying," he whispers, his voice low and seductive. "I know you better than anyone." His hands move down my waist, and my breathing becomes erratic as he drags them lower. "I know *this body* better than anyone else."

He cups my ass and a moan to slips out of me.

"You're wasting your time with Lucas," he whispers, brushing his lips against my ear.

"What makes you say that?" I ask, my defenses starting to crumble.

Grabbing my chin, he forces me to look at him. "Because the whole time you're with him, you'll wish you were with me instead. He'll never be able to give you what you want or make your body feel as good as I do."

"You're so arrogant," I whisper, even though he's not wrong. The other men I've been with could never pleasure me like he could. Not one of them could ever care the way he does—or reach the parts of me only Maddox seems able to.

It's safe to say Maddox Kamado has ruined me for other men. Not that I would *ever* admit that to him, though.

"Perhaps I am. But I'm only speaking the truth." He presses his lips on my neck, lightly sucking on it. "No one else can pleasure you like I can." He peppers kisses on my collarbone and across the tops of my breasts. Lifting my chin, he leans into me. "You're mine, Annalise."

Our lips are mere inches from each other. Unable to resist him any longer, I close my eyes, desperate to get a taste.

Then the restroom door swings open. Andrés and his wife barge through, killing the moment. Thankfully, they're too busy making out and groping each other to notice us.

"Couldn't wait until you get home, could you, Mrs. Navarro?" Andrés murmurs, guiding Katie into an empty stall as she bursts into a fit of giggles.

Not wanting to stick around to hear them bang, I adjust my dress and slip out of the restroom, Maddox following closely behind.

CHAPTER 23
Maddox

It became damn near impossible to keep my impure thoughts at bay from the moment I saw Annalise in that dress. The way it clings to every curve, every swell of her hips, every inch of that perfectly round, irresistible ass has my pulse hammering. And those red lips… I'm aching to taste them.

I came so close to finally tasting what I've been craving all these years, but of course we had to be interrupted. If only fucking Andrés could've kept it in his pants for a couple more hours, I wouldn't be having the worst case of blue balls I've ever had.

Lucas glowers at me, possessively wrapping his arm around Annalise. I'm sure seeing us come back at the same time raised some suspicions, but I don't give a shit. I wish he'd been the one who walked in on us, so he could see who Annalise really wants to be with.

"Everything okay?" he asks. "You were gone for a while."

"Yeah, sorry. I was on the phone with Mazi," she says, giving him a tight-lipped smile.

Elijah spots me from across the room and weaves through the crowd, heading my way. He nudges me with his elbow, wiggling his brows with a suggestive grin. "Sooo… what were you and Annalise doing in the restroom together?"

"Nothing," I reply flatly.

"Why are you being so secretive?" He crosses his arms, pinching his brows together. "I'm your best friend. Come on! Give me the details."

"There *are* no details," I mutter, scrubbing my hand down my face. "Andrés and Katie barged in and decided to get freaky the moment Annalise and I were about to kiss."

"Damn it," he sighs. "So you mean to tell me I spent all that energy talking to Hilton for nothing?"

"Wait—you were talking to him?" I tilt my head, brows furrowing together. "For what?"

"So you could get some action!" He throws his hands up. "He was about to check on her, but I had to keep him distracted and pretend like I was interested in getting to know him." Rolling his eyes, he lets out an exasperated sigh. "His favorite color is orange and he doesn't like ice cream, in case you were wondering." He shakes his head, wrinkling his nose. "Who the hell doesn't like ice cream? I knew there was something off about the guy."

My shoulders shake with laughter. Elijah may be an immature goofball, but he is one hell of a good friend. "So y'all are best buds now?"

"Yep." He nods. "I'm gonna make him a friendship bracelet."

"You never made me one," I pout.

He laughs, shoving me playfully. "Bro, shut your ass up."

"So, was Hilton losing it earlier?" I ask, a smirk tugging my lips.

"Oh, for sure. I didn't think it was possible for someone to get that red. The vein on his forehead was pulsating so hard, I thought it was going to burst."

My smile widens. "I wish I could've seen it. I'm glad he's getting a taste of his own medicine."

"He probably invited her tonight to rile you up, and now look at him."

Lucas steers Annalise away from our side of the room, and I can tell he's feeling insecure from the tight grip he has on her.

She glances my way and I meet her eyes with a soft smile. Lucas frowns slightly, noticing her lingering gaze. He quickly redirects her attention back to him.

Even though Annalise and I were interrupted tonight, I feel more at ease. I wasn't feeling worried about Lucas anymore. She may still be in denial, but I know deep down she still wants me. I just have to be patient.

"How's everyone doing tonight?" Adriana Garcia climbs onto the stage and the crowd erupts in cheers.

"Oh my God! Oh my God!" Annalise jumps up and down, squealing with excitement.

"Before we get started, I wanted to sing happy birthday to Chandler—who, by the way, is looking extra handsome tonight." She winks at him, blowing a kiss his way. He blushes furiously, a wide grin spreading across his face.

The servers come out with a cake and we all sing happy birthday to him, led by Adriana on stage.

When the candles are blown out, Adriana pulls the attention back to her. "I've been working on a new song that hasn't been released yet, and you all will be the first ones to hear it. It's called 'Always Be Mine.'"

The music swells through the speakers, a haunting melody wrapping around her voice as she takes the mic.

"All those years...

I thought I'd moved on.

But when I saw you again,

I knew I couldn't have been more wrong!"

The rhythm pulses through the floor, and her voice rises with raw emotion.

"No matter distance or time, you will always be mine!"

Everyone's eyes are on the stage, captivated by Adriana's angelic voice, but mine are on Annalise. I shoot her a smile and she returns it. A warm feeling blooms through my chest.

Not only do the lyrics deeply resonate with me, but hearing Adriana live again has me feeling nostalgic. I took Annalise to an Adriana Garcia concert for our first date.

I spot Annalise by the lockers and head her way. I have the biggest crush on her, and I've been trying to get her to go on a date with me for months, but she's turned me down every time. The rejections stung, but I didn't let it stop me. I'm hoping she'll say yes this time around.

"Hey, Monroe."

"What do you want, Kamado?" She continues pulling books out of her locker, not sparing me a glance.

"Sooo... I have front-row seats to the Adriana Garcia concert this weekend. Do you want to go with me?"

Her brow ticks upward. "You're quite persistent, aren't you? I thought you'd take a hint after I turned you down the first ten times."

"What can I say? When I want something, I go after it until I get it." I wink, earning an eyeroll from her. "Did I mention there will be backstage passes?"

She shuts her locker, her eyes widening. "Are you serious?"

"Yeah. But since you don't seem interested, I think maybe I'll ask someone else."

I start to walk away but she grabs my arm. "No, wait. I'll go with you. But don't read too much into it. I'm only agreeing to go because I've been dying to meet Adriana Garcia, and I couldn't get my hands on tickets."

I try my best to keep my cool, but I'm jumping with joy on the inside.

"If it means I get to spend time with you, I'll take it."

The party continues after Adriana's performance. Needing a break from the festivities, I escape to the rooftop. I lean against the cool railing of the balcony, gazing upon the night sky.

The sound of heels clicking against the floor catches my attention. I turn my head, a smile ghosting across my lips when I see it's the person I was hoping for.

The moon casts a glow on her beautiful tan skin and illuminates her sapphire and emerald eyes. The gentle breeze tousles her long brown hair as she walks toward the balcony.

"You following me now?"

"Oh, yeah, totally. I couldn't stand to be apart from you," she says, her tone laced with sarcasm.

"Clearly, since you left your bodyguard behind," I tease.

"I only came to see Adriana Garcia, so I'm ready to leave now." She digs in her purse, pulling out a joint. "Is it okay if I smoke? That's why I came up here."

I shake my head. "I don't mind."

She places it between her lips, lighting it up.

I watch her closely as she inhales and exhales, releasing a cloud of smoke that curls around us.

She holds out the joint to me. "Do you wanna take a hit?"

"Sure," I say, taking it from her. I take a puff but end up inhaling too much. The smoke burns my lungs and I break out into a fit of violent coughs. My hand tightly grips the railing as I gasp for air.

She laughs, patting me on the back. "You alright there, Dimples?"

Dimples.

A smile blooms on my face upon hearing that old nickname.

"Why are you smiling like that?" She looks at me, puzzled.

"Because you called me Dimples." I continue grinning at her like an idiot.

"Okay, so what?" She shrugs, a rosy blush touching her cheeks.

"You've only been calling me by my last name."

"It must have slipped out." She quickly glances away, taking another puff of her joint.

It may be a small victory, but I'll take it as a sign she's slowly warming up to me.

"I can never get enough of this view," she says, staring out at the Golden Gate Bridge sparkling over the water.

"Neither can I," I agree, my eyes on her. "It beats the view I had when I was living in Houston."

"What was it like living there?"

"It was pretty dope. There was always some kinda event going on, and the food was great. Tacos in Texas hit different. But the weather during the summer was unbearable. It feels good to be back in San Francisco. I missed it here."

"I missed it too."

I missed *you*.

"Are you ever going to tell me why you really left New York?" I angle my body toward hers.

"I already told you, I wanted to be closer to my family."

I let out a heavy sigh, not buying it. "I want the *real* reason, Annalise. You worked so hard to pursue your dream. I know you wouldn't have given it up that easily. I know your family wouldn't have let you, either."

She takes a long puff from her joint, then puts it out against the railing before tossing it in a trash can to the side.

A heavy sigh leaves her lips before she starts. "When I graduated from college, I had an internship lined up with Camille Dubois. I flew back home to visit my family, and Abuelo was extremely ill. The doctors ran a few tests on him and found a mass in his lung. He was later diagnosed with stage-three small cell carcinoma."

My gut twists with pain. Her grandfather, Emilio, is such a warm and gentle soul. It pains me knowing that he's battling this illness.

Gently, I place my arm on her shoulder. "I'm so sorry, Annalise. I know how much he means to you."

She remains silent, trying to fight back the tears.

"What's his prognosis?" I ask.

"The doctor said he has a thirty percent chance of surviving with treatment."

"I think he'll beat the odds," I say, trying to lift her mood. "He's got a lot of spunk in him."

"I hope so… I don't know what I would do without him." Her voice cracks and tears spill down her cheeks.

I bring her head to my chest, pulling her into a tight embrace as she sobs.

"Why him?" she wails. "He doesn't deserve this."

My heart aches seeing her in such a vulnerable state. I want to protect her and obliterate anything that caused her sadness.

I curse myself for not fighting harder for her back then. My anger prevented me from reaching out to her. Had I been there for her, she wouldn't have had to endure this pain alone.

Annalise is like a rose, beautiful and compelling. Her beauty often distracts people from seeing the thorns she tries to hide from the world. Many people wouldn't dare grasp a rose full of thorns for fear of the pain that it would cause, but I'd let her thorns pierce through every part of me. I see her for who she is and appreciate every part of her—thorns and all.

"I'm sorry for ruining your night." She sniffles, swiping the tears from her eyes. "You should go back down with your friends. I don't want to burden you with my problems."

My hands drift to her face. I cup her cheeks, staring deep into her eyes. "Don't ever feel like you're burdening me, Annalise. I'm here for you. Always. And you didn't ruin my night." I gently stroke her cheeks. "Being out here with you was the best part of it."

A small smile touches her lips, causing my heart to swell.

"There you are. I've been looking everywhere for you." Lucas's arrogant voice slices through the air.

Annalise pulls away from my embrace, quickly dabbing at the corners of her eyes.

He strides over to the balcony, deliberately placing himself between us. His eyes flick to her tear-streaked face, the pink tinge of her nose. "Is Kamado bothering you?" he asks, his tone sharp.

"No. We were just talking," she replies, shaking her head.

As much as I want to give him an earful and send him flying off the edge of this building, I resist. I don't want to upset Annalise and ruin the moment we shared earlier.

"I'll see you next week at Dauntless," I say, giving her a smile.

"Yeah. I'll see you around." She grins and gives me a small wave.

I slowly descend the stairs, lingering at the base and contemplating if I should rush back up and tell her that I'm still deeply, madly in love with her.

I've been lying to myself saying that I don't, but the truth is, I never *stopped* loving her.

Even if she doesn't say it back, I can't let another minute go by without her knowing.

With my heart pounding loudly in my chest, I race up the stairs—ready to profess my love for her.

But the words die in my throat.

Lucas's hands are in her hair and they're locked in a kiss.

How could she kiss him after the moment we just shared?

I feel my heart shatter into a million pieces at the sight before me, crushing me beyond repair.

CHAPTER 24
Annalise

Ever since I found out about Abuelo's diagnosis, I've pushed it to the back of my mind, not wanting to face reality. But tonight, all the emotions I've been suppressing came crashing through me as though a floodgate had been opened. In that moment, I forgot about the past I had with Maddox and let myself get lost in the familiar warmth of his embrace.

For the rest of the world, I put on a façade and keep my problems to myself. Maddox makes me feel safe enough to let my barriers down. He sees the parts I keep hidden from the rest of the world and the silent battles I fight alone.

I thought what I felt for Maddox was just pure lust, but being in his arms again has me doubting my feelings.

"Did you have a good time tonight?" Lucas asks after Maddox leaves us alone on the rooftop. He wraps his arms around my waist.

My body stiffens at his touch. "Yeah. I'm glad I decided to come," I say, forcing a smile. "Being able to see Adriana again was a great experience."

"You look so beautiful tonight," he says, snaking his hands through my hair.

Then, without warning, he crushes his lips to mine.

I'm shocked at first as his lips move against mine in a sloppy kiss. It takes a second to wake the hell up—but when I do, I kiss him back, hoping it extinguishes whatever I'm feeling for Maddox.

Everything I feel for him is so damn confusing. I don't want to trust him again after what he did, but I can't deny that he's become a safe space for me, just like he used to be.

And unfortunately for me, kissing Lucas isn't changing my feelings for him in the slightest. It doesn't help that when Lucas's lips first met mine, I didn't feel a single thing. Not a spark, or even a twinge of anything remotely romantic.

I felt more when Maddox was just standing in front of me. I can still feel his touch lingering on my skin, burning into the depths of my soul.

Lucas finally pulls away, a dazed grin on his face. "I've waited eight long years to do that. I've had a crush on you ever since I laid eyes on you in our ninth-grade history class."

Not knowing how to respond, I smile back at him.

And that's when I realize that kissing Lucas only makes me more confused about my feelings for Maddox.

The trees outside sway violently in the wind as the sound of thunder rumbles through the lobby. Driving to work today was terrifying. The rain was pouring down so heavily that I could barely see the road.

I'm extremely late, but I'm grateful that I made it in one piece.

The doors to the elevator are about to close so I race toward it, spotting Maddox inside.

"Hold the elevator!" I call out. He presses a button and the doors open again.

"Thank you." I smile at him, expecting him to return it or make some kind of flirty remark. Instead, he doesn't acknowledge my presence, and his eyes remain glued to his phone.

"Man, this weather is insane. It felt like I was driving through a hurricane," I say, attempting to start a conversation, but he continues scrolling through his phone.

Ever since we came back into each other's lives, we've been at each other's throats. Last weekend was one of the few times we'd had a normal conversation without getting into a heated argument.

We shared a moment on the rooftop at Chandler's party. We nearly kissed, and I can't for the life of me figure out what could have happened between then and now to explain his change in behavior.

In all the years I've known Maddox, he's never been one to remain silent. He's always been vocal and has never had trouble expressing himself. Something has to be seriously bothering him to act this way.

"Okay, what's wrong—" The elevator jerks, causing me to fall forward. "Shit!" I gasp, grabbing on to Maddox to steady myself.

It comes to a complete stop, and everything goes dark.

Using the flashlight on my phone, I shine it on the panel and press the emergency call button, but the only sound coming from the other end of the line is static.

Fucking great. I nearly died on the way to work today, and now I'll be stuck here for Lord knows how long. What a fantastic way to start my week.

Not wanting to be in complete darkness, I pull my water bottle out of my bag and place it on top of my phone to create a makeshift lantern. "We might as well pass some time, since I don't know when someone will come by to get us out. How's everything going with the collab?" I try again, hoping to get a response out of him this time.

He continues wearing a blank expression and starts watching videos on his phone.

"Are you seriously ignoring me?" I groan. "Weren't you the one who said we should be cordial?"

He rolls his eyes. "Good morning, Annalise. There. Are you satisfied now?"

"Why are you being such a freaking jerk?"

He straightens to his full height, brows furrowing with sharp irritation. "Oh, so it's okay for you to ignore me, but when I do it, I'm the bad guy?"

Dragging both hands down my face, I release a groan. My back thuds against the cold metal wall as I glare at him. "Ugh! I can't believe out of all people, I have to be stuck in an elevator with you!"

His arms fold across his chest as he steps forward, closing some of the distance between us. "Oh, I'm sorry. Would you rather be here with your boyfriend Lucas?"

"Oh my God! We went on *one* date. He's not my boyfriend."

His jaw tightens. "Didn't look that way to me."

"What are you talking about?" I ask, my brows drawing together.

"I saw you, Annalise!" There's a flame beneath his deep brown eyes. "I saw you kissing him."

Guilt pierces through me, making me regret the kiss more than I already do. The look on his face crushes me. The last time I saw him this broken was when I left him four years ago.

"Are you purposely trying to hurt me?" he asks, his voice cracking. "Are you trying to get back at me for something I didn't even do?"

I take a shaky breath, hands trembling at my side. "No, I-I don't know why I kissed him," I say. The words tumble out, frantic and tangled. "I've been so damn confused."

A bitter laugh escapes him as he throws his hands into the air. "Oh, you've been confused? How the hell do you think I feel, Annalise?" he yells. "You tell me you hate me, but your actions say otherwise. I never know where I stand with you!" His chest rises and falls rapidly as he stares at me, eyes blazing. "If you want to be with Lucas, then be with him. Stop playing with my emotions. Stop giving me all these damn mixed signals!"

I shake my head, stepping forward instinctively. "I don't want to be with him! I don't have feelings for him."

"Then what *do* you want?" he says, his eyes searching mine.

"I don't know!" I shout, voice breaking.

"You drive me fucking crazy, Monroe."

He yanks me close to him, crashing his lips onto mine, giving me my answer.

What I want is *him*.

CHAPTER 25
Maddox

Finally. After four long years of waiting and wondering when I would get to kiss Annalise again, it's finally happening. She crashes through the walls I had built around my heart, completely demolishing them.

Releasing all the feelings I've kept buried deep within me awakens every cell in my body, bringing me back to life. I don't know how I ever managed to survive without her.

The kiss is soft at first but becomes hungrier and more desperate, like all the years we lost are crashing into this one perfect moment. I expected her to pull away from me, but she's kissing me back with the same urgency, showing me she's been craving this as much as I have.

Deepening the kiss, I pin her against the cold metal wall of the elevator, tangling my hand in her hair and devouring those luscious lips.

Shivers of desire race through me hearing her soft whimpers as my tongue explores her mouth. I hook my hands underneath her thick thighs and press my erection against her panties.

"Maddox!" she moans, wrapping her legs around me tightly as I roll my hips against her.

Seconds later, our shirts are unbuttoned and my lips are on her neck while my hands graze her bare skin. She inhales sharply when my fingertips reach the base of her bra. Climbing my hand further, I groan in satisfaction at finding a metal barbell pierced through her nipple.

"When did you get this done?" I ask as I roll her hard nipples between my fingers.

"Last year," she answers breathlessly. "Do you want to see them?" She looks up at me through her thick lashes.

I nod, pulling my bottom lip between my teeth.

With her eyes locked on mine, she pulls down her bra, exposing herself to me.

My cock strains against my slacks at the sight of her perky breasts and pierced nipples on display. "You're so fucking sexy. I can't get enough of you." I lower my head and take her nipple into my mouth. She cries out, grabbing onto my hair as I switch back and forth.

Reclaiming her lips, I move my hand between her legs and groan in satisfaction when I feel her arousal. "You're fucking soaking for me, Monroe."

As much as I want to rip off her panties and plunge into her, I resist the urge. Seeing how fucking turned on I am *without* being inside her, I don't know how long I'll last once I feel her drenched pussy wrapped around my cock. When we make love again, I want to savor it. I want to make it last.

She slides her panties down, giving me more room to explore.

Loud moans pour from her mouth when she feels my fingers against her with no barrier. Her wetness increases, trickling down her thighs as I glide my hand through it.

My hand moves further down, stopping at her entrance as my thumb circles her swollen clit. She bites down on her bottom lip, staring at me with pleading eyes.

I pull her lip between my teeth and slip a finger into her, moving it in and out slowly.

"Maddox, please…" she whimpers.

"Do you want to come all over my fingers?" I whisper, continuing at my tortuously slow pace.

"Yes, please," she pants. "Please make me come."

"Spread your legs for me, Monroe." She willingly parts them and I thrust another finger inside her.

"Yes!" She grinds against my hand, her loud moans echoing through the elevator.

I wrap my hand around her throat, applying the perfect amount of pressure while fucking her with my fingers. Seeing the faces she makes brings me immense pleasure. I start imagining the feeling of her tight cunt around me.

Driving my fingers deeper, I rub against the spot that makes her toes curl while my thumb moves against her clit.

"Oh, fuck, Maddox!" she moans, gripping tightly onto my shirt as her walls clench around my fingers.

"So fucking beautiful," I murmur, watching as the orgasm crashes through her.

Just as she's coming down from her high, I lower myself to the ground, kneeling before her like the queen she is. My tongue laps at her pussy, feasting on her sweetness. She fists my hair with one hand and grabs onto the railing with the other as her legs tremble uncontrollably.

I suck on her clit then drag my tongue down her slit before pushing it inside. Her cum drips all over me and onto the floor as she shatters again and again.

Lifting my head from between her legs, I grin in satisfaction at seeing the pure ecstasy shining on her face.

Then the lights flicker on and the elevator rumbles back to life, beginning its ascent and breaking us out of our blissful haze.

"Fuck!" Annalise gasps, her eyes wide with fear.

She pulls her panties up and quickly readjusts her skirt while I fumble with the buttons of my shirt.

My shirt is only partially buttoned and Annalise's hair is still disheveled when the elevator reaches the top floor, where the main office is located. The doors slide open, revealing Veronica standing before us.

"Oh my goodness! Mr. Kamado!" Veronica's voice cracks, her hand flying to her mouth as she steps toward us. "My deepest apologies about the elevator! Our generator took a while to kick in. Are you okay?"

I am more than okay. Being trapped in the elevator with Annalise allowed me to finally do what I've been wanting to do since she walked back into my life.

"It's no problem, Mrs. Zhang."

"Happy to hear it. Now, let's go and talk business, shall we?" she says, gesturing to the conference room.

"Oh, of course. But I have to use the restroom first, if you don't mind."

I need to take care of myself as soon as possible because I am in fucking pain.

"Oh, that's fine!"

She turns to Annalise, suspicion written all over her face. "Ms. Monroe, please go fix yourself up. Your shirt is a mess and your makeup is smudged. It's not very professional for our workplace."

"Sorry. I got rained on," she says.

"Use an umbrella next time." Veronica scoffs as she walks off.

I shift my focus back to Annalise and my stomach twists at the sight of regret etched on her face. The atmosphere in the room feels thick and suffocating. I can sense the barrier between us rising once more.

She gazes down at the floor, shaking her head. "That shouldn't have happened."

CHAPTER 26
Annalise

My heart and soul were set ablaze when Maddox's lips touched mine again. It's been years, and no one has even come close to making me feel the way he does.

I've been in a constant state of denial since he came back into my life. I haven't wanted to believe that he could still have that much power over me. My head, my heart, my body… They all ache for his touch.

Every inch of me craved Maddox in that elevator, even though my mind was shouting at me to run the other direction. But there was this primal want—*primal need*—that refused to be silenced.

When his hands drifted down, exploring and grabbing like he used to, I was putty. There was no way to deny how badly I needed him and his expert touch. It was clear to me almost immediately that he remembers *exactly* how to fulfill my every desire. Every stroke of his fingers inside me, every flick of his tongue over my clit, had me wondering how I've gone so long without experiencing the earth-shattering orgasms that only he is capable of giving me.

Because he cheated. He broke your heart.
And he'll do it again the second you give him the chance.
Shit…

"That shouldn't have happened," I say, shaking my head and holding my fingers to my lips.

"What?" His face morphs into sadness, brows dipping together. "Annalise, you can't mean that."

He reaches out for me but I pull away from his touch at the last second. Squaring my shoulders, I swallow the boulder in my throat and look him dead in the eye.

"I shouldn't have kissed you." My arms wrap around my middle in a desperate attempt to protect myself from the man who already destroyed my heart once. "And I definitely shouldn't have let things go as far as they did. I don't want you getting the wrong impression. There's no chance for us again, Maddox."

The lie tastes like venom on my tongue, but I need to say it for the sake of my heart.

"No," he spits, shaking his head and taking a giant step toward me. "Fuck that."

"Excuse me?"

"*Fuck that*, Annalise. I refuse to believe that you truly think what happened in there was a mistake. I know you felt exactly what I did."

"I didn't," I deny. "It was a momentary lapse in judgment."

"You're saying that if I were to kiss you again"—he steps closer—"right here in front of everyone, you could honestly tell me that you would feel nothing?"

The look on his face tells me that he isn't bluffing.

I open my mouth to respond but Veronica pops her head out of the office, glaring at me.

"Ms. Monroe, stop distracting Mr. Kamado and get to work!"

"Yes, Ms. Zhang."

As soon as I leave here tonight, I'm going to look for another job. I can't keep working at Dauntless and run the risk of being alone with Maddox again. I don't trust myself. He came too close to destroying the shield around my heart—the one that's only there because of him.

It was easier to protect myself when he wasn't a part of my life, but now… it's damn near impossible. My feelings for Maddox grow the more I'm around him, and I don't want it to get to the point where I can no longer contain them.

It was bad enough having my heart crumble at the hands of him once. I don't think I'd survive if I gave him the chance to do it again.

"What's on your mind, *mi rosa*?" Abuelo asks. We're at the infusion center where he gets chemotherapy.

The last few days, I haven't been getting enough rest. My mind keeps replaying the kiss I shared with Maddox. "Nothing, Abuelo." I place my hand on top of his weathered one, giving it a light squeeze. "I just had a very long week."

He gives me a pointed look. "I raised you. You really think you can lie to me without me noticing?"

I don't answer him. Instead, I face the TV and pretend to be interested in whatever the weatherman is saying.

"We have four hours to kill. Talk to me," he urges.

I release a sigh. I know that if I don't tell him, he will keep bugging me about it. "It's Maddox… He's back in my life, and things have gotten so complicated."

Abuelo sits up straighter, brows shooting up in surprise. "He is? Where did you see him?"

"At Dauntless. He partnered with the company for a collab. I feel like I'm being punished. Not only do I have to work for La Diabla, but I have to see my ex again."

"What ever happened between you two? I know it took more than distance for a couple like you two to break up."

Wringing my hands together, I stare down at my lap as painful memories flash through my mind. "On our anniversary… I flew to Chicago to surprise him and saw Charlotte Jones come out of his room wearing his clothes. He… he cheated on me, Abuelo."

Abuelo taps his chin, his face unreadable. "Hmm."

Hmm? That's all he's going to say? I was expecting him to start cursing and shouting in Spanish. Anything other than *hmm*.

"Charlotte Jones. Isn't she the mean girl that was jealous of you and Maddox?"

"Yes. The same one. Why?" I ask, furrowing my brows.

"Just wondering." Abuelo shrugs. "So, what happened after you saw her? Where was Maddox?"

"He was still sleeping. I confronted her and she confessed that she slept with him. Said she only did it because he told her we weren't together anymore. I kept this from you and Mami because I was so crushed. It's still hard for me to talk about it now."

I check to see if Abuelo has fallen asleep because it's been a good minute since he responded, but he's wide awake and wearing the same unreadable expression.

Abuelo shakes his head. "Maddox loved you more than anything, Annalise. I don't think he would throw it all away after everything you two built."

"But he did, Abuelo. And I made the mistake of kissing him again the other day. I'm so stupid."

"Oh, *mi rosa*. You are not stupid." He reaches over and gives my hand a squeeze. "I know seeing what you did hurt you, but I think there may be more to the story."

"No, there isn't. He cheated on me. I don't care how many times he denies it. I know he did. That's all men do. They lie."

He crosses his arms. "So you're calling your abuelo a liar now, too?"

"No!" I groan. "You don't count. You're one of the few good ones in the world."

Leaning his head back on the recliner, he lets out a long sigh. "A love like the one you had with Maddox is rare to come by. Him being back in your life isn't a punishment, *mi rosa*. This is all part of God's plan—for you to rekindle the love that was lost. Perhaps you need to hear him out."

I'd convinced myself that Maddox betrayed me. That we were over. Since he came back into my life, he has shown how much he cared for me through his actions, and he's reminded me of the love we once had. It has me questioning if he was ever truly capable of cheating on me.

Over the last four years, I've been so consumed by anger and hatred that I didn't allow him to tell me his side of the story.

Abuelo is right. I need to hear Maddox out.

With shaking hands, I pull out my phone and begin typing a message.

Hey. Can we talk tonight?

My heart races as I hit send. I anxiously await his response, knee bouncing up and down, each passing second feeling like an eternity.

CHAPTER 27
Maddox

"**D**ude, why do you look so bummed? We just won a big game," Andrés says as he passes me another shot. We blew North Carolina State out of the water tonight and are throwing a party at our apartment to celebrate.

"Tomorrow is my three-year anniversary with Annalise and we're spending it apart." I tip my head back, downing the shot. "I had the whole weekend planned out for us, but she said she had too many projects to catch up on. I won't be able to see her for another month."

"I'm sorry, man. Long distance must be so hard," he says softly, placing a hand on my shoulder. "I definitely wouldn't be able to survive if I went that long without seeing Katie."

"I'm dying, man. I hate being away from her. We went from seeing each other every day to only once a month, if that."

If it weren't for my father, we wouldn't be in this predicament. The fact that I decided to pursue a career in basketball didn't sit well with him. During my senior year of high school, he kept pushing me to major in business, but I refused.

That's when he gave me an ultimatum—if I wanted to play college ball, I had to secure a full-ride scholarship, or he'd cut me off entirely. Millennium University was the only school that came through with the offer so, reluctantly, I accepted.

I had dreamed of living in New York with her—riding the subway, going to Broadway shows, and building a life together. Instead, I'm stuck in Chicago, hundreds of miles away, seeing her only through a screen for barely an hour a day. It's not what I imagined at all.

"Coach said NBA scouts are attending the next game." Andrés shifts the conversation in an attempt to cheer me up. "It'll be your time to shine. Maybe you'll get drafted to New York. That way, you wouldn't have to be apart from her."

"I hope so. I'm so ready to get out of Chicago."

"Hey, Chicago isn't so bad. You wouldn't have met me if you went to college elsewhere. And you gotta admit"—he nudges his shoulder against mine, his mouth lifting into a smile—"I'm pretty awesome."

A laugh bubbles out of me. "I guess."

"Come on, I need to redeem myself in beer pong," he says, pulling me away from the corner. "I made the mistake of part-nering up with Harrison and we got our asses handed to us."

The last thing I remember is winning a beer pong game with Andrés. Everything after that is a blur.

"Stop saying you love me!" Annalise shouts. "You *clearly* don't have a clue what it means to love someone. The only person you're capable of loving is yourself."

"How could you say I never loved you? Charlotte and I only slept together once in high school, and it happened way before you and I got together. I promise I haven't been with anyone but you. You are the only one I want, Rosie."

I've done everything in my power to make her feel loved, to make her feel special. My words and actions were wasted for her to say that I don't love her and for her to think that I would cheat on her.

"Enough! I'm *sick* of your lies!" she shouts, tears falling from her cheeks. "You're exactly like my father!"

An overwhelming heaviness settles in my chest. Her father—the man who put her and her family through so much—is the worst possible person she can compare me to. It's like a gut punch to know that she can even put me in the same category as someone like him.

How could she think that I would ever hurt her like that? I know the pain she lived through. I know how much it affected her. She has to know that I would never do that to her.

She has to…

With my heart left bleeding out on the sidewalk, I open up my apartment door to find Andrés in the kitchen ransacking the drawer.

"Sorry, I misplaced my wallet. I swear I'll leave as soon as I find it."

I mumble my acknowledgement, not caring enough to enunciate.

He shifts his attention to me, noticing my flushed face and bloodshot eyes. "Dude, are you good? Where's Annalise? I was almost scared to come home because I didn't wanna walk in on y'all banging in the kitchen." He lets out a laugh.

I grab the gift bag Annalise left for me and bring it to the couch. Reaching inside, I pull out the contents—a jar full of origami hearts and a hand-knit beanie and scarf.

Twisting the jar open, I pluck out one of the paper hearts and open it.

> *I love you because you always push
> me to follow my dreams.*

"Earth to Maddox," he says, waving his hand in front of my eyes that are still locked on the small piece of paper.

"Annalise broke up with me." My voice cracks, tears falling from my cheeks and onto the paper. "She hates me. I think I lost her forever."

"Wait, what? I don't understand." His brows furrow, lips parting in disbelief. "She flew all this way to see you. What happened?" He shuts the drawer and slides onto the couch.

"Apparently when she showed up, Charlotte came out of my room wearing my clothes. She accused me of cheating on her. I don't even know what the fuck she was doing in my room last night. Please tell me there's someone who can vouch that I didn't sleep with Charlotte."

He sighs. "I wish I could tell you, man. I left with Katie after we played beer pong, so I don't know what happened after that." He shakes his head, placing a hand on my shoulder. "This has to be a misunderstanding. I know you're not capable of doing something like that. Maybe you should go talk to Charlotte."

After I pull myself together enough to be seen in public, I barge though the girls' dormitory and demand someone to tell me where Charlotte's room is.

"She's in room 102." A short brown-haired girl points to the hall on the left.

I stomp down the hall, avoiding everyone's stares as I locate her room. "Charlotte, open up the fucking door!" I yell, pounding the door with my fist.

The door swings open and Charlotte stands there with a

towel slung across her shoulder and a bag of toiletries in her hand. "Oh, hey, babe. I was about to hop in the shower." She leans into me, placing her hand on my chest. "You're more than welcome to join me if you'd like."

I shove her off of me. "Do you have any idea what you've done?"

She scrunches her brows. "What are you talking about?"

"Annalise broke up with me because of *you*! She thinks I cheated on her. You destroyed our relationship!"

"I didn't know you were still together, I swear!" Charlotte throws her hands up in defense. "I was shocked when I saw her. You told me you broke up with her before we slept together."

"Stop lying!" I snap. "She's the love of my life. I would never do that to her."

"Maddy Bear, why would I ever lie to you?" she says, placing her hand on my cheek.

Who the hell does she think she is? Calling me by the nick-name Annalise gave me—which is something I'll probably never hear again.

"Don't fucking call me that!" I shout, swiping her hand away.

"Why are you being such a jerk? You were so loving and tender last night."

"Tell me the truth, Charlotte!" I bang my fist on the door, the impact making her flinch and jump back. "Why the fuck were you in my room last night? And why were you wearing my clothes?"

She rolls her eyes. "I told you already. We slept together. You ripped off my clothes and I needed something to wear, so you gave me yours."

"You're lying." I shake my head. "I would never do that to her. I love her too much."

"You really don't remember what happened?" she says, lifting her eyes to mine.

"I was fucked up, Charlotte. I don't remember jack shit."

She pauses for a moment, taking a deep breath. "Okay, so I might have made up the part about you telling me you broke up with Annalise…"

I knew it. I knew I didn't sleep with her.

"But I didn't lie about us having sex. I didn't want you thinking less of me for sleeping with you while knowing you were still with Annalise. I've been in love with you since high school. What we had back then was more than just a fling to me."

All the air leaves my lungs. The room starts spinning. Charlotte continues talking but I can't hear a word she's saying.

Fuck. Did I sleep with her last night? Did I mistake her for Annalise?

No—this can't be true. Charlotte can't be trusted. I have to find out the truth.

In the days that followed, I combed through social media posts and tried to make a list of everyone who attended the party. It was impossible to find out who all was there because there were so many people who came and went at different times. I know Annalise wouldn't believe my word alone, so I was desperate to find proof that Charlotte was lying.

I contacted everyone I could, asking if they saw me interact with Charlotte or if they saw her go into my bedroom. But no one seems to know a thing. I feel so helpless.

I call Annalise's cell, hoping this time I hear her voice on the end. But, just like the other hundreds of times I've called, it goes straight to voicemail.

It's been fourteen days since she left me. Fourteen days since my whole world came crashing down.

I've spent the last few days scrolling through pictures of us and replaying old videos. Knowing that this is all I have left of her only makes me feel worse. I'll never be able to hold her again or kiss those soft lips. I'll never be able to hear her laugh or hear her tell me she loves me.

We were supposed to build a life together. We were supposed to have a future. But it was all ripped away in the blink of an eye.

No. I refuse to believe this is the end for us. I refuse to give up on us so easily.

Sitting here wallowing in my misery isn't doing me any good. If she's not going to answer my calls, then I'll fly to her and make her talk to me.

Grabbing my phone, I book the first flight to New York. It costs triple the amount it normally would, but I don't give a shit.

I rummage through my dresser, pulling out clothes and packing them inside my duffle bag. The flight is in a few hours, so I have to haul ass if I want to make it on time.

Andrés stands in my doorway, eyeing the piles of clothes scattered all over my bedroom. "Dude, where are you going? We have a game tonight."

"I'm going to New York. I have to see Annalise. I miss her so fucking much, it hurts."

I pull a coat off of my hanger and try to stuff it in my bag, but Andrés grabs my arm. "NBA scouts will be at tonight's game, remember?"

Shaking him off of me, I shout, "I don't fucking care! I need to get her back. Nothing else matters if she's not in my life."

Andrés shakes his head, disappointment written on his face. "You're missing out on your chance to get into the *NBA*, Maddox. You've been working so hard for this. Don't throw it away."

Zipping up my duffle bag, I sling it over my shoulder and push past him.

Making it to the NBA means fucking nothing to me if I don't have her by my side.

I knock on Annalise's apartment door, hoping she's home. The door creaks open and I'm greeted by Mazikeen, her hazel eyes filled with malice.

"What the fuck are you doing here, asshole?"

"Is Annalise home?" I ask, trying to peek around her.

"Nope," she replies, crossing her arms. "She's studying at the library."

"I'll wait until she comes home then," I say, trying to step into the apartment.

She glowers at me, exhaling through her nose. "You really think showing up here will fix what you did? You cheated on her, you pig. I hate the fact that I've been right about you all along."

Heat flushes my cheeks and all the blood rushes to my ears. There's nothing I hate more than when people make assumptions about me. "You know nothing about me. You never even made the effort to try and get to know me when I was with Annalise. All you ever did was judge me for who I was in the past."

"The past?" She laughs in disbelief. "You're obviously still the same person! You wasted your time coming here."

"Mazi, let me talk to him." Annalise comes up from behind Mazikeen, placing a hand on her shoulder.

Her nose is red and her eyes are swollen from crying. My heart sinks knowing that it must be because of me. I'm supposed to be the one wiping her tears away, not the one causing them.

Dropping my bag on the floor, I pull her to my chest. Her body stiffens against me, her arms hanging at her sides.

"Oh, Rosie. I missed you so much. I need you in my life. I can't do this without you." I bury my face in her hair as tears stream down my face. "You are the love of my life. My soulmate. I would never throw that all away for Charlotte. For fucking *anyone*. You have to believe me." I reach out to cup her cheeks and stare deeply into her eyes—into the windows of her soul. The soul that is a part of my own. "I love you so fucking much. I'll transfer schools to be with you, if that's what it takes."

She shoves her hands inside the pocket of her hoodie, chewing on her bottom lip. "But your basketball scholarship—"

"I don't care," I say, shaking my head. "It doesn't matter to me. None of that matters if you're not in my life."

She swallows, staring back at me. "Maddox, I—"

"Don't do it, Annalise," Mazikeen cuts in. "Stay strong. He'll just keep trying to manipulate you."

I scrub my hand down my face. "Will you just shut up and let her talk?"

Her eyes blaze with fury. "What the fuck did you say to me, asshole? You really have a death wish, don't you?"

Ignoring her, I turn my attention back to Annalise, lacing her fingers with mine. "Come on, Annalise. Can you please give our relationship another chance?"

Annalise pulls her hands from mine, turning away from me. "Just give it up, Maddox. There will never be an *us* again."

"Look me in the eyes, then. Look me in the eyes and tell me you don't want to be with me. Tell me you don't love me anymore," I say, my voice shaking.

Squaring her shoulders, she lifts her eyes to mine. I don't recognize the empty look staring back at me.

"I don't love you anymore, Maddox. We're over. You need to move on with your life."

And just like that, my world ends once again.

We are over for good. My heart stops beating, and there is no way I can be revived again. Swallowing down the last of my withered pride, I give her a single nod.

"Then I'll leave you alone." I pick up my bag and sling it

over my shoulder. "I will always love you, Annalise. No matter how much time passes, I will always love you."

I walk out of her apartment hollowed out—an empty shell of who I was. Every hope, every dream I had with her shatters inside me. I did everything in my power to make her feel loved, but I clearly failed since she questioned my loyalty. I put my all into her and it wasn't enough.

From this day forth, I swear I will never fall in love again or get into a relationship. What's the fucking point? I'll just end up getting my heart broken.

CHAPTER 28
Maddox

Tonight is hands down the most embarrassing night of my entire career. I've lost games before, but it has never been this bad. Minnesota blew us out of the water and beat us by forty points at home.

Fans started leaving during the first half of the fourth quarter, and we threw out the bench for the rest of the game. Lucas and I have not been playing well together—go figure. Neither of us ever wanted to pass the ball to one another. If we keep playing like this, there's no way we'll make it to the championship round, let alone the playoffs.

He isn't entirely to blame, though. I haven't been in the right headspace since Annalise and I kissed. I tried turning my emotions off during the game, but it was hard considering the kiss happened less than twenty-four hours ago.

Every time we take one step forward, we take two steps back. It's giving me whiplash. I was in way over my head thinking everything would be okay after we kissed, but we clearly weren't on the same page.

I know if I reach out to her, she'll push me away even further, so I figured it's best to give her some space.

Despite what she said, I know she doesn't regret what happened. She wouldn't have kissed me the way she did. Her body wouldn't have reacted to my touch the way it did.

"So, how are things going with Annalise?" Chandler asks Lucas. He's been bonding with Lucas since he joined the Dragons. Even though Lucas and I made it evident that there's beef between us, only Elijah and Andrés know about our history.

"They're going really well. We kissed the other week," Lucas says, loud enough for me to hear. "And man, is she a good kisser." He glances over at me, shooting me a smug smile.

I roll my eyes as I chug down a bottle of water. I want to wipe that stupid fucking grin off his face and tell him that he definitely wasn't on her mind when my fingers and tongue were inside her. But I'll just let him continue to be delusional.

"You're a lucky man. She really is beautiful," Chandler says.

"I know. And fuck, that body of hers is smoking. Those tits and that ass. I can't wait to find out how good she is in bed. I bet she's a real freak in the sheets."

Red-hot rage flashes through me. Charging toward Lucas, I pick him up by his jersey and slam him into the lockers.

"What the fuck, Kamado!" Lucas winces, rubbing the back of his head.

"Keep running your mouth about her and see what the fuck happens!"

"Your threats don't scare me. We all know you're not going to do anything about it," he scoffs. "You need to learn how to keep your anger under control. It's not a good look for an MVP candidate."

I drop him to the ground, my gaze burning into him. "If I hear you disrespect my girl again, I will fucking end you, Hilton. Annalise isn't just some girl you take to bed. She's so much more than that. You don't deserve her, you piece of shit."

Lucas tips his head back, laughing. "Your obsession with her is really unhealthy. You need some serious help. She's moved on, man. You should too."

"Oh, you think she's moved on with you? Trust me, she's not thinking about you." I smile knowingly and that cocky grin slides off his face. "I don't know what the fuck Annalise sees in you, man. Wait until she hears about what you've been saying."

Shaking my head, I walk back toward my locker. I can't believe I felt threatened by someone as pathetic as Lucas.

"Who do you think she's going to believe? Me or the man who cheated on her?" he sneers.

My head whips around. "What the fuck did you say?"

"Maddox, walk away, man," Elijah warns, stepping in front of me and holding a hand to the center of my chest.

Lucas leans against the lockers, folding his arms. "She claims the breakup was because of long distance, but I highly doubt that's the case, given your reputation."

My mind goes blank and all I can see is red. I shove Elijah out of the way and lunge at Lucas, punching him square in the jaw.

Being able to unleash all the anger I've built up toward him over the years is exhilarating.

Lucas staggers backward, rubbing the side of his face. With fury igniting in his eyes, he comes at me swinging, striking me on my temple. All hell breaks loose and our teammates clamor around us, trying to pull us apart. I land a blow to the side of his mouth and blood gushes from his lip. Elijah and Andrés grab my arms, pulling me back before I cause any further damage.

"What the fuck is going on here?" Coach's booming voice fills the locker room. His eyes dart from Lucas's split lip to the welt forming on my temple.

"These two idiots are trying to kill each other," Darius says, shaking his head.

"Hilton. Kamado. My office. Now," Coach demands, his nostrils flaring and face reddened from anger.

We round the corner, following him into the office. He slams the door behind him. "First, both of you play like garbage tonight, and now this? What the fuck is the matter with you two?"

"He punched me first!" Lucas points at me accusingly.

"Yeah, to get you to shut the fuck up. All you ever do is run your damn mouth and spread lies about me," I say, glaring at him.

Lucas scoffs. "They're not lies. The world needs to know what a—"

"ENOUGH!" Coach slams his fist on the table, causing us to jump. I've seen Coach angry before, but not like this. "I don't give a shit who started the fight. I need y'all to grow up and stop acting like some goddamn teenagers."

Lucas and I remain quiet, staring down at the ground. Seeing the disappointment on Coach's face makes me feel small. He's been a father figure to me since I joined the Dragons, and he was one of the players I looked up to when I was growing up. Being able to work under him is an honor.

"Do you know how many people would kill to be in your spot? Being in the NBA is a privilege, and you two seem to be taking it for granted," Coach continues. "I need you two to work out whatever shit y'all have going on because I do not tolerate this on my team. Now, apologize to each other."

"You gotta be fucking kidding me," I mutter under my breath. Coach's eyes shift to mine, his face serious.

I inhale deeply and look at Lucas. "I'm sorry for hitting you, Hilton."

I'm sorry I didn't hit you harder.

"I'm sorry for what I said earlier," Lucas says, his tone lacking any remorse.

"If this happens again, there will be consequences," Coach says. "Do I make myself clear?"

"Yes, sir," we say in unison, nodding our heads.

Coach scrubs a hand down his face. "I feel like I'm a principal scolding children. Hilton, you are free to go. Kamado, stay back."

Lucas nods and steps out of the office, shutting the door behind him. Coach waits a few moments before turning to me.

"I know there's some bad blood between the two of you, but you gotta learn to ignore him."

"It's hard for me to keep my cool around him. He knows how to push my buttons and constantly provokes me until I snap," I say, squeezing my fingers.

Coach folds his arms across his chest, lifting a brow. "You think I liked every guy I played with? No. But I learned to put aside my feelings when I was on the court. Next time Hilton tries to rile you up, don't react. Remain professional."

"Yes, Coach."

"You are one of the best players this team—hell, the NBA—has seen in decades. Don't throw it all away over some stupid feud," he says, his voice softening. "Focus on the big picture. Focus on winning a championship for our team."

My chest tightens. Coach may be tough, but he has shown more appreciation for my hard work over the last few months than my father ever did during my twenty-two years of life.

"I won't let you down, Coach," I reply.

"I'm going to have a talk with him to make sure he doesn't press charges. Don't let this happen again. I don't want you ruining your career before it even starts."

"Yes, Coach." I nod.

"I found you!" I yank the blanket off of Isaiah and he squeals with laughter. We're playing hide-and-go-seek while Santiago uses the bathroom and Elijah cooks in the kitchen.

Once a month, Elijah tries to host something at his place.

Today he's making fried fish and gumbo—a recipe that was passed down from his grandmother, who grew up in Louisiana. Andrés has something going on with Katie's family, so he couldn't make it.

With everything going on with Annalise, and the fiasco with Lucas, hanging out with my boys is exactly what I need.

"I'm better at this game than you, Uncle Maddox. You took forever to find me." Isaiah flashes me a toothy grin.

I found him a minute after the game started, but he doesn't have to know that. "You sure are, kid. It's not easy for me to hide with how tall I am," I say, ruffling his hair.

"Food's ready," Elijah calls out as he sets the food down on his large kitchen island.

"Can we play again?" Isaiah asks.

"After we finish eating." I smile and take his hand, leading him to the kitchen.

I lift Isaiah onto the stool and settle next to him. Elijah's eyes are on me as I take a bite of the gumbo. "Do you have to do that every time?" I ask, rolling my eyes.

"Just wanna know if it's good." He shrugs and plops down on the stool next to me.

"Yes, it's delicious. Bless Grandma Callahan for coming up with this recipe."

Elijah's mouth tilts into a smile. "Not everyone can follow a recipe and make it good."

Santiago comes out of the bathroom cackling while staring at his phone. "Elijah, who is Riley and what did you do to her?"

Elijah arches a brow. "A cheerleader I hooked up with. Why?"

"She just tweeted: *Elijah Callahan's dick is so small you need a microscope to see it.* It already has over ten thousand re-shares."

I chuckle, shaking my head. I knew something like this would happen.

Elijah hops off the stool, plucking the phone out of Santiago's hands. "Let me see this shit." He presses his lips together as he frantically scrolls through the comments.

Santiago walks over to Isaiah and plants a kiss on top of his head. "Is the food good, mijo?"

"Yeah! Can we play hide-and-go-seek later? Uncle Maddox lost." Isaiah lets out a little giggle. "I think you will lose too, Papi."

"Geez, I think we need to stop hanging around you, Elijah. Your big ego is rubbing off on my son."

"Based on Riley's tweet, I guess that saying is true. Men with big egos have small…" I trail off.

Elijah sets down the phone, sliding it to Santiago. "*Please.* Lots of women can confirm that what she said isn't true—your sister included." He winks and stuffs his mouth with food.

"Shut the fuck up." I laugh, shaking my head. "Asami wouldn't want you even if you were the last man on earth. She can't stand you. That's why she doesn't want to invite you to her wedding."

Growing up, Elijah would often come over to my house. Asami didn't mind him at first, but once he hit puberty, he drove her insane. He would constantly try to flirt with her, but she never gave him the reaction he wanted.

"She doesn't want to invite me because if she saw me at the wedding she would know she made a mistake," Elijah smirks.

"You're an idiot. The day Asami wants you is the day hell freezes over." I laugh.

Elijah shrugs and takes another spoonful of gumbo.

"So what did you do that pissed Riley off enough for her to post that?" Santiago asks.

Elijah grabs a napkin, dabbing the corner of his mouth with it. "Look, I thought we had a mutual agreement. That this was just causal sex. We never agreed to be exclusive. So I hooked up with other girls. And one of them happened to be her cousin…"

"Bro…" Santiago and I say in unison.

Elijah throws his hands up. "How was I supposed to know they were related?"

"Maybe it's time you take a break," Santiago says, lifting his brow.

He laughs so hard he nearly chokes. "And join you in your celibacy? No thank you. I still can't believe it's been over a year since you had sex. I don't know how you do it."

Santiago takes a sip of water and shrugs. "Between work and having to take care of Isaiah, it's not something that's been on my mind. Plus, the next person I sleep with, I want to have a connection with."

I nod my head in agreement. "I feel you on that. Nothing compares to having sex with someone you love." My mind wanders off to the only person capable of making me feel that way.

"So what's going on with you and Annalise?" Elijah asks.

"It's complicated." I sigh, raking my hand through my hair.

"What's so complicated about it? Y'all were eye-fucking each other last week and came close to *actually* fucking. She clearly still wants you."

"We kissed a few days ago, and I thought—"

"Wait, what?" Santiago says, his eyes bulging out.

"Back the fuck up!" Elijah sits up straight, holding up his hands. "You kissed your ex-girlfriend and you failed to tell us. And we're *supposed* to be best friends?"

They're both staring at me with their arms folded across their chest.

"We were stuck in an elevator together, and it just happened."

"An elevator, huh?" Elijah waggles his brows. "I know for a fact y'all did more than kiss."

Blush creeps onto my cheeks, and I avert their gazes as

images of Annalise coming apart and the sound of her moans fill my mind. "Nope. We just kissed—that's all."

"I never keep secrets from you," Elijah says with a groan.

"Sometimes I wish you did, because I do not need to hear *everything* you tell me." I roll my eyes.

"So, what happened after y'all kissed?" Santiago asks.

I stare down at my lap, twisting my fingers. "She said she regretted what happened. I'm just giving her space right now."

"Have you told her how you feel? That you're still in love with her? And don't you dare deny it because we can all see it," Elijah says.

"No, I haven't. I was gonna tell her how I felt the night of Chandler's birthday, but then I saw her kissing Lucas…"

"Is that why you left so early?"

"Yeah… But now I don't even know when I should tell her. After how she reacted…" I trail off, scrubbing my hand down my face. "I don't know if I can."

"You need to tell her, man. Don't let another day go by without letting her know. Maybe hearing you say those words again will make her realize that you two are meant to be together," Santiago says, squeezing my shoulder.

He's right. I need to stop waiting for the right moment.

I fish my phone out to text her and see a new message notification from five minutes ago.

ANNALISE

Hey. Can we talk tonight?

My stomach flutters and a grin spreads across my face. The boys hover over my shoulders and stare down at the phone.

"Talk about a fucking sign!" Elijah beams.

"Can y'all please not stand over me?" I ask.

"Fine. But you better tell us every single detail."

"Whatever," I say, shaking my head.

Sure. Meet me at our spot tonight at 7? 

ANNALISE

Okay. I'll be there.

CHAPTER 29
Annalise

Soft pink and golden hues paint the sky, and the gentle breeze caresses my skin as I stroll along the rugged shoreline. Blissful memories wash over me and flutters form in the pit of my stomach when I near the secluded beach cove. I can feel Maddox's presence nearby, pulling me like a magnet to the place that belongs to us and only us.

This place was our sanctuary. We used to come here when we needed to escape from the rest of the world. Maddox and I would spend hours talking or just being together in silence, and we'd often lose track of time.

My heart hammers against my ribs when I see him standing inside the cove. He looks devastatingly handsome. The sunlight beams on his face, illuminating those beautiful brown eyes.

Maddox lifts his hand and places it on the wall of the cavern, his fingers tracing over the engraving of our initials and the heart surrounding it.

"You know, today would mark six years since I did this." Maddox turns to me, the corners of his mouth curving into a dimpled smile.

Heat flushes my cheeks and the flutters in my stomach intensify. Six years ago he told me loved me in this very spot, and later he carved our initials into the wall.

I step closer to him and my hand reaches up to trace over it. "I can't believe it's been that long."

"When was the last time you were here?" Maddox glances at me sidelong.

I tug at the hem of my shirt. "Gosh, I haven't been here since we left for college."

His hand brushes against mine, and instinctively I interlace my fingers with his. Electricity thrums through my veins at the simple touch. Alarms go off in my head, telling me to let go, but being here with him feels so right. I don't want to let go.

"This place holds a piece of us," he says. "I'd come here hoping one day I would see you again, and that you would come back to me."

There were a handful of times where I came back to San Francisco to visit and felt a pull toward the cove. I would drive around aimlessly, and before I knew it, I would end up near where we would typically park. Once I realized where I was, I would turn back around.

I wonder if it was his soul trying to reach for me.

He turns his body toward me, his eyes meeting mine. "I really missed you, Annalise. Not a day went by where you didn't cross my mind."

"I missed you too, Maddox," I say softly. His eyes glaze over at the admittance. "I've been living with anger since it all went down, and I'm tired of being mad at the world. I never gave you a real chance to explain to me what happened, but I want to hear you out."

Maddox takes a deep breath before he starts. "The night before you came, we had a huge party after the game to celebrate our win. A ton of people from our class showed up, and a lot of them came and went. It was impossible to keep up with who all was there."

"Was Charlotte there?" My stomach twists and I feel my throat dry up when her name leaves my lips.

"Yeah. I think she came with some friends, but I didn't talk to her at all." He takes a breath. "I was with Andrés and some of the other guys from the team the whole night. I tried my best to enjoy myself, but it was hard. All I wanted was to be with you for our anniversary, so I drank more than I normally do to mask how bummed I was."

"Do you remember anything from that night?"

Maddox shakes his head. "I remember playing beer pong with the guys, and that's pretty much it. Everything else is a blur."

I can see all the hurt in his eyes—the hurt that he's been carrying this whole time. All these years, I thought he was happy. He has his dream career and makes more money than I could ever dream of. But seeing him now, I know he's been hiding pain behind that success.

"I spoke to Charlotte after you left, but she kept trying to manipulate me. I even tried asking some people from school, but no one knew anything."

Tears cascade down his face and his voice starts to crack. "I was a mess when you left. I spiraled and started smoking and drinking more. Even came close to losing my scholarship."

My heart aches knowing that he almost lost everything he's been working toward his whole life because of what happened.

"I wish more than anything that I had proof I didn't cheat on you. I will never forgive myself for getting that wasted, but I hope you know that I would never do anything to jeopardize our relationship." Maddox cups my cheeks, his eyes boring into mine. "What we had was beautiful, Annalise. I would never destroy that."

I place my hand on top of his, gently caressing it. "Sorry for jumping to conclusions back then. I guess discovering my dad cheating on my mom fucked me up more than I thought. I was constantly worried that you would cheat in college, so when I saw Charlotte come out of your room, it was like my fears had come true."

"I hate that you compared me to him in your mind," he says softly. "I was devastated when you believed Charlotte over me, but I understand why you did. Your father put you through hell, and that's not something you heal from overnight." He takes a breath, chewing his lip. "I should have fought harder for us. For you. But I let my pride get in the way."

"There was always a small part of me that believed you would never cheat," I say, my eyes brimming with tears. "But I let the negative voices in my head overpower me. I was too weak to fight them."

Maddox leans in, placing his forehead on mine. "I'll do everything in my power to destroy those negative thoughts so you never feel that way again." He places a kiss on my forehead and pulls me into a warm embrace.

My heart thuds loudly and a huge weight lifts off my shoulders as all the anger and hatred leaves my body. In its place is something I haven't allowed myself to feel in years—love. I wait for the negative voices to tell me to pull away, but they're silent.

Maddox tucks a stray tendril of hair behind my ear and locks his eyes with mine. "I love you, Annalise. I've never stopped loving you."

The moment I hear those three little words from him again, the block of ice surrounding my heart completely melts away. I had convinced myself that I hated him. That I was better off without him. But that's far from the truth.

I feel three words clawing at my throat, begging to be said, but I swallow them down. My heart is still fragile and I'm not quite ready to admit how I feel. But knowing he loves me? That alone is enough to ease some of my worries.

At my silence, he places my hand on his chest, letting me feel his racing heart against my palm. "It's always been you, Annalise. It will *always* be you. No matter how much time passes, and no matter what happens between us, my heart will only ever be yours. When you're ready to take a chance on us again, I'll be waiting, no matter how long it takes. The stars aligned for our paths to cross again, and this time, I'm not letting you go."

Struggling to find the right words, I stand on my tiptoes, wrapping my arms around his neck, and press my lips to his. He kisses me back slowly and tenderly. Unlike our last kiss—which happened in the heat of the moment—this one feels different. It's filled with promises and second chances.

Pulling away, I grab his hands and lift my eyes to his. "I want to give us a chance again, Maddox. But I don't want to rush this. I want to take it slow."

His face splits into a wide grin and I can feel the warmth of his joy radiating through the cove. "We can take it as slow as you want, baby. I'm not going anywhere."

Waves crash against the shore and stars twinkle in the sky above us as we walk along the beach, hand in hand. We spent hours in the cove sitting next to each other and talking, just like we did all those years ago.

"If you're free next Saturday, would you, uh—wanna go on a, uh, date with me?" He rubs the back of his neck and gives me the same sheepish look as when he first asked me out seven years ago.

A playful smile tilts my lips. "I'd rather watch grass grow than go on a date with you."

Maddox chuckles, shaking his head. "I'm still as persistent as I was when I was fifteen years old. No matter how many times you reject me, I'll keep asking until you say yes."

Giggling, I lean forward and plant a kiss on his cheek. "Saturday is perfect. But can we go somewhere discreet?"

"Oh, so you're embarrassed to be seen around me? Got it." Maddox purses his lips and nods.

"No, you idiot." I laugh, knocking my shoulder against him. "You're a world-famous NBA player now. People recognize you everywhere you go. I'm not ready to tell my friends and family about us yet. And Veronica said there would be consequences if I get—"

"I'm just messing with you, Annalise," he says, a smirk sliding across his face. "I was already planning on taking you somewhere private for that very reason."

Bringing my hand to his lips, he places a soft kiss on top of it. "Thank you for giving us another chance."

CHAPTER 30
Maddox

Finally laying it all on the table and telling Annalise that I am still in love with her has me on cloud nine. Even though she didn't say it back, the fact that she wants to give us a chance is more than enough for me.

My cheeks hurt from all the smiling I've been doing, because for the first time in years, I am genuinely happy. Given how we left things and how she reacted when she saw me again, I thought the chances of us ever getting back together were slim to none. But now we can finally move forward and create new, beautiful memories together.

"Damn." I sigh at my reflection in the mirror. I've spent the last thirty minutes trying to style my hair, and it is not agreeing with me.

Tonight is the night of our date, and I've been a fucking nervous wreck all week long. The other day, I spent hours at the mall trying to find a new cologne and an outfit to wear. Because I couldn't decide what I wanted, I ended up leaving with five new pairs of pants, seven different shirts, two jackets, and four bottles of cologne.

I've taken her on countless dates before, but this one is

different. It's the start of a new chapter for us, and everything has to be perfect.

Even though she wants to give us a chance again, I know she isn't on the same level as I am. She's still in a fragile state, and I'm worried I'll say or do something to scare her off. Living in a world without her was unbearable, and I won't be able to survive if I lose her again.

"Wish me luck, Tsuki." Crouching down, I ruffle her soft fur and kiss the top of her head before slipping out the door.

My heart pounds loudly in my ears and my stomach twists in knots as I approach Annalise's apartment. Raising my hand, I rap my knuckles against her door. I inhale and exhale, attempting to calm my jitters while I wait for her.

I have no problem playing basketball in front of 20,000 people, but this? All of my confidence has flown out the window. I'm just as nervous as I was when I was fifteen, trying to impress the girl I've been in love with since third grade.

Annalise swings open the door and all the air leaves my lungs as I take her in. "Hey, Dimples," she says, smiling brightly.

Fuck, she looks incredible.

Her chestnut-brown hair is half-up and those luscious lips are covered in a soft pink gloss, making them more inviting.

The outfit she's wearing makes me want to cancel all my plans and take her right here and now. She's in a pair of flared jeans that hug her deliciously thick thighs and plump ass, and a green halter top that looks perfect against her tan skin.

Since she's not wearing a bra, I'm able to see the outline of her pierced nipples through her top. Thinking about the last time I had them in my mouth sends a rush of need straight to my cock. It doesn't help that the longer I stare at them, the harder they become.

"You're drooling," she teases.

My eyes lift to hers and she's wearing an amused look on her face. "I can't help myself," I say, rubbing the back of my neck and offering her a half-smile. "You look sexi-ful."

What?

Blush creeps across my cheeks. The date hasn't even started and I'm already acting a fool.

Annalise chuckles softly. "You look pretty sexi-ful yourself."

"These are for you." I bring my arm from behind my back and hand her the bouquet of fresh flowers that I carefully picked out. It's an arrangement of orchids, peonies, baby's breath, and roses—her favorite.

Her entire face lights up as she takes the bouquet from me and inhales deeply. "Maddox, these are so beautiful. Thank you. I can't wait for our date." She pushes up on her tiptoes and plants a kiss on my lips, settling my nerves.

Lively music pulsates through the air and colorful lights from the carnival rides surround us as I pull into the vacant parking lot. I step out of my car and round to the passenger side, opening the door for Annalise while extending my hand to her.

She takes it with a smile and I guide her toward the entrance, where a cheerful carnival worker greets us, letting us through with a wave. Under normal circumstances the carnival would've been filled with people, especially on a Saturday night in spring.

"You rented the whole carnival for us?" she asks, her sapphire and emerald eyes sparkling as she turns to look at me.

"Yeah. I remember how much you used to love going."

A few moments of silence pass, and suddenly the whole idea feels silly. I haven't been around Annalise in years. She's prob-ably grown out of that by now.

I rub my palms, slicked with cold sweat, on my jeans and

swallow down the lump in my throat. "If you're not, uh, into it anymore, we can, uh, do something else."

"Are you kidding me?" Pure joy radiates on her face and she throws her hands up, gesturing around us. "We have the whole place to ourselves and don't have to wait in any lines. This is perfect."

"The perfect date for the perfect girl." Leaning forward, I drop a quick kiss to her lips.

Taking my hand, she pulls me toward the attractions and stops in front of the one I was hoping to avoid—Terror Train. It's one of those rides where you go down this creepy tunnel and shit pops out at you.

Using the back of my hand, I wipe away the beads of sweat that trickle down my temple. "D-d-do we have to go on this one?" I ask, my voice trembling.

"We're going on all of them!"

Reluctantly, I follow her as she dashes inside and slides into the front seat.

The train lurches forward and I grip the bar in front of me, my knuckles turning white. Chills race down my spine as we enter the dark, ominous tunnel. My eyes dart to Annalise and she's just sitting there, as calm as can be, with her hands folded in her lap. It's as though we're going through some magical fairy garden instead.

We turn a corner and a woman with long black hair and no eyes pops out, shrieking at the top of her lungs.

"AHHH!" I scream, wrapping my arms around Annalise. She cackles, clearly entertained by my fear.

After what feels like an hour, the ride comes to a stop and I rush toward the exit like my life depends on it.

"I should've told the workers to shut this ride down for the night," I say, shaking my head.

Annalise clutches her stomach while laughter rumbles through her. "You are such a big baby."

"You're made different. I can't believe you didn't even flinch."

She shrugs like it's no big deal. "It wasn't even that bad."

Annalise walks over to look at the screen displaying the photos taken during the ride. She points to one where I'm mid-scream, my eyes wide with fear. "Oh, we have to get this one," she says, turning to the attendant. "Could you please print this for me?"

The attendant nods and presses the print button on her screen. The photo ejects and she hands it over. With a smile, Annalise takes the picture and places it inside her purse.

"Wanna go again?" she asks. A playful smile teases her lips.

"Absolutely not," I say, shaking my head. "It's my turn to choose." Taking her hand, I lead her toward the game booths and stop in front of Hoop Shoot.

There's something about carnival hoops that make them more challenging to shoot at than a regular basketball hoop. The worker tosses the ball to me and I stand behind the line.

"Since you're an NBA player, shooting from there would be too easy," he says, rubbing his chin.

"You're right, Sam." I nod, looking at his name tag. "There would be no fun in that." I start walking backward and he motions for me to continue.

"Keep going… Keep going… There you go!" He gives me the okay sign with his hand, signaling for me to stop. "Three shots in and you get the prize. You get four tries."

I dribble the ball and begin to plan my move.

"You got this, Dimples!" Annalise cheers me on, and I immediately get a boost of confidence.

I release the ball and watch as it arcs through the air. It sinks through the net and Annalise jumps with excitement.

A smile eases across my face as I reminisce on the days when she would cheer me on at my games. Hopefully, one of these days, she'll be sitting courtside and wearing my jersey.

The next shot goes in easily. The last one isn't as smooth, but it finds its way through the net. I jog over to Annalise and wrap my arms around her waist. She giggles as I pepper her with kisses.

"I should've made you do that with your eyes closed," Sam says, flashing me a toothy grin.

"I bet he would've made those, too," Annalise says.

Sam crouches down and pulls out a teddy bear, handing it to Annalise. "Here's your prize."

The bear is wearing a red Dragon's jersey with the number 24 stitched on it. And instead of my last name on the back, it says *Maddy*.

"Aw, Maddy Bear. This is so adorable!" She squeals, holding the teddy bear tightly to her chest.

"He can keep you company when I'm traveling for games," I say.

"I'll have him next to me while I'm watching you play on TV."

I break into a wide grin. The mere thought of her watching me while I'm on the road makes me swell with pride.

"I can't believe I used to call you Maddy Bear." She laughs, shaking her head. "We were so cringey."

"We were," I say with a smile. "But in the cutest way." I nudge her shoulder and press a quick kiss to her cheek.

We spend the rest of the night playing games in the booths, riding rides, and stuffing our faces with funnel cake and other carnival foods.

I lead her toward the Ferris wheel—our favorite spot—to end the night. They've updated it since the last time I was here. It's bigger and features an enclosed cabin with spacious seats.

The door slides open and we step inside.

I pull Annalise close to me, threading my fingers through hers.

"Tonight has been incredible," she says, resting her head on my shoulder. "Thank you."

"I'm glad you had a good time. I was worried that you would hate it and regret giving me a chance."

She turns her body toward me, glancing up. "I could never hate anything you plan for me. You always know what I like. I was expecting you to take me to a fancy dinner, but this"—she gestures around us—"beats fancy. Is that why you've been so nervous tonight?"

I nod, chuckling softly. "Yeah. I'm pretty pathetic, aren't I?"

"I think it's adorable, seeing you get all flustered." She presses a kiss to my cheek. "Reminds me of how you were when we first started dating."

The Ferris wheel comes to a stop at the top and I lean forward, tilting her chin. "How about we recreate our first kiss?"

My mouth swoops down to capture hers, and sparks ignite within me. No matter how many times we kiss, it always feels like divine ecstasy when our lips touch.

She fists my hair, bringing me closer to her and deepening the kiss. My hand slides up her thigh as I pull her bottom lip between my teeth.

I feel myself growing hard from the sounds she makes as I devour her lips.

Without breaking the kiss, I hoist her onto my lap. The caress of her lips on my mouth and her ass on my cock sets me aflame. My hand moves to her lower back and she grabs it, guiding it to her ass. I give it a squeeze and she moans against my lips.

I pull away from the kiss, locking my eyes with hers as my thumb brushes across her nipple. She parts her lips slightly and her eyes darken with desire.

"You wore this purposely to torture me, didn't you?" I say as I roll her nipple between my fingers.

"I like the way you look at me. I like seeing how turned on

you get," she whispers as she licks my earlobe, sending goose-bumps down my body.

"You always turn me on." I take her hand and place it on top of my aching bulge. "See what you do to me?"

She swipes her tongue across her bottom lip and strokes me through my jeans. "Damn, you're so hard."

I groan in satisfaction at feeling her hand on me instead of my own. I've spent the last couple of months fisting my cock in the shower while thinking of her.

My lips recapture hers, more demanding this time. She shifts in my lap so she's straddling my thighs. Grabbing her ass, I thrust my hips up and press my hardness against her core.

"Maddox…" she moans as she rolls her hips against me. "I need you inside me."

Fuck. The combination of the friction she's creating on top of what she just said almost makes me combust right then and there. I have to fight the urge to tear off her clothes and take her inside the Ferris wheel.

"Take me back to your place," she says, need and hunger swirling in her eyes.

CHAPTER 31
Annalise

As soon as we step through the door, Maddox crushes his lips against mine while his hands greedily explore my body. The prolonged anticipation since leaving the carnival has been unbearable. I desperately need to dull the ache between my legs.

With our lips still connected, he lifts me up in one fell swoop, gripping my ass tightly while he carries me down the hall.

We reach his bedroom and he lowers me to the ground, placing me in front of his floor-length mirror. He stands behind me, pressing his erection into my ass. One of his hands pops the button of my jeans and pulls down the zipper while the other unties the strings on the back of my top.

My shirt falls to the ground, leaving my breasts on full display. The insatiable look in his eyes sets my body on fire. He presses himself further into me, letting me know how much the sight of my body turns him on.

Soft moans escape my lips while he palms my breasts and squeezes my nipples between his fingers.

He brushes my hair to the side and shivers race down my

spine as he kisses my neck. "Take off the rest of your clothes. I want to see all of you."

I do as I'm told, discarding my jeans and drenched panties. His tongue darts out, swiping across his bottom lip as his eyes rake over my body.

"So beautiful and so *mine*."

With his gaze locked on me, he slowly slides his hand down my stomach. My breaths become shallower as he gets closer to where I need him most.

His hand dips between my legs, fingers gliding through the wetness. "Fuck, Annalise," he groans, his eyes fluttering shut as he rubs tight circles over my clit.

My legs start trembling at his touch. Reaching behind me, I wrap my arm around his neck to steady myself. His hand moves down to my entrance, slipping two fingers inside me with ease.

"Yes…" I moan in pleasure. I continue to watch our reflection in the mirror as he fucks me with his fingers. Getting to see the look in his eyes as he pleasures me further increases the wetness between my legs.

Just as the pressure starts building up, he pulls his fingers out of me. "I need to taste you again."

Taking my hand, he guides me to his bed and lays me down. He strips off his clothes before settling in next to me.

The oxygen leaves my lungs when I see him in all his glory. My eyes roam down his body, admiring every detail—from his broad chest to his sculpted arms and abs. He is truly beautiful. A masterpiece.

My gaze flicks down to his long, thick cock, and the throbbing sensation building between my legs intensifies when I see the precum dripping out of it. Reaching over, I stroke his hard length. He tips his head back, satisfied grunts leaving his lips.

Maddox leans down, gently kissing my lips before his mouth descends down my body. Whimpers of pleasure escape me as he takes my breasts in his mouth, his tongue caressing my swollen nipples.

He nestles himself between my legs, and hooks them over his shoulders, pulling me close to him. Slowly, he begins a tantalizing path of kisses, his warm breath teasing my skin as he traces his lips along my inner thigh.

Dipping his head between my legs, he holds my stare as his tongue moves along my dripping core in languid strokes. "You always taste so fucking sweet. I love eating your pussy," he murmurs. I cry out, fisting his hair as he continues to devour me like he's been starving for days.

Most men I've been with saw it as a chore or would skip it altogether. But not Maddox. Going down on me has always been one of his favorite things to do. He moans while sucking my clit, showing me just how much he's enjoying this.

Pleasure rips through me when he dives his tongue deep inside me as his fingers circle my clit. My hips buck off the bed and I come undone, writhing beneath him as he continues to fuck me with his tongue with such skill and precision. By the time he removes himself from between my legs, my body is limp—paralyzed from pleasure.

After my breathing settles to a normal rhythm, he reaches inside his nightstand and pulls out a condom.

Before he tears it open, I place my hand on his to stop him. "I'm on the pill," I whisper. "I want to feel you. Give me all of you, Maddox."

A tender smile blooms across his face, and he tosses it to the side. "I'm all yours, my love. Every part of me belongs to you." He laces his fingers through mine, kissing me tenderly while gliding his throbbing cock through my wet core. It's been years since I've had him. I don't want there to be any barriers between us.

Breaking the kiss, he positions himself near my entrance,

boring his eyes with mine. I can feel all the love emanating from him. "I love you, Annalise," he says before plunging into me.

Loud moans erupt from me as he stretches me out, pushing in another inch with each stroke until he's fully inside of me.

Once I get accustomed to his size, he increases the pace of his thrusts. I move my hips, matching his rhythm.

"*Fuucckk*, you're so tight," he murmurs against my lips. "I missed this. You feel so fucking good, babe."

"I m-missed this, t-too," I manage to say between moans.

I've spent years being deprived of him—having mediocre sex that left me unfulfilled. The pleasure of finally having him inside me again is indescribable. Maddox knows my body better than anyone else. He's spent years studying me like I was his favorite subject, and he knows exactly what I need. It's impossible for anyone to live up to him.

Maddox was my first, and losing my virginity to someone I was deeply in love with was an amazing feeling and something I will forever cherish. But it paled in comparison to how it feels now, our bodies reconnecting after being apart for so long. Making love to him again ignites a fire we've both longed to rekindle. He is my soulmate. My other half. Being with him fills that void that's been missing in my life.

Spreading my legs wider, he tucks my knees to my chest. The change in position allows him to penetrate me deeper.

"Oh, *fuck*, Maddox! Yes!" My nails rake his skin and my moans ripple through the room as he pounds into me relentlessly.

"Come for me, baby," he grunts as he continues to pump his cock into me.

My body convulses, my walls tightening around him. The orgasm crashes through me like a tidal wave, hitting me with force, and I come harder than I have in years. My body levitates to a land of euphoric bliss.

Maddox's breathing becomes ragged and he drives himself deeper, gripping my hips tightly. The feel of his pulsating cock inside me causes me to unravel once more. He collapses on top of me, releasing deep guttural moans as he comes apart.

After we come down from our high, he pulls me into an embrace and plants a kiss on my lips.

"So… does this mean I get a second date?" His lips curl into a a playful smile, dimples sinking into his cheeks.

A soft chuckle escapes me. "I think you already know the answer to that."

CHAPTER 32
Maddox

My heart flutters when I wake and find Annalise curled up in my arms. The morning sunlight filters through the blinds, casting a warm glow on her beautiful face. She's still in a deep slumber, a peaceful smile gracing her lips. I caress her silky waves and place a kiss on top of her head, wanting to savor this moment.

Last night was truly magical. We fit together perfectly, as if we were made for each other, and our bodies moved in harmony. With Annalise, it was never just about pleasure. What we share is far more intimate and visceral. Our lovemaking is filled with an immeasurable passion that feels as if it could reach across galaxies. We connect not only on a physical level, but also on emotional and spiritual ones. Two lost souls found each other again and became one.

The time apart made us realize how much we mean to each other. We were able to grow and reflect over the years and have come back stronger than ever.

I slide out of bed, careful not to wake her, and head to the kitchen. Pulling out my phone, I pull up the pancake recipe I have saved and gather ingredients from the fridge and pantry.

Game Changer

Annalise would always cook for me. For once, I want to be the one to wake *her* up with a nice meal. After the night we had, I know she'll wake up starving. I didn't expect for her to stay the night, but I went to the grocery store the other day in case she did.

Using the measuring cups and spoons I haven't touched before today, I carefully measure out the ingredients and place them in the mixer. Once the batter has a smooth, even texture with no clumps, I coat the pan with nonstick spray.

The first pancake cooks unevenly because I poured too much batter into the pan. So I pour less batter when making the next one, and end up burning it to a crisp.

"Fuck, why is this so hard? They always make it look so easy on TV," I mutter to myself. Perhaps I should've practiced first.

After a few more failed attempts, I slice up some Spam, throw it in the air fryer, and pop slices of bread in the toaster. I somehow manage to make sunny-side-up eggs, so at least this wasn't a complete and total disaster.

"Am I dreaming or is Maddox Kamado actually cooking?"

I turn around and see Annalise standing by the sink with Tsuki trailing behind her. She's dressed in nothing but my T-shirt, which fits her like a dress, ending a few inches above her knees. I've seen Annalise in everything from casual clothes to black-tie attire, but nothing compares to seeing her wear my clothes. It serves as a reminder that she is mine.

I rub the back of my neck and place the plates of toast, Spam, and eggs on the counter near the barstools. "I, uh, tried to make pancakes, but I failed miserably. You don't have to eat this if you don't want to. We can order delivery."

A small chuckle leaves her lips. "You are too adorable." She slides onto the bar stool and bites into a piece of Spam. "This is delicious. And you made spicy Spam?"

I settle next to her, the tension in my muscles easing up. "Are the eggs okay?"

"They're perfect." She leans in, pressing a swift kiss to my lips. "Thank you for making me breakfast. And for the mind-blowing sex last night."

My mouth lifts into a grin. "It was pretty damn mind-blowing." I slide my hand up her thigh. "Are you up for another round or have you had enough?"

She giggles and slaps my hand away. "I still need some more time to recover from last night. Let me enjoy this meal you made for me. This is a rare occurrence."

Grabbing a slice of Spam and some eggs, she lays it onto a piece of toast, folds it into a sandwich, and takes a bite. "*Mmm, so good.*"

"I promise I'll make you pancakes one day."

"I can teach you next time."

"Next time huh?" I lift a brow, a grin tugging at my lips. "So does that mean I should get used to waking up next to you again?"

"Perhaps. We'll have to see how the second date goes." A playful smirk dances on her lips.

"I promise you it'll be better than the first date."

She takes another bite of her Spam-and-egg toast. "I don't know. Seeing you scream like a baby during that Train Terror ride will be pretty hard to top."

"I'm glad you find humor in me being terrified," I deadpan.

She sits up straight, clapping her hands together. "Ooh! Can we go to a real haunted house one day? There are some where you're able to stay the night. That would be the ultimate date."

I take another bite of my food and shake my head. "Okay, I think all of those orgasms you had last night are fogging your brain."

"Trust me—my mind is perfectly clear. I think it would be fun," she says, her lips pulling into a smirk.

"I think we have different ideas of fun, sweetheart," I laugh, shaking my head. "Also, I think I may reconsider taking you on a second date. I'm beginning to question your sanity."

A laugh bursts from her. "I'm *joooking*. I enjoy a good scary movie, but I would never actually set foot in a real haunted house."

"I don't know who in their right mind would pay for that shit." I clear the rest of my plate and glance at the clock. It's a quarter to ten. "Damn it."

"What's wrong?"

I sigh, rubbing the back of my neck. "I have to head to practice soon. It starts at eleven."

"Oh. I'll help you clean up." She starts to get up but I grab her hand to stop her.

"Don't worry about it. I'll get it later. I wish I could skip it, but I don't want to give Coach another reason to be angry with me."

Annalise's brows draw together. "Another reason?"

Right. I haven't told her about what Lucas said about her. Talking about him isn't exactly my favorite subject, and there hasn't been a right time to tell her.

"Yeah, so… I kinda beat the living shit out of Lucas a couple of weeks ago." I let out a shaky laugh.

"What? What the hell happened?" Her eyes grow wide, round as saucers.

Anger simmers in my veins as Lucas's pompous face flashes through my mind. "I overheard him telling Chandler how he can't wait to find out what you're like in bed."

Her lips curl into a snarl and she crushes the empty water bottle near her. "What a fucking pig!"

"He started antagonizing me and said that I cheated on you and a bunch of other bullshit. So I fucking lost it."

She releases a groan, burying her face in her hands. "I can't believe I fell for his nice-guy act. You've been right about him all along. I was too much of an idiot to see it."

"You're not an idiot," I say, taking her hands and putting them in mine. "You see the good in everyone and give them the benefit of the doubt."

"Yeah, but that's not always a good trait to have. That's how you get fucked over. I'm just glad I ended things before it went any further."

I lower my gaze to the ground, a trembling breath slipping past my lips. "For a second, I thought I would lose you to him."

She shakes her head and gives my hand a squeeze. "I hope you know that I never felt anything for him. I thought going on a date with him would help me move on and get my mind off you. But it only made me realize how much I wanted to be with you." With her gaze locked on mine, she places her palm on my cheek. "You'll never lose me. I'm yours, Maddox. Always have been. Always will be."

A warm rush of emotions floods my chest as her words envelope me like a sweet symphony. They serve as a promise of forever and of our unbreakable bond.

I rest my forehead on hers and weave my fingers through her hair. "And I will always be yours."

I pull her close to me, kissing her soft pink lips. Every kiss we share is electric, sending zings down my spine and awakening every single nerve. Her lips part slightly and I thrust my tongue inside.

The moan she releases in my mouth has my cock throbbing with need. Lifting her up, I move her to the counter and pull my T-shirt over her head. She lets out a sharp cry when I place my mouth over her swollen peaks, licking and sucking in quick succession.

My hand moves between her legs and a deep groan rumbles through me when I find her panties soaked with arousal. "Do you still need time to recover? Or can you take my dick again?" Pushing her panties to the side, I slip two fingers in her with ease.

Her head falls back and unintelligible words slip through her lips.

"I'm gonna need you to speak clearly." I push my fingers deeper, hitting her sensitive spot while I rub her clit, and she lets out a strangled cry.

"Maddox!" she moans, tightening her grip on the counter.

The sight of her topless and moaning with my fingers inside her has my cock rock-hard. And she is so fucking wet. A small puddle is already forming on my counter.

I can't take it anymore. I need to be inside her. Pushing my shorts off, I release my aching bulge from its confinement.

I rip off her lace panties and drag the head of my cock through her dripping pussy. She squirms on the counter and her breathing becomes erratic. "You're still not giving me an answer." My fingers tug her nipples and she lets out a loud gasp.

"Fuck me, Maddox." She wraps her hand around my length and positions it near her entrance. "Don't hold back. Fuck me hard."

Her words awaken something primal within me. Spreading her legs wide, I grip her thighs and slam my cock into her tight cunt.

Her screams of pleasure ripple through the entire house as I fuck her senseless, pounding into her with deep, brutal thrusts.

My phone buzzes repeatedly on the counter, a flurry of messages lighting up the screen—it's the team group chat. I switch it to Do Not Disturb. I have more important matters to take care of.

After giving her multiple earth-shattering orgasms on my kitchen counter, I check my phone while Annalise rinses off in the shower.

DARIUS

Coach just called me and said practice is
canceled. Chandler got into a car accident.
They had to rush him to the hospital.

ELIJAH

Oh fuck, it must be bad. I pray that he'll be
okay.

ANDRÉS

Oh God. What's his condition? What hospital
are they taking him to?

DARIUS

I'm not sure. And Greenwich Memorial. I'm
heading there now.

My blood runs cold and bile rises in my throat. Chandler and
I aren't the best of friends or anything, but he's one of my nicest
guys I've ever met. He always remains positive and lifts up
everyone on the team after a loss.

I call Elijah's and he answers after the second ring.

"Dude, I just saw the text," I say. "I hope he's okay. Have
you left yet?"

"I hope so, too. And I'm getting ready now. Do you think
you could pick me up?" Elijah's voice sounds frantic on the
other line.

"Yeah, I can be there in twenty."

"Okay. Drive safe."

I sift through my drawers and pull out a pair of shorts and a
fresh T-shirt.

Annalise comes out of the bathroom, drying her hair on a
towel. "Everything okay?"

"It's one of my teammates, Chandler. He got in a car accident. I'm gonna go to the hospital to see him after I drop you
off."

"Oh my God!" she says, her hand flying to her mouth. "Is he
okay?"

"I don't know his condition… but I pray that he is."

I pull up to Elijah's luxury apartment building and shoot him a text to let him know I'm here. He lives in a penthouse suite in the heart of downtown—the perfect bachelor pad.

I lived in something similar when I was in Houston. But when I signed with San Francisco, I purchased a home in the suburbs with the intention of retiring in the city where I grew up —and in hopes that I would start a family one day. Maybe years from now Annalise and I will have miniature versions of ourselves running around that home.

A knock on my window pulls me out of my daydream. Elijah waves at me and I unlock the door to let him in.

"Thanks for picking me up," he says as he slides into the passenger seat. "I know I live close but I just got back from visiting my cousins in Sacramento, so I didn't feel like driving."

"Are you sure it's not an excuse to spend more time with me?" I ask, raising my brows.

He chuckles softly. "Yeah, you got me. I'm secretly in love with you."

"Sorry—my heart only belongs to Annalise." A wide grin spreads on my face as I think about the amazing weekend we've had together.

"Aw, look at you cheesing," he teases. "How was the talk y'all had?"

"It went really well. I finally told her how I feel, and she's willing to give us another chance. We—" I'm about to tell Elijah about our date, but then I remember she wanted to keep it between us.

He's my best friend and I know he wouldn't blab to anyone. But I'm not going to tell anyone until she's ready.

"I'm happy for you, man. But I'm also sad to lose my wingman." He sighs, his mouth dipping into a frown. "Andrés is married and Santiago prefers to be celibate. I have no one."

"Lucas will be a good replacement."

Elijah starts laughing so hard he snorts. His phone slips from his hand, clattering to the floor. "*Please*, he has no game. He'll end up scaring all the women away."

"Poor guy is gonna be in a relationship with his hand for the rest of his life."

"That's for sure." He reaches down and picks up his phone from the floor. "Who do these belong to?" A smirk dances on his face as he holds up a shiny gold hoop earring. One of the same earrings Annalise wore for our date.

I shrug and try to play it off, hoping he won't catch on. "Not sure. Probably Asami's."

"I've never seen her wear hoop earrings before. And I pay attention."

I scrunch my face up. "Why the hell are you so observant when it comes to my sister? Save that energy for the court."

"They're Annalise's, aren't they?" he says, smiling knowingly.

Unable to come up with anything, I roll down the window and wave over the valet driver.

A security guard escorts us to the VIP floor where Chandler is staying. The lobby is filled with most of our teammates. Coach is in the corner talking to Andrés.

"Do *not* mention the earring to Andrés," I whisper, shooting him a warning glare.

"I knew it was Annalise's!" he says, a little too loudly. "I wanna know every detail later."

I roll my eyes at him and approach Coach. "Hey, Coach. What's the update on Chandler?" Knots form in my stomach as I wait for his response.

"He's pretty banged up, but he's okay. He has a few broken

ribs and fractured his clavicle, so he's probably gonna be out of the rest of the season."

The knots in my stomach loosen and I blow out a breath of relief. "It's a bummer he won't be with us for the playoffs, but I'm so glad he's okay," I say.

"Thank God he's alive," Elijah says. "Can we see him soon?"

"He's still recovering from surgery but we should be able to see him soon," Coach says.

"I'm so glad his injuries weren't severe. I didn't know what to expect when I saw the text," Andrés says.

"Yeah, same. Driving is so scary. You never know if there will be a reckless driver on the road," I say.

Elijah and I plop down on the couch next to Andrés.

"It's gonna be tough without him on the court with us," Elijah says.

"Yeah, it will be. This means Lucas will be a starter now." I lean forward, rubbing my temples.

"Yeah. This fucking sucks," Andrés says, shaking his head.

Our team has built up such good chemistry over the season. We're familiar with each other's moves, and our bond is strong. Lucas throws our balance out of whack, and with him being a starter now, I'm not sure how it's going to work.

"So how was your weekend, Andrés?" Elijah asks.

"It was nice. Katie and I went to the orchestra and had a nice dinner after."

Elijah puts his arms around both of our shoulders. "Aw, look at both of my boys going on dates this weekend."

"I'm gonna fucking kill you," I say through gritted teeth.

Andrés sits up straight. "What the hell? You haven't taken any girls on dates since Annalise. Unless..."

Andrés has been out of the loop, so he doesn't know that we kissed in the elevator, or that we almost kissed again at Chandler's birthday. But I knew it wouldn't take him long to figure it out. He knows I swore off relationships after Annalise and I broke up.

"You were on a date with Annalise, weren't you?" he says, the puzzle coming together in his mind.

"He sure was!" Elijah blurts, grinning like an idiot.

I whack him on the back of his head.

"When did you two get back together?" Andrés asks. "Last time we talked about her, you said she hates your guts and you'd moved on."

I know these guys won't leave me alone until I tell them. I swear they can be so damn nosy sometimes. "Let's grab lunch later. I'll tell y'all everything then."

"Okay, but it'll be your treat since you wanna keep secrets from me," Andrés scoffs. "I was there for you during the breakup. I'm kinda hurt you didn't tell me."

"I didn't tell Elijah either," I say with a shrug. "He just got it out of me."

"There's nothing you can keep from me." Elijah smirks.

"You have a big fucking mouth," I say with a groan, rolling my eyes.

"Look who just showed up," Andrés says, and we follow his gaze. Lucas walks in alone, looking completely out of place.

I'm not sure why he showed up. I doubt Chandler would want to see him. They became friends when Lucas first joined the team, but that changed after the shit he pulled in the locker room. No one on the team cares for him. We just tolerate him. Which is why I'm worried about how things will be with him as a starter. He doesn't share the camaraderie that we all have with each other.

He speaks to Coach for a minute before approaching me. "Hey, Kamado. Can we talk?" Shoving his hands in his pockets, he fixes his gaze on the wall behind me.

"I have nothing to say to you, Hilton," I hiss, shooting him an icy glare.

"Can you please hear me out?"

The bruises on his face are starting to fade and I want nothing more than to give him fresh ones. But I'm already on thin ice with Coach.

Reluctantly, I get up from my seat and gesture toward the vending machines in the back corner. "Let's talk over there."

Once we've stepped away, Lucas stares at the ground and fiddles with his T-shirt. "I want to apologize for my erratic behavior."

"You think an apology is going to fix anything?" I scoff. "I want nothing to do with you."

"I'm truly sorry for the way I acted. What I said about Annalise was out of line." He lifts his eyes to mine and a hint of remorse shines through. "I'm sorry for how I treated you over the years. I've always been in love with Annalise, and I got jealous that she chose you over me in high school."

She didn't choose. You were never a fucking option.

"I thought I had a chance with her when I ran into her again and found out she was single. She ended it with me the day after Chandler's birthday party. She said she didn't see us as anything more than friends."

Annalise never told me when she ended things with Lucas. But knowing that she realized her feelings for me that day filled me with immense joy.

"I knew that wasn't the only reason. I saw the way she was looking at you that night. I was a fool to think that I could ever compete with you. I just want you to know that I am truly sorry. For everything. I hope one day we can start over and be friends. Or at least become acquainted with one another." He extends his hand to me. "Let's put this behind us."

He should get an Oscar for this performance, because I almost believe it. But I know his apologies are far from genuine. He hated me for years and now, all of a sudden, he has a change of heart? I don't buy his bullshit for a second. He will always be a snake.

I want to tell him to drop out of the NBA and move far away from San Francisco so I never have to see his pathetic fucking face again—but I choose to bite my tongue.

"For the sake of the team, I will be amicable with you. But you and I? We will *never* be friends," I snarl.

Lucas shoves his hand back in his pocket and his mask slips off. "Here I am, trying to be the better person, but of course you want to be immature and hold grudges."

My fists clench at my sides, and red-hot rage starts building in me. I take deep breaths to simmer it down and walk back toward my friends. I refuse to take the bait.

Andrés and Elijah ask me what the conversation was about, and I fill them in. They both agree that Lucas's apology is fake and he can't be trusted.

After thirty minutes, Chandler's parents come out to the waiting area to let us know we can go see him. Coach and Darius go in first, and I go in after with the guys.

Chandler is resting in bed, hooked up to an IV pump with his arm in a sling. His normally kempt blonde hair is disheveled and there are dark circles under his eyes. He is usually so full of energy and life, so it's hard seeing him like this. But I'm grateful that he's conscious and not hooked up to a ventilator.

His hospital room resembles a studio apartment. There's a pull-out couch on the side, a 65-inch TV, and a fridge and microwave in the corner.

"Hey, guys," he says, managing a weak smile. "I feel so loved, having the whole team come to see me."

We all take a seat on the couch next to him.

"Of course, man. We were all worried about you," I say.

"I was scared shitless when I received the news," Elijah says.

"I hate that I won't be playing with you guys," Chandler sighs. "This happened at the *worst* time."

"It is unfortunate, but we're just glad you're okay. How are you feeling right now?" Andrés asks.

Chandler holds up a control with a red button that's attached to a pump. "This thing has been a lifesaver. When I'm in pain, I just press this button and it delivers morphine. That way I don't have to bother the nurse."

"Is your nurse hot, by any chance?" Elijah asks.

"Really, dude?" Andrés shoots him a look and Elijah shrugs.

"Yeah, if you're into fifty-year-old men with receding hairlines." Chandler grins and a collective laugh ripples through the room.

"So, what happened? How did you get hit?" I ask.

"I was driving down 16th Street when this black SUV came out of nowhere and T-boned me."

"Fuck. Did they run a red light or something?" Elijah asks.

"I hope you win a huge lawsuit from this," Andrés adds.

"I was knocked unconscious, and by the time the cops arrived, they'd fled." Chandler grimaces and holds his side. He presses the button on his control and falls back into the pillow.

"That fucking asshole. I hope the cops catch him," I say.

"I hope so too." Chandler lets out a yawn and his eyelids start to droop.

"We'll let you get some rest," Andrés says, getting up from his seat. "Hope you feel better, man."

"Thanks for coming. Win the championship for me."

"We will." I nod.

He pulls up the covers and drifts off to sleep.

Once we're near the elevator, Andrés turns to me. "Don't forget—we're going to lunch. You're going to tell me everything."

"I'm gonna text Santiago to see if he wants to join," Elijah says with a grin on his face.

I scrub my hand down my face. "I can't stand you guys."

CHAPTER 33
Annalise

"**H**ey, Mazi!" Waddling toward her, I grab her bag and pull her in for a hug. "How was Colorado?"

"It was so beautiful!" she gushes. "It was my first time shooting a wedding in the snow. The shots came out phenomenal!" Pulling out her camera, she shows me some of the pictures she took over the weekend.

"Did you go on a date this weekend?" She nods toward the vase of flowers in the center of our breakfast table.

"Oh, no! I saw those when I went to the store and thought they were super pretty." I've bought flowers before, just because I love having fresh flowers in the house. But the bouquet Maddox got me isn't something you can find in a grocery store —nor would I ever spend that kind of money on flowers.

"Are you hungry? I'm about to make bourbon chicken and lo mein," I say, walking back to the kitchen.

"Yes, I'm starving. Are you okay? You're walking kinda funny." Mazi eyes me suspiciously.

My cheeks flame with heat. I'm still quite sore from the activities Maddox and I had over the weekend. Heat pools between my legs as I think about the way he made my body feel.

Game Changer

The way he ravished me on his kitchen counter has been replaying in my mind all day.

He said he leaves tomorrow for Chicago and will be on the road for the rest of the week, so I'll have to suffer during those days. I'd forgotten how much I missed sex. It's probably because I haven't had sex like that in years.

"The elevator was down yesterday so I had to take the stairs. You know how out of shape I am."

Mazi gives me a look that tells me she doesn't buy any of my bullshit, but doesn't prod any further. "I'm gonna go shower."

Once she's in her room, I pull out my phone and shoot Maddox a text.

> Mazi is suspicious.

MADDOX

> What gave it away?

> The extravagant yet lovely bouquet you gave me. And the way I'm walking. It's all your fault.

MADDOX

> You act like you don't enjoy feeling the soreness between your legs. It serves as a reminder that I was inside of you.

Fuck. My core pulses with need and my panties start to dampen. Thank goodness Mazi isn't around or the look on my face would be a dead giveaway.

I change the subject to prevent myself from getting even more turned on.

> How's Chandler? Is he okay?

MADDOX

> His car is totaled, and he has a few broken ribs and fractured his clavicle. But he's stable.

Oh God! That's a huge blessing. Hope he recovers soon.

MADDOX

Looks like he'll be out for the season, though. It was a hit-and-run.

Ugh. People are so irresponsible. Hopefully the police can pull the footage from cameras.

MADDOX

Yeah, hopefully.

Btw Elijah found your gold hoop earring in my car. I tried to lie and say it was my sister's, but he didn't believe me.

Damn it. I was wondering where it fell out.

MADDOX

I grabbed lunch with the boys after we visited Chandler and they all interrogated me. 🫣

Damn. So they all know now?

MADDOX

Yeah. Sorry. They were ruthless.

So much for keeping it a secret 😅. I guess I should tell Mazi soon.

MADDOX

Sending prayers your way. And don't tell her where I live because she might come and murder me in my sleep 😳.

Thanks. I'm gonna need it. And lol, I won't.

Setting my phone down, I pull the marinated chicken out of the fridge and place it into the frying pan. While the chicken is cooking, I add sauces to the lo mein in another pan and stir it up.

"*Mmm*, that smells so good." Mazi comes out of the room

with pajamas on and a towel wrapped around her head. "I'm so lucky to have a best friend who cooks for me."

I turn my head and smile at her. "It should be ready in a few." Hopefully being nicely fed will put her in a good mood so she doesn't go ballistic when I drop the bomb about Maddox.

Both of our phones buzz with a new text alert. We check and see a new text from Serena in our group chat.

> **SERENA**
>
> What are y'all doing? I was supposed to go on a date with Randall but we got into a huge fight 😫

> **MAZI**
>
> Let me guess. It was over some bullshit, as always 🙄

> **SERENA**
>
> I was studying with my friends, and he got mad at me because a guy was there too.

> What a dumbass 🤦‍♀️! Do you wanna come over? I'm cooking dinner. We can have a girls' night.

> **MAZI**
>
> Yes! Come over, please. We can watch Beauty Within, the new romcom that just came out on Netflix!

> **SERENA**
>
> Okay! I'll be there soon.

"I can't get over how good that bourbon chicken was," Serena says.

"Right? It's way better than what they have at the food courts in the mall. You would put them out of business," Mazi agrees.

A smile pulls on my lips. "Glad you ladies liked it."

We're sitting in the living room with face masks on, sipping on wine. Mazi and I are already almost done with our second glass, but Serena has barely put a dent in her first.

"This movie is kinda boring." Mazi groans.

"Yeah, I'm not feeling it either," I agree. "The love interest isn't doing it for me."

"Right? He's so cringey," Serena says, wrinkling her nose at the screen. "I brought this new card game I got the other day! Do y'all wanna play it?" Reaching in her bag, she pulls out a box that says *Unhinged*. It has a pink lip-bite icon on it and an 18+ sticker at the bottom.

"Ooh, this looks juicy!" Mazi guzzles down the last drops of her wine and sets her glass on the table.

"So we each pull out a card, and we all have to go around and answer. It's just a fun way to get to know each other," Serena says. "Do you wanna pull the first card?" She opens the box and hands it to Mazi.

"Yes, please!" she says, pulling a card from the middle. My muscles tense and my heart hammers in my chest. "What is your current body count?" Mazi reads from the card.

Okay, that one's not so bad. My pulse slows to a normal rhythm and I sink back on the couch, relaxing a bit.

"Geez, I'm too drunk to think right now. Twenty? Maybe thirty? Who knows?" Mazi says, laughing.

"I've only been with two," Serena says. "But I don't know if I count the first guy because he was really small and I could barely feel it."

"How small was it?" I ask.

She holds her two pointer fingers a couple of inches apart to show us. Mazi and I burst out laughing.

"Oh, babe, I'm so sorry you lost your virginity to a guy that had a dick the size of a peanut." Mazi pours more wine in her glass. I lift my glass to her, and she fills it up too.

"Did he at least go down on you?" I ask.

She shakes her head. "No. And Randall barely goes down on me, either. When he does, it's for five seconds, and then he wants to stick it in."

"What the fuck!" Mazi gasps. "So you've never orgasmed by getting eaten out? You are missing out!"

"I've never orgasmed. Period. At least not from a man…" Serena looks away and takes a sip from her glass.

Mazi and I both have the same expression, eyes wide and mouths hanging open.

"You've gotta be joking," I say, shaking my head.

"I wish I was," she sighs.

"It's time for you to get a new man." Mazi shakes her head.

Serena doesn't say anything and turns her attention to me. "What's your body count, Annalise?"

"Seven." *But only one of them has the ability to make me see stars when I orgasm.* "I went through a phase where I was on dating apps. It didn't make me feel too good after, so I stopped."

"We all need a hoe phase sometimes," Mazi says, raising her glass.

Serena pulls out the next card and reads it. "When was the last time you had sex, and where?"

Damn it. This was not how I wanted to tell Mazi. Maybe I can skip my turn without them noticing.

"I had sex two days ago. It was in his room. Nothing special." Serena shrugs.

A mischievous smile flickers across Mazi's lips. "I had sex yesterday. I hooked up with one of the bridesmaids in the limo."

"Ooh, scandalous!" I reach for a card in the box and pull it out. "What is your number-one sexual fantasy?"

"Wait, you didn't answer the question," Serena says.

Damn it.

Mazi and I are both drunk, so maybe I should just tell her

now. I might not have the courage to do it tomorrow, and I'd hate for her to find out from someone else.

I take a big gulp from my glass. "I had sex yesterday… on the kitchen counter."

She scrunches her nose. "On *ours*? I hope you wiped it with bleach."

"No. On his…"

"I *knew* you were on a fucking date!" Mazi shouts, slapping her thigh. "I was waiting for you to tell me. So, who was it?"

Goosebumps rise my skin and I feel the contents of tonight's dinner trying to resurface. "It was…"

Their eyes are on me, waiting for me to answer.

I gnaw on fingernails, averting their gaze. "It was Maddox."

The room is so quiet that you could probably hear a pin drop. Mazi's lips are pressed together in a tight line, and she has a death grip on her wine glass—she's probably imagining it's Maddox's neck instead. Her hazel eyes are filled with a fire so intense that it could incinerate me within seconds.

"Please tell me you were with someone else named Maddox, and not your ex who broke your fucking heart."

I chew on my bottom lip so hard, the taste of copper fills my mouth. "It was him." My voice comes out as a squeak.

A heavy sigh leaves her lips. "Annalise, why would you get back together with him? After everything he put you through?"

Noting the tension in the room, Serena sets her wine glass on the table and gets up from the couch. "I need to use the bathroom."

I chew on my bottom lip. "We're not officially back together. We're just giving it another shot and seeing where it goes."

I wasn't exactly lying. Maddox and I haven't put a label on our relationship, but we both know what we mean to each other. I'm not planning on seeing anyone else, and neither is he.

"Annalise, I know he was your first love, but he cheated on you," Mazi says, shaking her head. "That's unforgivable. You said so yourself, that you would never get back together with him. So what the hell changed?"

"Since he came back into my life, he's really been there for me. And I honestly don't believe he ever cheated on me."

Mazi sits up straight. "But you saw Charlotte come out of his bedroom!"

"I was so angry with him, I never gave him a chance to tell me his side of the story. We finally talked about it, and I have a feeling Charlotte wasn't telling the truth."

I fill Mazi in on everything Maddox told me about that night. I also tell her about all the things he's done for me that made me fall for him all over again—about him professing his love to me, and about our first date.

"I spent all those years trying to convince myself that I hated him. But when I saw him again, all the feelings I kept buried away resurfaced." Reaching over, I squeeze her hand. "I haven't been this happy in a long time. I'm sorry I kept this from you. But I know you have your reservations toward him. I was waiting for the right time to tell you."

Mazi squeezes my hand back, her face softening. "You really love him, don't you?"

"Yeah, I do." My heart clenches, warmth flowing through me like honey. It's the first time I've admitted it out loud. I am so deeply in love with Maddox Masashi Kamado. I always have been.

"If you're happy, then I'm happy too. I love you, Annalise Rose Monroe. You deserve all the happiness in the world, and I hope Maddox treats you like the queen you are."

The nerves in my stomach settle. I was expecting Mazi to scold me and unleash hell. But she took it a lot better than I thought she would.

"I love you too, Mazikeen Francesca Rivera." We pull each other into an embrace.

"But if he breaks your fucking heart again, I will castrate him. I don't care if I end up in prison."

I burst into a fit of giggles, even though Mazi is probably being dead serious.

"You can come out now, Serena!" Mazi calls out.

Serena comes out of the room and rejoins us on the couch. "We don't have to play anymore if y'all don't want to."

"Oh, no, we are still playing," I say, sitting up straight. I pick up the card I pulled out earlier, "So, Serena, what is your number-one sexual fantasy?"

"That's an easy one," she says, a wicked smile playing on her lips. "To join the mile-high club."

"That's my number-one, too," I say.

"I'm sure Maddox can help you fulfill it," Mazi says with a wink. "I've been a member of the mile-high club for a while now. It's exhilarating as hell, but not exactly comfortable. Maybe one day I'll get to do it in first class or on a private jet."

"I hope I can experience that one day. But Randall is such a prude, he would probably never go for it," Serena sighs.

"Honey, what do you even see in him?" Mazi asks.

"Honestly, I don't know anymore." Serena shakes her head. "Anyways, what's your number-one, Mazi?"

"With how kinky she is, she probably already fulfilled it." I snort.

"I haven't, actually. My number-one is to have sex while skydiving."

My face scrunches in confusion. "Huh? How would you even do that?"

She pulls a blanket over her lap and shrugs. "I'll figure out a way."

My phone dings with a text from Maddox.

MADDOX

So is Mazi on her way to murder me now? •••

No 😅. She took it surprisingly well. We're having a girls' night and playing a card game. We just discussed our number-one sexual fantasy.

MADDOX

Oh? So what's yours? 👀

To join the mile-high club 😏

MADDOX

I can make that happen 😜

CHAPTER 34
Maddox

Annalise is nestled between my legs as I watch her sketch with the new set of colored pencils I bought her. We're sitting together on a picnic blanket under a giant cherry blossom tree by a secluded lake in a town an hour away from San Francisco. Tsuki is rolling around on the grass, having the time of her life.

We took a horse-drawn carriage ride through the meadows earlier this afternoon and later indulged on gourmet sandwiches, fresh fruit, and wine—all prepared by the owner of the ranch.

The ranch owner and his son are huge NBA fans, so I was able to convince him to let us use the ranch for the day by offering courtside tickets for the rest of the season, a basketball autographed by all of the players—well, minus Lucas—and a meet and greet. I also purchased several cases of wine from him and promised to promote his business.

It feels nice to be away from the hustle and bustle of the city. There is no cell service out here, so we're able to disconnect and appreciate the beauty around us.

With Chandler being out, I've been under a lot of stress

lately. I put a lot of pressure on myself and overexerted on our road games. We won two out of three games, but I felt like a huge failure when we lost. If we have one more loss, we'll drop to number two in the league, and I can't have that.

Being away from San Francisco gives me the tranquility I need and the ability to cast away all my worries. Out here in the countryside, I'm not Maddox Masashi Kamado, the world-famous NBA player. I'm just a regular guy enjoying a date with his girlfriend.

Although we haven't formally labeled our relationship yet, in my heart she is undeniably my girlfriend, my soulmate, and the love of my life. I hope one day I'll get to call her my wife.

"That dress is turning out beautifully, Rosie." I place a kiss on top of her shoulder. Her mouth curves into a smile.

"Hmm. I don't know, it kinda looks plain. I feel like I need to add something." She taps her forehead with the colored pencil and sucks in her cheeks as she stares at the sketch.

A few moments pass and she sits up straighter, her face lighting up as though a lightbulb has gone off in her head. Pulling out a deeper shade of pink, she begins adding more to the piece.

I watch in awe as she adds intricate details to the dress, making it come to life. I can't draw to save my life, but she does it so effortlessly.

"You are so incredibly talented. I know celebrities will be fighting over who gets to wear this dress on the red carpet."

She lets out a small laugh and an adorable shade of pink tinges her cheeks. "Oh, please, you're just saying that. I'll never be good enough for celebrities to wear my designs."

Grabbing her waist, I turn her body so that she's facing me. "I'm not just saying that to make you feel good. It's the truth. If I sucked at basketball in high school, would you have lied to me and told me I'd make it to the NBA?"

"I'm pretty sure you've been practicing shooting baskets since you were in your mom's womb." She chuckles, shaking her head. "But no, I wouldn't have lied to you."

"I've always believed you were destined for greater things, ever since we first met when we were only eight years old," I say, smiling warmly as I meet her eyes. "Being a fashion designer is in your blood."

"This is what you need to be doing." I point to the dress she sketched. "Making your own designs and bringing them to life. Not performing every ridiculous task Veronica asks of you. As much as I love seeing you at Dauntless—which is the only reason why I've been dragging my feet through this collab—it kills me to not see you do what you love. To do what you were born to do."

Annalise smiles, her eyes glossing over. "I want to quit every single day, but I can't. It's too risky." She shakes her head. "I've been helping my mom cover some of the bills from Abuelo's treatment, so I need as much money as I can get."

"I'm not saying you should quit, but you should start somewhere. Maybe sell a few items online?"

She sits up straight, the smile slowly returning on her face. "I have thought of doing that before. Only problem is, there's really not enough room in the apartment to put my sewing machine and all of my materials."

"You can always use my place," I offer. "I have plenty of empty rooms."

"Trying to get me to move in with you on the second date, Dimples?" Her brows shoot up, a teasing smile pulling at her lips. "Don't you think that's a little fast?"

Wrapping my arm around her waist, I squeeze her tight and kiss the top of her head. "Is it a crime that I want to wake up next to you every day?"

"Well, it wouldn't be every day. You do have to travel for games, and I'll be all alone in that giant house."

A laugh bursts from me. "I'm trying to be romantic and you're getting technical on me. Plus, you wouldn't be alone. Tsuki would be with you."

At the mention of her name, she leaps on to our laps, covering us with kisses. "Hey, pretty girl," Annalise coos, scratching the spot behind Tsuki's neck that she loves so much. "You love me more than your daddy, don't you?" Tsuki barks in response. "I knew it."

"Please, that was a mere coincidence," I say, rolling my eyes. Tsuki moves close to Annalise, nuzzling her head against her.

"So, *when* you open up your own boutique, what will you name it?" I ask while I run my fingers through her hair.

Her smile widens, eyes sparkling with joy. "I would call it Thorny Roses."

"Thorny Roses. I love it!"

"Maybe I'll get Mazi to help me take pictures of the clothes to post on the website!"

"Yes! Now we're talking. I love seeing you get excited about something again."

"Thank you, Maddox. For lifting me up when I doubt myself."

"I will continue to lift you up. I hope one day you can see yourself the way I see you." Tilting her chin, I place a soft kiss on her lips. "Perfect."

She smiles and brings her lips back to mine once more.

"Do you wanna take a dip in the lake before we leave?" I ask.

"But we didn't bring swimsuits."

Shrugging, I strip off my clothes and jump into the lake, splashing water everywhere.

"Maddox, you got me wet!" She groans.

"Damn, already?" I flash her a suggestive smile and she shakes her head. "Come join me! The water feels perfect!"

"You are crazy." She hesitates for a moment before stripping down and jumping in.

A few days after our date, I schedule a meeting with Veronica to discuss the collaboration. Trang still hasn't come up with a single design that I like.

"What is it you wanted to discuss with me, Mr. Kamado?" Veronica says, motioning for me to sit down.

Shutting the door behind me, I take a seat on the leather chair opposite her. "The collaboration. I'm afraid it's not working out."

Her face pales. "W-what do you mean? I thought things have been going well." She chews on her bottom lip and bounces her knee under the table as she waits for my response.

Leaning forward, I rub my temples and let out a heavy sigh. "Ms. Zhang, I tried giving Trang a chance, but she continues to do the exact opposite of what I tell her."

Veronica swallows, the color in her face draining further. She now matches the white wall behind her.

"You told me Trang is the best, but I don't think she's the best person for this collaboration. I need to work with someone who understands my vision."

I should've had this conversation with Veronica months ago, when Trang first showed me her horrendous designs, but coming to Dauntless gave me an excuse to see Annalise—even though she gave me the cold shoulder during those first few weeks.

I don't need to use Dauntless as an excuse now that we've worked things out, but there's something so thrilling about keeping our relationship a secret while we're here. The stolen glances we exchange when no one is looking, the quick kisses in the elevator, and the way our hands brush against each other in passing keeps my heart racing.

Veronica reaches for her water bottle, taking large gulps from it. "So does this mean you still want to work with Dauntless for the collaboration?"

I nod. "Although it didn't work out with Trang, I would still love to collaborate with Dauntless."

A hint of color returns to her face and her shoulders relax. "I apologize, Mr. Kamado. Trang is the top fashion designer at Dauntless, and I truly thought she was the best person suited for the role. But you are valuable to us, and I don't want to continue wasting your time if you are not satisfied with Trang. I will work hard to find you someone more suited for the role."

I highly doubt that whoever she replaces Trang with will be able to capture my vision. There's only one person who is capable of doing that. "Perhaps the person you're looking for is someone who has been hiding in the shadows, waiting for her chance to shine."

Veronica shoots me puzzled look. "Sorry, I'm not following. Who are you talking about?"

"Ms. Monroe."

She starts to laugh, but covers it with a cough when I glower at her. "Mr. Kamado, this isn't a small project. This is a big one that will have a great impact on our company. I can't just give it to someone with absolutely no experience."

"She may not have been in the industry long, but her talent is immaculate. I know if you give her a chance, she will succeed. Everyone deserves a chance to prove themselves. If we were never given that chance, I wouldn't be in the NBA, and you wouldn't be running one of the top athletic brands in the nation."

Veronica stares at me, an unreadable expression on her face.

I glance at my watch to check the time, even though I'm not in a rush to be anywhere. "I must get going, but I'll return next week. In the meantime, I hope you take what I said into consideration."

Getting up from my seat, I walk toward the door. Veronica remains frozen in her seat, her eyes unblinking.

"Have a good day, Ms. Zhang." I give her a wave and shut the door to her office.

Annalise glances up from her desk and smiles at me, blush creeping on her cheeks.

Pulling out my phone, I shoot her a text.

> Hey Rosie, you going to lunch soon?

ANNALISE
> I can't. I'm just gonna snack on a banana and a granola bar. I have way too much to do, and I'm not trying to stay here late.

> Ah, okay. Well, come over after work. We can eat dinner together, and I can have you for dessert .

She shakes her head, smiling.

ANNALISE
> Lol. I can't stand you. Now I'm getting turned on at work and I'm not able to do anything about it.

> Are you already wet for me? 

ANNALISE
> Why don't you come find out, Mr. Kamado?

I suck in a breath, heat rushing to my groin.

> Don't tempt me, cause I'll do it.

She shoots me a wink and goes back to doing her work. I rush off to the restroom to try and collect myself before everyone notices that I have a raging boner.

Turning on the water faucet, I rinse my face. I take deep breaths, trying to calm myself and think of anything other than fucking her in every corner of the office, but it's impossible. I wait a few minutes before exiting the restroom.

The office has already cleared out for lunch, and Annalise is the only one there. She's munching on a protein bar while scrolling on her computer.

"Is everyone gone?" I ask, grabbing a chair and pulling it next to her.

"Yes, except the janitor. But what are you still doing here?" she hisses, shooting me a warning glare.

Leaning in, I kiss her and take her bottom lip in my mouth, sucking on it. "Doing what you asked and finding out how wet this pussy is for me."

Her lips part and those sapphire and emerald eyes darken when my hand disappears under her skirt. Instead of pushing it away, she spreads her legs wider.

"So fucking wet before I even touched you," I say, rubbing her through her panties.

She bites her lip to try to suppress her moans and grips her chair when I add more pressure. Her attention is no longer on work.

"I want you to show me," I whisper, my lips grazing her ears. "Show me how you would pleasure yourself if I wasn't here."

"Right here?" She gulps, looking around at the open space.

"Does Veronica lock the door during lunch?" I ask.

"Not usually. Only when we leave for the day."

Taking her hand, I pull us toward Veronica's office.

"This is crazy," she whispers, but she doesn't attempt to stop me when I pick her up and place her on top of Veronica's desk.

I plop down on the chair and sit in front of her. "Take off your bra and leave your top unbuttoned so I can see those perfect fucking tits."

Reaching behind her, she unclasps her bra and pulls it

through a sleeve. The blouse she's wearing is sheer, so I'm able to see those lovely pierced nipples through it.

She unbuttons her top, leaving the last three buttons.

"Now take off your panties," I demand.

Hiking up her skirt, she removes her lace panties.

My cock throbs with painful need seeing her glistening pussy on full display for me. "Touch yourself for me, Rosie. Imagine it's my hands instead of yours."

With both hands, she cups her breasts and tugs on her nipples. Keeping her eyes on me, she slowly slides her hands down her stomach.

Her mouth falls open as she moves her hands through the pool of wetness between her legs. She keeps her gaze fixed on me while she circles her swollen clit.

My tongue swipes across my bottom lip. "Fuck, that's hot."

When we were in college, she would send videos of her touching herself, and we'd video chat with each other as well.

Getting a front-row seat to it in real time feels like a reward. When her hand slides down to her entrance and she pushes two fingers inside, I feel like I'm going to pass out from being so turned on. My dick is practically screaming to be released.

"Maddox…" she moans, moving her fingers faster. "I'm so fucking wet for you. I want to feel your big cock inside of me."

Her words nearly send me over the edge. Unzipping my pants, I finally allow my cock to spring free. "Fuck yourself until you come, and then you can have this," I say, stroking myself.

An insatiable need grows in her eyes, and she licks her lips as she watches me.

Loud moans fill the room as she increases the pace, pumping her fingers faster. With her free hand, she pleasures her aching bud.

"Keep going, Rosie. You're doing so good. Once you make yourself come, I'll bend you over this desk and fuck you like you've been wanting me to." I continue to move my hand up and down my length, matching her rhythm. "I can't wait to be inside your tight pussy."

Her legs start shaking and she bucks her hips off the desk. "M-Maddox! I'm c-coming," she moans. She continues to move her fingers in and out as she rides out her orgasm.

Unable to hold back anymore, I stride over to her and replace her fingers with my cock.

Connecting her lips with mine, I swallow her moans as she comes around me. I can barely keep it together, feeling her clamp down on me.

The sound of footsteps echoes from outside the door and both of us widen our eyes in surprise. I begin to pull out of her, but the loud whirring of a vacuum fills the space.

She places her hand over her chest and sighs in relief. "Thank goodness. It's just the janitor."

"How much longer until they get back from lunch?" I ask, glancing at the clock.

"We have about twenty minutes."

"Do you think you can keep quiet?" I move in and out of her at a torturous rate.

"I'll try my best," she answers breathlessly. "Because I really want you to bend me over this desk, Mr. Kamado."

"I'm at your mercy, Ms. Monroe." I pull out of her and undo my tie, shoving it in her mouth to use as a gag.

A mischievous glint appears in her eyes when I reposition her so she's pressed down on the desk.

Hiking her skirt up, I spank her ass hard and slam myself into her.

"Oh, fuck!" She lets out muffled screams as I continue to hammer into her.

Objects clatter to the ground and the desk moves forward, scraping against the hardwood floor. The sound of my balls slapping against her ass fills the room.

"Is this how you like to be fucked?" Reaching over, I yank her hair as I continue to slam into her with deep, hard thrusts.

The tie isn't doing much to drown out her moans. Luckily the janitor is still is vacuuming.

How did I get so lucky to end up with a girl like her? She is perfect in every single way—smart, talented, beautiful. And behind closed doors, she's got a wild side that still blows my mind.

"This is my fantasy as much as it is yours. I've been wanting to bend you over this desk since the moment I saw you again. Do you know how many times I've fisted my cock while I thought of you?" Grabbing her ass, I push myself even deeper, filling her up completely.

"Oh, fuck, Maddox!" she cries out. Her entire body trembles and her walls tighten around me as she unravels again and again.

"Fuck!" I grunt. My cock pulsates inside her and I fall forward, letting out a deep, guttural cry as I erupt.

I wish I could stay like this forever, but I reluctantly pull out of her and we get dressed.

Swooping down, I capture her lips with mine. "Did you enjoy that, Ms. Monroe?"

"I sure did, Mr. Kamado." A seductive smile plays on her lips and she gives me a wink. "I'm not gonna be able to stop thinking about this."

"Well, I fully plan on checking off every fantasy of yours."

She laughs, and plants another kiss on my lips. "Oh, God, we made a mess in here."

The smell of sex permeates the air, and evidence of what we just did is all over Veronica's desk and floor.

There is only a Kleenex box in here, and we try our best to clean up, but it doesn't do much.

"I'm gonna bribe the janitor to do a deep cleaning in here," I say, scratching the back of my neck. "Come over after work?"

She nods, and I press a quick kiss to her lips before exiting the room. I spot the janitor, and Annalise sneaks back to her desk while I distract him.

"Ms. Zhang's office needs a deep cleaning. And if anyone asks, I left an hour ago." I pull out a wad of hundred-dollar bills, placing it in his hands.

"Your secret is safe with me." He gives me a curt nod and stuffs the money in his back pocket.

I've been dropping a lot of money lately to keep our relationship a secret and prevent people from talking, but it's worth every penny.

CHAPTER 35
Annalise

"Mi rosa, this dress is gorgeous!" Mom smiles proudly as she holds up the sage-green floral dress I just finished making.

"It has pockets, too!" I beam, showing her.

Over the last couple of weeks, I've been creating new designs for my line—dresses, blouses, and two-piece sets. I wanted to start off by doing a soft launch of my online store and selling a few pieces. I told my friends about the idea and they agreed to model my clothes, and Mazi is going to help with the photos.

Mom turned my bedroom into a storage room after I graduated high school, but she still kept my sewing machine and desk. After I told her about my plans to launch an online store, she was more than happy to let me use the space and told me I can come over whenever I wanted.

I could probably squeeze the desk and sewing machine in my own room, but there's no way I'd be able to fit all my materials in there—unless I plan on getting rid of my bed.

It had been months since I'd created anything. I hadn't

stepped foot inside a craft store or touched my sewing machine since I found out about Abuelo's diagnosis.

As I sit behind my desk, feeding the fabric through the machine and keeping my foot on the pedal, I finally start to feel like myself again.

Working at Dauntless is still a drag, but I don't let it affect me as much as it used to. Because now I have something to look forward to when I get off.

"It makes me so happy to see you smile. I'm so glad your passion is coming back." Mom hugs me and places a kiss on my cheek.

"Me too." Ollie nods. "I'm glad making clothes again has put you in a good mood. You've been so grouchy lately."

Picking up a pillow, I whack him in the face.

"Ow!" He picks it up and whacks me back.

"That's not the only reason she's been in such a good mood," Abuelo says, his mouth lifting into a smile.

"*Abuelooo.*" I narrow my eyes at him while Mom and Ollie exchange confused glances.

"I'm sure seeing Maddox again is contributing to her mood." Abuelo's smile widens.

"You two are back together?" Ollie sits up straight, his eyes widening with curiosity.

"When did this happen?" Mom crosses her arms, her lips curling downward. "How are you gonna tell Abuelo before you tell me?"

Staring at my lap, I twist my hands and avoid her burning gaze. "We're not officially back together. We're taking it slow and seeing where things go."

Maddox and I have definitely *not* been taking it slow, but my family doesn't need to know that. I had planned on waiting longer until I gave myself to him again, but making love to him again has brought us closer. I wasn't filled with regret the next day like I was with other guys.

Because Maddox isn't some guy that I'm just using for sexual pleasure—even though he excels at it. He is the love of my life, and my soulmate.

I fill Mom and Ollie in about seeing Maddox at Dauntless and how I fell for him all over again.

"I'm glad you two are working things out," Ollie says. "I've missed him."

"I know you did," I say, smiling softly.

Ollie was only seven when he met Maddox, and he really looked up to him. He would hog Maddox's attention when he came over. They would watch anime and play basketball together. Maddox was the one who taught Ollie how to play.

"You should call him over for dinner," Mom says.

"He just got back from traveling for games a few hours ago. He's probably tired."

"He won't be tired once you tell him I'm cooking dinner. I know he loves my food."

"Please invite him," Ollie begs.

"Fine." I roll my eyes and pull out my phone.

> Hey, if you're not too tired, my mom wants you over for dinner. She's making lechón asado and yuca frites.

MADDOX

> Hell yeah, I'll be there. I haven't had Cuban food in so long. Well, besides you 😋

> Lol I can't stand you.

MADDOX

> So did you decide to tell her about us, or did she find out somehow?

> Abuelo found out. I came to him for advice after we kissed because I was confused about how I was feeling. He was the one who pushed me to talk to you.

MADDOX

He's a good man. I owe him everything for that.

So does this mean I can tell my mom about us too?

Lol yes you can.

MADDOX

She's gonna be over the moon.

What time do you want me over?

Come over at 7.

MADDOX

Okay. I'll be there.

"He says he can come," I say, and everyone lights up with excitement.

"Do you want me to help you prep dinner, Mami?"

She waves me off. "I'm good. Thank you, baby. Go back upstairs and finish making your clothes."

The doorbell rings and Ollie perks up. "That must be Maddox!"

He sprints to the door and flings it open. I follow after him. "Hey! Maddox!"

"Ollie! My man!" Maddox says, pulling Ollie into a hug. "Man, you've gotten so tall. Are you already in high school?"

Ollie nods. "Yeah, I'm a freshman now."

"Wow, that's crazy. You were only in elementary school when I last saw you."

Maddox drops a quick kiss to my lips. "Hey, Rosie."

"Hey, Dimples," I say, my heart fluttering.

Taking his hand, I lead him to the dining room.

"*Hola*, Ms. Delgado. *Hola*, Señor Delgado." He greets them with a wave. "It smells delicious. Thank you so much for having me."

Mom sets her bowl down and Abuelo gets up from his seat. They both take turns hugging him.

"It's so good to see you, Maddox," Mom says.

"It's so good to see everyone," Maddox says with a grin.

"I'm glad to see you back with Annalise. You have always been so good to her," Abuelo says.

Maddox wraps his arm around my shoulder and plants a kiss on top of my head. "Well, I love your granddaughter very much, and she's good to me too."

My heart flutters wildly and a huge grin spreads across my face.

"The other guy she brought home was a *pendejo*." Abuelo shakes his head and takes a seat on the chair.

Maddox goes rigid against me, and his face falls. "She brought home another guy?"

I should interject, but I decided to play along. "Yeah, he was the CEO of a million-dollar company."

"Oh. I didn't know you dated anyone." His throat bobs. "Which company is it?"

We all shake with laughter and Maddox looks around, dumbfounded.

"We're just messing with you, babe." Tiptoeing, I press a kiss to his cheek. "I never brought home another guy, nor have I been in another relationship."

"That wasn't very nice. It felt like my heart was being ripped out of my chest," he says, shooting me a glare.

"I'll make it up to you later," I whisper, low enough that only he can hear. The corner of his mouth lifts into a smile.

Mom brings out the bowl of yuca frites and beckons for us to sit down.

"Ms. Delgado, this is fantastic," Maddox says, taking a large bite of the lechón asado.

"Thank you, Maddox. I'm so glad you are enjoying it. How's basketball going?" Mom asks. "That's so incredible that you're playing for the team you always wanted to play for."

"Yeah, it's a dream come true. One of my teammates, Chandler, is out due to injuries, so we're short one person. It's been tough, but we've been able to keep our number-one ranking."

"The championship will be yours this year. I've been watching you play. I haven't seen anyone play that well since Kyrie Lyons," Abuelo says.

"*Gracias*, Señor Delgado. That means a lot to me." Maddox's grin widens.

Maddox has always looked up to Kyrie, so I know how much that comment means to him.

"I'm so happy that you followed your dreams, Maddox." Mom smiles. "And *mi rosa*, once your clothing line takes off, you will be filthy rich and able to retire me."

"And I can drop out of school and live off of you," Ollie says with a mouthful of food.

Mom slaps him on the back of the head, and everyone breaks out in chuckles. "You are still going to school, young man. You can make your own money."

Ollie groans and rolls his eyes, grabbing a handful of yuca frites.

"Plus, if you drop out of school, you won't be able to see your little girlfriend," Mom says.

Ollie's cheeks turn a deep shade of red and he slinks lower in his seat.

"You have a girlfriend? Since when?" I set my fork down, eyes wide with shock.

"We always catch him talking on the phone with some girl late at night," Abuelo says, a teasing smile gracing his lips.

"I don't have a girlfriend. Amaya and I are friends."

"Friends who talk on the phone late at night?" I eye him curiously.

"Fine, I have a crush on her," Ollie groans. "But she'll never go for me. She's the prettiest and most popular girl in school."

"And you're just as great," I say. "I'm sure she likes you too, but if you choose to do nothing about it, you'll be stuck in the friend zone forever."

"But what if she rejects me?" Ollie stares down at his plate, pushing the food back and forth with his fork.

"Do you know how many times your sister rejected me before she said yes?" Maddox says, pulling a chuckle from everyone. "I wouldn't be here now if I didn't keep trying. I know it's scary to ask out a beautiful girl. I was so nervous when I approached her, I felt like I was going to throw up."

"Really? But you always seem so confident," Ollie says.

Maddox shakes his head. "In that moment, I lost all my confidence. But my point is, if you continue to let your fears prevent you from going after what you want, you'll live your life in regret and constantly wonder what if."

Even though Maddox isn't addressing me directly, his words strike a chord with me. If I had allowed those negative voices in my head to control me, I would have missed out on pursuing what my heart truly desires. A life without Maddox would have been a life full of regret.

"Thank you, Maddox—for the advice." Ollie smiles. "I think I'll, uh, ask her out on Friday."

"That's what I'm talking about!" Maddox holds his fist up and dabs it with Ollie's.

"My baby is all grown up." Mom sniffles, her eyes glazing over with tears. "It seems like it was yesterday when I held you in my arms and rocked you to sleep."

Ollie groans, turning his attention back to the food.

"You better not do anything more than kiss," Mom says,

pointing a fork at Ollie. "The only person I want to give me grandkids right now is Annalise."

I nearly choke on my food, and Maddox laughs next to me. "Mami, you need to slow down. We *just* started dating again."

"My mom said the exact same thing when I called her earlier to tell her about us." Maddox chuckles, shaking his head.

"Don't listen to them," Abuelo says, waving his hand. "Focus on your careers first. Babies can wait. But when it does happen, you two will have beautiful babies."

"We would, wouldn't we?" Maddox kisses me on the cheek and I melt into a puddle.

Having kids isn't something I'm opposed to. I've always pictured having them with Maddox one day.

However, I don't see myself being a mom for at least another decade. I want to succeed in my career and continue to build a life with Maddox first. When the day does come, I already know Maddox will make an amazing dad.

Over the next week, all of my free time is spent preparing for the soft launch of my online store. After work, I go over to Mom's house to finish working on my clothes. Maddox had offered me one of his empty rooms, but I didn't want to invade his place.

With Ivy's help, I created an Instagram for my shop and started posting sneak peeks of the clothing. She gave me a bunch of tips on marketing and ideas for content creation. My account currently has around a hundred followers, and although it's not a huge amount, seeing people commenting about how pretty my clothes are warms my heart.

Maddox begged me to let him give me a shoutout on his Instagram—which would probably give me a huge boost, since he has over twenty million followers—but I told him this is something I want to do on my own.

"I'm so excited for you to launch your shop tonight. You know, I'll be the first customer. I need to get my hands on that pink two-piece set." Ivy smiles and takes a sip out of her taro tea.

We stopped by Boba Guys after lunch, and now we're heading back to the office.

"Thank you, Ivy. I really appreciate all your support."

"You're welcome, queen. Don't forget about me once Thorny Roses blows up."

Rolling my eyes, I take a sip of my strawberry matcha latte. "I'm not going to forget about you. And I doubt it'll blow up."

"Sure it will. What are your plans for next week?"

Dauntless will be closed for a week for spring break, so I'm able to get a break from Veronica and her antics.

"I plan on utilizing that time off to make more clothes for my shop."

"Are you doing anything for your birthday?"

"I don't have anything planned." I shrug. "Probably just gonna have dinner with my family."

"And some birthday sex?" Ivy says, wiggling her brows.

Shaking my head, I sip the rest of my drink and toss it in a nearby trash can.

I fully plan on having birthday sex.

Ivy doesn't know about Maddox and me yet, but I think she's suspicious, since she's caught us staring at each other multiple times.

Veronica left Reginald in charge of the collaboration with Maddox. According to Maddox, he's a much better designer than Trang, but Maddox still isn't completely satisfied. He said the designs are nice, but they aren't *him*. They lack his personality.

After Trang got pulled from the collaboration, I sketched a few designs—T-shirts, windbreakers, hoodies—that matched his vibes and incorporated his Japanese culture. I haven't shown him the designs yet, because I know if he showed Veronica, she would shut it down as soon as she learned who designed them.

No matter what I do, she will never think I'm deserving of becoming a fashion designer. I hope one day I'll be able to prove her wrong.

"Why am I being blindfolded?" I ask as Maddox ties a black scarf around my eyes. "Are you going to tie me up, too?" My lips curve into a suggestive smile.

A deep laugh rumbles through him. "I plan on doing that later, love. You can't see anything, right?"

"Nope. It's pitch black. Please make sure I don't bump into anything."

"I won't." Taking my hand, he leads me through his house.

We turn left and walk a few steps before coming to a halt. Maddox unties the scarf and my heart skitters when I see what's before me.

He's completely transformed one of his empty rooms into an office space for me. The room is probably the size of my apartment, and is painted a sage-green color with a pastel-pink accent wall.

In the back is a desk with a top-of-the-line sewing machine, and hanging on the wall behind it is the name of my brand—Thorny Roses—in neon letters. It has everything I could ever want—a rack to place my rolls of fabric, a drawer to organize my threads, and so much more.

It even has a brand-new Kamado Tech desktop so I can use it to fulfill my online orders, and a massage chair for when I need a break.

"Happy early birthday, Rosie." He smiles.

Throwing my hands around his neck, I kiss him. "Thank you, Maddox! I love it so much. Gosh, you're the best boyfriend ever."

"Boyfriend, huh?" Maddox's face flushes to an adorable

shade of pink, and he flashes his dimpled smile. "Is that your way of telling me you want us to be official?"

I laugh and squeeze him tighter. "Maddox Masashi Kamado, will you be my boyfriend? Again?"

"I would love to." He lifts me up and kisses me tenderly, carrying me out of the room.

"Is my *boyfriend* taking me to his bedroom to fuck me while I'm blindfolded?"

"I do plan on fucking my *girlfriend*. But she needs to open her next gifts first."

"Gifts? As in plural?" I stare at him, wide-eyed. "Maddox, you have given me more than enough."

"You deserve the world, Rosie."

We enter his bedroom and he sets me down on the ground.

On the floor is a bag from Dior and a beautiful mocha-colored luggage set with a matching weekender and toiletry bag.

"Maddox, you didn't!" I pull the box from the Dior bag and open it. Inside is the white Lady Dior bag I've been eyeing for the longest time.

"Open the luggage," Maddox says, nodding toward it.

Crouching down, I unzip the luggage and find that it's full of swimsuits and beautiful outfits—perfect for a tropical vacation, all neatly folded.

"Remember how we talked about visiting Hawaii one day?"

"Yeah, I do."

We were supposed to plan a trip to Hawaii during winter break of our first year of college, but we never got a chance to.

"We leave in a couple of hours," Maddox says, smiling.

"What? People on the plane will recognize you!"

"They won't." He grins. "Because we're gonna take my private jet."

CHAPTER 36
Maddox

"**I** don't think I can go back to flying economy after this," Annalise says as she lies back on the plush leather seat of the private jet and stretches her legs.

"You'll never have to with me," I say, smiling.

We are headed to the beautiful island of Kauai, and we've been watching Disney movies together on the large-screen TV and indulging in gourmet meals. As much as I wanted to visit all of the islands, we're limited on time. With Kauai being the least touristy spot, it was the best option.

The regular season just ended, and we get a little break before playoffs start. Everyone else on my team is practicing and preparing. Coach was not too happy about me missing practice to go on a trip, but getting to put a smile on Annalise's face is worth facing his wrath.

"Have any other women been on your private jet?"

Sipping my champagne, I shrug my shoulders. "Just two others."

She narrows her eyes, folding her arms across her chest. "Who were they? Models? Actresses?"

I try my best to hold in my laughter. "None of the above. One is a chef and the other is a doctor."

"Oh. I thought you were just hooking up with these women. I didn't know you took them on trips, too." She lets out an adorable humph and turns her body toward the window.

Unable to hold back anymore, I burst out laughing. "The two other women are my mom and sister."

"You are a jerk for that!" Her scowl slips off her face and she playfully slaps my arm.

Reaching over, I grab her hips and pull her onto my lap so she's straddling me. "I'll make it up to you." I plant a kiss on her lips before moving to her neck.

"How do you plan on doing that?" Her breathing becomes ragged as my mouth moves to the curve of her breasts.

Slipping my hand under her dress, I grip her ass and push her farther down on my lap. She lets out a loud gasp as I press my erection against her lace panties.

"By making you a member of the mile-high club." Yanking her toward me, I crash my lips against hers.

She kisses me back roughly, tugging on my hair while she rocks her hips back and forth.

Lifting my shirt, she traces the hard lines of my abs with her fingers.

I break away from the kiss, shedding my T-shirt and tossing it onto the floor.

Reaching over, I untie the bow in the front of her dress and her breasts spill out. Bringing my mouth down, I lick and suck her hardened nipples while she continues to rub herself against me.

"Yes!" she moans. Her arousal seeps through her panties, dripping onto my shorts.

My hand moves between her legs and I push her panties to the side, sinking my fingers into her. I start pumping my fingers faster, but she grabs a hold of my hand.

"I want to feel your cock." She licks my earlobe, sending shivers down my spine.

"You'll get it soon." I thrust my hips up, earning another moan from her.

"I want to feel it in my mouth." Reaching between us, she strokes me over my shorts.

Fuck. Her words have me pulsating with need.

She grabs my hand and takes my fingers into her mouth, giving me a preview about what she's about to do to my cock.

Hopping off of my lap, she drops to the ground and kneels before me. She teases me first—planting kisses over my aching bulge—before peeling off my shorts along with my boxers.

Precum leaks from the tip, and she licks her lips at the sight of it.

Her mouth hovers over my cock while she pumps it in her hand.

My knuckles whiten around the armrest of the chair and beads of sweat drip down my brow. The anticipation is killing me. I have to physically restrain myself from pushing her head down and fucking her mouth.

"Annalise…"

"Yes?" She looks up at me through her thick lashes, a wicked smile dancing on her face.

"Please. You're killing me. I need to feel your pretty little lips wrapped around my—"

Her tongue swirls around the tip of my cock, silencing me.

With her eyes on me, she pushes her head further down, licking the underside of my shaft as she takes more of me in her mouth.

"*Fuck…*" I groan in satisfaction, my hands tangling in her hair. I'm at her mercy, and I love watching her take control of my body.

She bobs her head up and down and moans while she sucks me, sending vibrations down my cock.

"You look so pretty on your knees for me. And fuck, your mouth feels amazing, babe."

She moans at my praise and takes me deeper. I release a loud grunt when my cock hits the back of her throat. Drool leaks from the corner of her mouth and tears stream down her cheeks, but she continues to take as much as she can.

The sounds of her choking on my cock fill the cabin. She continues to pleasure me, every lick and suck bringing me closer to the edge.

"Fuck, don't stop." I tighten my hold on her hair as she sucks me harder and increases the pace.

Slamming my hips up, I fill her mouth with my cum as the orgasm hits me with force, blurring my vision.

She swallows every drop, licking me clean, and my body goes limp.

Removing her mouth from me, she climbs back onto my lap and a proud grin pulls at the corner of her lips.

"You've always been a pro at sucking my cock. Such a good girl." I brush my thumb across her swollen pink lips, and her smile widens.

Pressing a button on the side of the chair, I recline it all the way until I'm lying flat. "Now take off the rest of your clothes and ride my cock."

Blush spreads across her cheeks and she bites her bottom lip between her teeth. She pulls her dress over her head and slips off her soaked panties. "Don't you need time to recover?"

Shaking my head, I reclaim her lips and pull her body close to mine. The sight of her glorious naked body has me hard once again.

She grabs my cock, gliding the tip through her dripping wet core. "See what you do to me? Sucking your dick got me so fucking wet." Dragging my length to her entrance, she slowly pushes me into her.

The combination of the dirty words that just came out of her mouth on top of feeling her tightness wrapped around my cock nearly causes me to unravel once more. "I can't get enough of you, Annalise."

Taking her time, she slowly moves up and down my hard length, easing me into her inch by inch. Moans of pleasure escape her lips as I stretch her out.

"*Fuck...* I love your cock." She pants as she rocks her hips back and forth.

"Then show me. Show me how much you love it." I reach up, squeezing her breasts.

Resting her hands on my chest, she rides me hard and fast. Her breasts bounce up and down as she screams in pleasure.

"We would never be able to fuck on a regular plane with how loud you are." Wrapping my hand around her neck, I thrust my hips up, pushing myself deeper into her.

Choked moans leave her lips as I continuously pound into her. After a few moments, she regains her rhythm and our bodies move together in synchrony as the jet flies through the air.

We enter the land of orgasmic bliss together, and she continues to ride me as I come undone.

The feeling of her tightening around me has me coming harder than I did earlier.

After we get cleaned up and dressed, I drift off into a peaceful sleep with Annalise in my arms. Soon we'll be together in paradise and will have the freedom to go wherever we want without keeping our relationship a secret.

CHAPTER 37
Annalise

"Oh gosh, this is so good." I take another bite of the warm custard-filled malasada. After we landed, we stopped by our luxury condo to shower and drop off our luggage. It's right by the beach, and we even have a personal housekeeper—a sweet middle-aged lady named Lelani—who gave us a bunch of recommendations for food spots and places we must see.

We indulged in the best poké I've ever had in my life, and later stopped by the bakery and purchased a whole box of malasadas straight from the oven.

"These are fucking addicting," Maddox says, reaching for another one.

"Don't eat them all, now," I warn, shooting him a glare.

He wraps his arms around me and kisses my cheek. "Don't worry. I'll buy you more."

I lean against him as we watch the sunset at Hanalei Bay. The sunsets in California are beautiful, but they don't compare to this glorious sunset in Kauai.

"This is nice," he says, caressing my hair. "Being able to hold your hand out in public."

"It is. I miss being able to do stuff like this with you. If we did this back home, everyone would be swarming around you trying to get an autograph."

"That's going to be you once this shop takes off. Everyone will be wearing a Thorny Roses piece by the end of the year." He flashes me his dimpled smile.

"I'll be happy just having a few people wear my clothes."

My phone dings with a notification and I pull it out to check it. I texted my family when I landed, but I haven't touched it since. It's a message from Serena and Mazi.

SERENA

How's Hawaii so far?

MAZI

Are you a member of the mile-high club yet? 👀

I snap them a picture of the box of malasadas.

It's great. I'm never coming home. And yes lol. 😂

SERENA

I'm so jealous! 🥺

I check my emails and am surprised by what I find in my inbox. "Oh my gosh, Dimples! Ten orders have been placed for my shop!" Checking Instagram, I find that my number of followers has doubled—I now have four hundred.

"Rosie, that's incredible! See, I told ya your shop is gonna take off. I'm so fucking proud of you!" He lifts my chin and kisses me on my lips.

"Thank you, Maddox, for encouraging me to pursue my dreams again. For the office, for this trip, for everything. I promise once I make some money, I'll repay you."

Maddox has done so much for me—spoiling me and showering me with affection. I want to be able to give back to him, too.

He shakes his head and laces his fingers with mine. "You don't have to give me anything. I have you. You are all I need in this world."

Those three little words rise in my throat, but I swallow them down once again. Each day, the urge to say them to him grows stronger, yet I still can't bring myself to speak them. I'm afraid that once I utter those words, the voices in my head will return, trying to snatch away my happiness and convince me that I don't deserve love.

"You ready for playoffs?"

Maddox sucks in his cheeks. "Truthfully? I'm nervous as hell. I made it to playoffs last year when I was in Houston. But being back home? There's so much pressure on me, and I'm scared I'm gonna let everyone down." He grabs a handful of sand, letting it seep through his fingers. "Everyone compares me to Kyrie, but I don't think I can ever live up to him."

"Maddox, you are amazing. And you shouldn't compare yourself to anyone. Kyrie was a fantastic player, but so are you. You both changed the game of basketball, and you're going to lead the Dragons to the championships just like he did. I have faith in you."

A warm smile graces his lips and he kisses my forehead. "Thank you for always lifting me up."

Blush creeps on his cheeks and he scratches the back of his head. "Will you, um, come to my playoff game next Saturday? You can bring Ollie, too."

"I wouldn't miss it for the world," I say, squeezing his hand.

"Really?" The excitement in his voice and the way his face lights up squeeze my heart.

"Of course. I plan on attending every single game of yours. I'm gonna be the loudest one there."

"Promise me you'll wear my jersey. The only last name you

should be wearing is mine," he says, a teasing smile quirks on his lips.

A laugh bursts from me. "I was already planning to."

I roll over in bed and reach for Maddox, only to find the space next to me empty. Slipping on my shorts, I head to the living room to find it fully decorated. There are vases of flowers every-where, a large "Happy Birthday" banner hanging on the wall, and balloons and streamers dangling from the ceiling. In the kitchen, Leilani, the housekeeper, is preparing something that smells absolutely delicious.

Maddox is leaning against the wall wearing a lazy smile on his face. "Happy birthday, beautiful."

Racing toward him, I leap into his arms and give him a kiss. "Thank you, Maddox. Gosh, you spoil me so much."

"My girl deserves the best." He smiles against my lips.

"Breakfast is ready!" Leilani carries out two plates of loco moco—a traditional Hawaiian dish consisting of white rice, a hamburger patty, gravy, and a sunny-side-up egg—and sets them on the table.

"*Mahalo*, Leilani. This looks delicious!" Maddox says. We both take a seat and Leilani comes back with two glasses of freshly squeezed orange juice.

"You are too kind for cooking for us," I say.

"*Na'u ka hau'oli*," she says sweetly. "And happy birthday to you."

"*Mahalo*, Leilani."

She scurries off to the kitchen to clean up, and I dig in. "Wow, this is so good. Who knew this combo would be so tasty?"

"Right? Hawaiian food has been amazing so far. I wish I could have woken you up with breakfast, but I didn't want to burn this house down." He grins and takes another bite of food.

I reach over and squeeze his hand. "It's okay that you lack skills in the kitchen. You make up for it in other ways."

A suggestive smile tugs at his lips, and his hand grazes my thigh. "Oh? Are you talking about my skills in the bedroom?"

Heat pools between my legs as I think about all the ways he has pleasured me. "You are so cocky. But I'm talking about how thoughtful and caring you are. You've been so amazing to me, and I am so grateful to have you in my life again."

Blush creeps across his cheeks and his smile widens. Leaning forward, he pops a kiss on my lips. "I am, too. And I hope you like what I have planned for us today."

"I'm sure I will. What are we doing first?"

"First, we're gonna go shark cage diving."

"What?" My stomach starts churning, and I shoot Maddox a look to let him know he has completely lost his mind. "I'm all about adventure, but I'm not trying to die on my birthday. Have you not seen *47 Meters Down*?"

He waves me off. "That's just a movie. We'll be perfectly fine."

"If a shark breaks through the cage, I'm going to use you as bait to get away."

He folds his arms across his chest, frowning. "Wow—I was just joking about cage diving, but it's good to know you're willing to sacrifice me."

"I'm kidding. I would never do that." I laugh. "But what are we really doing?"

"You'll see. And I promise it doesn't involve sharks."

Wind whips through my hair and ocean water splashes me as our boat glides through the stunning Nā Pali Coast. The towering cliffs, lush valleys, and turquoise waters look like something straight out of a postcard.

Our captain, Kekoa, expertly maneuvers the boat into the heart of a glorious sea cave.

"This is Pukalani, which means *window to heaven*." He gestures toward the large circular opening above us.

Maddox and I tilt our heads back in awe, completely mesmerized by the breathtaking views. The vibrant blue sky stretches above us, illuminated by beams of sunlight cascading through the opening. It truly looks like a window to heaven.

Kekoa takes us through more sea caves before bringing the boat to a stop. "This is the perfect spot to snorkel," he says, handing us our snorkel gear.

Excitement bubbles in me as I buckle my life jacket and slip the mask over my face. It's my first time snorkeling, and I can't believe I get to do it in freaking *Hawaii*.

As we dive beneath the shimmering surface, a sea turtle swims past us. Maddox quickly retrieves his Kamado Tech Adventure Cam and captures the perfect shot of us with the turtle and other magnificent sea creatures in the background.

"Did you two have fun?" Kekoa asks, handing us towels as we return from our snorkeling adventure. We'd been having such a blast that we completely lost track of time.

I remove my snorkel gear and wrap the towel around my body. "Yes, it was gorgeous out there. I wish I could stay out here all day."

Maddox settles next to me and pulls me onto his lap. "I've been snorkeling before, but I have never seen views like this. I'm so glad I got to experience this with you, Rosie."

"Thank you for giving me this experience, Dimples."

Just when I thought my birthday couldn't get any better, Maddox surprises me with massages by the beach, followed by a helicopter ride to a waterfall where we're currently having a candlelight dinner beside the water.

After we finish our main course, our chef, Makoa, comes out with a ukulele singer and a cake. They all join together and sing "Happy Birthday" to me.

"Happy birthday, beautiful," Maddox says, kissing me on the cheek.

I shut my eyes and wish for Abuelo to be cancer-free, for me to have the courage to leave the job I hate, and for what I have with Maddox to last for an eternity.

Using my fork, I dig into the carrot cake—my favorite flavor —and pop it into my mouth. "Oh, this tastes like heaven."

Maddox takes a bite and hums in satisfaction. "My mom will always be my favorite chef, but Chef Makoa comes pretty close. Do you think I can pay him to move to San Francisco so I can eat more of his food?"

"And leave this?" I gesture to the scenery around us. "I don't think there would be enough money in the world for that. I'm already dreading leaving paradise."

"I am, too. What do you say we come back to Hawaii after basketball season is over? We can explore the other islands then."

"I would love that. One of the things I want to do is travel more. I've been to Cuba with my family, to a few cities in Cali, and Mazi and I went to Vegas during spring break last year. But there's still so much of the world I have yet to see."

Leaning in, he plants a soft kiss on my cheek. "We can see it together. Traveling is one of the greatest luxuries in life, and this trip is the first of many."

A smile spreads across my face and warmth fills me as I envision us traveling the world together. I imagine going to Paris and placing locks on the Love Lock Bridge above the Seine

River, visiting Japan during cherry blossom season to meet his grandparents, and staying in one of those glass domes in Norway as we watch the aurora borealis dance above us.

"Out of all the places you've traveled to, what has been your favorite?" I ask.

"Hawaii." He reaches over and strokes my cheek. "Because every other trip I've been on, the whole time I was wishing you were there with me. You are my favorite person, Rosie, and anywhere next to you is my favorite place to be."

Digging into his front pocket, he pulls out a red heart-shaped velvet box and places it in my hand.

"Maddox, you didn't have to give me another gift. You've already given me enough."

He shifts in his seat, watching me carefully as I open the box. My heart beats rapidly in my chest when I catch sight of the gold rose necklace he gifted me on our anniversary all those years ago. "I can't believe you still have this," I whisper, a rush of nostalgia washing over me.

As I lift the necklace from the box, I notice that he added diamonds on the stem and had our initials engraved on the leaves. The last time I saw the necklace, I had thrown it at him out of spite, and that was something I've always regretted.

"I held on to it, hoping one day I would be able to give it back to you," Maddox says softly. "All the mementos from our relationship—the ticket stubs, the handmade gift you made me, the jar full of love notes—I kept them all."

Butterflies swarm wildly in my stomach. "I did, too."

Sitting on my old bedroom floor is a box full of memories from the time we were together. As angry as I was with him, I couldn't bring myself to throw them away. I didn't want to completely erase him from my life.

"Can you put it on me?" I ask, handing the necklace to him.

Brushing my hair to the side, he clasps the beautiful piece around my neck and holds the rose pendant with his fingers.

"The diamonds I added symbolize the strength of my love for you, which continues to grow with each passing day."

Turning me toward him, he cups my cheeks and caresses my lips, sending jolts of electricity through my entire body.

The singer reappears and strums his ukulele to the tune of "I Won't Give Up" by Jason Mraz—our song—and begins to sing.

Maddox takes a bow and reaches for my hand. "Annalise Rose Monroe, may I have this dance?"

Smiling, I pinch the sides of my gown and curtsy. "You may."

The stars twinkle in the sky as we stare lovingly into each other's eyes and sway to the beat.

Maddox twirls me around and brings me back to his chest, nuzzling his face in my hair. "I missed being able to slow dance with you."

"I did, too. We haven't danced together since senior year, when we won prom king and queen."

"And now I have my queen in my arms again," he says, causing my smile to widen. "I hope you had a great birthday, Annalise."

"This has been the best birthday I've ever had. And it's not because of the gifts or this trip. It's because I got to spend it with you."

His warm brown eyes sparkle under the soft glow of the moonlight and his dimples carve hollows into his cheeks. "I plan on spending the rest of your birthdays with you, Rosie."

He plants a kiss on forehead, the warmth of his lips lingering as I nestle my head against his broad chest. I breathe him in, wanting to savor this moment.

CHAPTER 38
Maddox

"How was Hawaii?" Okāsan asks as she places the spread of sushi rolls and sashimi in front of me. "It was beautiful," I say. And the food was so delicious."

Okāsan glares at me and I slink down in my seat. Grabbing the chopsticks, I pop a piece of sashimi in my mouth. "But not as good as yours!"

She smiles and settles into the chair next to me.

"Did you take surfing lessons?" Asami asks.

"We did. And I got my ass whooped by the waves. My dignity was taken away."

I thought with me being an athlete, I would be a little better at it, but I was clearly wrong. I could tell our surfing instructor was trying to hold back from laughing when I kept falling. Annalise was a lot more graceful than I was and managed to stay on the board for a longer period of time.

"Please tell me you have videos of this." Asami laughs.

Scrolling through my phone, I show my family the video of my failed attempt at surfing. Okāsan and Asami burst into giggles, and Otōsan's lips twitch into a small smile.

"Did you go whale watching?" Okāsan asks.

I nod. "It was a phenomenal experience. It was so hard leaving Kauai. I was tempted to retire early and move there."

Asami slips a piece of sashimi in her mouth. "You should've invited Annalise over for dinner tonight. I miss her."

A big grin takes over my face. "You'll see her tomorrow at the game."

Excitement builds within me at the thought of seeing her in my jersey tomorrow while she cheers me on. When we were in high school, her presence in the crowd always eased my nerves and gave me the confidence to perform my best.

Asami lets out a squeal and her eyes light up. She and Annalise were very close when we were together, but lost touch once we split. I know Asami is more than thrilled to rekindle their friendship.

"I can't wait to see her! Watching your games will be less boring now."

I roll my eyes. "Okay, says the girl that's on the edge of her seat during the entire game."

"I'm so happy we will get to see Annalise more now." Okāsan squeezes my shoulder. "Make sure you bring her over for dinner next time."

"Yeah—we don't care about seeing you, we wanna see her!" Asami reaches for the last big piece of sashimi, but I beat her to it.

"Hey, you greedy ass!"

I shrug. "I have a big game tomorrow. Need to make sure I eat enough to build up my energy."

"How are you feeling about the game tomorrow, Masashi?" Okāsan asks.

"I'm pretty nervous, but I have a lot of faith in my team. We play against LA first, so I think we have a good chance of advancing to the next round."

"You will, Masashi," she says, smiling widely. "The championship is yours this year! I just know it."

Swallowing, my eyes flicker to Otōsan. "Otōsan, will you, um, come to my game? It's the first time in a decade that the Dragons have advanced to playoffs. It would mean a lot to me if you were there."

Otōsan reaches for a glass of water and gulps it down. My stomach twists in knots as I wait for his response.

He pushes his glasses up the bridge of his nose. "I can't. Kamado Tech is about to release our new VR. There's still a lot of work that needs to be done."

"Of fucking course," I mutter under my breath.

I thought that with me playing for our hometown, and with it being the playoffs, he would change his mind—but I was wrong. I feel like a fucking idiot for even asking him.

Okāsan narrows her eyes at him, her arms folded across her chest. "Can't you spare a couple of hours to be there for your son?"

"It's okay, Okāsan," I say, rising from my seat. "I don't even know why I bothered asking. Nothing will ever be more important to him than his job."

Otōsan clears his throat. "That's not true. I have a deadline to meet. You have to understand."

Heat crawls up my spine. I am beyond fed up with his excuses. "When are you going to accept the fact that I have no desire to take over your company? You supported Asami. Why can't you do the same for me?"

Asami gets up from her seat and scratches the back of her neck. "I'm gonna use the bathroom…"

"You never thought I'd make it to the NBA, but I did. I fought for every inch of it. Basketball was never just a hobby for me. It's my passion. My purpose." All of the anger I've kept bottled up for years erupts at this moment. "You know how much it means to me, yet you've never showed up for a single one of my games!" My voice trembles, cracked and raw. "Why am I not good enough for you?" The words hang heavy in the air.

Otōsan stares down at his plate and remains silent.

Walking over to Okāsan, I plant a kiss on her cheek. "Thanks for dinner. I'll see you tomorrow. *Daisuki*, Okāsan."

"*Daisuki*, Masashi," she says softly.

I storm out of my parents' house and slam the door behind me. Pulling out my phone, I call the one person who always makes me feel better.

"Hey, can you come over? I need to see you."

"What happened, Maddox?" Annalise runs her fingers through my hair as I rest my head on her lap.

"I got into it with my dad." I let out a sigh. "I asked him to come to my game tomorrow. He used work as an excuse, like always."

"Has he attended any of your games since you joined the league?"

"Nope." I clutch a pillow as the heat rises in me. "I thought he would take me seriously when I played ball in college, but he didn't. Then I thought he would start supporting me now that I'm in the NBA, but he still hasn't shown up to a single fucking game."

I stare up at the ceiling, blinking away the hot, angry tears that threaten to spill.

Her brows knit together, a scowl appearing on her face. "He's ridiculous! You're literally the number-one player in the league and so freaking successful. I don't understand what his problem is."

"I guess he's still upset with me about not wanting to take over Kamado Tech, but I want nothing to do with it. I don't want to carry on his legacy. I want to build my own." I sit up straighter, fingers twisting in my lap as a tear slides down my cheek. "I don't know what else to do to prove my worth to him. All I ever wanted was for him to be supportive of me the way he's supportive of my sister."

She reaches over and gently swipes the tear away with her thumb. "For what it's worth, I'm incredibly proud of you. I remember those thrilling nights watching you play in high school. And now I get to witness your dream come true as you take the court in the NBA for the team you've always wanted to be a part of."

My heart swells with warmth, and the anger that once consumed me starts to dissipate.

"You may have grown up with a silver spoon in your mouth, but you busted your ass to get where you are now," she continues. "Many people would've given up, but you never did. I truly admire your strength. I always have. It's one of your best qualities. Screw your dad for not seeing how extraordinary you are."

"God, I love you so much." Wrapping her in my arms, I place a kiss on her temple. "Thank you for always being there for me, Rosie. It truly means a lot to me. When I have kids of my own, I'm going to let them be whoever they want and do whatever it is that makes them happy."

Annalise places a gentle kiss on my lips. "You're gonna make an amazing father one day, Dimples."

CHAPTER 39
Annalise

I descend the stairs of the Golden Gate Center with Oliver and we maneuver through the crowd to get to our seats. The arena is filled with fans wearing red San Francisco Dragons T-shirts and donning jerseys of their favorite players. The majority sport Maddox's number, twenty-four.

As we approach our row, Asami spots us and her face lights up. "Annalise! Oh my God!"

She rushes toward me, pulling me into a tight hug and squeezing me so hard I feel like my insides are going to burst. "It's so good to see you."

"It's good to see you too, Asami."

"We have so much catching up to do!" She turns to Ollie and gives him a wave. "Hey, Oliver! Didn't recognize you for a second. You've doubled in size."

He smiles shyly and gives her a wave.

"Hi, Annalise and Oliver!" Izumi says as we walk toward our seats.

"Hi, Mrs. Kamado," I say, pulling her into a hug.

"Masashi is going to be happy to see you. I bet he will score a lot of points tonight because of you." A broad grin lights up Izumi's face.

Chuckling, I take my seat next to Asami. "So, Maddox told me you got engaged! Let me see the ring!"

She holds out her left hand, and her gorgeous emerald-cut ring sparkles beneath the light.

"Wow, he did a good job. It is stunning!"

"Soon you'll have a ring on your finger, too." Izumi smiles, lifting her brows.

"Okāsan, they *just* got back together." Asami groans, rolling her eyes.

I smile to myself as I picture Maddox getting down on one knee. "So, who's the lucky guy?"

"His name is Hotaru. He's an associate at Jin and Simmons Law Firm." Scrolling through her phone, she pulls up a picture of the two of them in Paris.

"Wow, he is dreamy. You two make a lovely couple!"

"Thank you. So do you and my brother. Even though you're way better looking than he is."

A chuckle erupts from my chest. "So, what else is new with you?"

"I passed my boards recently, and I'm now a licensed dermatologist. I started working with Dr. Eun-ji Bae a couple of weeks ago, and she has been such an incredible mentor."

"That's wonderful, Asami!" I beam. "Do you plan on opening your own clinic one day?"

"Yes, that's the plan! I'd also like to develop my own skin-care products."

"I can totally see that becoming a huge success!"

"You think so?" She rubs the back of her neck.

"Oh, for sure. Success runs in the Kamado family." I smile.

Asami chuckles. "So, how's everything going with your online shop? All the clothes you have on there are so cute! I need to order everything."

"It's going pretty well!" I reply, a grin spreading across my face. "I thought it would take me a while to get orders in, but I shipped out items to ten different customers yesterday, and I've already got a few new orders today. I'm really hoping they leave good reviews. That would give my shop a big boost."

"Girl, I'm sure they will leave you raving reviews. You are talented as hell," she says, flashing me a warm smile.

"Thank you, Asami. If only I could quit my job so I can focus on my shop. Working at Dauntless leaves me drained." I let out a groan and slump back in my seat.

Asami squeezes my hand. "I can only imagine. One day, you will be able to leave that place and be your own boss."

A few months ago, I thought I was stuck working at this dead-end job, and had accepted the fact that I would never become a fashion designer. But now, my future is looking bright again. My shop is growing every day, and my passion for creating clothes has come back.

Maddox's constant encouragement reminds me of what I am capable of and has brought back my confidence. He's silenced the voices in my head that were telling me to give up on my dreams.

Those dreams once felt so far out of reach, but now I feel myself getting closer to making them a reality.

The lights dim and red strobe lights dance across the floor.

"Everybody, get on your feet and make some noise for your *San Francisco Draaagooonsss*!" the announcer bellows.

"All I Do Is Win" by DJ Khaled blasts from the speakers, and the announcer introduces the starting five players as they come out one by one.

"Everyone, get loud for number twenty-four, your shooting guard and MVP, Maddox Kamado!"

The energy in the crowd is palpable, and the whole arena fills with chants of his name.

"I love you, Maddox!" someone shouts.

"Have my babies!" another voice calls out.

"He is so hot," a girl sitting behind me says.

"I know. I wish I was a basketball so I could be touched by him."

I let out a snicker and Asami sticks her finger in her mouth, making a gagging sound.

I don't blame them. Maddox looks extremely hot in his uniform. It shows off his large biceps and muscular legs. How lucky am I to have him all to myself?

Maddox scans the crowd and when his eyes land on me, he flashes me his infectious dimpled smile. I smile back at him, giving him a thumbs up and mouthing "good luck."

He shoots me a wink and I instantly become flustered.

Ollie gives me a look. "You two are gross."

I shove him playfully. "Don't be a hater."

The game begins, and Darius and the center from Los Angeles stand in the middle, preparing for tip-off.

Darius leaps in the air, knocking the ball in the Dragons' possession. Elijah catches it and passes it to Maddox.

The players from Los Angeles surround him but he quickly maneuvers through them, making his way toward the goal.

One of the players is onto him but he fakes left, shooting the ball from the three-point line. The ball swishes through the net, earning the Dragons their first goal.

"Hell yeah! Let's go, Maddox!" I jump up and down excitedly, clapping my hands and cheering him on with the others.

He blows me a kiss as he jogs past me.

"Oh my God! I think I'm going to faint! Maddox Kamado just blew me a kiss," the fangirl behind me screams.

Asami and I shake with laughter.

Adrenaline pumps through my veins as the game continues. The Dragons are demolishing Los Angeles, and they have a twenty-point lead by halftime.

I watched Maddox play countless times when we were

together, and I was always in awe of how unbelievably talented he is. Seeing him today, playing with the pros, fills me with pride and leaves me speechless. He dominates the court, and you can see the fire and passion in his eyes. Every shot, block, and pass he makes is executed effortlessly.

He is the king, and the court is his kingdom. Maddox Kamado is a force to be reckoned with and will become a legend one day.

San Francisco blew LA out of the water, beating them by thirty-five points. I wait for the crowd to clear before making my way to the court to where Maddox is standing.

"You were amazing out there, Dimples." I throw my arms around him and nearly kiss him before realizing we aren't alone.

"You were my good-luck charm," Maddox says, causing blush to spread across my cheeks.

"Hey, Maddox! You killed it out there," Ollie says.

"Hey, Ollie! Thank you so much for coming." Maddox gives him a side hug. "You need to try out for your school's team next year. Maybe one day we can play together on this court."

"Won't you be retired by then?" Ollie teases, earning a chuckle amongst the team.

"Hey! I'm not that old!" Maddox glares at him.

Elijah throws his arms around Maddox's shoulders. "You're gonna be a veteran by then."

"We're the same age." Maddox rolls his eyes.

"Thanks for showing up tonight, Annalise. He would've played like shit if you hadn't been here," Andrés teases.

I chuckle. "Oh, I'm sure he would've played fine. But it was a great game. I think y'all will be able to sweep LA."

Elijah leaves Maddox's side and walks over to Asami.

"Asami, baby. Thanks for coming out to support me." He flashes her a cheeky grin.

Asami rolls her eyes. "I did not come here for you."

Elijah taps his chin. "That's funny, because I could feel your eyes on me during the entire game. Bet you were impressed by the shots I made."

Asami scrunches her face and holds up her left hand. "I'm engaged, you moron."

"To the wrong man. I can give you everything he can't," Elijah drawls.

Andrés scrubs his hand down his face. "Oh, God, I'm getting secondhand embarrassment."

"Elijah, leave my sister alone. Go terrorize someone else."

Elijah chuckles and stalks off to the locker room, blowing Asami a kiss on the way out.

Asami shudders. "Remind me why you're best friends with this guy."

Maddox shakes his head. "I ask myself that every day."

"I'm going to drop Ollie off, but I'll see you tonight," I whisper.

"Can't wait." He lightly brushes his hand against mine on his way to the locker room.

Izumi pulls me in for a hug. "Please come by for dinner next week. I'll be happy to have you."

"You know I'll be there. I can never turn down your food." I turn to Asami and give her a hug. "It was so nice catching up with you again. We need to hang out soon."

"Oh, yes, please! Let me know the next time you're free!" Asami says.

I'm walking toward the exit with Ollie when I feel a tap on my shoulder.

I turn around to see Lucas standing before me.

"Hey, Annalise." He smiles. "How are you?"

Anger courses through my veins when I think about what he said about me.

"How are you? Really?" I let out a short, bitter laugh. "You think you can just strike up a casual conversation as if nothing happened?"

Lucas furrows his brow. "I'm not following."

I shake my head. "I thought you were my friend. I can't believe I was so blind."

He continues to stare at me, dumbfounded. "What are you talking about? We *are* friends."

"If we were friends, you wouldn't have gone around telling everyone how you can't wait to find out how good I am in bed!" I snap, my face flushing with anger.

His face pales. "Did Kamado tell you that? Because it's not true." Lucas grabs my arm. "I care about you, Annalise. I would never disrespect you like that."

I yank my arm away. "Oh, cut the bullshit, Lucas! You always act like you're such a good person, but you're not. I finally see you for who you really are. A pathetic, selfish man who's always been jealous of Maddox."

"*Me*, jealous of *him*?" He lets out a laugh. "He's the one who's jealous. That's why he's making up these lies. I mean, look how he acted when he saw us at dinner together. Don't you see how toxic and controlling he is?"

"Toxic? Why don't you take a long, hard look in the mirror? You are the *epitome* of toxic," I say, my voice sharp with anger.

Grabbing Ollie's arm, I tug him toward the exit. "Come on. Let's go home."

"You must have zero self-respect if you plan on getting back with that womanizing asshole," he spat.

Something in me snaps. All those years when he talked shit about my man, I let it slide. But I'm not going to do that this time.

Spinning around, I march toward him and slap him across the

face. "*You* are the one with zero self-respect. Stop spreading lies about Maddox and work on yourself."

Lucas holds his cheek, staring back at me in shock.

"And don't ever speak to me again," I add before storming off.

As we exit the arena, Ollie whispers to me, "Wow. That was awesome."

I smile to myself, feeling liberated after finally doing what I should've done years ago.

"You slapped him?" Maddox asks, wearing an amused grin on his face.

"Yeah. I made sure to slap him hard, too." A smile blooms on my face when I think about the red mark I left on Lucas's cheek.

"I'm mad that I missed it. I would've paid money to see that. Maybe I can ask the security guards to give me the footage…"

A loud laugh escapes me. "Well, I hope he'll leave us alone after this."

"Oh, I'm sure he will. I'd be pretty damn embarrassed if I were him. I wouldn't be surprised if he moves far away from San Francisco after this."

"I don't understand what his problem is," I say, shaking my head.

"He's obsessed with you. He's upset that he will never have you. I don't blame him. I know I would be." Maddox wraps his arms around my waist and places a kiss on my temple.

My fingers twist the blanket in my lap. "I don't know. I feel like his hatred for you runs deeper than that."

He cocks his head to the side. "What would be the reason, then? I mean, I'm only an asshole to him because I'm just giving him back the same energy he gives me. But I've never spread rumors about him like he did with me."

"I don't know…" My voice trails off.

"Do you want to watch a romcom with me?" I ask, changing the subject.

"I'm always in the mood for romcoms." He grins.

I reach in my pocket to put my phone on silent when a notification catches my eye: *Raven Vogel tagged you in a reel.*

My heart lurches and my hands shake as I click on the notification.

Raven Vogel has over a million followers and is a big-time fashion influencer. Her platform consists of videos and photos of her in stunning outfits. She often promotes different brands to help them grow.

The reel begins to play.

"You guys, I think I found my new favorite shop. Look how cute this dress is!" She twirls in front of the camera, showing off my blush midi dress.

"Oh, shit. Is that one of the dresses you made?" Maddox asks, glancing at my phone.

I nod excitedly. "Yes! And the video already has so many comments and likes."

Raven continues to show off the other items she bought from my shop while raving about them. *"The price is so affordable for how good the quality is. Make sure you check out Thorny Roses. You can find the link to the clothes I bought in my bio."*

I go back to my Instagram profile and see that I've had a surge of new followers.

"That's my girl!" Maddox beams. "I'm so proud of you, Rosie." He drops a kiss to my lips and my heart swells.

I've been so used to things going wrong—but with Maddox back in my life and my shop flourishing more than I ever imagined, I finally feel like I'm on the right path.

I just pray that this happiness doesn't get snatched away from me.

CHAPTER 40
Maddox

Los Angeles is giving it their all tonight. We have won the last three games, and if they lose this one, they'll be eliminated from the playoffs. We were in the lead until the third quarter of the game, but they caught up to us and we're currently tied.

The time on shot clock is ticking down, and we need to make some moves to break the tie and send them home.

Kingsley Ross leaps up for a two-pointer, but Darius blocks it clean, sending the ball flying across the court. I sprint after it, snatching the ball before the other team can get to it and racing across the court.

Quickly scanning my surroundings, I spot Elijah positioned near the goal and launch the ball his way. He catches it seamlessly and executes an effortless Euro step, sinking the ball into the net.

A player from LA scrambles toward the ball and attempts to make it to the other side in time, but the buzzer goes off—securing our victory.

"Fuck yeah!" I shout, pumping my fist in the air,

"We're going to the conference semifinals, baby!" Andrés cheers.

Elijah does a celebratory dance and removes his jersey, twirling it in the air, which elicits excited screams from several women.

My eyes land on Annalise and my stomach does somersaults. Her hair is pulled back into a ponytail, and she's wearing my jersey and a massive smile on her face. It takes all my willpower not to run over and kiss her in front of everyone.

Seeing her in the crowd, cheering me on while I play, gives me strength. I feel invincible.

"You played well tonight," a deep voice says from behind me.

I turn around and come face-to-face with the legend himself —Kyrie Lyons.

"Mr. Lyons, w-what an honor. Thank you."

Kyrie has been in attendance at some of the regular-season games and all the games during the playoffs, but this is the first time he's approached me.

Back when I was in high school, I had the chance to meet him during a meet and greet, and I was a complete nervous wreck—which is exactly how I'm feeling now.

I no longer feel like the confident shooting guard who just won a big game.

"You can call me Kyrie. Calling me *mister* makes me feel old. I may be retired, but I'm only in my forties."

He lets out a chuckle and I join him, relaxing a little.

"You made a lot of noise during your rookie year," he says. "I remember when I saw you on TV. I was like hey, I know that kid!"

My eyes widen in shock. "Wait—you remember meeting me?"

He nods. "Sure do. Your ambitious nature made quite the impression on me."

"I can't believe you remember me. That was so long ago."

"I've been rooting for you ever since. Your talent will take you far, and the Dragons are lucky to have someone like you on their team."

The corners of my mouth lift into a big grin, and prides washes over me.

I can't believe I received a compliment from Kyrie freaking Lyons.

"Wow. That means a lot coming from you."

"Keep up the good work and bring home that championship." He pats me on the back.

"I will, sir."

We reserved Blackout tonight to celebrate our win. The entire team is here, joined by their closest friends and significant others.

The only person that's missing is Lucas. I think he knows better and chose to stay away—especially after what happened with Annalise. If only I could have been there to witness her slapping him across the face.

Annalise walks in with Mazikeen following closely behind her. She looks absolutely ravishing in her tight black dress.

"Hey, Rosie." I wrap my arms around her, pulling her into an embrace while resisting the urge to kiss her. The other guys on our team suspected we were together when they saw her at the first playoff game, but I have neither confirmed nor denied it.

"Hey, Dimples." She flashes me a smile, causing my heart to skip a beat.

"Hi, Maddox." Mazikeen gives me a small smile and waves.

I blink twice. "Wait. You're actually speaking to me without sounding hostile?"

She rolls her eyes. "Look, Kamado. I just want to apologize

for being a complete and total bitch to you. I shouldn't have judged you for who you were before you dated Annalise. I know you care a lot about her, and I can see how happy you make her."

I never thought I'd see the day where Mazikeen Rivera would be nice to me—let alone apologize to me. I had won over Annalise's family and wanted her best friend to like me as well, but I had accepted that it might never happen. The fact that she was finally willing to accept me means a lot.

"I appreciate the apology, Mazikeen. Perhaps we can start over."

I extend my hand to her to call a truce, and she shakes it.

"I would like that."

"Aw!" Annalise places her hand on her cheek. "Look at my best friend and my boyfriend finally getting along."

I let out a laugh.

Mazikeen narrows her eyes and points a finger at me. "But if you ever break her heart, I will fucking crush your skull."

She's a whole foot shorter than me, but she still terrifies me.

I wrap my arm around Annalise's waist. "Trust me—that'll never happen."

"Oh, shit. It's like a high school reunion." Elijah approaches us, wearing a goofy grin on his face.

"What's up, Rivera? Long time, no see." He throws his arm around Mazikeen's shoulders.

She makes a face and shrugs him off.

"Dang. Are you still only into women?" he asks.

"No, I still like men too. You're just not my type," she says, smoothing her hand down the front of her dress.

Elijah blows air out of his cheeks. "Oh, whatever. I'm *every-one's* type."

"If that were the case, then why are you the only player here without a date?" Mazikeen gestures around us. Every single player, besides Elijah, has a woman in their arms tonight.

"It is odd that you didn't show up with anyone. Does this

mean you're done fucking around and ready to get into a committed relationship?" I ask, cocking a brow.

Elijah lets out a snort. "You're not even drunk yet, and you're already spewing bullshit. Don't count on me going on double dates with you anytime soon."

He refocuses his attention to Mazikeen. "And for your information, I had several options tonight. I couldn't make a decision."

She lets out a disgusted groan. "I'm gonna need some alcohol in me to survive a night being around this idiot."

He rolls his eyes and motions for the server to come to us.

The server pours us a round of shots and we all raise our glasses. "To success! And to friendships!" Elijah cheers.

We clink our glasses together in unison and down the shots.

"Let's take a photo together to remember this moment!" Annalise smiles and takes her phone out of her purse.

Since I'm the tallest one out of the group, I'm in charge of capturing the photo. We all crowd together and I snap the pic.

"Aw, it's just like old times," Elijah says.

"We were never friends in high school." Mazikeen groans.

"We can become friends…" A devilish grin slides across his face. "With benefits."

"Not gonna happen, Callahan," she mutters, rolling her eyes.

I pinch the bridge of my nose. "Bro, can you go the rest of the night without hitting on someone?"

He lets out a laugh. "I just love annoying her."

I shake my head and wave at the server to order more drinks.

After sharing a few more drinks and laughter with our friends, Annalise and I move to the dance floor. My hands are on her hips as we move in sync with the beat.

The way she's moving her body has me growing hard against her.

Amused by the effect she has on me, she presses her ass farther back, causing a curse to leave my lips.

Brushing her hair to the side, I bring my lips near her ear. "Are you trying to make me fuck you in the middle of the dance floor?"

"Maybe," she whispers in a low, seductive tone while continuing to rub her ass against my straining cock.

The club is dark, and everyone else is too preoccupied to pay us any mind.

Moving my hands up, I cup her breasts, and she lets out a gasp. She moans quietly as I roll her nipples with my fingers.

Then I trail a hand down to her inner thigh, slowly sliding it upward. Her breath hitches when my hand reaches the hem of her dress.

After checking again to make sure no one is watching, I slide my hand farther up, rubbing her over her already soaked panties.

My hands move faster, and she grows wetter with every stroke.

Pushing her panties aside, I trace the heat of her, my fingers quickly slick with her desire.

My fingers rub tight circles over her swollen clit, and she bites down on her bottom lip to suppress her moans.

I slip a finger inside her drenched pussy with ease, moving it in and out slowly. "Do you enjoy this? Being finger-fucked out in the open where anyone can see?"

"*Yes*," she moans. I add another finger, pumping them fast. "Oh, Maddox! That feels so good."

Plunging my fingers deeper, I rub them against her walls and she grips the back of my neck to brace herself.

Using my thumb, I stimulate her clit while my fingers thrust inside her. I can tell she's getting close by the way her legs tremble and her breathing becomes erratic.

I continue to pleasure her until she comes on my fingers, her arousal dripping down her thighs.

Removing my fingers from her, I readjust her dress. Her eyes darken as she watches me lick them clean.

I take her hand and pull her away from the dance floor, leading her into an empty restroom. A sly smile spreads across her lips when I lock the door behind us. Thankfully, the club has individual private restrooms, so I don't have to worry about anyone walking in and seeing what I'm about to do to her.

"I can't go another minute without being inside you. I need you now." Grabbing the back of her head, my hands tangle in her hair as I crush my lips against hers.

She kisses me back with hunger, thrusting her tongue inside my mouth while she fumbles with my belt buckle.

Her hands dip inside my briefs and she strokes my hard length.

"*Fuck…*" I hiss against her lips.

I pull down the front of her dress and lower my mouth, sucking her hardened nipples.

Turning her around, I push her against the counter and slide her panties off.

I keep my eyes locked on hers in the mirror as I position the head of my cock near her wet entrance.

Grabbing her ass, I slowly push myself inside, groaning in pleasure when I feel her wetness wrap around me.

I pull out of her and then drive my length inside her all at once.

Her loud moans bounce off the walls as I pick up the pace of my thrusts. She moves her ass back, matching my rhythm.

"I love watching you fuck me," she says, gazing at our reflection in the restroom mirror.

"Yeah? I love it too, baby." Fisting her hair, I yank her head back and hammer into her, driving myself deeper with each thrust.

"Oh, fuck, Maddox!" she cries out, her knuckles whitening around the counter. "Don't stop!"

I let out a groan, feeling my balls tighten as I watch myself pound into her tight pussy. The sound of her moans and the faces she makes is bringing me closer to the edge.

I continue to move inside her, and when her walls clamp down on my dick, I'm a goner.

"Fuck, Annalise!" I collapse onto her, my fingers gripping her ass as I flood her pussy with my release.

After we get cleaned up and do our best to make ourselves look presentable, we head back out to mingle with our friends.

"What were you two up to?" Elijah lifts his brows, smiling at us knowingly.

"Just exploring other parts of the club," I say.

"More like exploring Annalise," Mazikeen chimes in. "Next time y'all fuck in public, put a gag on her. We could hear her moaning over the loud music."

Heat flames Annalise's cheeks and I let out a cough.

"W-wait what? Are you serious?" Annalise says, her eyes flicking from Mazikeen to Elijah.

They both laugh hysterically, earning an eye roll from Annalise and me.

"Y'all make it so damn obvious." Elijah shakes his head, taking a sip out of his drink.

"I need to pee." Mazikeen gets up from her seat. "Which one did y'all fuck in, so I can avoid it?"

"Honestly, I wasn't paying attention." I look at Annalise, grinning.

She lets out a soft chuckle and Mazikeen wrinkles her nose.

"You two are gross."

"A little more to the left. *Yes*, that's the spot. Oh, fuck, that hurts." I grunt as Annalise digs her thumb into my shoulder, releasing the tight knot.

Tomorrow night is the first game of the conference semifinals, and we're facing off against Seattle. Their star player, Thomas Everett, is a fucking beast on the court, and beating Seattle will be way more challenging than LA.

I've been overdoing it during practice, and the large knot that formed on my shoulder has been causing discomfort to my arms and neck.

"Does that feel better?" she asks, plopping down next to me on the couch.

I roll my shoulders back. "Yes, much better. Thank you." Pulling her close, I plant a kiss on her cheek.

She rests her head on my shoulder, threading her fingers through mine. "How are you feeling about the game tomorrow night?"

"My stress levels have been through the roof." I blow air out of my cheeks. "The first round was a breeze, but Seattle will give us a run for our money."

I let out a heavy sigh, fixing my gaze on my lap. "There's been so much weight on my shoulders lately. If we get eliminated after this round, I'm going to be so disappointed in myself."

"Have you forgotten who you are?" She arches a brow, folding her arms over her chest.

I lift my eyes to meet hers.

"You are Maddox *freaking* Kamado. This is only your second year in the NBA, and look at how much you've achieved. You are the number-one player in the league, you're in the running for MVP, and the Dragons have advanced to the playoffs for the first time in decades—because of *you*."

Tsuki scoots onto my lap and barks.

"See? Even Tsuki agrees with me," she says, rubbing the fluffy Samoyed's head.

I let out a small chuckle as my worries fade away and my mood lifts. "Thanks for always believing in me, Rosie."

"Always." She kisses me softly on the lips.

"What do you feel like watching?" I ask, grabbing the remote.

She glances at the time on her phone. "Ooh! *The Scoop* should be on right now!"

The Scoop is a talk show hosted by Zoey Hartman. She is the main source for the latest celebrity gossip and scandals.

I let out a groan. "I'd rather watch a scary movie than listen to Zoey Hartman talk."

She cocks her brow. "Oh? So we can watch *The Ring*?"

"Oh, fuck no! That gave me nightmares for years."

She chuckles, and I flip through the channel to find her requested show.

"I wonder if she's gonna give us an update about what's going on with S.T.O.R.M."

S.T.O.R.M. is a pop group consisting of five women—Sasha, Tori, Olivia, Rainey, and Morgan. The rest of their world tour was recently canceled, and people are speculating that Rainey slept with Sasha's boyfriend.

I only know this because Annalise told me—I never keep up with celebrity gossip. I've only caught snippets of *The Scoop* when she mentioned it, or when photos of me with an actress— or some other celebrity—got leaked.

Thankfully, I haven't been the subject of her conversations as of late.

"Good evening, everyone! Welcome to *The Scoop!*" The crowd cheers as Zoey struts onto the stage wearing a hot-pink dress.

"Tonight, I've got the *juiciest* gossip of the season—so buckle up." She flashes a sly smile, clearly savoring the moment.

I relax a little—until the giant screen behind her flickers to life.

A massive photo of *me* fills the screen.

I spoke too soon.

"What the fuck?" I jolt upright, heart hammering.

"The most eligible bachelor, Maddox Kamado, who is notorious for his skills both on and off the court…" Zoey says, pausing for dramatic effect. I can feel my heart racing and I glance over at Annalise, who is nervously chewing on her fingernails.

"…is officially off the market!" Zoey declares, grinning.

The photo of me then fades away, replaced by another image that drains all the color from my face. On the screen behind her is a photo of Annalise and me standing on the tarmac next to my private jet, kissing passionately.

And, just like that, our relationship has been exposed to the entire world.

CHAPTER 41
Annalise

Nausea swells in the pit of my stomach when I think about how my privacy will be violated. I knew it was only a matter of time before the secret was out. Maddox is a world-famous basketball star and almost everything he does is documented. Those private, intimate moments we shared really helped us rebuild our relationship, and I wanted to savor them with him for a while longer.

Loud gasps ripple through the crowd as Zoey reveals the photo.

"I know—I was shocked, too. I'm sad I'm not the one he's settling down with." Zoey sighs and the crowd roars with laughter.

"Maddox has never been seen traveling with another woman, so it must be serious. Sources are saying the girl in the photo is his high school sweetheart, Annalise Monroe."

"Oh, this is a fucking disaster." I lean back, scrubbing my hand down my face. "You don't think it was anyone from your cabin crew, do you?"

Maddox flicks off the TV. "I hope not. It took a while for me to find a good crew. I'd hate to fire them. But it could've been anyone… People are aware that I have a private jet. I'll talk to my publicist to see if she can find out who's behind this."

"What if we were followed on our other dates, too? What if they took photos of us skinny dipping?" My pulse races, my palms slick with sweat as the possibility of those photos being leaked crosses my mind.

Maddox shakes his head. "I don't think so. We were in the middle of nowhere. Plus, those photos would've been leaked a while ago." He reaches for my hand, giving it a squeeze. "You have nothing to worry about, Rosie."

"Nothing to worry about?" I stare at him in disbelief. "I have *everything* to worry about. I could lose my job."

Veronica's warning rings in my ears. *"Mr. Kamado is our client and having a sexual relationship with him is strictly prohibited. So unless you want to be out of a job, I highly suggest you refrain from getting involved with him."*

After Raven posted the viral video of the clothing she got from my shop, the number of orders I received tripled. But I still wasn't making enough to quit Dauntless—especially after subtracting the cost of the materials.

If I increased my prices, I would make a whole lot more, but I want my clothes to be affordable to everyone.

"I don't think Veronica will fire you over this. She needs an assistant, and I don't think anyone else could last as long as you have. It takes a special kind of person to be able to put up with her bullshit daily." Maddox grins.

I let out a small chuckle. "True. Ivy did say Veronica's previous assistants never lasted longer than a month."

Leaning forward, he kisses my forehead. "We'll get through this. It's us against the world."

"Hopefully it'll blow over soon." I sigh.

"Until it does, stay off social media. And no more watching *The Scoop*."

I did the opposite of staying away from social media. The moment I woke up, I grabbed my phone and scrolled through Instagram. Photos of us from high school have resurfaced, and the hashtag *maddalise* is currently trending. There are some positive comments talking about how we make such a cute couple, but amongst those are negative ones.

"What does he see in her? She's not even that pretty."

"She's probably a gold digger."

"Why is he with her? She's a nobody."

Heat rises in me as I scroll through all the comments.

Maddox stirs next to me and rubs his eyes. "Good morning, beautiful." He kisses me softly on my lips.

"Ugh, people are so rude!" I groan.

He peeks over at my screen and sees the comments.

"*Annaliiise,*" Maddox groans. "I told you to not look at those things." Grabbing my phone, he tucks it under the pillow.

I chew on the inside of my cheeks. "I can't help myself. I hate that people are saying these things about me."

"Don't pay attention to those trolls. They're nothing but losers hiding behind a keyboard," he says, trying to reassure me.

But all of those negative comments are getting to me. Maddox's hard work and talent is what made him famous, and I want the same for me, too. I want to be recognized for being a fashion designer, but now I fear that people will only ever see me as a famous basketball player's girlfriend.

They'll probably think that the only reason I become successful is because of him.

Everyone's eyes are on me, and indistinct whispers fill the room when I step into the office. Ever since our relationship leaked over the weekend, I've been dreading coming back to work.

I clear my throat and avoid their gazes as I walk to my desk.

"I'm kinda upset I found about this out online, and not from you," Ivy pouts. "I thought we were work besties."

"I'm sorry. Only a handful of people knew about it. I was still figuring things out between us and wanted to keep things private."

"I get it. But I kinda suspected there was something going on."

I raise a brow, intrigued. "How so?"

She smirks. "Well, for starters—he's hot as fuck. It was only a matter of time before you gave in. And don't act like I haven't seen the way you two sneak glances at each other when you think no one's watching. Pluuus"—she draws out the word, giving me a knowing look—"you've been in a *much* better mood lately. So, I figured it has to be because you're getting some good dick."

Blush creeps across my cheek. "*Ivyyy…*"

She lets out a laugh. "I'm very observant."

Veronica's door swings open, and my stomach twists into knots when her eyes land on me. I can feel the heat of her stare from across the room.

"Ms. Monroe. My office. Now."

Wiping my palms on my skirt, I try to focus on my breathing to prevent myself from losing it as I walk toward her.

When I enter her office, she slams the door behind us.

"I specifically told you not to have any kind of relationship with Mr. Kamado and you went and did it anyway!" Her face reddens with anger, the vein on her temple pulsating.

"I'm s-sorry, Ms. Zhang." I stare at the ground, unable to meet her eyes. "I can't help how I feel about him. I didn't expect this to happen."

She folds her arms across her chest. "So, what you're saying is that this job isn't important to you?"

"No, of course it's important to me! I am very grateful for this job and to be able to work for this company. You have been such a great boss."

Hearing my own words makes me want to throw up. Kissing Veronica Zhang's ass is the last thing I want to do.

"I should be firing you for insubordination," she snaps.

Bile rises in my throat and my chest tightens. I feel like I'm suffocating.

"But I'm not going to."

"You're not?" I stare at her, stunned, the words leaving my mouth before I can stop them.

She quirks a brow, cool and composed as ever. "I don't think Mr. Kamado would be too pleased if I fired his girlfriend. And the last thing I need is for him to pull out of this collaboration." Her voice is sharp, every syllable a warning. "Consider yourself lucky, Ms. Monroe. Because if it weren't for that deal, I wouldn't have even let you through the front doors this morning."

"Thank you. For, um… not firing me." I manage a weak smile, scratching the back of my neck.

She doesn't return the smile. Instead, she leans forward slightly, eyes narrowing. "Now that you're in the public eye, please avoid any scandals. If you do anything to ruin the reputation of Dauntless, I won't only fire you, but I'll make damn sure you never work in fashion again. Do I make myself clear?"

"Yes, Ms. Zhang," I reply, the oxygen finally returning to my lungs.

"Now, go and fetch me my coffee before I change my mind." Veronica shoos me off.

Nodding, I exit her office and pull my phone out to shoot Maddox a text.

Good news. I still have a job.

MADDOX

That's great! I knew it wouldn't happen.

She warned me not to get into any scandals or she'll fire me.

MADDOX

Damn. So I guess we can't fuck in her office again, huh? 😌

Lol def not.

MADDOX

My flight lands soon. Do you want to get some Italian tonight? I've been craving the pasta alla Trapanese from Louisa's. It's a bit far from my place, so it wouldn't taste the same once reheated.

You sure it's a good idea?

MADDOX

It'll be fine. It's a mom-and-pop shop. I've been there before and no one pays me any mind. They just let me eat in peace.

Okay. I'll see you tonight.

"See? I told you it would be nice and quiet here." Maddox pops a forkful of creamy pasta in his mouth. "You should learn to trust me more."

I thought our date would be full of interruptions—people approaching him for pictures or autographs—but, to my surprise, everyone keeps to themselves.

Occasionally I see a few people glance our way, but no one bothers us.

"I'm glad I'm able to fully enjoy my meal." Twirling my

fork, I take another bite of the delicious pasta. "So do you think y'all will be able to sweep Seattle, too?"

The Dragons won the last two games and will advance to the Western Conference Finals if they are able to win the next two— which would allow them more time to recover before the next round.

Maddox clicks his tongue. "I don't know. We've been neck and neck during the last two games, and never really had a big lead." He tilts his head back and groans. "I wish Chandler hadn't gotten injured. I hate admitting this, but Lucas isn't a bad player. It's just…"

"You don't trust him?" I add, finishing his thought.

"Yeah. There have been plenty of times when he's been wide open, but I refuse to pass it to him."

"Don't be too hard on yourself, babe," I say, my voice soft. "Anyone would act the same if they were in your position."

He releases a sigh. "I know, but I gotta learn to work with him if I want to win."

"So, what's the update on Chandler? Did they ever find out who hit him?"

"Unfortunately not. It's crazy that there was no camera footage from his accident. It's a pretty busy street, so you would think there would be."

I tear off a piece of bread and dip it in the pasta sauce. "Do you think maybe it wasn't an accident?"

Maddox lifts his brow. "What, like someone purposely hit him?"

I shrug. "Maybe whoever is behind it doesn't want the Dragons to win. I'm guessing whoever did it probably exposed our relationship too, in hopes that it would throw you off your game and make you lose."

He lets out a laugh, nearly choking on his food, "Okay, I think you watch wayyy too much TV. Now, I can't explain why someone exposed us, but I highly doubt those two things are correlated. Hit-and-runs are pretty common."

"I don't know what I would do if anything happened to you," I say, worry tightening in my chest. "Chandler got lucky, but it could've been worse."

Leaning forward, he kisses me on the cheek. "Nothing's going to happen to me, Rosie. You and I are both going to live long and healthy lives."

I offer him a smile but it doesn't reach my eyes. A gnawing unease twists in my gut, and no matter how hard I try, I can't shake the sense that something awful is looming just out of sight.

"How was everything?" Our waitress Gianna approaches, setting the check on the table.

"Oh, it was the best pasta I've ever had!" I gush. "I will definitely be coming back."

She gives me a smile. "I'm so glad to hear. Thank you for dining at Louisa's."

Maddox leaves a couple of hundred-dollar bills on the table as we exit the restaurant. When we turn the corner to head to the parking garage, paparazzi suddenly appear out of nowhere. The flashes from their cameras blind us as they bombard us with a flurry of questions.

"Maddox, is it true that you two are expecting?"

"What? Where are they getting this from?" I whisper to Maddox.

"Did your parents force you two to break up back then because she didn't come from a wealthy family?" another reporter asks.

"No, now if you will excuse us…" Wrapping his arm around my waist, Maddox tries to push through, but they continue to crowd us.

"Annalise, are you only with Maddox for his money and fame?"

My fists clench at my side and heat spreads through me like

wildfire. I want to grab their cameras and smash them on the ground, but I remember what Veronica said about getting involved in any scandals. I need to protect my image.

"Annalise, did you come up with a plan to win him back when you found out he's in the NBA?"

"Enough!" Maddox shouts. His booming voice demands authority and they quiet down.

He grabs a microphone from one of them. "And to clear up this false narrative you all keep spreading, *I* was the one who pursued *her*. The moment I saw her again, I realized that I'd never stopped loving her, and that I had to win her back. Letting her go was the biggest mistake I ever made."

His lips swoop down to meet mine, and the moment our lips touch, everything around us disappears. The shouts from the paparazzi and the clicks from their camera fade away in the distance.

CHAPTER 42
Maddox

The video of me speaking outside the restaurant and kissing Annalise went viral. Everyone around the world is shipping us, and people are calling us the "it couple."

I've even had fans message me to say our love story inspired them and gave them the courage to go after "the one that got away."

Annalise's shop has been blowing up, and she's been working overtime to keep up with orders. With our crazy schedules, we haven't had much time to go on dates.

But to me, any time I get to spend with her is valuable—even if I'm just helping her pack orders, like I am now.

Building the office for her was one of the best decisions I ever made. I love coming home to her after a long, grueling day of practice. I gave her the code to my house after we got back from Hawaii, and she's been spending almost every night here since then. Every now and then she'll go back to her apartment to spend time with Mazikeen.

With her around, my house finally feels like a home.

She passes me a pile of clothes and I carefully place them inside a box and seal it with packing tape.

"That should be the last of it." She gets up from the floor, rubbing her back. "My whole body hurts. I think I overdid it. Thanks for helping me, Maddox. I'm sure this is the last thing you want to do after coming home from practice."

Getting up, I place a kiss on her lips. "I don't mind at all. I love being able to help you. Seeing how much your shop is flourishing makes me so happy. I'll continue to be your assistant until you open your own physical store and get some official help—which will be soon, at the rate you're going."

I wish I could buy her a space for a boutique so she can finally leave Dauntless. But I know that's something she wants to do on her own, and I have faith that she will make it happen.

She fidgets with the hem of her shirt. "What if people are only buying my clothes because I'm your girlfriend? I'm worried that once we're no longer a hot topic, they'll stop."

"We will *always* be a hot topic," I say, smiling at her. "But you being my girlfriend has nothing to do with the success of your shop. That's all you. I mean, would you purchase clothes you didn't like just because they were made by a famous person's girlfriend?"

She shakes her head, making a face. "Hell no. That would be a waste of money."

"Exactly." Taking her hand, I lead her to the bathroom. "Come on. Let's go take a bath."

The limo pulls up to Annalise's apartment and I shoot her a text to let her know we're outside. We defeated Seattle after six games and have advanced to the Western Conference Finals. I can't believe we are *that* much closer to the championship.

The limo door opens, and Annalise slides in with Mazikeen

and their friend Serena. Annalise has brought her up before in conversation, but we haven't officially met.

"Hey, Dimples." Annalise pops a kiss on my lips, and my stomach immediately flip-flops. "I hope you don't mind that I invited Serena. She passed her boards and is officially a registered nurse!"

I pull Annalise onto my lap and wrap my arms around her. "I don't mind at all." My mouth curves into a smile and I extend a hand to Serena. "Nice to meet you. And congrats on passing your boards! That's incredible."

"Thank you so much!" She beams. "And congrats on advancing to the next round! I'm glad I'm able to fully enjoy the games now."

Elijah sets down his drink and scoots next to Serena. "Nice to meet you. I'm Elijah."

"You don't have to introduce yourself—I know who you are." She chuckles. "But it's nice to meet you, too."

Andrés waves from his seat. "It's nice to meet you, Serena. This is my wife, Katie."

Katie smiles at her warmly and gives a wave.

"Wow. I never thought I'd be partying with the San Francisco Dragons. This is definitely a treat after busting my ass in nursing school."

"If I ever become hospitalized, I want you as my nurse," Elijah says, flashing her a cocky smile.

"Dude, can you stop hitting on everything that moves?" Andrés lets out a groan.

"Leave her alone. She's taken," Annalise chimes in.

"Yeah, to a sorry excuse of a man," Mazikeen mumbles.

Serena scratches the back of her neck. "He said he was too tired to come out and celebrate with me. He sent me a total of five texts telling me I better not dance with other guys." She rolls her eyes. "I've never given him a reason not to trust me, yet he still acts like this."

"Sounds like he has a lot of insecurities," I say.

"Oh, he for sure does." Mazikeen sits up straight. "She is *way* out of his league. He's as ugly on the outside as he is on the inside."

"Mazi…" Annalise hisses, giving her a *look*.

Mazi clears her throat. "Sorry. That was mean. But I can't stand how he treats you, Serena."

"Part of me wants to leave him, but part of me wants to stay and see if he'll change," she says, her voice laced with an unspoken sadness. "We've been together for almost four years now, and I'd hate to start over."

"We just want you to have the love you deserve," Annalise says softly.

"Have fun tonight, and celebrate your accomplishments!" I say. "Elijah, pour us some shots."

"You got it!" Elijah grabs a bottle of tequila and pours it into shot glasses, passing them around. "To us moving on to the next round, and to Serena becoming a nurse!"

We all let out cheers, clinking our glasses and downing the warm liquid.

He pours another round of shots, but Serena holds up her hand when he passes one to her. "Oh no—I'm good with one. I'm a super lightweight."

I laugh, shaking my head in disbelief. "There's no way one shot is enough to get you drunk."

Turns out, one shot was all she needed, because Serena is currently dancing on top of a table, waving her hands in the air.

"And this is why we call her One-Shot Wonder," Annalise says with a laugh.

"That's impressive." I let out a chuckle. "I would save a fuck-ton of money if my tolerance was that low."

Santiago walks in the club—we've rented Blackout again—and greets me with a hug. "Hey, man! Sorry I couldn't make it to the game, but congratulations!"

"Thanks, man!"

"Hey, Annalise! So good to see you." He walks over and gives her a one-armed hug.

"It's good to see you too, Santiago! How's the little guy doing?"

"Oh, he's getting so big. He just turned four a couple of months ago." He pulls out his phone and pulls up a picture of Isaiah at an indoor kiddie park, sporting a birthday hat and cake smudged on his face.

"He's so cute! He's literally your twin." Annalise beams down at the photo. "Have you found a stepmom for him yet?" she adds jokingly.

Santiago chuckles. "Nah, it's just been me and him. I'm not really interested in—" Something catches his attention and he looks as though he's been placed under a spell. "Whoa. Who is that?"

I follow his gaze and see Serena dancing on the table, swaying her hips to the beat. "That's Annalise's friend, Serena."

"She's gorgeous." He smiles, blush spreading across his face.

It's been a while since I've seen him look at anyone like that. Isaiah has been Santiago's number-one priority, and he's always said he wants to put all his focus on his son.

"You should try and shoot your shot." I grin, patting him on the back.

"I think I will."

"I thought you said you weren't interested in dating anyone," I say, cocking a brow at him.

"I wasn't… until now."

"Are you not gonna tell him?" Annalise whispers.

I shake my head. "Where's the fun in that? And who knows

—maybe they'll hit it off and Serena will leave her shitty boyfriend."

Annalise lets out a giggle. "Maddox Masashi Kamado, you are a big hopeless romantic, you know that?"

I place a kiss on her temple. "That's because I have you, the girl of my dreams."

A huge grin appears on her face and her cheeks turn an adorable shade of pink.

After the club closes, we move the party to Elijah's penthouse. Serena and Santiago have spent the last hour getting cozy and talking to one another while Annalise and I observe from a loveseat on the balcony.

"Aw, are we witnessing a love story unfold?" Annalise places her hand on her chest as she watches them through the glass door.

"I think he's fallen in love already. Look how smitten he is," I say, wrapping my arm around her shoulders.

"Santiago is a good guy. He would give Serena what she deserves."

"Yeah, he would. After what Gabriela put him through, I hope he can open up his heart and allow himself to love again."

Elijah slides open the balcony door and sticks his head out. "Get in here, ya lovebirds. I set up the karaoke machine."

"We'll be there in a minute. I gotta warm up my vocals," I say.

He shuts the door and I refocus my attention on Annalise. "Are you ready for me to serenade you, Rosie?"

"I'm not looking forward to having my ears bleed," she teases.

My phone buzzes with a new text alert. I glance at the screen —it's a video message from an unknown number.

Weird. It must be spam.

I hesitate to click on it, worried that it might be a virus, but curiosity gets the better of me.

The video starts off with a blank screen, but what appears in the next few seconds has all the color draining from my face and my blood running cold.

Someone recorded us having sex on my private jet.

CHAPTER 43
Maddox

The video isn't just a short clip where the quality is so bad you can't see who the people are. It's several minutes long and you can see our faces, clear as day. It starts off with Annalise going down on me, and continues with us having sex.

I try to respond but receive a notification saying the text message can't be delivered.

"Fuck! Fuck! *Fuck!*" I yell, slamming my phone down onto the seat.

"Oh, God, this can't be happening." Annalise leans forward, shaking her head.

I thought our relationship being exposed caused enough

chaos, but if this sex tape gets released, it would be an apocalypse.

Annalise and I have worked so hard to get where we are in our careers. She's one step closer to fulfilling her dream of opening her own shop. And for me, winning a championship is so close I can almost taste it.

Everything we've built would be destroyed if this gets out.

I didn't take Annalise seriously when she speculated that someone was trying to ruin my career. But this threat further proves that someone has been plotting my downfall. Who knows what else they're capable of?

I hate that Annalise has been dragged into all of this. One thing I feared was that all of this might be too much for her, and she would leave me.

We're happier than ever, and the thought of it being stripped away kills me.

"I need to reach out to my cabin crew and find out who the fuck installed a hidden camera. I'm probably going to have to fire all of them." I rake my hand through my hair. "Talk about the fucking timing. This is such a catastrophe."

Annalise gnaws on her fingernails. "Do you think you can offer them a large sum of money to not release this?"

I shake my head. "I don't think this is about money. I'm sure they paid someone from my crew a fuck-ton of money for that video."

"We should go to the police station tomorrow morning," she says. "Maybe they can find out who this sick fuck is."

We head back inside, where Elijah, Andrés, and Santiago are singing "Bye! Bye! Bye!" by NSYNC at the top of their lungs.

"Hey, we're gonna head home. I'm not feeling too good. Think I might be getting sick," I tell them. Which isn't a total lie, because I do indeed feel sick.

Elijah frowns and pauses the music. "What? But we didn't

even get to sing together. Come on, at least finish this song with us."

"Another time," I say, managing a weak smile.

"So when can I expect to hear back?" I ask, handing the police officer behind the desk the report I just filled out.

She rolls her eyes, annoyed that I've interrupted her endless scrolling through social media. "A month or two, give or take."

"Two months? Are you kidding me?" My eyes widen in disbelief. "I need you to start working on this now!"

Setting her phone down, she narrows her eyes at me. "Just because you're a famous basketball player, doesn't mean you get special privileges. We have thousands of cases that take priority over yours. You think you're more important than murder cases and kidnappings?"

Heat pulses through my veins. "I never said I'm more important. I just need this to be escalated. My privacy has been violated."

She cocks a brow. "If you were worried about your privacy, maybe you should've chosen a different career." She raises her hand, shooing me away. "Now, move along, pretty boy."

"*Kono kusottare*," I mumble, shaking with anger as I walk out of the station.

"Well, she sure was a lot of help," Annalise says.

"Yep. We're never gonna hear back from her."

I open the passenger door for her and she slides into the seat.

Rounding the car, I open the driver's side, get into my seat, and turn on the ignition.

"Now what are we gonna do?" She sighs.

I drive toward the main road and let out a shaky exhale. "I'm gonna have to throw the game."

Her brows cinch together. "Maddox, no! I can't let you do

that. You've worked so hard to get where you are now. This is supposed to be the year you take home a championship."

"But what about you?" I say, my voice low. "Annalise, you're finally catching a break with this shop of yours, and you're so close to making your dreams a reality. This sex tape would ruin your image before the world even gets a chance to discover your talent. How selfish would I be to take that away from you?"

Reaching over, she places her hand on top of mine. "We don't know if they will actually release it. What if it's some kinda sick joke?"

I shake my head. "I'm not willing to take that risk."

She pauses for a few moments, staring out the window. "Wait… What if we ask your dad for help? He's the owner of the largest technology company in the entire world. I'm sure he can find out who sent you that video."

The muscle in my jaw tightens. "I don't want his help."

Even though Otōsan is the one person who could help figure this out—since the cops were useless—he's the last person I want to ask.

My relationship with him has been rockier than ever. I haven't spoken to him since we got into it during dinner. I've been avoiding going over to my parents' house because I don't want to see him.

Okāsan begged me to reconcile with him, but I don't see a point in trying. It's been this way ever since I was a kid. It's a hard pill to swallow, but I'm trying to accept that we will never have the relationship I yearn for.

"Maddox, don't be stubborn," Annalise says. "He can track down whoever is behind this. I know you have your differences, but—"

My knuckles whiten around the steering wheel. "I said I don't want his help!" I snap. "Just leave it alone."

"What the hell is your problem? All I did was make a

suggestion! You don't have to be such a fucking jerk." She folds her arms across her chest and turns her body toward the window.

The remainder of the car ride was spent in silence. When we arrive home, Annalise storms inside and heads straight to the bathroom.

Grabbing her makeup bag, she starts gathering her cosmetic and skin-care products.

"Annalise, what are you doing?"

"I'm going back to the apartment." She doesn't look at me and continues to pack her stuff.

Gently, I place my hands on her shoulders. "I'm sorry I snapped at you. With everything going on, I've been under a lot of stress lately. I shouldn't have taken it out on you."

Her eyes remain fixed to the floor, but she doesn't pull away from me.

"I hate that you're in this predicament because of me. First with your privacy being invaded from the news of our relation-ship getting out, and now this sex tape threat."

I sink to the cold tile floor, bringing my knees to my chest and wrapping my arms around them. "I feel like I'm making your life more complicated than it should be. If you weren't with me, you wouldn't be in this mess."

"Maddox, this isn't your fault." She drops to the floor and pulls me into her. My head rests on her chest while she threads her fingers through my hair. "And don't you think for a second that this is going to push me away. I love—" She clears her throat, her cheeks turning pink. "I love being with you."

Even though she didn't exactly say the words I want to hear, it's enough to send my heart into a frenzy.

"We're going to find this sick bastard and take him down. We're not going to let them win and destroy our future."

She presses her lips to mine, kissing me gently.

"I'm not going anywhere, Maddox. We'll get through this. Together."

I gaze at my reflection, and what stares back is a haunting image. Dark circles rim my eyes and the pallor of my skin is almost ghastly.

Sleep eluded me the last few nights, and I have a feeling I won't get much more of it until I find out who's behind this.

Even though someone from the cabin crew most likely provided the video, I highly doubt they were the person behind the threats.

My guess is that it's probably someone from another team who doesn't want to see the Dragons win. Or it could be an old hookup acting out of spite, bitter that I never wanted anything more.

Walking back to my locker, I strip off my pre-game suit and change into my uniform. As I grab my phone to lock it up, I receive another text message from Unknown.

UNKNOWN

Don't even think about trying anything tonight. I will be watching.

If you don't make sure the Dragons lose, the whole world will see that video.

You wouldn't want everyone seeing your girlfriend's smoking hot body, now, would you?

"You motherfucker!" I throw my phone in my locker and slam the door shut.

Fury builds within me at the thought of some disgusting low-life pervert jacking off to Annalise.

Andrés looks over at me. "You good, bro?"

Taking a deep breath, I try to keep the rage within me from exploding. "Yeah. There's this asshole who keeps leaving nasty comments about me and Annalise on my page. I blocked him, but he ended up making another account."

"Just ignore those idiots," Elijah says. "It doesn't matter what any of them say because you and Annalise are the cutest couple ever. Seeing the two of you together almost makes me wanna get into a relationship."

"Really?" Andrés and I say in unison, staring at him in disbelief.

"Fuck no." Elijah rumbles with laughter. "I'm never giving up my freedom."

"If you're with the right person, you won't feel like you're trapped," I say. "Don't you want someone to share your life with?"

"The only thing I want to share with someone is my bed." Elijah flashes a cheeky grin.

Andrés slips his shorts on, rolling his eyes. "Well, at least one of y'all stopped fucking around. Crazy how a few months ago, you were talking about how great being single is. Now look at you."

I shrug my shoulders. "I was just waiting for my girl to come back into my life."

"Alright, everyone, listen up." Coach walks in, his booming voice silencing the chatter in the locker room. "I need everyone to bring their A game tonight. I don't want to see any of you slacking. The energy y'all brought during the first two rounds? I need y'all to unleash it tenfold tonight. This is Houston we're talking about."

Elijah, fired up, chimes in. "We're gonna crush them and send them home crying tonight!"

Everyone on the team gathers close, stacking our hands in a unified tower. "Let's go, Dragons!" we shout in unison as we lift our hands up.

As we step onto the court, the crowd erupts in roars of excitement.

"We love you, Maddox!" a group of fans calls out, waving posters decorated with my face and name.

I manage to give them a weak smile, giving high fives as I pass, but inside, waves of guilt crash over me like a relentless tsunami.

They're all going to fucking hate me after tonight.

I'm standing at the three-point line and the defenders from the Houston Phoenixes have me surrounded.

Andrés is standing at the opposite end, waving his arms in the air and signaling for me to pass it to him. Ignoring him, I continue to fight off the defenders and purposely let the ball slip from my fingers.

"What the fuck, Kamado?" Coach shouts from the sideline, frustration evident on his face.

A player from the Phoenixes grabs the ball and makes a fast break across the court. He slam dunks the ball, and Houston now has a twenty-five point lead.

A collective groan passes through the crowd, and my gut wrenches seeing people rising from their seats and heading toward the exit.

Coach pulls me out of the game and subs in Marcus James— one of the bench players.

Chills race down my spine when I meet Coach's eyes. He looks as though he wants to strangle me.

"Kamado, what the hell is going on with you?" he shouts, his voice shaking with rage. "You're missing shots left and right and causing multiple turnovers!"

I exhale a shaky breath. "I'm sorry, Coach. I have a lot going on right now…"

This only pisses him off more. The heat of his fury is enough to incinerate the entire arena. "I don't give a fuck what you have going on! Don't bring your problems to the court."

Unable to reply, I simply nod.

"The fourth quarter just started, and they may be in the lead, but it's not impossible for us to beat them. I need you to get it together and show them who the MVP is!"

"Yes, Coach."

After a couple of minutes pass, I jog back onto the court.

The ball is in Elijah's hand, and he redirects us as he dribbles down the court.

Alex Hui—my old teammate—stands in front of me with a smug look on his face as he's guarding me. We used to be good friends when I played for the Phoenixes, but once I signed with the Dragons, he started treating me like I'm his worst enemy.

I'm sure seeing me play like trash tonight fills him with satisfaction.

"Wow, Kamado. Even the benchwarmer is playing better than you tonight," he snickers. "Guess your girlfriend's pussy is so good that you can't seem to focus on anything else."

Heat surges through me as I clench my jaw, but I bite back the words and stay silent.

Peering over his shoulder, he licks his lips when he spots Annalise sitting courtside. "Maybe I'll see for myself how good it is. It'll be my reward when we eliminate your sorry-ass team from the playoffs."

"Shut the fuck up!" I snarl, shoving my shoulder into him.

He lets out a laugh. "I bet she'll dump your ass once she sees what a loser you are. That's probably why your old man still isn't showing up to your games. I bet he's embarrassed to see what a failure you turned out to be."

The single thread that has been holding me back from losing control finally snaps. I am already in a bad mood, and he hits me in my weakest spot. I confided in him about my situation with Otōsan when we were friends, and he's deciding to use it against me.

I strike him in the face and he crumbles to the ground, a sharp yelp escaping his lips as blood gushes from his nose.

The referee marches toward us, blowing his whistle. "Kamado, that's a technical foul!"

A smile spreads across Alex's lips.

"Exit the game now," the referee says, pointing his finger toward the door on the left with a giant Exit sign looming above it.

I leave the arena feeling defeated as I catch a glimpse of thousands of eyes filled with disappointment. My coach, my team, the fans—I've let every single one of them down.

CHAPTER 44
Annalise

Abuelo and I stroll through Golden Gate Park, admiring the gorgeous spring flowers that have just blossomed. He's been bringing me here since I was little. We used to come every year, and over time, it turned into a tradition.

He becomes winded and pauses to catch his breath, holding onto a nearby tree.

"Do you need me to grab the wheelchair?"

I keep one in the back of my car, but he's always been too prideful to use it. The doctor recommended he use a portable oxygen tank when he has to walk long distances, but Abuelo refuses that too.

"My legs still work," he says, shooting me an icy glare.

I release a sigh. "You'll be able to enjoy the park more without getting tired."

He lets out a huff, rolling his eyes. "I don't need it."

Plopping down on an empty bench, I pat the spot next to me. "Let's sit down and take a little break then."

"Fine," he says, settling next to me.

"Thank you," I say, smiling at him. "You can be so stubborn sometimes, you know?"

He chuckles. "You are one to talk. I keep telling you to quit working for La Diabla and focus on your shop, but you choose to stay. You've been so exhausted and stressed out lately, *mi rosa*."

I chew the inside of my cheeks. "Work isn't the only thing stressing me out."

Abuelo sits up straight, lines of worry creasing his face. "What's going on? Are you and Maddox having problems? I may be an old man, but I can still take him on if he's hurting my granddaughter."

I chuckle at the image of Abuelo trying to smack Maddox with his *chancla*. "No, Abuelo. He's been good to me."

"Good, because I like the two of you together," he says, smiling. "So, tell me, what's got you so stressed out?"

I release a long breath. "It seems as though life has been testing us lately. Things were going so well, but then we had to deal with the fiasco of our relationship being exposed—which I'm glad I didn't get fired for." I lean forward, burying my face in my hands. "But now we're faced with this new threat…"

Abuelo's brows shoot up. "There's someone threatening you?" He grabs my shoulder, fear igniting in his eyes. "*Mi rosa*, are your lives in danger?"

"No, it's not a death threat. But it is something that can ruin our careers." I glance around, lowering my voice. "Someone has a video of us being intimate… and they threatened to release the video unless Maddox threw the game—which he ended up doing last night."

"I knew something was off when I watched the game on TV," he says, shaking his head. "It seemed as though he was playing poorly on purpose. Have you two gone to the police about this?"

I nod. "Yeah, but they were no help at all. We submitted a report but we haven't heard back, and I don't think we're going to. I suggested we ask his father for help, but Maddox is still upset with him, so he doesn't want to ask him." I let out a defeated sigh. "He worked so hard to get where he is, and now he could lose everything. I don't know what to do, Abuelo. I feel like his father is the only person who can help us, and I've been contemplating asking him myself. But I don't want Maddox to be upset with me."

"I don't think he'll be upset with you," Abuelo says, patting me gently on the back. "You would be helping him save his career. Perhaps this will also mend his relationship with his father."

I cut things off with my own father a long time ago, and I have no desire to make amends with him. But it's different for Maddox.

Despite their complicated relationship, he still loves his father. And even though he pretends like he doesn't care, I can see how heavily it weighs on him to not speak to him.

Abuelo rises from the bench, reaching for my hand. "Come on. Let's finish our walk."

Bundles of nerves form in my gut as I sit in my car, staring at the Kamados' mansion. Mr. Kamado's black Mercedes sits in the driveway. I circled the neighborhood about five times before I finally decided to park. I'm tempted to drive home before he notices me sitting in the driveway, but I know this has to be done.

With a deep breath to steady myself, I open the car door and head toward their front door, my footsteps heavier than usual. I've only ever exchanged a few words with Satoshi Kamado, so coming here and asking him for help is a lot for me.

Swallowing the lump in my throat, I press a finger to the doorbell.

After a few moments, the door swings open with a creak, revealing Mr. Kamado. His eyes widen in surprise. "Annalise? Is

Masashi with you?" He steps forward, peaking around to look for Maddox.

"No, it's just me," I reply.

His expression turns solemn. "Oh. I was hoping to see him again. I tried calling him, but he won't talk to me."

"I'm sure he'll come around eventually. He just needs more time."

"Is Masashi hurt? Is he in trouble?" he asks, his voice tinged with concern.

"There's someone trying to blackmail him. I need you to help me find out who's behind this."

Satoshi nods, opening the door wider to let me pass. "Come on in."

CHAPTER 45
Maddox

My knee bounces under the table as I sit in front of Roger Hudson, the NBA commissioner. He's the person responsible for overseeing fines and disciplinary action against players.

He steeples his hands underneath his chin, staring at me with beady eyes. "After carefully reviewing your case, the League Office has come to an agreement in regards to your technical foul in game one against the Houston Phoenixes."

Pausing, he takes a sip of water.

I adjust my tie, feeling suffocated as I wait for his response.

"Because of the severity of your actions, you will be fined $15,000. Violence in the NBA will not be tolerated."

The air returns to my lungs and I relax a little in my seat. I was expecting to pay a larger amount—or worse, face suspension. "Understood. I am deeply sorry for my actions, and I am aware that it was a poor error in judgment. I'll learn to keep my temper under control, and I assure you it won't happen again."

Rising from my seat, I stick my hand out for him to shake it and smile at him. "Hopefully this will be the last time we meet during my career."

He doesn't take my hand, nor does he return the smile.

Clearing my throat, I shove my hand in my pocket. "Well, if that's all, then I will be on my way. Have a good day—"

He cocks a brow. "I'm not done yet, Mr. Kamado. You will also be suspended for two games."

Clouds fill my vision and my throat goes dry. "You can't be serious! These games are crucial. I need to play! Please reconsider."

"My decision is final," he says, his voice firm.

"But if I'm not there, we might not make it to the final round," I protest.

He simply shrugs and replies, "Not my problem. You can go now, Mr. Kamado."

Trying hard to keep my cool, I pivot on my heel and make my way out of the building.

Once I'm in my car, I finally let loose the frustration that's been building up inside me.

"Damn it! Damn it! *Damn it!*" I yell, pounding my palm on the steering wheel.

"I bet he's embarrassed to see what a failure you turned out to be."

Alex's words ring loudly in my head.

This is supposed to be the year I bring home the championship trophy and win the MVP award.

Otōsan would've finally told me he's proud of me, and realized that my choice to pursue a basketball career wasn't a huge mistake.

Now, I don't think I'll ever hear him utter those words to me.

I will not only be a failure to Otōsan, but to the whole world.

My phone lights up with an incoming call from Annalise, and I press the green button to answer it. "Hey, Rosie."

"Hey, Dimples. How did it go?" she says softly.

Despite the sour mood I'm in, hearing her voice puts a smile on my face.

"They fined me and suspended me for two games." I sigh, raking my hand through my hair.

"Two games? That's just cruel!"

"If Chandler weren't injured, they'd probably have a better chance without me. If we lose these next two games, we have to win four in a row, and I don't see that happening." I exhale, the weight of defeat heavy in my chest.

"Don't lose hope, Maddox. It may seem impossible, but I know you're capable of making the impossible happen."

I stare out the window, shaking my head. "I don't know if I have any hope left, Annalise. Everything is so fucked. What if this person makes me throw the next game I play in? I don't think they'll stop until the NBA drops me."

She lets out a heavy sigh on the other line. "I'm sorry, Maddox. I hate that this is happening to you."

"Will you still be with me if I'm not an NBA player?"

She lets out a laugh, and I can picture her eyes rolling. "That's not gonna happen, but don't be ridiculous. I'll be with you regardless of what your career is."

"Even if it's flipping burgers at In-N-Out?"

"Yes. I'm sure they'll make you a manager in no time."

I chuckle softly. "Do you have any plans when you get off work?"

"I actually made plans for us tonight. Meet me at my apartment at seven. Make sure you wear long pants, long sleeves, and closed-toe shoes."

I scrunch my brows. "What the hell are we doing?"

"Just trust me."

"Are we almost there?" I glance over at Annalise as we cruise down the highway.

Her eyes flick to her phone. "Yeah. You're gonna take the next exit and then make a right on 27th Street."

Annalise continues to direct me until we reach our destination. I park next to a grey building marked by a bold blue sign that reads Wreck It. A towering sledgehammer stands next to it.

"Is this one of those rage rooms?" I ask.

She nods. "Yeah. I saw an ad for it the other day and thought it would be fun. I figured we could both use some de-stressing."

Leaning forward, I pop a kiss on her lips. "You are the best."

After we sign the waivers, the worker gives us hard hats and goggles and leads us to our rage room.

The room is filled with several different objects—monitors, game consoles, glass bottles, and more.

"Alright, so you have an hour. Feel free to use any of those objects"—the worker points to the side, where baseball bats, sledgehammers, and golf clubs line the floor—"but please, don't use them on each other."

Annalise gives him a smile. "I'll try my best not to."

The guy chuckles. "Have fun!"

Grabbing a glass bottle, I chuck it against the wall. A small wave of relief washes over me seeing it shatter into hundreds of pieces.

Annalise picks one up too, and a smile tilts her lips when she smashes it.

I grab the sledgehammer and swing it down onto a computer monitor with all my strength. The sharp sound of impact echoes in the room. I smash it repeatedly, completely destroying it to the point where the monitor is unrecognizable.

With every swing and strike against the inanimate objects, the anger simmering inside me—toward my father, the blackmailing, being suspended—begins to dissipate.

By the end of our session, I feel the tension melting away, and the stress I've been carrying is replaced by a profound sense of tranquility.

"I really needed that. Thank you, Rosie." I say, wrapping my arms around Annalise. "I had a lot of fun."

"I'm glad you did." Getting on her tiptoes, she plants a kiss on my lips. "I had too much fun."

"Were you imagining the objects as Veronica's face?"

"Oh, one hundred percent." She lets out a laugh. "All of that wrecking burned all my energy. I'm starving now."

"Wanna get some In-N-Out, go back home, and watch a movie?" I pull the car door open for her and she climbs inside.

"Fuck yeah!" She smiles.

Rounding the car, I climb into the driver's side and put in the directions to the nearest In-N-Out.

Even on a weeknight, the drive-through line is long, wrapping around the building. Reaching over the console, I lace my fingers through Annalise's.

"So, I have some news," she says.

"Oh? What is it?"

"Bay City Marketplace reached out and asked if I would be interested in having a pop-up shop for my clothing line." A huge smile stretches across her face and her eyes light up with pure joy.

"Wow, babe, this is huge!" I beam, giving her hand a squeeze. "When is this supposed to happen?"

"It'll be the last weekend of the month, so a few weeks from now. If it goes well, they'll continue allowing me to use the space on the weekends. I do have to pay a fee, but it'll be a great alternative until I have enough money saved up to open up my own boutique."

"I am so fucking proud of you. You'll be able to leave Dauntless in no time."

"I think I'm finally catching my break." Her face splits into a wide grin. "Having an online shop is great, but it will make me so happy seeing people buy my clothes in person."

"You're gonna sell out within the first hour."

The car behind me blares his horn. "You're holding up the line!" he shouts.

I was so excited about Annalise's big news, I didn't even realize the line had moved. "What do you wanna eat?"

"I'll take a combo number two with a Coke."

"Animal style?" I ask.

She nods.

"Thank you for choosing In-N-Out. What can I get for you?" the worker says through the intercom.

"Can I get a Double-Double combo with a Sprite, and a combo number two with a Coke? Make it animal style."

"Okay. Will that complete your order?"

"Should I ask them if they're hiring, too?" I whisper to Annalise.

She shakes her. "You're an idiot."

I pull my car up and the worker—a teenage boy—pushes open the window. "Okay, sir, your total will be—*no fucking way!*" His eyes widen and he does a double take when he sees me. "Maddox Kamado, going through a drive-through? I have to be dreaming."

Chuckling, I shrug my shoulders. "I like the food here. And just because I'm famous doesn't mean going through a drive-through is beneath me." I fish out a couple of hundreds from my wallet and hand them to the kid. "Keep the change."

"Thank you." He smiles at me with a mouth full of braces.

"Can I get your autograph?" he asks, handing me a napkin and a pen.

"Sure," I reply, taking the pen from him and scribbling my autograph on the napkin.

"I'm going to frame this. I can't believe I got to meet my favorite player tonight."

I thought everyone would hate me for how badly I fucked up the last game, but seeing how happy this kid is brings me joy.

"Here's your order," he says, handing us the bag of food. "Have a great night!"

"You too, kid!"

"Man, this smells so good!" Annalise says, taking the bag from my hands.

"I know. I can't wait to dive in."

Annalise's phone starts ringing and she grabs it from her purse. "Oh, it's my mom."

"Tell her I say hi."

She swipes the phone to answer it. "*Hola*, Mami. Maddox says hi."

There's a beat of silence before Annalise speaks again.

"Wait, wait, slow down! W-what happened?" Annalise sits upright. The smile slides off her face and her expression turns serious.

The paper bag crumbles in her hand and her face loses its color. "I'll be right there."

She hangs up the phone, her hands shaking as she sets it down. "My abuelo, he…" She swallows, tears forming in her eyes. "He collapsed. They're rushing him to the hospital."

CHAPTER 46
Annalise

When I arrive at the hospital, Maddox drops me off at the emergency room, then goes to look for parking. Rushing through the doors, I find Mom frantically pacing around the waiting room and Ollie sitting on a chair with his head hung low.

Since I got the call from Mom saying she found Abuelo lying on the bathroom floor unconscious, I've been riddled with anxiety. Images of him lying in a hospital bed hooked up to a machine in a comatose state flashed through my mind on the over here.

"W-where's Abuelo?" I ask her, my voice trembling. "Is he a-awake yet?"

Mom nods. "He regained consciousness when we arrived at the ER. They're taking him for a CT scan right now."

"Oh, thank God he's awake. I thought he—" I shake my head, tears stinging the back of my eyes. "I was so scared, Mami."

She pulls me into a hug, caressing the back of my head. "I know, baby. I know. We just gotta pray that the CT comes back negative."

Maddox walks through the door with the In-N-Out bags in his hands and greets Mom and Ollie. "Do you guys need anything? Water? Snacks?"

Mom gives him a small smile. "No, we're fine, thank you. I can take Annalise home later, Maddox. You don't have to stay."

Maddox settles in the chair next to me. "It's okay. I want to be here." He takes my hand and rubs his thumb over my palm in soothing circles.

I rest my head on his shoulder, thankful that he decided to stay. I needed him here by my side.

He takes out my cheeseburger and hands it to me, but I shake my head. "I don't have much of an appetite right now."

"Okay. If you get hungry later, I'll leave and get you some fresh food."

"Thank you, Dimples."

A young black-haired woman with tan skin and wide brown eyes approaches with a clipboard in her hands. "Are you Mr. Delgado's family?"

"Yes. I'm his daughter, and these are my kids." Mom gestures to me and Ollie.

"His oncologist, Dr. Pham, came by and ordered some more scans. Once he's done, we will take him upstairs. He has a room on the fifth floor in bed twenty-seven."

Maddox walks up to the nurse and whispers something to her.

She nods and heads back to the nurses' station to speak to another nurse, who I assume is the charge nurse. The woman lifts the phone and punches in a series of numbers.

After a few minutes, the charge nurse approaches us. "A room opened up for him on the seventh floor. You may follow me."

We ride the elevator up to the seventh floor and, unlike the other floors where you can just walk in, this floor is badge-access only.

The charge nurse swipes her badge and we follow her into the room. The room is larger than the living area in my apartment with Mazi. It has its own microwave and fridge, with a large sofa by the window.

"Thank you," I whisper to Maddox.

He smiles at me and gives my hand a squeeze.

Half an hour later, a transporter rolls Abuelo into the room. He has a huge bruise on the side of his face, and looks as though he hasn't slept in days.

"*Mi rosa!*" His face breaks into a huge smile when he sees me.

Walking up to him, I wrap my arms around his frail body and place a kiss on his cheek. "Hi, Abuelo."

He scans the room, his eyes landing on Maddox. "You brought Maddox with you? Don't tell me I ruined date night."

Maddox lifts his hand, giving Abuelo a wave. "*Hola*, Señor Delgado. You didn't ruin anything. How are you feeling?"

"I'm feeling fine. I'm sure they will release me soon. Don't worry about me. Go back and enjoy your night."

I shake my head. "I'm not leaving you."

Ollie pulls up a chair and sits on the other side of him. "Does your head hurt? Do you remember falling?"

"It hurts a little, and no, I don't remember much. I picked up my toothbrush and turned on the sink, and next thing I know, I'm in the hospital."

"Do you need me to call the nurse to get you some pain medicine?" I ask.

Abuelo shakes his head. "No, I'm okay, *mi rosa*. I've had worse pain than this before."

A few moments later, there's a soft knock on the door. "Come in!" Abuelo calls out.

Dr. Pham walks in, her expression unreadable. She turns her attention to Maddox. "Sir, do you mind stepping outside the room?"

Abuelo raises his hand. "No, it's okay. He's family. He can stay."

Maddox rises from his seat. "Oh, it's okay. I'll give you some privacy. I'm gonna go to the vending machine to grab snacks. Y'all want anything?"

Mom and I shake our heads.

"Can you get me some Cheetos and a Coke?" Ollie asks.

"You got it." Maddox steps out of the room, shutting the door behind him.

"So, you suffered a mild concussion from the fall. But thankfully, the CT of the brain was negative for intracranial hemorrhage."

"Does that mean he's going to be okay?" I ask.

Dr. Pham clears her throat, unable to meet my gaze.

The room falls silent, and all I can hear is the pounding of my heart and my labored breathing. I grip the white hospital sheets tightly, my mind racing with endless possibilities about what her answer might be.

"I have reviewed his scans, and they're showing that the cancer has metastasized to his other organs. There's a tumor in his brain, which most likely caused him to collapse."

"No. There has to be a mistake," I say, shaking my head in disbelief. "I just went to the park with him a few days ago. He was fine."

Mom stands from her seat. "Can we be more aggressive with chemo?"

Dr. Pham stares at the ground, shaking her head. "I'm afraid chemotherapy isn't an option anymore. His cancer is far too advanced."

She walks over to Abuelo and places a hand on his shoulder. "I'm so sorry, Mr. Delgado."

Abuelo's throat bobs and his eyes brim with tears. "How much time do I have left?"

"A month. Maybe a few weeks. I'm not entirely sure," she answers softly.

"There must be something you can do!" I shout.

"We did the best we could," Dr. Pham says softly, "but his body didn't respond to chemo."

"Then we will find another doctor!"

Abuelo gives my hand a squeeze. "*Mi rosa*, it's okay."

"No, it's not okay!" I shout, my voice breaking as the tears fall from my cheeks. "You can't die! You can't!"

I stumble out of the room, feeling as if the weight of a thousand bricks is pressing down on my chest, stealing the breath from my lungs.

Maddox spots me as I make my way to the exit, and he chases after me.

"Annalise, what happened?" he asks, his eyes filling with concern as he places his hands on my shoulders.

"The cancer has spread to his other organs. There's nothing else they can do. I'm gonna lose him, Maddox."

When Abuelo was first diagnosed, I knew his chances of survival were low, but I held on to hope, praying that he would beat the odds.

He was there for me when I scraped my knee while learning how to ride a bike, when I got my license, and when my father left us. He's been there for me through every moment in my life.

He was supposed to be the one walking me down the aisle when I get married and to be around when I start a family of my own. The thought of living in a world without his warm hugs and infectious laughter is too much for me to bear.

Maddox pulls me tightly against him, his strong arms enveloping me as I crumble into a torrent of tears. My sobs wrack my entire body, echoing the deep agony inside of me.

"I'm so sorry, Annalise. Your grandpa is such a kind and wonderful soul, and has always treated me like family. It isn't fair that this is happening to him." He caresses my hair, placing a kiss on top of my head. I can feel tears of his own falling down. "I can't even begin to fathom what you're going through. I know how much he means to you."

"The doctor says he only has a few weeks left. What am I supposed to do without him?"

Placing his hand on my cheek, he gently strokes it with his thumb. "Try to make the most of the precious time you have left together. He'll need you by his side now more than ever."

CHAPTER 47
Maddox

My heart squeezed painfully in my chest when I saw Annalise in such a broken state. I felt useless—there was nothing I could say or do that would take her pain away.

If only I had the cure to cancer, so her grandpa could live longer and be there during all the special moments in her life.

Emilio Delgado may not be related to me by blood, but I considered him my family. He means a great deal to me. Both of my grandparents live in Japan, so I only saw them once a year growing up, when I would visit with my family. Emilio is the closest thing I have to a grandparent, and he's always made me feel like I belong.

I'm absolutely gutted upon receiving the news that he only has a few weeks to live, but I have to try my best to stay strong for Annalise.

Quietly, I open the door to his hospital room, careful not to wake him.

Emilio is in the bed and Annalise is lying in a recliner next to him, both in a deep slumber. Tiptoeing inside, I open the closet and set down a bag of Annalise's clothes and toiletries that I retrieved from my house earlier.

Walking over to Annalise, I pull the blanket over her body and plant a kiss on top of her head.

Emilio's eyes flick open and he lets out a yawn.

"*Lo siento*, Señor Delgado. I didn't mean to disturb you."

He waves his hand. "No, it's okay. I've been sleeping too much anyway."

I settle down in the chair next to him. "Is there anything I can get for you? Do you need the nurse?"

"No, I am okay. Thank you."

He sits up straight, angling his body toward me. "Maddox, I want you to know that I really appreciate you. Thank you for everything you've done for Annalise. You are an extraordinary young man."

"And Annalise is an extraordinary young woman," I reply, my gaze shifting over to her. "I love your granddaughter very much."

"I know you do," he says, the corners of his mouth lifting into a smile. "Many people are scared of death, but I am not." Reaching over, he places his hand on my shoulder. "I can leave this world knowing she'll be in good hands."

Tears well up in my eyes and I blink, trying to hold them back. "I promise I will always take care of her."

I want to make sure I live up to the standards he set for me. I will love Annalise with everything I have to make him proud. She deserves the kind of love that moves mountains, and I'm going to try my hardest to give it to her.

CHAPTER 48
Annalise

Abuelo gets discharged from the hospital a few days later and is sent home on hospice. Veronica allows me to take the rest of the month off. It's without pay, but I want to make sure I'm by his side during his last moments.

It takes everything in me not to burst into tears when I'm around him. I want to stay strong for him, even though I feel like falling apart. I don't want our last memories to be filled with sadness.

From morning to night, I stay by his side. He tells me stories about growing up in Cuba, and how he met Abuela.

He grows weaker with each passing day, his once-vibrant spirit fading like a dwindling flame. It's heartbreaking to witness him wither away as the cancer takes over his body.

I get up from the bed in my old room and walk over to Abuelo's room to check on him.

He's already awake, lying in bed and reading the Bible.

"*Buenos días*, Abuelo."

"*Buenos días, mi rosa*. Come on in," he says. "I want to read this verse to you. It is my favorite one."

Crawling into bed with him, I curl up beside him like I did when I was a kid. He begins to read the verse out loud.

" *'No weapon formed against you shall prosper. And every tongue which rises against you in judgment, you shall condemn.'* Every time the enemy poisons your mind with negative thoughts and uncertainty, or you are feeling weak, I want you to refer back to this verse," he says, lifting his eyes to mine. "Let it be a reminder that He will always be there to protect you against all harm."

Shutting the Bible, he hands it to me with trembling hands. "This was Abuela's Bible. I want you to have it."

"Thank you, Abuelo." I take it from him, holding it against my chest.

"His Word has helped me during my toughest times. It helped me cope with my diagnosis. I know that it can help you, too."

Reaching over, he places his hand on top of mine. "My sweet granddaughter, continue to blossom like the beautiful rose you are, and promise me you'll never stop chasing your dreams. *Te amo mucho, mi rosa.*"

I nod, my eyes brimming with tears. "I promise. *Te amo mucho*, Abuelo."

Mom and Ollie walk in, and we all huddle together in bed.

Abuelo wraps his arms around mine and Ollie's shoulders. "I am so blessed to be a part of this family. And you all are the greatest gifts I could ever ask for."

Ollie rests his head on Abuelo and he sobs onto his chest. "I don't want you to die, Abuelo. You can't leave us. There's still so much we need to do together. Still so much we need to talk about."

I'm unable to stop the flood of tears from bursting through upon seeing Ollie break down.

Mom wraps her arms around her middle, to try to prevent

herself from crying, but she breaks down as well. "We need you here, Papi."

A single tear trickles down his cheek. "I'll always be with you," he whispers.

I can feel him slowly slipping away. His heartbeat slows, and his breaths become shallower and more ragged.

He draws in one final breath, and his heart stops completely.

I cry out in agony as he leaves this world and leaves me behind.

I had finally managed to escape from the relentless rip current I'd been caught in, and I was so close to reaching the shore, where happiness awaited. But now I'm being dragged back into the water, drowning and drifting away into the abyss.

Every day I wake up hoping this is a horrible nightmare, and that Abuelo is still alive and healthy. When I saw his cold, lifeless body in the casket, that's when reality hit. This isn't a nightmare—this is *real*. He lost his battle with cancer, and he is gone forever.

I'll never get to argue with him again when he's being overly stubborn, or go on strolls with him through Golden Gate Park during the springtime.

I hate this cruel world for taking him away from me. There was so much I wanted to do with him, but now I will never have that chance.

The days following his death were spent in bed. I would sleep even if I wasn't tired, and would only leave to go eat or use the bathroom.

Now, Tsuki lays her head on my chest, letting out a whimper. I rub her soft head as I scroll through my phone, looking at pictures and videos of Abuelo.

I've been staying with Maddox for the last couple of weeks.

Mazi and Serena have been texting me to check in, but I've been avoiding them.

I click on the video I recorded of Abuelo last year on his birthday, before he got sick.

Candles shaped like the number sixty-five are placed on top of the tres leches cake I made for him. He's sitting at the table with a huge smile on his face as we sing "Happy Birthday" to him.

Sixty-five. That's the age when most people retire and find the freedom to do whatever they want and spend more time with their loved ones. Abuelo only got to enjoy a few months of retirement before he was diagnosed with cancer.

My heart aches thinking about the life he could've had. He wanted to start traveling more—since he'd only traveled to a few cities in America and Canada after moving here from Cuba—and pick up gardening. But now he's six feet under ground and only exists in my memory.

"Oh, Abuelo, I miss you so much." I wrap my arms around Tsuki, sobbing onto her.

The sound of the front door opening and closing fill the quiet house.

Maddox appears in the doorframe with a duffle bag on his shoulder and carry-on luggage in his other hand. "Hi, Rosie."

Tsuki's head perks up and she leaps out of the bed to greet him, panting and wagging her tail excitedly.

His suspension is over now, and he just got back from Houston. The Phoenixes are still in the lead, but if the Dragons can win the next two games, they'll move on to the finals.

I wanted to be there for him to support him, but I didn't have it in me to go.

"Hi," I reply flatly, my eyes staying glued to my phone. I open up the Instagram app and scroll through my feed.

He sets his duffle bag down and walks toward the bed, leaning down and giving me a quick kiss.

Pushing one of the pillows to the side, he sits down on the edge of the bed. "Do you wanna catch a movie tonight? I'll suck it up and watch a scary one with you."

I shake my head. "I don't feel like watching a movie."

"Do you want to go out to eat? Go bowling?" he asks, his voice hopeful.

"I don't want to go anywhere. I just wanna be alone."

He places his hand on top of mine. "Annalise, I know you're hurting right now. But please let me take you out to get your mind off of things."

I sit up straight in bed, yanking my hand away from him. "Are you trying to tell me I should just forget about him?"

"No. I would never tell you to forget about him," he says, his brows dipping together. "The death of a loved one is not something you can easily move on from. I just want to put a smile on that beautiful face of yours."

Anger swirls inside me. "You don't understand how hard this is for me. You never will. You may not have the best relationship with your father, but at least he's still around. Please stop forcing me to do things with you."

His throat bobs. "You're right. I'm sorry for pushing you to go out when you're not ready."

I don't say anything to him, refocusing my attention back on my phone. A post from a gossip page, The Daily Tea, grabs my attention.

The first photo on the post is an image of Maddox and me in high school with the caption: "The real reason why they broke up."

My body surges with heat when I swipe to the next photo and see an image of Charlotte. There's a small paragraph next to the photo saying that we broke up because Maddox cheated on me with her.

"What the hell?" Maddox says, glancing at my phone. "This

shit is getting out of hand. I'm going to hire a private investigator. This has to end."

He continues talking, but I don't hear him. Everything around me fades and all I can see is Maddox pounding into Charlotte. She moans his name as he grips her ass, driving himself deeper.

"You foolish girl. Falling for his tricks again."

I shake my head, trying to push that negative voice out of my head.

No—he didn't cheat on me. He loves me. He's shown how much he cares about me. He would never hurt me.

"There's no proof of his faithfulness to you. He's a liar, just like your father. He's going to continue to cheat on you and deceive you."

I close my eyes, trying to drown out the voices, but they become deafening.

"No one will ever love you."

"You are worthless. That's why your father left you. Why your abuelo left you. Maddox will leave you, too."

A chilling wave of ice courses through my veins, inching its way toward my heart and enveloping it in a frigid embrace.

"I have to go," I say, pushing myself off the bed.

Maddox stares back at me, a look of confusion plastered on his face. "Where are you going?"

Ignoring him, I leave his bedroom and head to the entrance, grabbing my purse off the entryway table.

I head for the door but he gets to it first, his tall frame blocking me. "Is it because of that post?"

I slip on my sandals and sling my purse over my head. "Please let me leave."

"God, you don't know how sorry I am," he says, placing his hands on my shoulders. "First the blackmail with the sex tape, now this. I hate that you are dealing with this because of me. I promise you I'm going to find a way to put an end to this."

"How can I believe you'll stay true to your promise, when you couldn't even stay true to me?" I snap, my voice trembling with rage.

"What? Annalise, I love you more than anything in this world. I would never hurt you."

He cups my cheeks, but I push his hands off me. "You must still be cheating on me now, hooking up with other women while you travel to different cities for your games."

He shakes his head. "This is exactly what they want. To destroy us. We can't let them win."

"I should've spent more time with Abuelo these last few months," I say, voice cold as steel. "But instead, I was spending it with *you*. I regret letting you back into my life."

A world of hurt flashes across his face as my words cut through him like a blade.

He steps aside, his shoulders slumping as I open the door. I shut it behind me, sealing him off from my world once more.

CHAPTER 49
Maddox

Dribbling the ball, I race across the court as the shot clock ticks down the last seconds of the game. I do a quick scan and spot Andrés standing by the goal, unguarded.

With only three seconds left, I pass the ball to Andrés and he slams it in the net, beating the buzzer.

Roars from the crowd fill the arena as everyone celebrates our win. We defeated the Phoenixes and are moving on to the championship round.

This is a big moment for me. I should be overwhelmed with an insurmountable amount of joy. But how can I be, when the most important person in my life isn't here to celebrate with me?

My eyes move to the crowd of fans celebrating. The spot next to Okāsan and Asami where she usually sits is filled by someone else tonight.

It's been weeks since I've heard from Unknown, so I assume they were just trying to see if I would fall for their twisted games. But I should've known they had another trick up their sleeve. They went after something that would damage me far more than my career.

I can deal with never playing in the NBA again, but losing her? I will never be able to recover from that.

"I regret letting you back into my life."

Her words replay in my mind on an endless loop, twisting the knife in my heart.

I want to reach out to her, but I know I'll be met with silence.

Elijah walks up to me, slinging his arm around my shoulders. "I feel like I'm on top of the world right now. A week from now, we're gonna get our rings and hold that championship trophy."

"Yeah, I can't wait," I reply, my tone lacking enthusiasm.

Elijah cocks his brow. "What's going on with you, bro? We're about to make history. You should be more excited."

"Nothing's going on," I say, forcing a smile. "I'm just exhausted and ready to go home and pass out. These games have been brutal."

"Come on, Maddox. I'm your best friend," he says softly, his face etched with concern. "You know you can talk to me about anything."

"Don't worry about me. I'm fine." I give him a wave and head to the lockers. "I'll see you at practice."

"Do you want some more?' Okāsan asks after I take my last bite of wagyu.

It's been a while since I came over here for dinner, and the only reason I came today was because she told me Otōsan would be working late.

I know seeing him would only further upset me and put me in a worse emotional state than I already am. With the first game of the finals being tomorrow, I can't afford that.

"No, I'm okay, thank you. I'm already getting pretty full."

Okāsan lifts a brow. "Okay, what's wrong?"

"Nothing's wrong." Getting up from my seat, I gather all the plates and head to the kitchen.

Okāsan follows after me, walking twice as fast to keep up with my long strides. "Don't lie to me, Masashi. You normally eat three times as much, so I know something is wrong. Is it because of Otōsan?"

I shake my head, placing the dishes in the sink. "No, it's not. I don't really care about trying to win him over anymore."

"Is everything okay with Annalise?" She continues to prod. "I know she hasn't been showing up to your games because she's grieving, but did you two get in a fight?"

Turning on the water, I start rinsing off the plates and release a heavy sigh. "She told me she regrets letting me back into her life."

"What brought this on?" Okāsan asks, her voice full of concern.

Grabbing a plate, I start scrubbing it with a sponge. "Someone told the press that the reason we broke up back then was because I cheated on her." I grip the edge of the sink, my chest heaving as tears fall down my face. "She's the love of my life, Okāsan. Life without her is meaningless. But if she doesn't want to be with me, what am I supposed to do?"

Okāsan turns the water off and wraps her arms around me, rubbing soothing circles on my back as I sob onto her shoulder.

"Oh, Masashi, I don't believe that Annalise meant what she said. She's in a vulnerable state after losing her grandpa, and seeing that post must have been triggering to her. I know she loves you very much. She needs you now more than ever, so don't give up on her."

Her grandpa's words echo in my head.

"I can leave this world knowing she'll be in good hands."

I promised him I would look after her and take care of her when he's gone, and I intend on keeping that promise. I can't let him down.

My phone dings and I spring up from the couch, hoping it's a text from Annalise—but it's a text from Elijah, in our group chat with the team.

I sent her a bouquet of flowers last night in hopes that she would reach out to me, but she hasn't.

Releasing a sigh, I sink back onto the couch. I don't want to bombard her with calls and texts because I know that would only make her angry.

Tsuki walks toward me with Annalise's pink scrunchie in her mouth.

She sets it on my lap and starts whimpering.

"I know. I miss her too," I say, petting her soft fur.

I open Instagram and scroll through it. I haven't been on it since The Daily Tea made that post. I switched my account to private and turned off my message requests, since my inbox was filled with hateful messages.

The fans didn't seem to care back then when I was sleeping around, but the claims of me cheating have ruined my image. Multiple people unfollowed me, and I noticed there were less fans sporting my jersey during the last game. Unknown wanted to ruin my image, and he succeeded.

My feed is mostly filled with highlights from the last game and predictions about which team will win the championship.

I'm about to get off the app when I see a post from Bay City Marketplace. The post features a list of all the new vendors that will be there—Thorny Roses being one of them.

I glance at the time. The marketplace closes around five p.m., so if I leave now, I can swing by before practice.

This could go one of two ways. Either she'll be happy to see me and will want to be with me again, or she'll tell me to leave and then never speak to me again.

I'm hoping for the former rather than the latter.

"Come on, Tsuki. Let's go outside before I leave." Getting up from the couch, I walk to the door leading to the backyard and open it, letting her out.

I head to my bedroom and change into my clothes for practice. Grabbing my sneakers, I stuff them in my duffle bag.

I'm opening my drawer to find a pair of socks when I hear the front door creak open. "Okāsan, is that you?"

Maybe she wanted to drop off some food for me before the game. I walk out to the living room and call out her name again, but there's no response.

My heart hammers against my ribcage and goosebumps prickle my skin. The only other person who knows the code to get inside my house is Annalise, but I know it can't be her.

As I fumble through my pockets, my fingers finally grasp the cool surface of my phone. My heart races as I begin to dial 911. Suddenly, a calm, almost chilling voice comes from behind me.

"Don't even think about it, unless you want your walls to be painted with your dog's blood."

A knot tightens in my chest when I turn my head around and see Lucas standing there with a gun pointed at me.

"Hello, Maddox," he says, a sinister smile stretching across his face.

"Lucas? W-what are you doing here?"

"You're smart. I think you can figure it out."

The puzzle pieces in my brain start coming together. "It was you, wasn't it? You were the one who leaked my relationship with Annalise, and the one who's been blackmailing me with the sex tape."

Tucking the gun in his elbow, he brings his hands together, clapping slowly. "Congratulations. Perhaps if you weren't so busy screwing Annalise, you would've figured it out sooner. I don't blame you, though." He pauses, licking his lips. "I would be banging that smoking hot body of hers nonstop."

I step forward with my fists balled at my sides. "Don't fucking talk about her like that, you sick son of a bitch!"

"Maybe I should pay her a visit," he says, another smile sliding onto his face. "I would love to hear more of those pretty sounds she makes when she comes."

"If you lay a hand on her, I will fucking kill you."

He lets out a cold laugh, leveling his gun at me once more. "I don't think you're in any position to make threats, Kamado."

"Are you really that jealous of my relationship with Annalise? Is that why you're doing this?" I snap, my voice rising. "When are you gonna get it through your thick skull that she will never want you?"

"You're really dense if you think this is just about Annalise. It's much more than that." His eyes grow cold and dark. "You took *everything* from me. You ruined my life!"

I stare at him, dumbfounded. "What the fuck are you talking about? *You're* the one trying to ruin *my* life!"

"You're just getting what you deserve!" he snaps, his voice brimming with fury. "You've made my life miserable ever since I met you. When you transferred to my school in first grade, everyone wanted to be your friend instead of mine."

Memories of elementary school come rushing back. Being in a new environment was terrifying for me, so I tried my best to make friends with everyone. I remember trying to talk to Lucas, but he would always ignore me.

I shake my head slowly. "Lucas… I didn't have any control over that. It's not as though I went around telling people not to be friends with you. Are you seriously telling me you have a vendetta against me because of *that*?"

"It's because of *everything*!" he snaps, voice shaking with frustration. "In high school, I busted my ass training and even stayed after hours to practice after everyone left. But no matter how hard I tried, I could never play as well as you."

I throw my arms out in exasperation. "That was in high

school! Why the hell does that matter now? You're in the NBA, for crying out loud!"

"It doesn't just end with basketball. You continued beating me at everything. I had the biggest crush on Annalise for years, and when I finally worked up the courage to ask her to home-coming, you beat me to it." He takes a slow step forward, his fingers curling tighter around the gun. "I thought she was gonna be a fling, like all the other girls you'd been with, but I was wrong. I had to spend the rest of high school watching you be with the girl I was in love with."

For a second, I feel the smallest amount of sympathy for him. If the roles were reversed, and I had to see Annalise with Lucas every day, I would be devastated. I got a small taste of it when I saw them kissing, and that was enough to ruin me.

"It was never-ending!" he spits, his voice trembling with rage. "You won prom king while I stood there clapping like a fool. I was so close to being valedictorian until you swooped in and stole that, too!" His jaw clenches, lips curling into a bitter sneer. Years of resentment surge to the surface. "You were always the star while I was stuck in the shadows. All I wanted was to be the best at something, but I never could because of *you*! I always came in second place." He shakes his head slowly, exhaling hard through his nose. "I can't stand the fact that you're living the life I dreamed of."

All this time, I thought his obsession was with Annalise. But it wasn't with her at all.

It was with *me*.

"Why do you feel the need to always compare yourself to me? You made it to the NBA. You have talent. You can make a name for yourself, and be your own person." My voice comes out low and calm. I'm hoping it has the power to change the course of the situation.

But the bitterness in his eyes only deepens.

"And yet you're the one in the running for MVP. You're the

one fans chant for. You're the face on every screen, the name in every headline. I'm so sick and tired of watching you get everything you want!"

His expression darkens, shadows swallowing whatever humanity is left in his eyes. "At first, I only wanted to ruin your career." He pauses, eyes locked on mine, unblinking. "But then I realized… that wouldn't be enough."

The cold mechanical *click* of the gun being cocked echoes through the air. His finger settles on the trigger with a terrifying calm. "As long as you're alive, I will always be miserable."

A chilling wave of fear crashes through me, paralyzing me. I have never felt so powerless in my entire life.

"Lucas, please don't do this. Getting rid of me is not going to solve anything."

"That's where you're wrong." His voice is flat now. Final. "My life will finally be better with you out of the picture."

As I stare directly into the cold, unforgiving barrel of Lucas's gun, the reality of my imminent demise looms over me like a dark cloud.

The sharp *crack* of gunshots pierce the air, and the last thing I see is Annalise's sapphire and emerald eyes sparkling as she smiles at me while the world around me slips away.

CHAPTER 50
Annalise

Salsa music fills the air as I stroll through the vibrant streets of Havana with Abuelo by my side. Gleaming vintage cars are parked along the cobblestone streets next to the colorful pastel buildings.

Abuelo pauses, a distant look softening his eyes. Slowly, the corners of his mouth lift into a nostalgic smile. "I met Abuela on this very street. I was walking home from the grocery store and was so distracted by her beauty that I didn't notice a biker coming from behind me. He ended up knocking me over, and all of my groceries were destroyed."

My eyes widen, hands flying to my mouth. "Oh my gosh, Abuelo, did you get hurt?"

"Yeah. I had a bunch of cuts and bruises. Abuela lived around the corner, so she nursed my wounds and cooked dinner for me. It wasn't long before I fell in love with her."

"Now that is one epic meet-cute," I say with a smile.

"Let's go down that road," he says, pointing to the left, where there's a bright light illuminating the street. "There's a shop with the best *pastelitos*!"

He rounds the corner and I follow him. But as I take a step

forward, an invisible barrier halts me in my tracks, pressing against my chest. I strain against it, pushing with all my might, but I can't break through.

"Abuelo!" I call out.

He doesn't so much as glance back, his figure growing smaller as he strides down the road, the space between us stretching wider.

"Abuelo! Please, come back!" I plead, desperation creeping into my tone, but the words seem to evaporate into thin air.

The blare of my alarm pulls me out of my dream. I'm no longer in Havana with Abuelo, but in my cold bedroom, all alone.

Rolling over to the side, I grab my phone, knocking over my ashtray in the process. It clatters to the ground, scattering ashes and used joints all over the hardwood floor.

"Damn it," I sigh as I throw the covers off and force myself out of bed.

I crouch down on the ground and pick up the joints off the floor. Then I straighten and walk to my door, turning the knob. I peek out and find Mazi standing by the kitchen counter, sipping on some coffee.

I've been trying to avoid human interaction as much as possible. After dinner, I lock myself in my room and don't come out until the next morning. I don't have it in me to engage in any conversations, and I'm tired of seeing the stares of pity. Everyone feels like they need to walk on eggshells around me.

"Good morning," Mazi says when I walk out into the kitchen.

"Good morning," I reply, my tone flat and dry.

I open the cabinet that hides our trash can and discard the joints.

"These came for you last night." She nods toward the vase of red roses sitting on our kitchen counter.

Maddox's messy handwriting is scrawled on a small card sticking out of the bouquet. I pull it out to read it.

No matter how much you push me away, I'm never giving up on you, Rosie. I love you with all my heart and all my soul, and I will continue to fight for us.
Love, Maddox

My gut twists when I think about the last time we saw each other. He wore the same pained look on his face then as he did when I broke his heart all those years ago.

I miss the way his soft brown eyes light up when he sees me, and the way his dimples sink into his cheeks when he smiles. I miss the way his hands fit in mine and the feel of his soft lips caressing my skin. I miss *him*.

I want to reach out to him and tell him I didn't mean what I said, but then the image of him screwing Charlotte flashes through my mind, and I'm reminded why I shouldn't.

I set the card down, grab a mug from the cabinet, and pour myself a cup of coffee.

"Are you excited for your pop-up shop today?" Mazi asks. "I have to leave to go to a photo shoot soon, but I'll stop by afterward to support you."

Picking up my phone, I glance at the date. My mind has been in a fog. I didn't even realize the event was today.

I take a sip out of my mug. "I'm not going anymore."

"What?" Mazi sets her coffee down, widening her eyes. "But Annalise, this is a huge opportunity, and you've been so excited about it."

I shrug my shoulders. "I don't care to go anymore."

"Annalise, please. This could be your way out. I know you don't want to keep working for Veronica."

I shake my head. "I don't see the point in going, Mazi. Even if it turns out to be a success, I know it'll be short-lived. Nothing good in my life ever lasts. Misery always seems to follow me."

Mazi walks over to me, resting her hand on my shoulder. "I know your world fell apart when you lost your abuelo, but he wouldn't want you to keep living like this. He would want you to be happy."

"I'm going to email them and cancel," I mumble as I walk toward the couch.

"Annalise, don't—"

"Just drop it, Mazi. Okay?"

She lets out a defeated sigh and grabs her purse. "I'll see you later tonight."

As soon as the door closes behind her, I take out my phone to draft an email to the marketplace manager. The living room fan's breeze sends a chill down my spine, prompting me to rise and switch it off. In my distraction, I accidentally topple over a box on the coffee table filled with Abuelo's belongings—his cherished photo albums, a favorite watch, a scarf I knitted for him, and other mementos.

As I carefully gather everything and return it to the box, my gaze falls upon the Bible he had gifted me. It lays open nearby, with Isaiah 54:17 highlighted.

No weapon formed against you shall prosper.

The memory of Abuelo reading me this verse before he passed flashes through my mind. *"Every time the enemy poisons your mind with negative thoughts and uncertainty, or you are feeling weak, I want you to refer back to this verse."*

Fresh tears spring to my eyes as I reflect on how I've been acting since he passed. I've shut everyone out and lost the will to do anything besides eating and sleeping. In my grief, I've become spiritually weak and have allowed those negative voices to consume me. I've been headed down a dark path and am starting to become someone I don't recognize.

The Bible opening to this very verse must have been a message from above.

I retrieve my phone from the couch and delete the email I'd drafted.

Heading to my room, I start boxing up clothes to prepare for the pop-up shop.

I made a promise to Abuelo that I would keep pursuing my dreams and make him proud.

The pop-up shop is going well so far. I've sold most of my items, and I've enjoyed conversing with the customers and helping them choose clothes that complement their skin tone and figure.

"Do you have this in a medium?" a young woman with light brown hair asks as she holds up a lavender sundress. "I graduate next month and this dress would be perfect."

"No, but I should have some more in stock next week on my online shop." I smile and hand her my business card.

"Thank you so much!" She beams, taking the card from me.

"I hope you have a great rest of your day."

"Thanks. You too!" She gives me a smile and goes off to explore other shops.

For the first time in weeks, I'm finally feeling happy—but it quickly dissipates, morphing into anger when I see Charlotte walk in.

"It's nice to see you're still designing clothes. You were always the best dressed in high school." She picks up a blouse, running her hands along the soft fabric.

"I'm getting ready to close," I say, my voice cold. "So you can leave now." I start gathering the clothes that are left, refusing to make eye contact with her.

"Wait, please—I came here to talk to you."

My fist clenches around the shirt I'm holding. "What's there to talk about, Charlotte? My boyfriend fucked you on the night before our anniversary, and now the whole world knows about it."

"That's what I came here to talk to you about." She shuffles her feet, chewing on her bottom lip. "Maddox, he…" Clearing her throat, she fixes her gaze to the ground. "He never cheated on you. We didn't sleep together. It-it was all a lie."

"Did Maddox reach out and tell you to come say this?" I ask, glaring at her.

She shakes her head. "No, I came here on my own. I saw on Instagram that you were having a pop-up shop, and wanted to come here and talk to you. I haven't spoken to Maddox in years, I swear."

"If you didn't sleep together, then why the hell did you come out of his room wearing his clothes?" I say through gritted teeth.

She inhales deeply, her hands twisting the hem of her shirt. "When I was at the party, I heard his roommate Andrés and his girlfriend talking about how you were flying in the next morning to surprise him. I waited until everyone left, and stayed behind at his apartment. I wanted to get him to sleep with me, but he was too passed-out drunk. So I devised a plan to trick you into thinking he cheated on you with me."

Rage consumes every fiber of my being. My heart is beating so loudly, I can hear it pounding in my ears.

"I-I should've told you the truth sooner, but I couldn't find the courage," she continues, unable to meet my eyes. "It's been eating at me these last few years. I feel so guilty about what I did. I was a horrible person."

"You are un-fucking-believable!" I snap. "What was the point in all of this?"

"I thought, with you out of the picture, Maddox would finally want to be with me. It was stupid to think he would ever love anyone but you," she says, shaking her head. "You don't know how sorry I am. I wish I could take it back." She takes a step forward, lifting her eyes to mine. "Will you f-forgive me?"

It takes everything in me not to slap her across her conniving face.

"Forgive you?" I scoff. "You manipulated me into thinking Maddox cheated on me. Do you have any idea how much damage you caused because of your lies? You destroyed our relationship. You destroyed *me*."

"I was young and stupid. I swear I'm not that person anymore. Please find it in your heart to forgive me," she pleads, her eyes welling up with tears.

I let out a bitter laugh. "I'm not giving you that satisfaction. You don't deserve my forgiveness. Now, please get the hell out of my face."

Her bottom lip quivers and she turns on her heel, walking out of the shop.

Guilt sinks in my gut. Maddox has done everything in his power to show me how much he loves me, but I threw it all away and believed her lies.

I need to tell him how sorry I am. He needs to know how much I love him.

Gathering the rest of the clothes, I head to the parking lot. After I throw the box inside my trunk, I pull out my phone and search for tickets for tonight's game. Once the tickets are purchased, I start the ignition and drive to the stadium.

The usher scans my ticket and lets me through. The game doesn't start for another hour and a half, but they allow fans to observe the players practicing before it starts.

I walk down the steps toward the floor of the arena and the usher calls after me. "Excuse me, miss, you need to stay in your section."

Ignoring her, I continue on.

She catches up to me and grabs my arm. "I'm going to need you to go back to your seat or I'm calling security to escort you out."

"No, please! I need to talk to Maddox." I scan the area for him but he's nowhere to be found.

She lets out a sigh, giving my arm a tug. "Come on. Let's go."

"Let me go!" I yell, trying to yank free from her grasp.

"Annalise?" Elijah turns his attention toward me. He passes the ball to Darius and jogs up to me.

"It's okay," he tells the usher. "She's my friend. And Maddox's girlfriend."

The usher lets go of my arm. "Oh, I'm so sorry. I didn't know who you were."

She clears her throat and heads back upstairs.

"Where's Maddox? I need to see him."

Worry etches across Elijah's face. "I don't know. He hasn't shown up. Andrés and I tried calling him, but he won't answer."

Fear clamps down on my chest. What if something happened on his way here? What if he's hurt?

This is the first game of the championships. No matter what's going on between us, Maddox would never miss it.

Elijah drags a hand through his hair. "You know what's weird? Lucas hasn't shown up either." He lets out a nervous laugh. "I just hope they're not trying to kill each other."

My heart pounds harder, the sound echoing in my ears. The horrifying image of Maddox lying lifeless on the cold ground flashes in my mind.

I shake my head quickly, forcing the thought away. Lucas might be awful, but a killer? *He couldn't be.*

"I'm going to his house," I say, already backing away. "I need to make sure he's okay."

Elijah nods quickly. "Please call me the second you know."

As I'm rushing out of the stadium, my phone buzzes in my pocket. The screen lights up with a call from Maddox's dad.

"Hello?"

"Annalise, I was able to track down the person behind the blackmail. Whatever program they used to block their number was highly encrypted, and it took me a while to hack into their system."

"So who's behind all of this?" My grip tightens around my phone, the anticipation growing.

"It's Lucas Hilton—the guy Maddox went to high school with. His location is pinging at Maddox's house. I'm on my way there now."

The blood drains from my face, bile burning in my throat.

If he's behind this, then my suspicions were true. Chandler's accident wasn't an accident after all. With Chandler out of the picture, Lucas got exactly what he wanted—a spot in the starting five.

A chill races down my spine. If he could do that to Chandler, then who knows what else he's capable of?

I end the call and take off for Maddox's house, praying I'm not too late to stop whatever Lucas has set in motion.

CHAPTER 51
Maddox

A piercing whine fills my skull, drowning out everything around me. Heavy footsteps thud across the floor and the sound of voices fills the room, but they're distant —like I'm underwater.

The sharp metallic tang of blood saturates the air. My vision steadies just enough to find Lucas sprawled on the ground, his face twisting in agony. He clutches his arm, crimson leaking fast between his fingers.

My hands frantically sweep over my body, checking to find blood or a wound, but there's nothing.

A shaky breath escapes me, air flooding back into my lungs as the weight of what just happened crashes down. I was inches from death.

Just moments ago, Lucas stood in front of me with a gun aimed at my chest. One pull of the trigger and I wouldn't be standing here.

A tall man wearing a bulletproof vest grabs Lucas's arms, cuffing them behind his back. He winces in pain, leaving a trail of blood as he gets dragged away.

A pair of hands lands on my shoulders, causing me to jump.

"Mr. Kamado, are you hurt? Do you need to go to the hospital?" a young paramedic asks me.

I shake my head. "No, I'm—I'm okay."

"I need to do a quick assessment on you to be sure."

Pushing myself off the floor, I get up to follow her.

"How did you guys know to come?" I ask as we walk out the door. "I didn't even get a chance to dial 911."

"Masashi!"

I look ahead and see Otōsan pushing past everyone and rushing toward me.

"Otōsan?" I widen my eyes, shocked to see him there.

He yanks me toward him, wrapping his arms around me tightly. "Thank God, you are alive. When I saw Lucas's location at your house, I was so worried. I thought I was going to lose you."

I stare back at him, confusion written all over my face. "You had Lucas's location? But how?"

"Annalise approached me a few weeks ago and asked if I could help track down the person who was blackmailing you. It took me a while to crack the code, but it seems as if Lucas was using some program to send you anonymous texts through his phone. Once I was able to get into his system, I was able to access his location. Detective Takeda works at the San Francisco police department, and he's a good friend of mine. So I called in a favor."

A wave of gratitude crashes over me—for Annalise, for Otōsan. I told Annalise I didn't want his help, but if she hadn't gone to him, I would've been leaving here in a body bag while Lucas walked away untouched.

"*Arigato*, Otōsan. You saved my life," I rasp, my throat tight.

"You are my son. There is nothing I wouldn't do for you," he whispers, eyes shining with conviction. "I've been such a horrible father to you." His voice fractures, breaking under the weight of his words.

Then, something in him crumbles. His shoulders cave as though the admission has gutted him and he folds in on himself, clutching his sides as if holding himself together. "*Gomenasai. Gomenasai. Gomenasai.*" His body shudders as raw sobs tear free.

In my twenty-two years, I have never seen Otōsan display this much emotion, let alone have I imagined him apologizing to me.

"It's okay," I say softly, touching his shoulder.

He shakes his head. "No, it's not okay. It was wrong of me to dismiss your passion for basketball and push you to take over my company so you can continue my legacy. I promise I will be more supportive of you and will stop putting work first."

Using the back of his hand, he swipes his tears away and lifts his gaze to meet mine. "You are extraordinary, Masashi. I am so proud of the man you've become, and I know you will continue to succeed."

My eyes brim with tears, and a warmth flows through me as all the negativity I've harbored toward Otōsan fades away. After going through a near-death experience, I no longer want to hold onto any grudges. I want to let go and move forward.

Otōsan pulls me into his arms once more. "I love you so much, Masashi. I'm sorry I ever made you doubt that."

"I love you too, Otōsan."

A faint, nervous chuckle escapes him. "I'm not looking forward to telling your Okāsan about this."

I can't help but smirk. "Yeah. She's probably going to force me to move back in with you guys."

A deep laughter rumbles in his chest, and soon I'm laughing too. For the first time, the bond I've been aching for feels like it's finally beginning to take root.

The paramedic clears her throat. "I need to do a set of vitals on you."

I give her a nod and follow her to the ambulance.

She shines a penlight in my eyes. My gaze follows as she moves it in every direction. Then she wraps a blood pressure cuff around my bicep and places her stethoscope on my chest, asking me to take deep breaths.

The sharp slam of a car door echoes across the front yard. Annalise rushes out, her face pale with panic. "Maddox!"

I rip the cuff from my arm and bolt toward her. The paramedic mutters a curse behind me as I break free.

Annalise collides into me, arms wrapping tight, her breath ragged against my chest. "Oh, God," she chokes out, tears shining in her eyes. "When I saw the police cars and ambulance outside, I was so scared. I thought I was too late."

I kiss the top of her head and caress her soft hair as she sobs into me. "It's okay, baby. Everything is going to be okay. Lucas is going to go away for a long time. He can't hurt us anymore."

She shakes her head, pressing trembling fingers to her lips. "I can't believe I went on a date with him. That I kissed him. Oh, I feel so sick."

"Don't beat yourself up about it, Rosie. There's no way you could've known. Even I didn't think he was capable of trying to take my life."

Tears well in her eyes as her voice cracks. "I'm so sorry, Maddox. For the way I treated you."

I brush my thumb gently across her cheek, wiping the tears away. "You don't have to apologize, my love. You were dealing with a tragic loss."

"I'm not only sorry for that. I'm sorry for *everything*. Charlotte came to the pop-up shop today."

My brows shoot up. "She did?"

She nods. "She confessed to everything. She overheard Andrés talking to Katie about my plan to surprise you, and then came up with her own plan to deceive me into thinking you had betrayed me."

Anger claws its way through my chest, my jaw tightening. Four years. *Four years* stolen from us because of Charlotte's lies.

"I can't believe she carried that lie for so long," I mutter, shaking my head in disbelief.

"Maybe she wanted to free her conscience," Annalise whispers.

Relief floods through me. The truth is finally out, and those unwanted memories will no longer haunt her.

Her eyes glisten as she takes my face in her hands. "What I said before—that I regret letting you back into my life? I didn't mean it. Not for a second."

Her voice breaks, raw and achingly tender. "You are the best part of my life. My world is brighter because you are in it. I love you, Maddox. I am so deeply, hopelessly in love with you. Every piece of me has always been yours."

Fireworks erupt in my chest upon hearing her utter those three little words after all these years.

She pulls me into her arms, her lips crashing against mine. We drown into each other, and nothing else matters.

When we finally break for air, I rest my forehead against hers. "I love you, Annalise. Nothing will ever come between us again."

CHAPTER 52
Maddox

Sweat drips down my brow, my heartbeat pounding in time with the ball echoing against the hardwood. The New York Werewolves' shooting guard, Clay Duncan, launches a three. My gut twists as I watch it arc high.

If he sinks it, we're finished. It would put New York in the lead by five points, and there's no way we could catch up with only a few seconds left in the game. We would have to kiss the championship goodbye.

The ball clanks off the rim. Relief slams through me. Andrés quickly snatches the rebound and fires it to me.

I take off down the court, defenders closing in, my heart hammering in my throat. One chance. No time left.

I release the shot.

The ball rattles around the rim—once, twice—teasing, mocking. My jaw grinds against my mouth guard, eyes locked on the clock.

Then it drops. The buzzer sounds.

For a second, the world stops as I register what just happened.

We won. We *fucking* won. The championship is ours. Everything I've worked for has led to this very moment.

The entire arena erupts in deafening cheers as confetti rains down.

My teammates rush toward each other, delivering chest bumps and back slaps.

"Fuck yeah! We are the champions, baby!" Elijah shouts.

Gabriel Amato—owner of the San Francisco Dragons—smiles proudly as he comes out with the trophy.

He presses the golden trophy into my hands. I hoist it high, pride surging as the cameras flash.

This moment has been my dream since I was a kid. But it didn't come easy. I think back to the sixth-grade boy who didn't make the team. To the seventh-grader who sat on the bench, invisible. No matter how many times I failed, I never gave up.

My failures didn't break me. They built me.

Every setback, every rejection, every early morning on the court has carved me into who I am today.

Standing here today, on the same court as the greats, with the trophy raised high, is proof that no dream is too far out of reach if you're willing to keep fighting for it.

My family and Annalise push past the reporters, surrounding me in a whirlwind of hugs. My heart swells. This moment is theirs as much as it is mine.

"Congratulations, Masashi. You made history tonight. We are so proud of you." Otōsan beams, his eyes shining with pride. He hasn't missed a single game since we reconciled—not even the ones in New York.

Okāsan cups my cheek. "It feels like just yesterday I took you to your first game. And now… look at you. I am so happy for you, Masashi."

"I guess you don't suck after all," Asami teases with a grin.

I raise my brows. "I was gonna offer to pay for your honeymoon, but I guess I should put that money elsewhere."

"Masashi, you are the *GOAT*!" she says, her tone full of sarcasm.

I laugh, rolling my eyes.

Annalise steps forward, her smile radiating joy. "You were amazing out there, Dimples. I had no doubt you would win the championship. I'm so glad I was here to witness it."

I thread my fingers through hers, holding tight. "Thank you for always believing in me—for inspiring me to chase this dream. I wouldn't have been able to do this without you by my side."

Her eyes glisten with adoration. "You are phenomenal, Maddox. Your hard work and determination brought you here. I've never been prouder."

"I may have won the championship, but having you in my life is the greatest prize of all."

Lifting her chin, I capture her lips with mine, savoring the sweetness of this glorious moment.

The whole team, along with our friends and family, gathers at Blackout to celebrate our victory.

Drunk out of his mind, Elijah slings his arms over mine and Andrés's shoulders, swaying as he belts out "We Are the Champions" by Queen.

We laugh and join in, soaking up the joy of this moment.

"Here's to winning more championships! And to a lifetime of friendship!" I cheer, raising my glass of champagne.

We clink glasses and I take a sip of the bubbly liquid, the celebration fizzing through me just like the drink.

The last couple of months have been a relentless roller coaster, but it finally feels like the storm has passed. My suspicions about Lucas buying his way into the NBA turned out to be true. His father, Benjamin Hilton—one of the wealthiest men in

San Francisco—paid our general manager, Gary Thompson, a hefty sum to secure Lucas a spot on the team.

But that wasn't all. With Benjamin's money, Lucas hired someone to follow me—the same person who hit Chandler with the car and bribed one of my flight attendants to install a hidden camera on board.

Now, the truth is out. Lucas and his father will be spending the rest of their pathetic lives behind bars.

As for Charlotte, she posted a public video admitting she'd tricked Annalise into thinking I cheated on her. My reputation's finally been restored, and Annalise and I are back to being the *it* couple.

"So, I've got some news," Andrés says, pulling his wife close with an arm around her waist. "Katie and I are expecting a baby."

"Wow! I'm so happy for you two! Congratulations!" I say, hugging both of them.

"Congratulations, man!" Santiago beams. "There's no greater joy than being a parent. Your life's about to change in the best way."

Andrés grins, pointing at me and Elijah. "Now you two need to hurry up, so all of our kids can have playdates."

Elijah and I exchange a shared look of panic.

"Yeah… You're on your own with that," I say quickly. "I don't plan on having any kids for a *looong* time."

Annalise nods in agreement. "Yep. We plan on traveling as much as we can."

I smile, pressing a kiss to her cheek.

"And seriously," I add, grinning at Elijah, "you think *he's* ready to be a dad? He can barely take care of himself."

The group bursts into laughter.

"Man, fuck y'all. I would make a *great* dad," Elijah protests, though he's laughing too.

Santiago shakes his head, chuckling. "You watched Isaiah for one hour while I went to the dentist. One hour. When I came back, he'd eaten an entire box of Oreos. That was the *first* and *last* time I left you alone with my kid."

Elijah shrugs, unbothered. "He's a cute kid. I just couldn't say no to him."

We stayed at the club a couple more hours, drinking, laughing, and soaking it all in.

I snake my arm around Annalise's waist and lean in, lowering my voice so only she can hear. "Wanna get out of here?"

She arches her brow. "You don't wanna spend some more time with your friends?"

I shake my head. "Nah. I wanna spend some alone time with my girl."

Blush warms her cheeks as her smile blooms. I take her hand, and together we slip out of the club and into the night.

I link my arm around Annalise, guiding her gently as we walk along the rugged shoreline, the waves crashing softly beside us.

As we approach the beach cove—our spot—a soft glow flickers inside, casting a golden light against the stone wall and cutting through the darkness of the night.

Annalise slows, her brows furrowing. "Did someone find our spot?" she asks, disappointment flickering in her voice.

I fight back a grin. "I hope not. Come on—let's go tell them they're trespassing."

I jog ahead, and I hear her footsteps quickly follow behind.

"Maddox, wait!"

I reach the entrance to the cove and she tugs my arm, pulling me back. "Let's just go home."

But then she peeks around me and lets out a surprised gasp. "Oh… Maddox!"

Game Changer

The glow of candles dances across the cave walls, and rose petals are scattered in soft trails on the ground.

I turn to face her, taking both of her hands in mine while I stare into her eyes.

My voice trembles as I begin. "Annalise… Before I met you, I didn't think true love existed." I swallow, blinking back the emotions surging inside. "But you showed me what love really is. You changed how I see the world, and how I see myself. You've been my rock through everything. You helped mold me into the man I am today."

Her eyes are already brimming with tears, her fingers trembling slightly in mine.

"I fall more in love with you every single day." Tears cascade down my cheeks as I smile at her. "You are my past, my present, and my future. When I look into your eyes, I see forever."

I reach into my pocket, pulling out the small velvet box. Her breath catches as I sink to one knee.

She covers her mouth as I open the box, the diamond ring glistening beneath the starlight, glowing with a promise.

"Our souls found their way back to each other," I say, my heart pounding. "And I want to spend every single day proving just how much I love you."

I smile up at her, eyes shining with everything I feel. "Annalise Rose Monroe, will you marry me?"

She chokes back a sob, her smile radiant through the tears. "Yes! A million times yes!"

With trembling hands, I slide the ring onto her finger. She throws her arms around me and our lips meet in a kiss—deep and full of promise.

Annalise isn't just the love of my life. She is my *game changer*. The moment she walked into my life, everything shifted. With her, the world made sense in a way it never had before. In her, I found my soulmate, and the truest love I've ever known.

EPILOGUE
Annalise

SEVEN YEARS LATER

A flutter of joy dances in my chest as I spot it—a dreamy little boutique painted in pastel green, with rose vines tumbling down its walls. Then I see it—the name glinting in gold-plated letters: Thorny Roses. My boutique. In Paris. On the iconic Champs-Élysées, nestled among the world's most prestigious brands.

When I told Veronica I was quitting so I could put all of my focus on my shop, she laughed in my face. She told me I would fail. That I would amount to nothing.

Normally her words would've affected me, but I wasn't the same weak girl I had been when she hired me. Her words didn't break me. They fueled me to keep going and prove her wrong.

I opened my first boutique in San Francisco six years ago, and since then, Thorny Roses has blossomed beyond my wildest dreams. Shops have sprung up across the country, and now I've made my mark in the fashion capital of the world. Celebrities grace the red carpet in my gowns, and my designs have been spotlighted in top fashion magazines everywhere.

Little five-year-old me would've been so proud. I stopped letting my doubts destroy my dreams.

Maddox wraps his arms around my waist, pressing a gentle kiss to the top of my head. "You have changed the world of fashion, Rosie. I'm so proud of you. I know your abuelo would be, too."

A soft smile tugs at my lips as my fingers trace the ink etched into my skin—Abuelo's favorite Bible verse wrapped around a dagger, framed with blooming flowers: *No weapon formed against you shall prosper.*

I miss him every single day. And although he isn't physically with me, I can feel his presence. Protecting me. Guiding me through life.

Taking Maddox's hand, I push open the door to the shop and step inside.

I am filled with bliss upon seeing customers admiring my clothing—the clothes that once only existed in my sketchbooks.

A woman with long raven hair smiles at her reflection in the mirror as she holds an emerald-green satin gown against her body.

"Pierre, what do you think?" she asks the man next to her.

He smiles at her, pure adoration in his eyes. "You would look beautiful in it, my darling."

"I agree," I say. "It brings out your eyes."

The woman spins around, her eyes widening in shock when she sees me. "Oh my goodness! You're Annalise Rose Kamado!"

Heads turn at the sound of my name, and customers stop browsing the clothes to approach me.

"I absolutely love your designs," one of them gushes. "They're so chic and beautifully made."

"I would buy the entire store if I could," another customer chimes in.

"Oh, thank you so much," I reply, placing my hand over my heart. "I'm so happy that you all love my clothes."

I point to a pale-blue chiffon gown with pearls on the bodice that's displayed on a mannequin. "This gown here was inspired by a design I created when I was thirteen."

"Gosh, you are so talented," a young woman says while beaming at me.

After chatting with the customers and sharing stories about my designs, I wave goodbye to them and leave the shop with Maddox.

A wide grin stretches across his face. "My wife is so famous."

"Oh, shut up." I laugh, blush spreading across my cheeks. "You know I hate being called that."

He chuckles softly. "But you know it's true. Didn't I tell you we would be the ultimate power couple?"

Shaking my head, I laugh as the memory of him saying those words over a decade ago flashes through my mind.

What he said is true. Both of us are thriving in our careers. The San Francisco Dragons are still undefeated champions, and MVP trophies with his name engraved on them are displayed on a shelf in our home.

After everything that went down with Lucas, Maddox wanted to start fresh. He sold his mansion and built a new one right next to our secret spot, so it could belong to us forever.

"Come on. Let's go get some macarons."

The Eiffel Tower sparkles against the night sky as we stroll across a bridge overlooking the Seine River.

I crouch down, drawn to the array of locks attached to the bridge—each one a silent love story.

"The bridge isn't complete without us adding our own," Maddox says with a smile.

He reaches into his pocket and pulls out two intertwined

heart-shaped locks—one blue, one green—engraved with our initials. "I wanted it to match your gorgeous eyes that I love so much."

I smile up at him, my heart full. All these years of marriage, and he never fails to make me swoon. "I love you so much, Dimples."

"I love you too, Rosie," he says softly, his eyes glistening.

Hand in hand, we attach our locks to the bridge, a heartfelt symbol of our everlasting love and the unbreakable bond we share.

The distance and time between us never changed the way I felt about him. My heart never stopped beating for Maddox. Fate brought us back together and gave us a second chance at love.

My life without Maddox was a sky full of darkness. Being with him brought back the light, filling my world with an endless galaxy of stars.

THE END

初志貫徹

Thank You For Reading

If you enjoyed *Game Changer*, it would mean the world to me if you left a review on goodreads, Amazon or any social media platform to help spread the word. Your support truly means everything. Thank you for taking the time to read Maddox and Annalise's story.

Acknowledgments

First and foremost, I would like to thank God for being my guiding light and blessing me with the gift of writing. Although I discovered what my true passion is later in life, being able to express myself through my writing and share it with the world has brought me the utmost joy.

Game Changer will always be a story that holds a special place in my heart. In 2020, I came up with the title and characters and published it on Episode Interactive in 2022. If you're here from Episode, thank you for all the love and support you've given me over the years and for following me on my writing journey. I hope you enjoyed the novel version and reading the spicy scenes that weren't on Episode.

Despite being horrible at sports and being the last person to get picked for teams in gym glass, I always wanted to write a basketball romance. Growing up, I always loved watching the Houston Rockets play. Even though we haven't won a championship in three decades, I still have hope.

Maddox and Annalise will forever be my favorite characters because I put pieces of myself in them and their story. Like Maddox, I'd often sought validation from my parents and wanted them to be proud of me more than anything. If you're a child of Asian immigrant parents, I'm sure you can relate. I'm also a huge baby when it comes to anything scary. The Ring still haunts me to this day.

Like Annalise, it was once my dream to become a fashion designer. I'm sure there's a sketchbook full of my designs lying somewhere in my parent's house. Her struggles with insecurity are something I relate to deeply, and I wanted to write about her journey in overcoming the battles within her mind.

When I was ten, I lost my grandpa to lung cancer. He was my protector—the person I admired most. Then, in my twenties, my uncle was diagnosed with the same disease, and we lost him far too soon, in his fifties. Losing two family members to cancer was devastating, and writing about my experience became a way for me to process that grief.

Game Changer was originally going to be a strangers to lovers story where Maddox is a player and Annalise is the one who "changes him". I decided to make it a second chance romance because, at the time, I was going through a breakup with my then-boyfriend—who's now my fiancé. That experience made me realize that no matter what happens, he'll always be the one I love, and there will never be room for anyone else in my heart.

To my fiancé, my soulmate, and my real life book boyfriend —I can't even begin to express my gratitude for you. Thank you for your constant support through this journey, for always lifting me up when I wanted to give up and delete my whole manuscript, for listening to me ramble about my story ideas, and for pushing me to become the best I can be. Thank you for being an amazing dad and for keeping our crazy toddler entertained when I'm writing. I love you and our little family to the moon and back. Our second chance at love led to forever.

To my mom—the strongest and bravest woman I know. Thank you for raising my sisters and me, for your unconditional love and for all of your sacrifices. Thank you for being the best grandmother to my son, and for cooking me all of your delicious meals. I'm so lucky to have you as my mom, and I hope one day I can give back even a fraction of what you've given me.

To my sisters—thank you for being there for me through every step of my life and for keeping me grounded. I didn't have a lot of friends growing up, but that didn't matter because I had you two. I am so incredibly blessed to have y'all in my life and for the bond that we share. Also I'm sorry if I scarred you with my spicy scenes.

To Bri and Juju—when I joined the Episode community, I thought I would just use the platform to promote my stories. Little did I know it would bring me my best friends for life. I'm forever grateful for Episode for bringing me you two because having y'all as friends feels like winning the lottery. I'm patiently waiting for y'all to write a novel. I know the world's gonna love it! It's not fair that y'all live so far from me, but I am so grateful we're able to take trips together. The amount of love I have for you two is immeasurable. Thank you for always being my safe space and your endless support.

To Nicolle—I'm so glad a friendship blossomed from those awful read for read days. Can you believe it's been almost 6 years? You've been with me since day one, back when I had no idea what I was doing. Thank you for all the times you helped me figure out coding, for letting me spam you every time I think of a new story idea, and for supporting me since the beginning of my writing journey. I love you bunches.

To Sandi—even though we both left the Episode community, I'm so grateful that you were one of the few people I stayed in touch with. I love how we can go weeks to months without talking, and then end up talking for hours when we do. I always knew you were meant to write novels when I first read your stories on the app. I beg of you to publish a book, because you are too talented to keep your beautiful writing hidden from the world. Thank you for supporting me over the years. I love you so much and hope one day I can fly across the world to visit you.

To Leigh—I would be completely lost without you. Thank you for reading the first messy draft of Game Changer, for helping me fix it to make it flow better, for giving me advice to help me grow as a writer, and for letting me spam you with text during random hours of the day. Writing a novel is not an easy task, and I'm so glad to have you alongside me throughout this whole process. You are an amazing friend and one hell of a writer. I love you loads!

To Jahnetta and Ty—thank you for being my biggest hype women, for getting me to leave the house to go on foodie adventures, and always being there for me when I want to vent about work or life in general. Y'all would always tell me that working in healthcare isn't what I'm meant to be doing and that I should write a book. I finally did it! Thank you for pushing me to get out of my comfort zone. I love y'all both so much.

To Ify—our writing sessions really helped me stay motivated. I appreciate you so much for taking your time to read my manuscript and giving me feedback. Thank you for always reassuring me when I doubt myself and don't think my writing is good enough. I love you so much, and I can't wait until you put your debut novel out into the world.

To Day—you were the first friend I made when I came back from my hiatus, and although I no longer write on Episode, I am so grateful to have met you. Thank you for always lifting me up by sending me Bible verses and prayers. Thank you for always reminding me to put my trust in God when the enemy is attacking my mind. You were the very first person to read Game Changer, and your positive feedback and excitement fueled me to keep going. I love you lots and I'm blessed to have you as my friend.

To Elle—sliding into your DMs and asking if you can alpha read Game Changer was one of the best decisions I ever made. I not only gained insight from a reader's perspective on how to improve my novel, but an amazing friend. Thank you for being my guide during this indie author journey and for always rooting for me. You are the sweetest human being and I am eternally grateful for you.

To my editor Megan—thank you for making Game Changer

the best it can be with your copy and line edits. I appreciate your attention to detail so much, and I promise to cut back my use of "arch a brow" for book 2. I'm so glad I came across your profile, and that we're able to bond over books, writing, and mommy things. I can't wait to work on future projects together.

To my cover artist (@dana_i_nana) and discreet cover designer (@kjaspersendesigns)—thank you for all the time and effort y'all put into creating the cover of my dreams. Both covers are so stunning and y'all captured my vision perfectly. Thank you both for being so amazing to work with!

To all the artists who worked on Game Changer (@pilitella, @bluusuu, @joe___lx, @rizzy.art, @talitarogs, @sleynir, @_minacchiii, @sketch.efe, @mspa.art, @aartis—thank you for bringing Maddox and Annalise and my ideas to life.

To everyone in the bookish community—I appreciate all the sweet DMs and comments y'all would leave me. It really kept me going when I was feeling burnt out or wanted to give up. Thank you for your support during my journey as a debut author.

To my readers—it means the world to me that y'all took a chance on me and my first book. Writing a novel has been something I've been dreaming about for years, thank you from the bottom of my heart for reading Game Changer. I hope you loved Maddox and Annalise as much as I do and that their story resonated with you all.

Love,
Cindy

About the Author

Cindy Ta is a Vietnamese-American author from Houston, Texas. She loves writing swoony, steamy contemporary romances—full of deep emotion, unforgettable moments, and men who yearn.

When she's not writing, you'll find her curled up on the couch cuddling with her dog while reading a good book, indulging in new foods, and traveling to new destinations to create memories with her husband and their two kids.

Connect with me to stay up to
date on my upcoming releases!